More Praise for Robert B. Parker and Spenser!

"We are witnessing one of the great series in the history of the American detective story."
　　　　—R.W.B. Lewis, *The New York Times Book Review*

"The sassiest, funniest, most-enjoyable-to-read-about private eye around today. . . ."

　　　　　　　　　　　—*The Cincinnati Post*

The Godwulf Manuscript

"Crackling dialogue, plenty of action, and expert writing. . . . Tough, wisecracking, unafraid, and unexpectedly literate—in many respects the very exemplar of the species."
　　　　　　　　　　　—*The New York Times*

Mortal Stakes

"Spenser is Boston's answer to James Bond. . . . His first person recital of his detective work makes for fast, amusing reading."

　　　　　　　　　　—*The Pittsburgh Press*

"Freshness, humor, taste and tension!"

　　　　　　　　—John D. MacDonald

Promised Land

"Parker writes exciting, genuinely witty stories populated by wacky characters. . . . Delightful."
　　　　　　　　　—*The Grand Rapids Press*

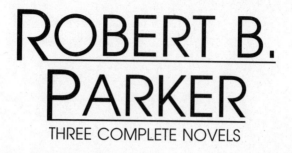

ROBERT B. PARKER

THREE COMPLETE NOVELS

ROBERT B. PARKER

THREE COMPLETE NOVELS

The Godwulf Manuscript

Mortal Stakes

Promised Land

WINGS BOOKS

New York • Avenel, New Jersey

Contents

The GODWULF MANUSCRIPT

This, like everything else, is for Joan, David and Daniel

CHAPTER ONE

THE OFFICE OF the university president looked like the front parlor of a successful Victorian whorehouse. It was paneled in big squares of dark walnut, with ornately figured maroon drapes at the long windows. There was maroon carpeting and the furniture was black leather with brass studs. The office was much nicer than the classrooms; maybe I should have worn a tie.

Bradford W. Forbes, the president, was prosperously heavy—reddish face; thick, longish, white hair; heavy white eyebrows. He was wearing a brown pin-striped custom-tailored three-piece suit with a gold Phi Beta Kappa key on a gold watch chain stretched across his successful middle. His shirt was yellow broadcloth and his blue and yellow striped red tie spilled out over the top of his vest.

As he talked, Forbes swiveled his chair around and stared at his reflection in the window. Flakes of the season's first snow flattened out against it, dissolved and trickled down onto the white brick sill. It was very gray out, a November grayness that is peculiar to Boston in late fall, and Forbes's office seemed cheerier than it should have because of that.

He was telling me about the sensitive nature of a

college president's job, and there was apparently a lot to say about it. I'd been there twenty minutes and my eyes were beginning to cross. I wondered if I should tell him his office looked like a whorehouse. I decided not to.

"Do you see my position, Mr. Spenser," he said, and swiveled back toward me, leaning forward and putting both his hands palms down on the top of his desk. His nails were manicured.

"Yes, sir," I said. "We detectives know how to read people."

Forbes frowned and went on.

"It is a matter of the utmost delicacy, Mr. Spenser"— he was looking at himself in the glass again—"requiring restraint, sensitivity, circumspection, and a high degree of professionalism. I don't know the kind of people who usually employ you, but . . ."

I interrupted him.

"Look, Dr. Forbes, I went to college once, I don't wear my hat indoors. And if a clue comes along and bites me on the ankle, I grab it. I am not, however, an Oxford don. I am a private detective. Is there something you'd like me to detect, or are you just polishing up your elocution for next year's commencement?"

Forbes inhaled deeply and let the air out slowly through his nose.

"District Attorney Frale told us you were somewhat overfond of your own wit. Tell him, Mr. Tower."

Tower stepped away from the wall where he had been leaning and opened a manila file folder. He was tall and thin, with a Prince Valiant haircut, long sideburns, buckle boots, and a tan gabardine suit. He put one foot on a straight chair and flipped open the folder, no nonsense.

"Carl Tower," he said, "head of campus security. Four days ago a valuable fourteenth-century illuminated manuscript was stolen from our library."

"What is an illuminated manuscript?"

Forbes answered, "A handwritten book, done by monks usually, with illustrations in color, often red and gold in the margins. This particular one is in Latin, and contains an allusion to Richard Rolle, the fourteenth-century English mystic. It was discovered forty years ago behind an ornamental façade at Godwulf Abbey, where it is thought to have been secreted during the pillage of the monasteries that followed Henry the Eighth's break with Rome."

"Oh," I said, "that illuminated manuscript."

"Right," Tower said briskly. "I can fill you in with description and pictures later. Right now we want to sketch out the general picture. This morning President Forbes received a phone call from someone purporting to represent a campus organization, unnamed. The caller said they had a manuscript and would return it if we would give a hundred thousand dollars to a free school run by an off-campus group."

"So why not do so?"

Again Forbes answered. "We don't have one hundred thousand dollars, Mr. Spenser."

I looked around. "Perhaps you could rent out the south end of your office for off-street parking," I said.

Forbes closed his eyes for perhaps ten seconds, inhaled audibly, and then went on.

"All universities lose money. This one, large, urban, in some ways undistinguished, loses more than most. We have little alumni support, and that which we do have is often from the less affluent segments of our culture. We do not have one hundred thousand dollars."

I looked at Tower. "Can the thing be fenced?"

"No, its value is historical and literary. The only market would be another university, and they would recognize it at once."

"There is another problem, Mr. Spenser. The manuscript must be kept in a controlled environment. Air-conditioned, proper humidity, that sort of thing. Should it be kept out of its case too long, it will fall apart. The loss to scholarship would be tragic." Forbes's voice sank at the last sentence. He examined a fleck of cigar ash on his lapel, then brought his eyes up level with mine and stared at me steadily.

7

"Can we count on you, Mr. Spenser? Can you get it back?"

"Win this one for the Gipper," I said.

Behind me Tower gave a kind of snort, and Forbes looked as if he'd found half a worm in his apple.

"I beg your pardon?" he said.

"I'm thirty-seven years old and short on rah-rah, Dr. Forbes. If you'll pay me, and do your Pat O'Brien impressions somewhere else, I'll see if I can find the manuscript."

"This gets us nowhere," Tower said. "Let me take him down to my office, Dr. Forbes, and lay it all out for him. I know the situation and I'm used to dealing with people like him."

Forbes nodded without speaking. As we left the office he was standing at his window, hands clasped behind his back, looking at the snow.

The administration building was cinder block, with vinyl tile, frosted glass partitions, two tones of green on the corridor walls. Tower's office was six doors down from Forbes's and not much bigger than Forbes's desk. It was done in beige metal. Tower got seated behind his desk and tapped his teeth with a pencil.

"It's really slick how you can charm a client, Spenser."

I sat across from him in the other chair. I didn't say anything.

"Sure," he said, "the old man's kind of a ham, but he's a damn good administrator, and a damn fine person."

"Okay," I said, "he's terrific. When I grow up I want to be just like him. What about the Godwulf Manuscript?"

"Right." He took an eight-by-ten color print from his manila folder and handed it to me. It showed an elegantly handwritten book lying open on a table. The words were in Latin and around the margins in bright red and gold were drawn knights and ladies and lions on their hind legs, and vines and stags and a serpentine dragon being lanced by an armor-clad hero on a plump and feminine horse. The first letter at the top left on each page was elaborately drawn and incorporated into the design of the margins.

8

"It was taken three nights ago from its case in the library's rare book room. The watchman punched in there at two and again at four. At four he found the case open and the manuscript gone. He can't say positively that it wasn't there at two, but he assumes he would have noticed. It's hard to prove you didn't see something. You want to talk to him?"

"No," I answered. "That's routine stuff. You or the cops can do that as well as I could. Have you got a suspect?"

"SCACE."

"SCACE?"

"Student Committee Against Capitalist Exploitation. Revolution at the far-left fringe of the spectrum. I don't know it the way courts want it known; I know it the way you know things like that if you're in my line of work."

"Informer?"

"Not really, though I've got some contacts. Mostly, though, it's a gut guess. It's the kind of thing they'd do. I've been here for five years. Before that I was with the Bureau for ten. I've spent a lot of time on radicals, and I've developed a feel for them."

"Like the late director developed a feel for them?"

"Hoover? No, he's one reason I quit the Bureau. He was a hell of a cop once, but his time came and went before he died. I got enough feel about the radical kids not to classify them. The worst of them have the same things wrong that zealots always have, but you can't blame them for getting rigid about some of the things that go on. That ain't Walt Disney World out there." He nodded out his window at the blacktop quadrangle where the slush was beginning to collect in semi-fluid patterns as the kids sloshed through it. A thin and leafless sapling leaned against its support stake. It was a long way from home.

"Where do I find SCACE? Do they have a clubhouse with college pennants on the wall and old Pat Boone records playing day and night?"

"Not hardly," Tower said. "Your best bet would be to talk to the secretary. Terry Orchard. She's the least unpleasant of them, and the least unreasonable."

9

"Where do I find her?"

Tower pressed down an intercom button and asked someone to bring him in the SCACE file.

"We keep a file on all college organizations. Just routine. We're not singling SCACE out."

"I bet you've got a thick one on the Newman club," I said.

"Okay, we don't pay as much attention to some as others, granted. But we're not persecuting anybody."

Tower's door opened and a post-coed blonde in high white boots came in. She was wearing something in purple suede that was too short for a skirt and too long for a belt. Above that was a scarlet satin long-collared shirt with puffed sleeves and a deep neck. Her thighs were a little heavy—but perhaps she thought the same of me. She laid a thick brown file folder on Tower's desk, looked me over like the weight guesser at a fair, and left.

"Who was that," I asked, "the dean of women?"

Tower was thumbing through the file. He extracted a typewritten sheet.

"Here," he said, and handed it across. It was a file on Terry Orchard: home address: Newton, Mass. college address: none. Transient.

"Transient?" I said.

"Yeah, she drifts. Mostly she lives with a guy named Dennis Powell, who's some kind of SCACE official. She also used to live sometimes with a girl over on Hemenway Street. Connelly, Catherine Connelly. It's all there in the file."

"Yeah, and the file is a year old."

"I don't have the staff. The kids come and go. They're only here four years, if that. The real romantic radicals like to think of themselves as free floaters, street people. They sleep around on floors and sofas and Christ knows where else. Your best bet would be to get her after class."

Again the intercom, again the purple skirt.

"See if you can get Terry Orchard's schedule from the registrar's office for me, Brenda." All business. Competent.

Professional. No hanky-panky. No wonder he lasted ten years with the Feds.

She was back in about five minutes with a Xerox copy of an IBM printout of Terry Orchard's schedule. She had a class in the psychology of repression that ended at three in Hardin Hall, fourth floor. It was 2:35.

"Picture?" I asked Tower.

"Right here," he said. He looked at the massive watch on the broad, snakeskin band that he wore. It was the kind they call a chronometer, which will tell you not only the time but the atmospheric pressure and the lunar cycle.

"Three o'clock," he said. "Plenty of time; Hardin Hall is two buildings away across the quad. Take the elevator to the fourth floor. Room four-o-nine is to your left, about two doors down the corridor."

I looked at the picture. It wasn't good. Obviously an ID shot. Square face, rather thick lips, and hair pulled tight back away from her face. She looked older than the twenty her file had said she was. But most people do in ID shots. I reserved judgment.

"Okay," I said. "I'll go see her. How about a retainer? Forbes telling me how indigent you all were has me nervous."

"One will come to you in the mail from the comptroller. A week's worth in advance."

"Sold," I said. I gave him back the file and the picture.

"Don't you want it?"

"I'll remember," I said. We shook hands. I left.

The corridors were beginning to fill with students changing classes. I pushed through into the quadrangle. The thin elm sapling I'd seen from Forbes's window wasn't as lonely as I thought. Five cousins, no less spindly, were geometrically spaced about the hot top quadrangle. Three sides of the quadrangle were bordered with gray-white brick buildings. Each had wide stairs leading up to multiple glass-door banks. The buildings were perfectly square, four stories high, with gray painted casement windows. It looked like corporate headquarters for White Tower Hamburgers. The fourth side opened onto the street, where MBTA trains rumbled.

Under one of the saplings a boy and girl sat close together. He was wearing black sneakers and brown socks,
flared dungarees, a blue denim shirt and a fatigue jacket with
staff sergeant's stripes, a Seventh Division patch, and the
name tag Gagliano. His thick black hair blossomed out from
his head in a Caucasian afro and the snow streaked the rose-
colored lenses of his gold-rimmed glasses. The girl had on bib
overalls and a quilted ski parka. On her feet were blue suede
hiking boots with thick corrugated soles and silver lacing
studs. Her blond hair was perfectly straight and halfway to
her waist. She wore a woven leather headband to keep it out
of her eyes. I wondered if it was a mark of advancing years
when you no longer wanted to neck in the snow.

A black kid in a Borsalino hat came out of the library
across the quadrangle. He had on a red sleeveless jumpsuit,
black shirt with bell sleeves, high-heeled black patent leather
boots with black laces. A full-length black leather trench coat
hung open. A Fu Manchu mustache swept to the chin on each
side of his mouth. Two kids in football jackets exchanged
looks as he went by. They had necks like pilot whales. A slim
black girl in an Angela Davis haircut and huge pendant earrings trailed a gentle scent of imported bath soap past me as I
went into Hardin Hall, the third building on the quadrangle.

The elevator that took me to the fourth floor was covered with obscene graffiti that some proprietous soul had
tried to doctor into acceptability, so that phrases like "buck
you" mingled with the more traditional expletives. It was a
losing cause, but that didn't make it a bad one.

Room 409 had a blond oak door with a window in it,
just like the other six classrooms that lined the corridor on
each side. Inside I could see about forty kids facing a woman
seated up front at a table. She wore a dark maroon silk
granny dress with a low scooped neckline. The dress was covered with an off-white floral design that looked like hydran-
gea. Her long black hair was caught back with a gold bar-
rette. She wore large round horn-rimmed glasses, and was
smoking a corncob pipe with a curved amber stem. She was
speaking with great animation and her hands flashed with

large rings as she spoke and gestured. A number of students were taking notes, some watched her closely, some had their heads down on the desk and were apparently asleep. Terry Orchard was there, back row, looking out the window at the snow. She looked like kids I'd seen before, the real goods, faded Levi jacket and pants, faded and unironed denim shirt, hair pulled back tight in a pigtail like an eighteenth-century British sailor. No make-up, no jewelry. On her feet were yellow leather work shoes that laced up over the ankle. She wasn't built so you could tell from where I was, but I would have bet my retainer that she wouldn't be wearing a bra. There are kids that get their anti-establishment milkman's overalls in the Marsha Jordan Shop with their own charge card. But Terry wasn't one of them. Her clothes exclaimed their origin in Jerry's Army–Navy Store. She was better-looking than her picture, but still looked older than twenty.

CHAPTER TWO

THE BELL RANG and the teacher stopped—apparently in midsentence—put her corncob pipe in her mouth, folded up her notes, and started out. The kids followed. Terry Orchard was one of the first out the door. I fell in beside her.

"Excuse me," I said, "Miss Orchard?"

"Yes?" No hostility, but very little warmth either.

"My name is Spenser and I'd like to buy you lunch."

"Why?"

"How about, I'm a Hollywood producer casting for a new movie?"

"Get lost," she said without looking at me.

"How about, if you don't come to lunch with me I'll break both your thumbs and you'll never play pool again?"

She stopped and looked at me. "Look," she said, "what the hell do you want anyway? Why don't you go hang around down at the convent school with a bag of candy bars?"

We were down one flight of stairs now and turning toward the next flight. I took a card out of the breast pocket of my jacket and handed it to her. She read it.

"Oh, for crissake," she said. "A private eye? Jesus. Is that corny! Are you going to pull a gat on me? Did my old man send you?"

"Miss Orchard, look at it this way, you get a free lunch and half a million laughs afterward talking to the gang back at the malt shop. I get a chance to ask some questions, and if you answer them I'll let you play with my handcuffs. If you don't answer them, you still get the lunch. Who else has been out with a private eye lately?"

"A pig is a pig," she said. "Whether he's public or private, he works for the same people."

"Next time you're in trouble," I said, "call a hippie."

"Oh, crap, you know damn well . . ."

I stopped her. "I know damn well that it would be easier to argue over lunch. My fingernails are clean and I promise to use silverware. I'm paying with establishment expense money. It's a chance to exploit them."

She almost smiled. "Okay," she said. "We'll go to the Pub. They'll let me in dressed this way. And this is the only way I dress."

We had reached the ground level and headed out into the quadrangle. We then turned left out onto the avenue. The buildings around the university were old red brick. Many of the windows were boarded, and few of the rest had curtains. Along the avenue was some of the detritus that gathers at the exterior edge of a big university: used-book shops, cut-rate clothing stores featuring this year's freaky fashions, a porno shop, a school of astrology-reading in a store-front, a term-paper mill, three sub joints, hamburger, pizza, fried chicken joints, and a place selling soft ice cream. The porno shop was bigger than the bookstore.

The Pub was probably once a gas station. It had been painted entirely antique green, glass windows and all. The word Pub was gold-leafed on the door. Inside were a juke box, a color TV, dark wooden tables and high-backed booths, a bar along one side. The ceiling was low and most of the light came from a big Budweiser sign in the rear. The bar was mostly empty in midafternoon; a group in one booth was playing cards. In the back a boy and girl were talking very softly to one another. Terry Orchard and I took the second booth from the door. The table top was covered with initials scratched with penknife and pencil point over a long period of time. The upholstery of the booth was torn in places and cracked in others.

"Do you recommend anything?" I asked.

"The corned beef is okay," she said.

A fat, tough, tired-looking waitress wearing sneakers came for our order. I ordered us both a corned beef sandwich and a beer. Terry Orchard lit a cigarette and blew smoke through her nostrils.

"If I drink that beer you're an accomplice. I'm under twenty-one," she said.

"That's okay, it gives me a chance to show contempt for the establishment."

The waitress set down two large schooners of draft beer. "Your sandwiches will be out in a minute," she said, and shuffled off. Terry took a sip.

I said, "You're under arrest." Her eyes flared open, and then she smiled, grudgingly, over the glass.

"You're nowhere near as funny as you think you are, Mr. Spenser, but you're a hell of a lot better than I figured. What do you want?"

"I'm looking for the Godwulf Manuscript. The university president himself called me in, showed me his profile, dazzled me with his elocution, and assigned me to get it back. Tower, the campus cop, suggested you might help me."

"What is a Godwulf Manuscript?"

15

"It's an illuminated manuscript from the fourteenth century. It was in the rare book room at your library; now it isn't. It's being held for ransom by an unidentified campus group."

"Why did Super Swine think I could help?"

"Super Swine—you must be an English major—he thought you could help because he thinks SCACE took it, and you are the secretary of that organization."

"Why does he think SCACE took it?"

"Because he has an instinct for it, and maybe because he knows something. He's not just a storefront clotheshorse. When he's not getting his nails manicured and his hair styled with a razor, he is probably a pretty shrewd cop. He didn't tell me everything he knows."

"Why not?"

"Sweetie, no one ever tells me everything he knows; it is the nature of the beast."

"You must get a swell view of life looking at it through a keyhole half the time."

"I see what's there."

The waitress brought our sandwiches, large, on dark bread, with pickles and chips. They were sweet pickles, though. I ordered two more beers.

"What about the manuscript?" I asked.

"I don't know anything about it."

"Okay," I said, "tell me about SCACE then."

Her face was less friendly now. "Why do you want to know about SCACE?"

"I won't know till I've learned. That's my line of work. I ask about things. And people don't tell me anything, so I ask about more things, and so on. Now and then things fall into place."

"Well, there's nothing to fall into place here. We're a revolutionary organization. We are trying to develop a new consciousness; we're committed to social change, to redistribution of wealth, to real liberty for everyone, not just for the bosses and the rip-off artists."

Her voice had become almost mechanical, like the

16

people who do telephone canvassing for dance studios. I wondered how long it had been since she'd actually thought about all those words and what they really meant.

^ "How would you go about getting these things instituted?"

"By continuous social pressure. By pamphleteering, by marching, by demonstrating our support for all causes that crack the establishment's united front. By refusing to accede to anything that benefits the establishment. By opposing injustice whenever we find it."

"Making much progress?" I asked.

"You bet your life. We're growing every day. There were only three or four of us at first. Now there are five times that many."

"No, I meant injustice."

She was silent, looking at me.

"I haven't made much progress that way either," I said.

A tall, big-boned blond kid wearing a plaid shirt and Levi's came into the Pub and looked around. He was clean-shaven and wild-haired, and when his eyes got used to the dimness he headed over to us and slid in beside Terry Orchard. He picked up her half-filled glass, drained it, set it down, and said to her, "Who's this creep?"

"Dennis," she said, "be nice."

He squeezed her arm hard with one hand and repeated the question. I answered for her.

"My name's Spenser."

He turned his head toward me and looked very hard at me. "I'm talking to her, not you, Jack. Shut up."

"Dennis!" She said it with more emphasis this time. "Who the hell do you think you are? Let go of my arm."

I reached over and took hold of his wrist. "Listen, Goldilocks," I said, "I bought her a beer and you drank it. On my block that entitles you to get your upper lip fattened."

He yanked his hand away from me. "You think maybe the long hair makes me soft?"

"Dennis," Terry said, "he's a private detective."

17

"Freaking pig," he said, and swung at me. I pulled my head out of the way and slipped out of the booth. The punch rammed against the back of the booth; the kid swore and turned toward me. He was not planning to quit, so I figured it best end swiftly. I feinted toward his stomach with my left hand, then hooked it over his lowered guard and turned my whole shoulder into it as it connected on the side of his face. He sat down hard on the floor.

Terry Orchard went down on her knees beside him, her arms around his shoulders.

"Don't get up, Dennis. Stay there. He'll hurt you."

"She's right, kid," I said. "You're an amateur. I do this kind of thing for a living."

The big old tough waitress came around and said, "What the hell is going on? You want the cops in here? You want to fight, go outside."

"No more trouble," I said. "I'm a movie stunt man and I was just showing my friend how to slip a punch."

"And I'm Wonder Woman and if you do it again, I'm calling the blues." She stomped off.

"The beer offer still holds," I said. The kid got up, his jaw already beginning to puff. He wouldn't want to chew much tomorrow. He sat down in the booth beside Terry, who still held his arm protectively.

"I'm sorry, Mr. Spenser," she said. "He isn't really like that."

"What's he really like?" I asked.

His eyes, which had been a little out of focus, were sharpening. "I'm like I am," he said. "And I don't like to see Terry sitting around boozing with some nosy goddamn gumshoe. What are you doing around here anyway?"

The left hook had taken some of the starch out of him. His voice was less assertive, more petulant. But it hadn't made him any sweeter.

"I'm a private detective looking for a stolen rare book, the Godwulf Manuscript. Ever hear of it?"

"No."

"How'd you know I was a private cop?"

"I didn't till Terry said so, but you got the look. If your hair were much shorter it would be a crew cut. In the movement you learn to be suspicious. Besides, Terry's my woman."

"I'm not anybody's woman, Dennis. That's a sexist statement. I'm not a possession."

"Oh, Christ," I said. "Could we cut the polemics a minute. If you know of the manuscript, know this also. It has to be kept in a climate-controlled atmosphere. Otherwise it will disintegrate. And then it will be worthless both to scholars and to you, or whoever the book-nappers may be. The university hasn't got the money to ransom it."

"They got the money to buy football players and build a hockey rink and pay goddamn professors to teach three hours a week and write books the rest of the time."

"I'm not into educational reform this week. Do you have any thoughts on where the missing manuscript might be?"

"If I did I wouldn't tell you. If I didn't I could find out, and when I found out I wouldn't tell you then either. You aren't peeking over the transom in some flophouse now, snoopy. You're on a college campus and you stick out like a sore thumb. You will find out nothing at all because no one will tell you. You and the other dinosaurs can rut around all you want—we're not buying it."

"Buying what?"

"Whatever you're selling. You are the other side, man."

"We aren't getting anywhere," I said. "I'll see you."

I left a five on the table to cover the lunch and left. It was getting dark now and the commuter traffic was starting. I felt the beer a little, and I felt the sadness of kids like that who weren't buying it and weren't quite sure what it was. I got my car from where I'd parked it by a hydrant. It had a parking ticket tied to the windshield wiper. Eternal vigilance, I thought, is the price of liberty. I tore the ticket up and drove home.

CHAPTER THREE

I WAS LIVING that year on Marlborough Street, two blocks up from the Public Garden. I made myself hash and eggs for supper and read the morning's *New York Times* while I ate. I took my coffee with me into the living room and tried looking at television. It was awful, so I shut it off and got out my carving. I'd been working on a block of hard pine for about six months now, trying to reproduce in wood the bronze statue of an Indian on horseback that stands in front of the Museum of Fine Arts. The wood was so hard that I had to sharpen the knives every time I worked. And I spent about half an hour this night with whetstone and file before I began on the pine. At eleven I turned on the news, watched it as I undressed, shut it off, and went to bed.

At some much later time, in the dark, the phone rang. I spiraled slowly upward from sleep and answered it after it had rung for what seemed a long time. The girl's voice at the other end was thick and very slow, almost like a 45 record played at 33.

"Spenser?"

"Yeah."

"It's Terry . . . help me."

"Where are you?"

"Eighty Hemenway Street, apartment three."

"Ten minutes," I said, and rolled out of bed.

It was 3:05 in the morning when I got into my car and headed for Hemenway Street. It wasn't till 3:15 when I got there. Three A.M. traffic in Boston is rarely a serious problem.

Hemenway Street, on the other hand, often is. It is a

short street of shabby apartment buildings, near the university, and for no better reason than Haight-Ashbury had, or the East Village, it had become the place for street people. On the walls of the building Maoist slogans were scrawled in red paint. On a pillar at the entrance to the street was a proclamation of Gay Liberation. There were various recommendations about pigs being offed scrawled on the sidewalk. I left my car double-parked outside 80 Hemenway and tried the front door. It was locked. There were no doorbells to push. I took my gun out, reversed it, and broke the glass with the handle. Then I reached around and turned the dead lock and opened the door from the inside.

Number three was down the hall, right rear. There were bicycles with tire locks lining both walls, and some indeterminate litter behind them. Terry's door was locked. I knocked; no answer. I knocked again and heard something faint, like the noise of a kitten. The corridor was narrow. I braced my back against the wall opposite the door and drove my heel, with 195 pounds behind it, against the door next to the knob. The inside jamb splintered, and the door tore open and banged violently against the wall as it opened.

Inside all the lights were on. The first thing I saw was Dennis Goldilocks lying on his back with his mouth open, his arms outspread, and a thick patch of tacky and blackening blood covering much of his chest. Near him on her hands and knees was Terry Orchard. Her hair was loose and falling forward as though she were trying to dry it in the sun. But it wasn't sunny in there. She wore only a pajama top with designs of Snoopy and the Red Baron on it, and it was from her that the faint kitten sounds were coming. She swayed almost rhythmically back and forth making no progress, moving in no direction, just swaying and mewing. Between her and Dennis on the floor was a small white-handled gun. It or something had been fired in the room; I could smell it.

I knelt beside the blond boy and felt for the big pulse in his neck. The minute I touched his skin I knew I'd never feel the pulse. He was cool already and getting colder. I turned to Terry. She still swayed, head down and sick. I could smell something vaguely medicinal on her breath. Her breath was heaving and her eyes were slits. I pulled her to her feet, and held her, one arm around her back. She was almost all the way under. I couldn't tell from what, but whatever it was, it was an o.d.

I walked her into the bathroom, got her pajama shirt off, and got her under the shower. I turned the water on warm and then slowly to full cold and held her under. She quivered and struggled faintly. The sleeves of my jacket were wet up past the elbows and my shirtfront was soaked through. She pushed one hand weakly at my face and began to cry instead of mew. I held her there some more. As I held her I kept listening for footsteps behind me. The door had made a hell of a lot of noise when I kicked it open, and the gunshot must have been a loud one long before that. But the neighborhood was not, apparently, that kind of neighborhood. Not the kind to look into gunshots and doors splintering and such. The kind to pull the covers up over the head and burrow the face in the pillow and say screw it. Better him than me.

I got a hand up to her neck and felt her pulse. It was quicker—I guessed about sixty. I got her out of the shower and across to the bedroom. I didn't see a robe, so I pulled the blanket off the bed and wrapped it around her. Then we waltzed to the kitchen. I got water boiling and found some instant coffee and a cup. She was babbling now, nothing co- herent, but the words were intelligible. I made coffee with her balanced half over one hip, my arm around her and the blan- ket caught in my fist to keep her warm. Then back to the living room to the day bed—there were no chairs in the kitchen—and sat her down.

She pushed aside the coffee and spilled some on her- self and cried out at the pain, but I got her to drink some. And again some. And one more time. Her eyes were open now and her breath was much less shallow. I could see her rib cage swell and settle regularly beneath the blanket. She finished the coffee.

I stood her up and we began to walk back and forth across the apartment, which wasn't much of a walk. There was the living room, a small bedroom, a bath, and a kitchenette, barely big enough to stand in. The living room, in which the quick and dead were joined, held only a card table, a steamer trunk with a lamp on it, and the studio couch on whose bare mattress Terry Orchard had drunk her coffee. The blanket I had pulled off the bed had been its only adornment, and as I looked into the bedroom I could see a cheap deal bureau beside the bed. On it was a candle stuck in a Chianti bottle beneath a bare light bulb hanging from a ceiling.

I looked down at Terry Orchard. There were tears running down her cheeks, and less of her weight leaned on me.

"Sonova bitch," she said. "Sonova bitch, sonova bitch, sonova bitch."

"When you can talk to me, talk to me. Till then keep walking," I said.

She just kept saying sonova bitch, in a dead singsong voice, and I found that as we walked we were keeping time to the curse, left, right, sonova bitch. I realized that the broken door was still wide open and as we sonovabitched by on the next swing I kicked it shut with my heel. A few more turns and she fell silent, then she said, half question—

"Spenser?"

"Yeah."

"Oh my God, Spenser."

"Yeah."

We stopped walking and she turned against me with her face hard against my chest. She clenched onto my shirt with both fists and seemed to be trying to blend into me. We stood motionless like that for a long time. Me with my arms around her. Both wet and dripping and the dead boy with his wide sightless eyes not looking at us.

"Sit down," I said after a while. "Drink some more coffee. We have to talk."

She didn't want to let go of me, but I pried her off and sat her on the day bed. She huddled inside the blanket, her wet hair plastered down around her small head, while I made some more coffee.

We sat together on the day bed, sipping coffee. I had

the impulse to say, "What's new?" but squelched it. Instead I said, "Tell me about it now."

"Oh, God, I can't."

"You have to."

"I want to get out of here. I want to run."

"Nope. You have to sit here and tell me what happened. From the very first thing that happened to the very last thing that happened. And you have to do it now, because you are in very big trouble and I have to know exactly how big."

"Trouble? Jesus, you think I shot him, don't you?"

"The thought occurred to me."

"I didn't shoot him. They shot him. The ones that made me take the dope. The ones that made me shoot the gun."

"Okay, but start with the first thing. Whose apartment is this?"

"Ours, Dennis's and mine." She nodded at the floor and then started and looked away quickly.

"Dennis is Dennis Powell, right?"

"Yes."

"And you live together and are not married, right?"

"Yes."

"When did the people come who did this?"

"I don't know exactly—it was late, about two thirty maybe."

"Who were they?"

"I don't know. Two men. Dennis seemed to know them."

"What did they do?"

"They knocked on the door. Dennis got up—we weren't asleep, we never go to sleep till very late—and asked, 'Who is it?' I couldn't hear what they said. But he let them in. That's why I think he knew them. When he opened the door they came in very fast. One of them pushed him against the wall and the other one came into the bedroom and dragged me out of bed. Neither one said anything. Dennis said something like, 'Hey, what's the idea?' Or 'Hey, what's going on?' One of them had a gun and he held it on both of us. He never said anything. Neither one. It was spooky. The other guy reached in his coat pocket and came out with my gun."

"Is that your gun on the floor?" I asked.

She wouldn't look but nodded.

"Okay, then what?" I asked.

"He handed my gun to the first man, the man with the gun, and then he grabbed me and turned me around and put his hand over my mouth and bent my arm up behind me and the other man shot Dennis twice."

"With your gun?"

"Yes."

"Then what?"

"Then—" She paused and closed her eyes and shook her head.

"Go on," I said.

"Then the man that shot Dennis made me hold the gun in my hand and shoot it into Dennis. He held my wrist and squeezed my finger on the trigger." She said it in a rush and the words nearly ran together.

"Did he have on gloves?"

She thought a minute. "Yes, yellow ones. I think they might have been rubber or plastic."

"Then what?"

"Then the one who was holding me made me lie down on the bed. I didn't have anything on but my top. And the other one poured some kind of dope in my mouth and forced it shut and held my nose till I swallowed it. Then they just held me there with a hand over my mouth for a little while. Then they left."

I didn't say anything. If she'd invented that story coming out of a narcotic coma, she was some kind of special species and nothing I could handle. She might have hallucinated the whole thing, depending on what she had taken. Or the story might be true.

"Why did they make me shoot him after he was dead?" she asked.

I discovered as I answered that I believed her. "To

hook you on a paraffin test. When you fire a handgun cordite particles impregnate your skin. A lab man puts paraffin over it, lets it dry, peels it off, and tests it. The particles show up in the wax."

It took a minute to register. "A lab man, you mean the police?"

"Yes, honey, the police."

"No, can't we get out of here? I'll go home. You won't say anything. My father will pay you. He has money. I know he can give you some . . ."

"Your boyfriend, dead in your apartment, killed with your gun, you gone? They'd come and get you and bring you back. Do you know a lawyer?"

"A lawyer, how the hell would I know a freaking lawyer?" She looked desperately toward the door. "I'm splitting, screw this scene." Her voice had gotten harsh and tough with fright, and I noticed her lapse into the jargon of her peer group as her fright increased. When she'd been clinging to me she talked like a young girl in college. When she wanted to get away from me her voice and language changed. I held her against me with my arm around her shoulder.

"Listen," I said. "You are in trouble enough to pull up over your head and tie a knot in. But you're not in it alone. I'll help you. It's my line of work. I'll get you a lawyer in a bit. Then I'll call the cops. Before I do, though—" She started to speak and I squeezed her. "Listen," I said, "When the cops come don't say anything, don't talk to them, don't argue with them, don't be hostile, don't be smart. Do not say anything to anybody till you talk to the lawyer. His name is Vincent Haller. He'll see you soon after you go downtown. Talk only with him present and say only what he says you should. Have you ever been busted?"

"No."

"Okay. It's not anywhere near as bad as you think it is. No one will hurt you. No one will grab you under a bright light and hit you with a hose. You'll be okay, and you won't be in long. Haller will take care of you."

She nodded. I went on.

"Before I make my call—do you have any idea why the men did this?"

"No."

"Do you use drugs?"

"Yes."

"Do you know what they gave you?"

"No. It tasted like paregoric and smelled like ether. It wasn't anything I'd tried. Whatever it was, was a downer though."

"Okay. Get dressed. I'm going to call."

CHAPTER FOUR

THE FIRST OF Boston's finest to arrive were two bulls from a radio car. They came in, told us not to touch anything, got our names, frisked me, took my gun, and looked closely at us till the homicide people came. They came, as they always do, in large numbers: technicians, photographers, someone from the medical examiner's. Two guys in white coats to carry out the corpse and some dicks to investigate the crime and question the suspects. In this case the crew was led by the commander of the homicide bureau, Lieutenant Martin Quirk. I'm six foot one and he was taller than I was, taller and thicker. His hands and fingers were thick and his lips were thick and his nose was broad. His thick black hair was cut close. He was clean-shaven at four A.M. and his shoes gleamed with dark polish. His shirt was freshly ironed and his tie neatly knotted. His suit was immaculate and sharply creased. He wore a Tyrolean hat with a feather in it and a white raincoat, which he never took off. His face was pockmarked and there was a short scar at one corner of his mouth.

He stood now looking at me with his raincoat open and his hands in his hip pockets. "This is sure a lucky break for us, Spenser, having you on this to help us out. We need slick professionals like yourself to straighten us out and all. Keep us from forgetting to look for fingerprints, missing clues, and stuff."

"I didn't plan to get into this, Lieutenant. The kid called me for help, and I came over and found her. And him. She was badly drugged. I got her sobered up a little and called you."

"How did she know you?" Quirk asked.

"I'm on a case that she's involved in."

"What case?"

"Looking for a missing rare manuscript stolen from a university."

"What university?"

"If it seems pertinent, I'll tell you."

"If I want to know, you'll tell me." Quirk's voice squeezed out sharp and flat like sheet metal.

"I'll tell you if you need to know it. I don't make a living telling cops everything they want to know about clients."

"I don't make a living taking crap from hole-in-the-wall shysters like you, Spenser."

A thin, blue-jowled sergeant named Belson drifted in between Quirk and me.

"Come on, Lieutenant, this don't get us far. Both the girl and the victim are university students, and there's a fair bet that it's the same university that hired Spenser."

Quirk looked at me, then Belson. "Do you know him?" he asked, nodding at me.

"Yeah, he used to work out of the Suffolk County D.A.'s office about five years ago. I hear he got canned."

"Okay, get his story." He turned to me. "You're not working for the D.A. now, boy, you're working my side of the street, and if you get in my way I'll kick your ass right into the gutter. Got that?"

"Can I feel your muscle?" I said.

28

Quirk looked at me without saying anything, then turned away and walked over to the girl.

Belson shook his head and pulled out a notebook.

"Start up with the lieutenant, Spenser, and you'll end up looking like you went through a pepper mill."

"I won't be able to sleep without a night light," I said.

Belson shrugged. "Okay. Start from the beginning. You're in the business. I don't have to lead you."

I told him, omitting, mostly from stubbornness, the name of my client, but including, because it was sure to come out anyway, the incident in the Pub that afternoon, when I had knocked the kid down.

Belson shook his head again. "How could anyone get mad at a sweetheart like you? I would have thought he'd have been hypnotized with the way you're so agreeable."

I let that go.

"You're sure you might not have been hustling his chick just a little, Spenser? And maybe you were over here hustling her again and he came home and caught you, and an argument developed?"

"Yeah, and I pulled out my fourteen-dollar Saturday night special and let fly at him. Come off it, Belson. You're just talking for the hell of it. You know I didn't do it. You know I wouldn't use a piece of cheap tin like that gun. If I had, you know I would have covered it better than this."

"Okay, maybe I don't like you for it. I've known you a long time, and it's not your style. But it could happen. You got nothing against girls, I can recall. It could be his gun and you had to take it away from him and it went off. Lotta people get killed by people in a way that ain't their style."

"And I shot him four times in the chest getting it away from him?"

"Could be to cover it up, make it look different."

"You're fishing, Frank," I said.

"Maybe."

"Have you heard the girl's story yet?"

"Nope, lieutenant's getting that now."

"He's going to love it," I said.

"Of course you got it before you called us," Belson said.

"She was way under from something. I had to bring her out."

"And then you had to ask her what happened and then she had to tell you. And then you had to fix up a story maybe."

"Wait till you hear the story. You don't think I'm smart enough to work up something like that. You guys are cops, not priests. Calling you isn't a ritual act. I called you as soon as my judgment told me it was both feasible and prudent."

Belson set fire to a half-smoked cigar before he said anything. Then he said, "You talk good for a dumb slug; feasible and prudent, my, my."

From the other side of the room Quirk spoke over his shoulder without turning his head. "Belson, bring the private license over here."

Belson nodded me toward Quirk and I walked over. Quirk was straddling the only straight chair in the room, with his forearms crossed on the back. Before him Terry Orchard was on the couch. She had on a denim shirt and Levi's again, but her hair was still wet and tight on her skull. She looked awfully small.

"Spenser," he said without looking up. "She says she won't say anything unless you say it's all right. She says you told her not to talk to us without a lawyer."

"Right enough, Lieutenant. I knew you wouldn't want to take advantage of her when she was confused, or perhaps in a state of shock."

"We're going to take her in."

"I thought you might."

"We'd like you to come along, too," Quirk said.

"I wouldn't miss it," I said.

Terry looked at me with her eyes very wide and dark. I said to her, "Haller will be there. Just do as I said."

The assistant M.E., a small man with thick glasses and gray curly hair, came over to Quirk.

"I'm through," he said. "If you are too, we'll haul him off."

"Any opinions, Manny?" Quirk asked.

"Yeah, I'd guess he was shot in the chest."

"That med school training really gives you insight," Quirk said. "Anything that I need to know that you can tell me now?"

"Shot sometime within the last five or six hours, cause of death presumable gunshot. I don't see any other signs. Got any corroborative testimony?"

Quirk looked at Belson.

"Spenser says the kid was dead when he arrived at three fifteen and that the blood had gotten tacky and the skin was cool," Belson said.

The assistant M.E. said, "That seems about right, but it could be a couple hours earlier for all I can prove here."

Quirk nodded. "Okay, thanks, Manny." And then to the two white-coated interns, "Take him away."

They bundled Dennis Powell onto the stretcher. He'd already started to stiffen and he was getting awkward to handle. They straightened his arms out down by his side, put his ankles together, wrapped the tarp around him, and strapped him into the stretcher. Then they dollied him out. They had to stand him up to get him out the apartment door, and when they did the top of him lolled against the straps. Terry made a noise and looked away. The stretcher bumped down the stairs and out to the ambulance. A few curious early risers stood around staring. The two harness bulls who'd showed up first kept them away from the door. A little fat dick in a long blue overcoat with a button missing came in after letting the stretcher out.

"Nothing, Lieutenant. Nobody heard nothing, nobody saw nothing, nobody knows nothing. Half of them are god-damn faggots, anyway."

"Jesus Christ," Quirk said. "Just give me information; don't review the witnesses' sex life for me."

"Okay, Lieutenant. I mean I figured that being as they was faggots you might not want to take their word. You know how these goddamn perverts are."

"No, I don't know, and I don't want you to tell me. Stay around, ask questions. See what you can find out about these two. Try to remember you're on the homicide squad, not the vice squad. When I want a fag count, I'll let you know."

The dick hustled out. Quirk shook his head. Belson was looking up at the ceiling, puffing the cigar butt that was barely clearing his lips by now.

"Take 'em downtown, Frank." Quirk said to Belson. "I'll clean up here and be along."

As we started out I said to Belson. "I'm still double-parked out there. Let me get it off the street before some zealous meter maid gets it hauled off."

Belson said. "Why don't you follow me downtown. Then we won't have to drive you back later."

I nodded and grinned. "See? I told you you didn't think I did it."

"I don't think anything," Belson said. "But you'll be down to look out for the little girl."

Belson took Terry into the squad car and they drove off. I got my car out from behind another white and blue police car with the seal of the city on the side, and followed Belson's car up Hemenway to Boylston, down Boylston to Clarendon, right on Clarendon, then up the Stanhope Street Alley and in behind headquarters.

CHAPTER FIVE

WE WENT IN the back door, off Stanhope Street by the parking area that says RESERVED FOR PRESS. There were no cars there. You only go in the front door if you're newsfilm material. If they put the arm on you in a disadvantaged neighborhood you go in past the empty press lot.

The Homicide Division was third floor rear, with a

view of the Fryalator vent from the coffee shop in the alley and the soft perfume of griddle and grease mixing with the indigenous smell of cigar smoke and sweat and something else, maybe generations of scared people. Vince Haller was leaning against one of the desks outside Quirk's frosted glass cubicle. He was wearing a white double-knit suit, and over one shoulder he carried a camel's-hair coat with big leather buttons. His gray hair was long and modish and he had a big Teddy Roosevelt mustache. He was a couple of inches taller than I was, but not as heavy.

"Gentlemen?" he said in his big actorish voice.

I gave him a wave and Belson said, "Hello, Vince."

"I'd like a chance to talk to my client."

Belson looked at Terry Orchard. "Is this man your attorney?"

She looked at me and I nodded. She said, "Yes."

"You can talk with her at my desk there." Belson nodded at a scarred and cluttered desk outside Quirk's enclosed cubicle. "We'll stay out of earshot."

"Has she been charged, Frank?" Haller asked.

"Not yet."

"Will she be?"

"I don't know. The lieutenant will be along in a minute. He takes care of that stuff. We'll want to talk with her a lot, though, either way."

"Has she been advised of her rights?"

Belson snorted. "Are you kidding. If she were shooting at me with a flame thrower I'd have to advise her of her rights before I shot back. Yes, she's been advised."

"Have you, Miss Orchard?"

"Yes, sir." She was numb and scared, and entirely submissive.

"Okay, come over here and we'll talk." She did and Belson and I stood silently watching them. I suddenly realized how tired I was. I'd slept about three hours. As we stood there, Quirk came in with two other dicks. He looked over at Haller and Terry Orchard, said nothing, and walked into his cubicle. Belson went in after him.

"Stick around," he said. And closed the door. The two dicks sat down at desks, and looked at nothing.

At the other end of the office a black cop with thick hands and a broken nose was talking into a telephone receiver cradled on one shoulder. An old guy in green coveralls came through dragging a cardboard carton with a rope handle and emptying the ashtrays and wastebaskets into it. Haller was still talking to Terry. And I thought about all the times I'd spent in shabby squad rooms like this. Sometimes it felt like all the rooms I was ever in looked out onto alleys. And I thought about how it must feel to be twenty and alone and be in one at 5:30 A.M. and not sure you'd get out. The steam pipes hissed. I wanted to hiss back.

More than that I wanted to run. The room was hot and stuffy. The air was bad. I wanted to get out, to get in my car and drive north. In my mind I could see the route, over the Mystic Bridge up Route One, north, maybe to Ipswich or Newburyport where the houses were stately and old and the air was clean and cold and full of the sea. Where there's a kind of mellowness and a memory of another time and another America. Probably never was another America though. And if I headed out that way I'd probably be sitting around the police station in Ipswich, smelling the steam pipes and the disinfectant and wondering if some poor slob deserved what he was getting.

Quirk came out of his office. And looked at Haller. Then turned to me.

"Come in and talk."

I did. I told the same story to Quirk that I had to Belson. Exactly the same way. Quirk listened without a word. Looking straight at me all the time I talked. When I was through he said, "Okay, wait outside."

I did. He called Terry Orchard in. Haller went with her. The door closed. I sat some more. The dick at the end of the room still talked into the phone. The two that had come in with Quirk continued to sit and look elaborately at nothing. The sun had come up and shone into one corner of the room. Dust motes drifted in languidly.

"I can't stand it anymore," I said. "I'll confess, just don't give me the silent treatment anymore."

The two detectives looked at me blankly. "Confess what?" one of them said. He had long curly sideburns.

"Anything you want, just no more of the cold shoulder."

Sideburns said to his partner, "Hey, Al, ain't he a funny guy? Right before you go off duty after working all night it's really great to have a funny guy like him around so you can go home happy. Don't you feel that way, Al?"

Al said, "Aw, screw him."

More silence. I got up and walked to the window. There was a heavy wire mesh across it so suspects wouldn't jump out, drop three stories to the ground, and run off. The windows were grimy, with a kind of ancient grime that seemed to have sunk into the glass. Three floors below a thin Puerto Rican kid with pointed shoes came out of the back of the coffee shop with a bucket and poured hot dirty water into the street. It steamed in the cold briefly. I looked at my watch. 6:40. The kid had got up awful early to come in and mop the floor. I wondered how late tonight he'd be there.

Belson came out of Quirk's office with Terry, through the squad room, and out. Haller came out too, and walked over to me.

"They've gone down to the lab. I think they'll book her," he said. I didn't say anything.

He said, "Quickly, I wanted to check her story with you. She was asleep with her boyfriend in their apartment. Two men apparently known to Powell entered. Shot Powell, forced her to shoot Powell's body, drugged her, and left. She called you. You came. Sobered her up, got her story. Called the cops."

"That's it," I said.

"She knows you because the university employed you to find a missing rare book."

"Manuscript," I said.

"Okay, manuscript. . . . You got in touch with her because the campus security man suggested that an organization she was part of might have taken it. She had your card. In trouble, she called you."

"Right again," I said.

"As stories go it's not a winner," Haller said.

"I know," I said.

"She's convincing when she tells it, though," said Haller.

"What's its effect on Quirk?" I asked.

"Hard to say. He doesn't show much, but I don't think he's easy about it. I think he'll book her, but I don't think he's sure she's guilty."

"What do you think?" I asked.

"All my clients are innocent."

"Yeah," I said, "of something, anyway."

While we waited, the shift changed. Al and Sideburns left. The black cop with the phone departed. The day people came in. Faces shaved, wind-reddened. Smelling of cologne. Some of them had coffee in paper cups they'd bought on the way in. It smelled good. No one offered me any. Belson came back into the office with Terry. They went back into Quirk's office. Haller with them. Quirk yelled from inside.

"Spenser, come in. You might as well hear the rest."

I went in. It was crowded in there. Quirk was behind his desk. Terry in a straight chair beside it. Belson, Haller, and I standing against the wall. Quirk's desk was absolutely bare except for a tape recorder and a transparent plastic cube that on all sides contained pictures of a woman, children, and an English setter.

Quirk turned the recorder on. "All right, Miss Orchard, your story and Spenser's match. But that proves nothing much. You had plenty of time to arrange it before we were called. Can you think of any reason why two men would wish to come and kill Dennis Powell?"

"No, I don't know—maybe." Terry spoke barely above a whisper, and she seemed to sway slightly in the chair as she spoke.

"Which is it, Miss Orchard?" Quirk's voice was almost

entirely without inflection and his thick, pockmarked face was entirely impassive. Terry shook her head.

Haller said, "Really, Lieutenant, Miss Orchard is about to fall from the chair." When Haller talked, the orange level light on the recorder flared brightly.

"Which is it, Miss Orchard?" Quirk said again, as if Haller hadn't spoken.

"Well, I think he was involved in the manuscript."

"Which manuscript?"

"The one that Mr. Spenser is looking for, the whatchamacallit manuscript."

I said, "Godwulf," and Quirk said, "Is it the Godwulf Manuscript, Miss Orchard?"

She nodded.

Quirk said, "Say yes or no, Miss Orchard; the recorder can't pick up signs."

"Yes," she said.

"How was he involved?"

"I don't know, just that he was, and some faculty member was. I heard him talking on the phone one day."

"What did they say?"

"I can't remember."

"Then why do you think it involved the theft of a manuscript?"

"I just know. You know how you remember having an idea from a conversation but don't remember the conversation itself, you know?"

"Why do you think a faculty member is involved, Miss Orchard?"

She shook her head again. "Same reason," she said.

"Do you think one of the men who you say killed Powell was a professor?"

"No."

"Why not?"

"I don't know. They didn't look like professors."

"What did they look like?"

"It's hard to remember. It was so fast. They were both big and had on dark topcoats and hats, regular felt hats, like businessmen wear. The one who shot Dennis had big side-burns, like Prince Albert, you know, along his jaw. He was sort of fat."

"Black or white?"

She looked startled. "White," she said.

"Why would the theft of a manuscript cause two big white men in hats and topcoats to come to your apartment at two thirty A.M. and kill Powell and frame you?"

"I don't know."

"Why—" Quirk stopped. Tears were running down Terry Orchard's face. She made no sound. She sat still with her eyes closed and the tears coming down her face.

I said, "Quirk, for crissake . . ."

He nodded, turned to Belson.

"Frank, get a matron and book her."

Belson took her arm. She stood up.

There was no sign that she heard him, or that she heard anything.

Belson took her out. Haller went with her.

Quirk said, "So far you're out of it, Spenser. I got nothing to hold you for. But if something does come up I want you to be where I don't have to look for you."

I got up. "There are whole days at a time, Lieutenant, that go by without me ever giving a real goddamn about what you want."

Quirk took my gun out of his desk and handed it to me, butt first. "Beat it," he said.

I put the gun away, went down the stairs three flights and out the front door. There were no cameramen, no TV trucks. It was cold and the wet snow-rain had frozen into gray lumpy ice. I went around the corner, got in my car, drove home, drank two glasses of milk, and went to bed.

CHAPTER SIX

THE PHONE WOKE ME again. I squinted against the brutal bright sunlight and answered.

"Spenser?"

"Yeah."

"Spenser, this is Roland Orchard." He paused as if waiting for applause.

I said, "How nice for you."

He said, "What?"

I said, "What do you want, Mr. Orchard?"

"I want to see you. How soon can you get here?"

"As soon as I feel like it. Which may be a while."

"Spenser, do you know who I am?"

"I guess you're Terry Orchard's father."

He hadn't meant that. "Yes," he said. "I am. I am also senior partner of Orchard, Bonner and Blanch."

"Swell," I said. "I buy all your records."

"Spenser, I don't care for your manner."

"I'm not selling it, Mr. Orchard. You called me. I didn't call you. If you want to tell me what you want without showing me your scrapbook, I'll listen. Otherwise, write me a letter."

There was a long silence. Then Orchard said, "Do you have my address, Mr. Spenser?"

"Yeah."

"My daughter is home, and I have not gone into the office, and we would very much like you to come to the house. I expect to pay you."

"I will come out in about an hour, Mr. Orchard," I said, and hung up.

It was a little after noon. I got up and stood a long time under the shower. I'd had about four and a half hours' sleep and I needed more. Ten years ago I wouldn't have. I put on my suit—I wasn't sure you could get onto West Newton Hill without one—made and ate a fried egg sandwich, drank a cup of coffee, and went out. I should have made the bed. I knew I would hate finding it unmade when I came back.

It was cold and bright out. It took five minutes for the heater in the car to get warm enough to melt the ice on my windows, and another five minutes for it to melt. I had no ice scraper.

By the Mass Turnpike it is less than ten minutes from downtown Boston to West Newton. From West Newton Square to the top of West Newton Hill is a matter of fifty thousand dollars. Status ascends as the hill rises, and at the top live the rich. It is old rich on West Newton Hill. Doctor rich, professor rich, stockbroker rich, lawyer rich. The new rich, the engineer rich, and the technocratic rich live in developments named after English kings in towns like Lynnfield and Sudbury.

Roland Orchard looked to be a rich man's rich man. His home was large and white and towering as one came up the hill toward it. It occupied most of the lot it was built on. New rich seem to want a lot of land for a gardener to manicure. Old rich don't seem to give a damn. Across the front and around one side of the house was a wide porch, empty in the winter but bearing the wear marks of summer furniture. Above the door was a fan-shaped stained glass window. I rang the bell. A maid opened the door. Her black skin, devoid of make-up, shone as though freshly burnished. Her almond-colored eyes held a knowledge of things that West Newton Hill didn't want to hear about.

She said, "Yes, sir."

I gave her one of my cards. The one with only my name on it.

40

"Yes, Mr. Spenser. Mrs. Orchard is expecting you in the study."

She led me down a polished oak-floored hall, past a curving stairway. The hall—it was more like a corridor—ran front to back, the depth of the house. At the far end a floor to ceiling window opened out onto the backyard. The coils of a grapevine framed the window. The rest was dirty snow. The maid knocked on a door to the left of the window; a woman's voice said, "Come in." The maid opened the door, said "Mr. Spenser," and left.

It was a big room, blond wood bookcases built in on three walls. A fieldstone fireplace covered the fourth wall. There was a fire going, and the room was warm and smelled of woodsmoke. Mrs. Orchard was standing when I came in. She was darkly tanned (not Miami, I thought, West Palm Beach, probably) and wearing a white pants suit and white boots. Her hair was shag cut and tipped with silver, and the skin on her face was very tight over her bones. She had silver nail polish and wore heavy Mexican-looking silver earrings. A silver service and a covered platter on a mahogany tea wagon stood near the fire. A chiffon stole was draped over the back of the couch, and a novel by Joyce Carol Oates lay open on the coffee table.

As I walked toward her she stood motionless, one hand extended, limp at the wrist, toward me. I felt as if I were walking into a window display.

"Mr. Spenser," she said. "It's very nice of you to come."

"That's okay," I said.

I didn't know what to do with her hand, shake it or kiss it. I shook it, and the way she looked made me suspect I'd chosen wrong.

"My husband had to go into the office for a bit; he should be back soon."

I said, "Uh huh."

"He might have stopped off at the club for handball and a rubdown. Rolly works very hard to stay in shape."

"Uh huh."

41

"What do you do, Mr. Spenser? You look to be in excellent condition. Do you work out?"

"Not at the club," I said.

"No," she said. "Of course not."

I took off my coat. "May I sit down?" I said.

"Oh, I'm sorry, of course, sit down. Will you have some coffee, or tea? I had some sandwiches made up. Would you like one?"

"No, thank you, I ate before I came. I'll take coffee though, black."

"You must pardon me, Mr. Spenser, my manners are really much better. It's just that I've never been involved with policemen and all. And I have never really spoken to a private detective before. Are you carrying a gun?"

"I thought I'd risk West Newton without one," I said.

"Yes, of course. You're sure you won't have a sandwich?"

"Look, Mrs. Orchard, I spent most of last night with your daughter and a corpse. I spent the rest of last night with your daughter and the cops. The last I knew she was in jail for murder. Your husband says she's home. Now he and you didn't get me out here to make sure I was eating properly. What do you want?"

"My husband will be along soon, Mr. Spenser; he'll explain. Rolly handles these things. I do not." She looked straight at me as she talked and leaned forward a little. She had large blue eyes, and she wore eye shadow, I noticed. I bet the eyes got her a lot that she wanted. Especially when she looked right at you and leaned forward a little as she talked. She turned slightly on the couch and tucked one leg under the other, and I got the long line of her thigh and the jut of her sharp breasts. Her body looked lean and tight. A little sinewy for my taste. She kept the pose. I wondered if I was supposed to bark.

She picked up the book. "Do you read much, Mr. Spenser?"

"Yeah," I said.

"Do you enjoy Miss Oates?"

"No."

"Oh, really? Why on earth not?"

"I'm probably insensitive," I said.

"Oh, I don't think so, Mr. Spenser. What little I've heard Terry say of you suggests quite the contrary."

"Where is Terry?"

"In her room. Her father has asked that she talk with no one except in his presence."

"How's she feel about that?"

"After what she's gotten herself into and what she's putting us through, she's learning to do what she's told."

There was a triumphant undertone in Mrs. Orchard's voice. I said nothing.

"Would you put another log on the fire, Mr. Spenser? It seems to be going low, and Rolly always likes a blazing fire when he comes in."

It was a way of establishing relationships, I thought, as I got a log from the basket and set it on top of the fire—get me to do her bidding. I'd known other women like that. If they couldn't get you to do them little services, they felt insecure. Or maybe she just wanted another log in the fireplace. Sometimes I'm deep as hell.

The door to the study opened and a man came in. He wore a dark double-breasted blazer with a crest on the pocket, a thick white turtleneck sweater, gray flared slacks, and black ankle boots with a lot of strap and buckle showing. His hair was blond and no doubt naturally curly; it contrasted nicely with his tan. He was a slender man, shorter than I by maybe an inch and maybe ten years older. Under the tan his face had a reddish flush which might be health or booze.

"Spenser," he said, and put out his hand, "kind of you to come." I shook hands with him. He wasn't being the top-exec-used-to-instant-obedience. He was being the gracious-man-of-affluence-putting-an-employee-at-ease.

He said to his wife, "I'll have coffee, Marion."

She rose and poured him coffee. She put several small triangular sandwiches on a plate, put the coffee cup in the little depression on the plate that was made to hold it, and placed it next to a red leather wing chair.

Orchard sat down, carefully hiking his trouser legs up at the knee so they wouldn't bag. I noticed he had a thick silver ring on his little finger.

"I'm sorry to have kept you waiting, Spenser, but I don't like to stay out of work if I can help it. Married to the job, I guess. Just wanted to make sure everything was running smoothly."

He took a delicate sip of coffee and a small bite of one of the sandwiches.

"I wish to hire you, Mr. Spenser, to see that my daughter is exonerated of the charges leveled against her. I was able to have her released on bail in my custody, but it took a good deal of doing and I had to collect a number of favors to do it. Now I want this mess cleared up and the suspicion eliminated from my name and my home. The police are working to convict. I want someone working to acquit."

"Why not have Terry join us?" I said.

"Perhaps later," Orchard said, "but first I want to speak with you for a time."

I nodded. He went on. "I would like you to give me a complete rundown of the circumstances by which you became involved with Terry up to and including last night."

"Hasn't Terry told you?"

"I want your version."

I didn't want to tell him. I didn't like him. I did like his daughter. I didn't like his assumption that our versions would differ. I said, "Nope."

"Mr. Spenser. I am employing you to investigate a murder. I want a report of what you've discovered so far."

"First, you may or may not be hiring me. You've offered. I haven't accepted. So at the moment I owe you nothing. That includes how I met your daughter, and what we did."

"Goddammit, Spenser, I don't have to take that kind of insolence from you."

44

"Right," I said, "you can hire another Hawkshaw. The ones with phones are in the yellow pages under SLEUTH."

I thought for a moment that Orchard was going to get up and take a swing at me. I felt no cold surge of terror. Then he thought better of it, and leaned back in his chair.

"Marion," he said, "I'll have some brandy. Would you join me, Mr. Spenser?" I looked at my watch; it was two thirty. He really handled stress well. I decided what the flush under the tan was.

"Yeah. I'll have some. Thank you."

Marion Orchard's face looked a little more tightly stretched over her good bones as she went to the sideboard and poured two shots of brandy from a decanter into crystal snifters. She brought them back to us, handed one to me and one to her husband.

Orchard swirled it in his glass and took a large swallow. I tried mine. It was the real stuff okay, barely liquid at all as it drifted down my throat. A guy who served brandy like that couldn't be all bad.

"Now look, Spenser. Terry is our only child. We've lavished every affection and concern on her. We have brought her up in wealth and comfort. Clothes, the best schooling, Europe. She had her own horse and rode beautifully. She made us proud. She was an achiever. That's important. We do things in this family. Marion rides and hunts as well as any man."

I looked at Marion Orchard and said, "Hi ho, Silver."

Orchard went on. I was not sure he'd heard me.

"Then when it came time for college, she insisted on going to that factory. Can you imagine the reaction of some of my associates when they ask me where my daughter goes to school and I tell them?" It was a rhetorical question. I could imagine, but I knew he wasn't looking for an answer. "Against my best judgment I permitted her to go. And I permitted her to live there rather than at home." He shook his head. "I should have known better. She got in with the worst element in a bad school and . . ." He stopped, drank another large slug from his snifter, and went on. "She never gave us any trouble till then. She was just what we wanted. And then in college, living on the very edge of the ghetto, sleeping around, drugs. You've seen her, you've seen how she dresses, who she keeps company with. I don't even know where she lives anymore. She rarely comes home, and when she does it's as if she were coming only to flaunt herself before us and our friends. Do you know she appeared here at a party we were giving wearing a miniskirt she'd made out of an old pair of Levi's? Now she's gotten herself involved in a murder. I've got a right to know about her. I've got a right to know what she'll do to us next."

"I don't do family counseling, Mr. Orchard. There are people who do, and maybe you ought to look up one of them. If you'll get Terry down here we'll talk, all of us, and see if we can arrange to live in peace while I look into the murder."

Orchard had finished his brandy. He nodded at the empty glass. His wife got up, refilled it, and brought it to him. He drank, then put the glass down. He said, "While you're up, Marion, would you ask Terry to come down."

Marion left the room. Orchard took another belt of brandy. He wasn't bothering to savor the bouquet. I nibbled at the edge of mine. Marion Orchard came back into the room with Terry.

I stood and said, "Hello, Terry."

She said, "Hi."

Her hair was loose and long. She wore a short-sleeved blouse, a skirt, no socks, and a pair of loafers. I looked at her arms—no tracks. One point for our side; she wasn't shooting. At least not regularly. She was fresh-scrubbed and pale, and remarkably without affect. She went to a round leather hassock by the fire and sat down, her knees tight together, her hands folded in her lap. Dolly Demure, with a completely blank face. The loose hair softened her, and the traditional dress made her look like somebody's cheerleader, right down to loafers without socks. Had there been any animation she'd have been pretty as hell.

Orchard spoke. "Terry, I'm employing Mr. Spenser to clear you of the murder charge."

She said, "Okay."

"I hope you'll cooperate with him in every way."

"Okay."

"And, Terry, if Mr. Spenser succeeds in getting you out of this mess, if he does, perhaps you will begin to rethink your whole approach to life."

"Why don't you get laid," she said flatly, without inflection, and without looking at him.

Marion Orchard said "Terry!" in a horrified voice.

Orchard's glass was empty. He flicked an eye at it, and away.

"Now, you listen to me, young lady," he said. "I have put up with your nonsense for as long as I'm going to. If you . . ."

I interrupted. "If I want to listen to this kind of crap I can go home and watch daytime television. I want to talk with Terry, and maybe later I'll want to talk with each of you. Separately. Obviously I was wrong; we can't do it in a group. You people want to encounter one another, do it on your own time."

"By God, Spenser," Orchard said.

I cut him off again. "I want to talk with Terry. Do I or don't I?"

I did. He and his wife left, and Terry and I were alone in the library.

"If I told my father to get laid he would have knocked out six of my teeth," I said.

"Mine won't," she said. "He'll drink some more brandy, and tomorrow he'll stay late at the office."

"You don't like him much," I said.

"I bet if I said that to you, you'd knock out six of my teeth," she said.

"Only if you didn't smile," I answered.

"He's a jerk."

"Maybe," I said. "But he's your jerk, and from his point of view you're no prize package either."

"I know," she said.

"However," I said, "let's think about what I'm

supposed to do here. Tell me more about the manuscript and the professor and anything else you can remember beyond what you told Quirk last night."

"That's all there is," she said. "I told the police everything I know."

"Let's run through it again anyway," I said. "Have you talked with Quirk again since last night?"

"Yes, I saw him this morning before Daddy's people got me out."

"Okay, tell me what he asked you and what you said."

"He started by asking me why I thought two big white men in hats would come to our apartment and kill Dennis and frame me."

That was Quirk, starting right where he left off, no rephrasing, no new approach, less sleep than I had and there in the morning when the big cheeses passed the word along to let her out, getting all his questions answered before he released her.

"And what did you answer?" I said.

"I said the only thing I could think of was the manuscript. That Dennis was involved somehow in that theft, and he was upset about it."

"Can you give me more than that? How was he involved? Why was he involved? What makes you think he was involved? Why do you think he was upset? What did he do to show you he was upset? Answer any or all, one at a time."

"It was a phone call he made from the apartment. The way he was talking I could tell he was upset, and I could tell he wasn't talking to another kid. I mean, you can tell that from the way people talk. The way his voice sounded."

"What did he say?" I said.

"I couldn't hear most of it. He talked low, and I knew he didn't want me to hear, you know, cupping his hand and everything. So I tried not to hear. But he did say something about hiding it . . . like 'Don't worry, no one will find it. I was careful.'"

"When was this?" I asked.

"About a week ago. Lemme see, I was up early for my

Chaucer course, so it would have been Monday, that's five days ago. Last Monday."

The manuscript had been stolen Sunday night.

"Okay, so he was upset. About what?"

"I don't know, but I can tell when he's mad. At one point I think he threatened someone."

"Why do you think so? What did he say that makes you think so?"

"He said, 'If you don't . . .' No . . . No . . . he said, 'I will, I really will. . . .' Yeah. That's what it was . . . 'I really will.' But very threateny, you know."

"Good. Now why do you think it was a professor? I know the voice tone told you it was someone older, but why a professor? What did he say? What were the words?"

"Well, oh, I don't know, it was just a feeling. I wasn't all that interested; I was running the water for a bath, anyway."

"No, Terry, I want to know. The words, what were his words?"

She was silent, her eyes squeezed almost shut, as if the sun were shining in them, her upper teeth exposed, her lower lip sucked in.

"Dennis said, 'I don't care' . . . 'I don't care, if you do.' . . . He said, 'I don't care if you do. Cut the goddamn thing.' That's it. He was talking to an older person and he said cut the class if the other person had to. That's why I figured it must be a professor."

"How do you know he wasn't talking about cutting a piece of rope, or a salami?"

"Because he mentioned class or school a little before. And what could they be talking about angrily that had to do with salami?"

"Okay. Good. What else?"

There wasn't anything else. I worked on her for maybe half an hour more and nothing else surfaced. All I got was the name of a SCACE official close to Powell, someone named Mark Tabor, whose title was political counselor.

"If you think of anything else, anything at all, call me. You still have my card?"

"Yes. I . . . . my father will pay you for what you did last night."

"No, he won't. He'll pay me for what I may do. But last night was a free introductory offer."

"It was a very nice thing to do," she said.

"Aw, hell," I said.

"What you should try to do is this," I said. "You should try to keep from starting up with your old man for a while. And you should try to stay around the house, go to class if you think you should, but for the moment let SCACE stave off the apocalypse without you. Okay?"

"Okay. But don't laugh at us. We're perfectly serious and perfectly right."

"Yeah, so is everyone I know."

I left her then. Said good-bye to her parents, took a retainer from Roland Orchard, and drove back to town.

CHAPTER SEVEN

DRIVING BACK to Boston, I thought about my two retainers in the same week. Maybe I'd buy a yacht. On the other hand maybe it would be better to get the tear in my convertible roof fixed. The tape leaked. I got off the Mass Pike at Storrow Drive and headed for the university. On my left the Charles River was thick and gray between Boston and Cambridge. A single oarsman was sculling upstream. He had on a hooded orange sweat shirt and dark blue sweat pants and his breath steamed as he rocked back and forth at the oars. Rowing downstream would have been easier.

I turned off Storrow at Charlesgate, went up over Commonwealth, onto Park Drive, past a batch of ducks swimming in the muddy river, through the Fenway to Westland Ave. Number 177 was on the left, halfway to Mass Ave. I parked at a hydrant and went up the stone steps to the glass door at the entry. I tried it. It was open. Inside an ancient panel of doorbells and call boxes covered the left wall. I didn't have to try one to know they didn't work. They didn't need to. The inner door didn't close all the way because the floor was warped in front of the sill and the door jammed against it. Mark Tabor was on the fourth floor. No elevator. I walked up. The apartment house smelled bad and the stair landing had beer bottles and candy wrappers accumulating in the corners. Somewhere in the building electronic music was playing at top volume. The fourth flight began to tell on me a little, but I forced myself to breathe normally as I knocked on Tabor's door. No answer. I knocked again. And a third time. Loud. I didn't want to waste the four-flight climb. A voice inside called out, "Wait a minute." There was a pause, and then the door opened.

I said, "Mark Tabor?"

And he said, "Yeah."

He looked like a zinnia. Tall and thin with an enormous corona of rust red hair flaring out around his pale, clean-shaven face. He wore a lavender undershirt and a pair of faded, flare-bottomed denim dungarees that were too long and dragged on the floor over his bare feet.

I said, "I'm a friend of Terry Orchard's; she asked me to come and talk with you."

"About what?"

"About inviting people in to sit down."

"Why do you think I know what's her name?"

"Aw, come off it, Tabor," I said. "How the hell do you think I got your name and address? How do you know Terry Orchard is not a what's his name? What do you lose by talking with me for fifteen minutes? If I was going to mug you I would have already. Besides, a mugger would starve to death in this neighborhood."

"Well, what do you want to talk about?" he asked, still standing in the door. I walked past him into the room. He said, "Hey," but didn't try to stop me. I moved a pile of mimeographed pamphlets off a steamer trunk and sat down on it. Tabor took a limp pack of Kools out of his pants pocket, extracted a ragged cigarette, and lit it. The menthol smell did nothing for the atmosphere. He took a big drag and exhaled through his nose. He leaned against the door jamb. "Okay," he said. "What do you want?"

"I want to keep Terry Orchard out of the slam, for one thing. And I want to find the Godwulf Manuscript, for another."

"Why are the cops hassling Terry?"

"Because they think she killed Dennis Powell."

"Dennis is dead?"

I nodded.

"Ain't that a bitch, now," he said, much as if I'd said the rain would spoil the picnic. He went over and sat on the edge of a kitchen table covered with books, lined yellow paper, manila folders, and the crusts of a pizza still in the take-out box. Behind him, taped to the gray painted wall with raggedly torn masking tape, was a huge picture of Che Guevara. Opposite was a day bed covered by an unzipped sleeping bag. There were clothes littered on the floor. On top of a bureau was a hot plate. There were no curtains or window shades.

I clucked approvingly. "You've really got some style, Tabor," I said.

"You from *House Beautiful* or something?" he said.

"Nope, I'm a private detective." I showed him the photostat of my license. "I'm trying to clear Terry Orchard of the murder charge. I'm also looking for the Godwulf Manuscript, and I think they're connected. Can you help me?"

"I don't know nothing about no murder, man, and nothing about no jive ass manuscript." Why did all the radical white kids from places like Scarsdale and Bel-Air try to talk as if they'd been brought up in Brownsville and Watts? He stubbed out his Kool and lit another.

"Look," I said. "You and Dennis Powell roomed together for two years. You and Terry Orchard are members of the same organization. You share the same goals. I'm not the cops. I'm free-lance, for crissake, I'm labor. I work for Terry. I don't want you. I want Terry out of trouble and the manuscript back in its case. Do you know where the manuscript is?"

"Naw, man. I don't know anything about it."

He didn't look up from the contemplation of his Kool. His voice never varied. Like Terry, he showed no affect. No response to stimulus. It was as though he'd shut down.

"Tell me this," I said. "Does SCACE have a faculty adviser?"

"Oh, man, be cool. SCACE ain't no frat house, baby. Faculty adviser . . . Man, that's heavy."

"Do any faculty members belong to SCACE?"

"Maybe. Lot of people belong to SCACE. That's for me to know and you to guess."

"What's the big secret?"

"Lots of dudes can get in trouble for joining organizations like SCACE. The imperialists don't like opposition. The fat cats don't like organizations that are for the worker. The superoppressors are scared of the revolution."

"You forgot to mention the capitalist running-dog lackeys," I said.

"Like you, you mean? See what happened to Terry Orchard? The pigs have framed her already. They'll do anything they can to stamp us out."

"Look, kid, I don't want to sit up here and argue Herbert Marcuse with you. The cops are professionals. You can sit here in your hippie suit and drink wine and smoke grass and read Marx and play revolution like Tom Sawyer ambushing the A-rabs all you want. That bothers the cops like a tick fly on an elephant. If they wanted to stamp you out, they'd come in here and stamp and you'd know what a stamping was. They don't have to get frilly and frame some twenty-year-old broad to get at you. They've got guys in the station house in Charlestown that they keep in a cage when they're not on duty."

He gave me a tough look. Which isn't easy when you weigh 150 pounds.

"How about a faculty member that might be associated with SCACE?"

He let the smoke from his cigarette out of his nose and mouth slowly. It drifted up around his head. Long years of practice, I thought. He looked straight at me with his eyes almost closed for a long time. Then he said, "Where would the movement be now if someone had saved Sacco and Vanzetti?"

"Sonova bitch," I said. "You're almost perfect, you are, a flawless moron. I don't think I've ever seen anyone stay so implacably on the level of absolute abstraction."

"Screw you, man," he said.

"That's better," I said. "Now we're getting down where I live. I've got no hope for you, punk. But I promise you that if that kid gets burned because you don't tell me what you could tell me, I will come for you. You martyr that kid and I'll give the movement another martyr."

"Screw you, man," he said.

I walked out.

I went back down the four flights of stairs, as empty as when I went up. Some sleuth, Spenser, a real Hawkshaw. All you've found out is you get winded after four flights of stairs. I wondered if I should go back up and have a go at shaking some information out of him. Maybe later. Maybe he'd stew a little and I could call on him again. I didn't even know he knew anything. But talking to him, I could feel him holding back. I could even feel that he liked knowing something and not telling. It added color to the romance of his conspiracy. Out in the street the air was cold and it tasted clean after the mentholated smoke and the stale air of Tabor's room. A truck backfired and up on Mass Avenue a bus ground under way in low gear.

My next try was the campus. The student newspaper was located in the basement of the library. On the blond oak door cut into the cinder block of the basement corridor an inventive person had lettered NEWS in black ink.

Inside, the room was long and narrow. L-shaped black

metal desks with white Formica tops were sloppily lined up along the long wall on the left. A hand-lettered sign made from half a manila folder instructed the staff to label all photographs with name, date, and location. The room was empty except for a black woman in a red paisley dashiki and matching turban. She was fat but not flabby, hard fat we used to call it when I was a kid, and the dashiki billowed around her body like a drop cloth on the sofa when the living room's going to be painted. A plastic name plate on her desk said FEATURE EDITOR.

She said, "Can I help you?" Her voice was not cordial. No one seemed to be mistaking me for a member of the academic community.

I said, "I hope so."

I gave her a card. "I'm working on a case, and I'm looking for information. Can I ask you for some?"

"You surely can," she said. "All the news that's fit to print, that's us."

"Okay, you know there's a manuscript been stolen."

"Yep."

"I have some reason to believe that a radical student organization, SCACE, is involved in the theft."

"Uh huh."

"What I'm looking for are faculty connections with SCACE. What can you tell me?"

"Why you want to know about faculty connections?"

"I have reason to believe that a faculty member was involved in the theft."

"I have reason to believe that information is a two-way go, sweetie," she said. "Ah is a member ob de press, baby. Information is mah business."

I liked her. She was old for a student, maybe twenty-eight. And she was tough.

"Fair enough," I said. "If you'll drop the Stepin Fetchit act, I'll tell you what I can. In trade?"

"Right on, brother," she said.

"Two things. One, what's your name?"

"Iris Milford."

"Two, do you know Terry Orchard?"

She nodded.

"Then you know she's a SCACE member. You also may know she's been arrested for murder." She nodded again.

"I think the manuscript theft and the murder are connected." I told her about Terry, and the murder, and Terry's memory of the phone call.

"Someone set her up," I said. "If someone wanted her out of the way they'd just have killed her. They wanted to kill Powell. They wouldn't go to the trouble and take the risk just to frame her. And they wanted to kill Powell in such a way as to keep people from digging into it. And it looked good—a couple of freaky kids living in what my aunt used to call sin. On drugs, long-haired, barefooted, radical, and on a bad trip, one shoots the other and tells some weird hallucinogenic story about guys in trench coats. The Hearst papers would have them part of an international sex club by the second day's story."

"How come you're messing it up, then? If it's so good. How come you don't believe it?"

"I talked to her right after it happened. She's not that good a liar."

"Why ain't it a trip? Maybe she really thinks she's telling you true. You ever been on a trip?"

"No. You?"

"Baby, I'm fat, black, widowed, pushing thirty, and got four kids. I don't need no additional problems. But she could think it happened. Got any better reason for thinking she's not guilty?"

"I like her."

"All right," she said. "That's cool."

"So, what do you know?"

"Not a hell of a lot. The kid Powell was a jerk, sulky, foolish. On an ego trip. Terry, I don't know. I've been in classes with her. She's bright, but she's screwed up. Jesus, they're so miserable, those kids, always so goddamn unhappy about racism and sexism and imperialism and militarism and capitalism. Man, I grew up in a tarpaper house in Fayette,

Mississippi, with ten other kids. We were trying to stay alive; we didn't have time to be that goddamn unhappy."

"How about a professor?"

"In SCACE, you got me. I do know that there's a lot of talk about drug dealing connected with SCACE."

"For instance?"

"For instance, that Powell was dealing, and had big connections. He could get you smack, anything you wanted. But especially smack. A kid that can get unlimited smack is heavy in some circles."

"Mob connection?"

"I don't know. I don't even know whether he really could get a big supply of smack. I just tell you what I hear. Kids like to talk big—especially to me, because I live in Roxbury, and they figure all us darkies are into drugs and crime, 'cause we been oppressed by you honky slumlords."

"I want a professor," I said. "Try this. Name me the most radical faculty members in the university."

"Oh, man, how the hell do I know? There's about thirty-five thousand people in this place."

"Name me anyone, any that you know. I'm not the Feds. I'm not going to harass them. They can advocate cannibalism for all I care. I only want to get one kid out of trouble. Make me a list of any you can think of. They don't have to be active. Who is there that might be involved in stealing a manuscript and holding it for ransom?"

"I'll think on it," she said.

"Think on it a lot. Get any of your friends who will think on it too. Students know things that deans and chairmen don't know."

"Ain't that the truth."

"How about an English professor? Wouldn't that be the best bet? It was a medieval manuscript. It was important because it referred to some medieval writer. Wouldn't an English professor be most likely to think of holding it for ransom?"

"Who's the writer it mentions?" she asked.

"Richard Rolle."

"How much they want for him?"

"A hundred thousand dollars."

"I'd give them some dough if they'd promise not to return it. You ever read his stuff?"

I shook my head.

"Don't," she said.

"Can you think of any English professors who might fit my bill?"

"There's a lot of flakes in that department. There's a lot of flakes in most departments, if you really want to know. But English . . ." She whistled, raised her eyebrows, and looked at the ceiling.

"Okay, but who is the flakiest? Who would you bet on if you had to bet?"

"Hayden," she said. "Lowell Hayden. He's one of those little pale guys with long, limp blond hair that looks like he hasn't started to shave yet, but he's like thirty-nine. You know? Serious as a bastard. Taught a freshman English course two years ago called The Rhetoric of Revolution. You dig? Yeah, he'd be the one, old Dr. Hayden."

"What's he teach besides freshman English?"

"I don't know for sure. I know he teaches Chaucer, 'cause I took Chaucer with him." I felt a little click in the back of my head. Something nudged at me. A Chaucer class had been mentioned before. I tucked the inkling away. I knew I could dredge it up later when I had time. I always could.

"Mrs. Milford, thank you. If you come up with anything, my number's on the card. I have an answering service. If I'm not there, leave a message."

"Okay."

I got up and looked around the basement room. "Freedom of the press is a flaming sword," I said. "Use it wisely, hold it high, guard it well."

Iris Milford looked at me strangely. I left.

The corridor in the basement of the library was almost empty. I looked at my watch. 5:05. Too late to find anyone in the English Department. I went home.

In my kitchen I sat at the counter and opened a can of

beer. It was very quiet. I turned on the radio. Maybe I should buy a dog, I thought. He'd be glad to see me when I came home. The beer was good. I finished the can. And opened another. Where was I? I ran over the last couple of days in my mind. One: Terry Orchard didn't kill Dennis Powell. That was a working hypothesis. Two: the missing manuscript and the murder were two parts of the same thing, and if I found out anything about one, I'd know something about the other. That was another working hypothesis. What did I have in support of these hypotheses? About half a can of beer. There was that click I had when I talked with Iris Milford. Chaucer. She's had a Chaucer course with Lowell Hayden. I drank the rest of the beer and opened another can. It came back. Terry was up early for her Chaucer course the day Dennis had been telling some professor on the phone to cut his class. I looked at my face, reflected in the window over the sink. "You've still got all the moves, kid," I said. But what did it give me? Nothing much, just a little coincidence. But it was something. It suggested some kind of connection. Coincidences are suspect. Old Lowell Hayden looked better to me all the time. I got another beer. After three or four beers everything began looking better to me.

I got a pound of fresh scallops out of the refrigerator and began to make something called Scallops Jacques for supper. It was a recipe in a French cookbook that I'd gotten for a birthday present from a woman I know. I like to cook and drink while I'm doing it. Scallops Jacques is a complicated affair with cream and wine and lemon juice and shallots, and by the time it was done I was feeling quite pleasant. I made some hot biscuits for myself, too, and ate the scallops and biscuits with a bottle of Pouilly Fuissé, sitting at the counter. Afterward I went to bed. I slept heavy and for a long time.

CHAPTER EIGHT

I SLEPT LATE and woke up feeling very good, though my mouth tasted funny. I went over to the Boston Y.M.C.A. and worked out in the weight room. I hit the light bag and the heavy bag, ran three miles around their indoor track, took a shower, and went down to my office. I was glistening with health and vigor till I got there. You never felt really glistening in my office. It was on Stuart Street, second floor front, half a block down from Tremont. One room with a desk, a file cabinet, and two chairs in case Mrs. Onassis came with her husband. The old iron radiator had no real control and the room, closed for three days, reeked with heat. I stepped over the three-day pile of mail on the floor under the mail slot and went to open the window. It took some effort. I took off my coat, picked up the mail, and sat at my desk to read it. I'd come down mainly to check my mail, and the trip had been hardly worth it. There was a phone bill, a light bill, an overdue notice from the Boston Public Library, a correspondence course offering to teach me karate at home in my spare time, a letter from a former client insisting that while I had found his wife she had left again and hence he would not pay my bill, an invitation to join a vacation club, an invitation to buy a set of socket wrenches, an invitation to join an automobile club, an invitation to subscribe to five magazines of my choice at once-in-a-lifetime savings, an invitation to shop the specials on pork at my local supermarket, and a number of less important letters. Nothing from Germaine Greer or Lenny Bernstein, no dinner invitations, no post cards from the Costa del Sol, no mash notes from Helen Gurley Brown. Last week had been much the same.

I stood up and looked out my window. It was a bright day, but cold, and the whores had emerged, working the Combat Zone, looking cold and bizarre in their miniskirts, boots, and blond wigs. Being seductive at twenty degrees was heavy going, I thought. Being horny at twenty degrees wasn't all that easy either. Things were slow for the whores. It was lunchtime, and the businessmen were beginning to drift down from Boylston and Tremont and Back Bay offices to have lunch at Jake Wirth's or upstairs in the Athens Olympia. The whores eyed them speculatively, occasionally approached one, and were brushed off. The businessmen didn't like to look at them and hurried off in embarrassment when approached, visions of the day's first Bloody Mary dancing in their heads.

I closed the window, threw most of the mail away, locked the office, and headed for my car. The drive to the university was easy from my office, and I was there in ten minutes. I parked in a slot that said RESERVED FOR UNIVERSITY PRESIDENT and found my way to Tower's office. The secretary was wearing a pink jumpsuit this day. I revised my opinion about her thighs. They weren't too heavy; they were exactly the right size for the jumpsuit. I said, "My name's Spenser. To see Mr. Tower." She said, "Yes, Mr. Spenser, he'll be through in a minute," and went back to her typing. Twice I caught her looking at me while she pretended to check the clock. You haven't lost a thing, kid, I thought. Two campus cops, in uniform, looking unhappy, came out of Tower's office. Tower came to the door with them.

"This is not Dodge City," he said, "you are not goddamn towntamers—" and shut the outer office door behind them as they left. "Dumb bastards," he said. "Come on in, Spenser."

"I'll see you again on the way out," I said to the secretary. She didn't smile.

"What have you got, Spenser?" Tower asked when we were in and sitting.

"A bad murder, some funny feelings, damn little information, some questions, and no manuscript. I think your secretary is hot for me."

Tower's face squeezed down. "Murder?"

"Yeah, the Powell killing. You know about it as well as I do."

"Yeah, bad. I know, sorry you had to get dragged into it. But we're after a manuscript. We're not worried about the murder. That's Lieutenant Quirk's department. He's good at it."

"Wrong. It's my department too. I think the manuscript and the murder are connected."

"Why?"

"Terry Orchard told me."

"What?" Tower wasn't liking the way the talk was going.

"Terry remembers a conversation on the phone between Dennis Powell and a professor in which Dennis reassured the professor that he'd hidden 'it' well."

"Oh, for crissake, Spenser. The kid's a goddam junkie. She remembers anything she feels like remembering. You don't buy that barrel of crap she fed you about mysterious strangers and being forced to shoot Dennis, and being drugged and being innocent. Of course she thinks the university's involved. She thinks the university causes famine."

"She didn't say the university. She said a professor."

"She'll say anything. They all will. She knows you're investigating the manuscript, and she wants you to get her out of what she's gotten herself into. So she plays little-girl-lost with you, and you go panting after her like a Saint Bernard dog. Spenser to the rescue. Balls."

"Tell me about Lowell Hayden," I said.

Tower liked the conversation even less. "Why? Who the hell is employing who? I want to know your results, and you start asking me questions about professors."

"Whom," I said.

"What?"

"It's whom, who is employing whom? Or is it? Maybe it's a predicate nominative, in which case . . ."

62

"Will you come off it, Spenser. I got things to do."

"Me, too," I said. "One of them is to find out about Lowell Hayden. His name has come up a couple of times. He's a known radical. I have it on some authority that he's the most radical on campus. I have it on authority that Powell was pushing heavy drugs and had heavy drug connections. I know Hayden had an early Chaucer class on the morning that Powell was talking to a professor about cutting his early morning class."

"That adds up to zero. Do you know how many professors in this university have eight o'clock classes every day? Who the hell is your authority? I know what's going on on my campus and no one's pushing heroin. I don't say no one's using it, but it's isolated. There's no big supplier. If there were, I'd know."

"Sure you would," I said. "Sure, what I've got about professors and Lowell Hayden adds up to zero, or little more. But he is all I've got for either the murder or the theft. Why not let me think about him? Why not have a look at him? If he's clean, I won't bother him. He probably is clean. But if he isn't . . ."

"No. Do you have any idea what happens if it gets out that a P.I. in the employ of the university is investigating a member of the university faculty? No, you don't. You couldn't." He closed his eyes in holy dread. "You stick to looking for the manuscript. Stay away from the faculty."

"I don't do piecework, Tower. I take hold of one end of the thread and I keep pulling it in till it's all unraveled. You hired me to find out where the manuscript went. You didn't hire me to run errands. The retainer does not include your telling me how to do my job."

"You'll stay the hell away from Hayden, or you'll be off this campus to stay. I got you hired for this job. I can get you canned just as easy."

"Do that," I said, and walked out. When you have two retainers you get smug and feisty. In the quadrangle I asked a boy in a fringed buckskin jacket where the English Department was. He didn't know. I tried a girl in an ankle-length o.d. military overcoat. She didn't know either. On the third try I got it; first floor, Felton Hall, other end of the campus.

Felton Hall was a converted apartment building, warrened with faculty offices. The main office of the English Department was at the end of the first floor foyer. An outer office with a receptionist/typist and a file cabinet. An inner office with another desk and woman and typewriter, secretary in chief or administrative assistant, or some such, and beyond that, at right angles, the office of the chairman. The receptionist looked like a student. I asked to see the chairman, gave her my card, the one with my name and profession but without the crossed daggers, and sat down in the one straight-backed chair to wait. She gave the card to the woman in the inner office, who did not look like a student and didn't even look one hell of a lot like a woman, and came back studiously uninterested in me.

Somewhere nearby I could hear the rhythm of a mimeograph cranking out somebody's midterm or a reading list for someone's course in Byzantine nature poetry of the third century. I got the same old feeling in my stomach. The one I got as a little kid sitting outside the principal's office.

The office was done in early dorm. There was a travel poster with a picture of the Yugoslav coast stuck with Scotch tape to the wall above the receptionist's desk, the announcement of a new magazine that would pay contributors in free copies of the magazine, the big campy poster of Buster Keaton in *The General,* and a number of Van Gogh and Gauguin prints apparently cut off a calendar and taped up. It didn't hold a candle to my collection of Ann Sheridan pinups.

The mannish-looking inner-office secretary came to her door.

"Mr. Spenser," she said, "Dr. Vogel will see you now."

I walked through her big office, through two glass doors, and into the chairman's office, which was still bigger. It had apparently once been the dining room of an apartment, which had been divided by a partition so that it seemed almost a round room because of the large bow window that looked out over a recently built slum. In the arch of the bow was a large dark desk. On one wall was a fireplace, the bricks painted a dark red, the hearth clean and cold. There were books all around the office and pen and ink drawings of historical-looking people I didn't recognize. There was a rug on the floor and a chair with arms—Tower had neither.

Dr. Vogel sat behind the desk, slim, medium height, thick curly hair trimmed round, black and gray intermixed, clean-shaven, wearing a black pin-striped double-breasted suit with six buttons, all buttoned, pink shirt with a wide roll collar, a white tie with black and pink stripes, and a diamond ring on the left little finger. Whatever happened to shabby gentility?

"Sit down, Mr. Spenser," he said. I sat. He was looking at my card, holding it neatly by the corners before his stomach with both hands, the way a man looks at a poker hand.

"I don't believe I've ever met a private detective before," he said without looking up. "What do you want?"

"I'm investigating the theft of the Godwulf Manuscript," I said, "and I have only the slightest of suggestions that a member of your department might be involved."

"My department? I doubt that."

"Everyone always doubts things like that."

"I'm not sure the generalization is valid, Mr. Spenser. There must be circles where theft surprises no one, and they must be circles with which you're more familiar than I. Why don't you move in those circles, and not these?"

"Because the circles you're thinking of don't steal illuminated manuscripts, nor do they ransom them for charity, nor do they murder undergraduates in the process."

"Murder?" He liked that about half as well as Tower had.

"A young man, student at this university, was murdered. Another student, a young woman, was involved and stands accused. I think the two crimes are connected."

"Why?"

"I have some slight evidence, but even if I didn't, two major crimes committed at the same university among people belonging to the same end of the political spectrum, and probably the same organization, is at least an unusual occurrence, isn't it?"

"Of course, but we're on the edge of the ghetto here. . . ."

"Nobody involved was a ghetto resident. No one was black. The victim and the accused were upper-middle-class affluent."

"Drugs?"

"Maybe, maybe not. To me it doesn't look like a drug killing."

"How does it look to the police?"

"The police don't belabor the obvious, Dr. Vogel. The most obvious answer is the one they like best. Usually they're right. They don't have time to be subtle. They are very good at juggling five balls, but there are always six in the game, and the more they run the farther behind they get."

"Thus you handle the difficult and intricate problems, Mr. Spenser?"

"I handle the problems I choose to; that's why I'm freelance. It gives me the luxury to worry about justice. The cops can't. All they're trying to do is keep that sixth ball in the air."

"A fine figure of speech, Mr. Spenser, and doubtless excellent philosophy, but it has little relevance here. I do not want you snooping about my department, accusing my faculty of theft and murder."

"What you want is not what I'm here to find out. I'll snoop on your department and accuse your faculty of theft and murder as I find necessary. The question we're discussing is whether it's the easy way or the hard way. I wasn't asking your permission."

"By God, Spenser . . ."

"Listen, there's a twenty-year-old girl who is a student in your university, has taken a course from your faculty, under the auspices no doubt of your department, who is now out on bail, charged with the murder of her boyfriend. I think she did not kill him. If I am right, it is quite important that we find out who did. Now, that may not rate in importance up as high as, say, the implications of homosexuality in

Shakespeare's sonnets, or whether he said *solid* or *sullied,* but it is important. I'm not going to shoot up the place. No rubber hose, no iron maiden. I won't even curse loudly. If the student newspaper breaks the news that a private eye is ravaging the English Department, the hell with it. You can argue it's an open campus and sit tight."

"You don't understand the situation in a university at this point in time. I cannot permit spying. I sympathize with your passion for justice, if that is in fact what it is, but my faculty would not accept your prying. Violation of academic freedom integral to such an investigation, sanctioned even implicitly by the chairman, would jeopardize liberal education in the university beyond any justification. If you persist I will have you removed from this department by the campus police."

The campus police I had seen looked like they'd need to outnumber me considerably, but I let that go. Guile, I thought, guile before force. I had been thinking that more frequently as I got up toward forty.

"The freedom I'm worried about is not academic, it's twenty and female. If you reconsider, my number's on the card."

"Good day, Mr. Spenser."

I got even. I left without saying good-bye.

On the bulletin board in the corridor was a mimeographed list of faculty office numbers. I took it off as I went by and put it in my pocket. The mannish-looking secretary watched me all the way out the front door.

CHAPTER NINE

I WALKED THROUGH the warm-for-early-winter sun of midafternoon across the campus back toward the library. In the quadrangle there was a girl in a fatigue jacket selling brown rice and pinto beans from a pushcart with a bright umbrella. Six dogs raced about barking and bowling one another over in their play. A kid in a cowboy hat and a pea jacket hawked copies of a local underground paper in a rhythmic monotone, a limp and wrinkled cigarette hanging from the corner of his mouth.

I went into the reading room of the library, took off my coat, sat down at a table, and took out my list of English professors. It didn't get me far. There was no one named Sacco or Vanzetti; none had a skull and crossbones by his name. Nine of the names were women; the remaining thirty-three were men. Lowell Hayden's name was right there after Gordon and before Herbert. Why him, I thought. I didn't have a goddamn thing on him. Just his name came up twice, and he teaches medieval literature. Why not him? Why not Vogel, why not Tower, why not Forbes, or Tabor, or Iris Milford, why not Terry Orchard if you really get objective? Like a Saint Bernard, Tower had said. Woof. Why not go home and go to bed and never get up? Some things you just had to decide.

I got up, put the list back in my pocket, put on my coat, and headed back out across campus, toward the English Department. Hayden's office was listed as fourth floor Felton. I hoped I could slip past Mary Masculine, the super-secretary. I made it. There was an old elevator to the left of the foyer, out of sight of the English office. It was a cage affair, open shaft, enclosed with mesh. The stairs wound up around it. I took it to the fourth floor, feeling exposed as it crept up. Hayden's office was room 405. On the door was a brown plastic plaque that said DR. HAYDEN. The door was half open and inside I could hear two people talking. One was apparently a student, sitting in a straight chair, back to the door, beside the desk, facing the teacher. I couldn't see Hayden, but I could hear his voice.

"The problem," he was saying in a deep, public voice, "with Kittredge's theory of the marriage cycle is that the order of composition of *The Canterbury Tales* is unclear. We do not, in short, know that 'The Clerk's Tale' precedes that of 'The Wife of Bath,' for instance."

The girl mumbled something I couldn't catch, and Hayden responded.

"No, you are responsible for what you quote. If you didn't agree with Kittredge, you shouldn't have cited him."

Again the girl's mumble. Again Hayden: "Yes, if you'd like to write another paper, I'll read it and grade it. If it's better than this one, it will bring your grade up. I'd like to see an outline or at least a thesis statement, though, before you write it. Okay?"

Mumble.

"Okay, thanks for coming by."

The girl got up and walked out. She didn't look pleased. As she got into the elevator I reached around and knocked on the open door.

"Come in," Hayden said. "What can I do for you?"

It was a tiny office, just room for a desk, chair, file cabinet, bookcase, and teacher. No windows, Sheetrock partitions painted green. Hayden himself looked right at home in the office. He was small, with longish blond hair. Not long enough to be stylish; long enough to look as though he needed a haircut. He had on a light green dress shirt with a faint brown stripe in it, open at the neck, and what looked like Navy surplus dungarees. The shirt was too big for him, and the material bagged around his waist. He was wearing gold-rimmed glasses.

I gave him my card and said, "I'm working on a case involving a former student and I was wondering if you could tell me anything."

He looked at my card carefully, then at me.

"Anyone may have a card printed up. Do you have more positive identification?"

I showed him the photostat of my license, complete with my picture. He looked at it very carefully, then handed it back.

"Who is the student?" he said.

"Terry Orchard," I said.

He showed no expression. "I teach a great many students, Mr."—he glanced down at my card lying on his desk—"Spenser. What class? What year? What semester?"

"Chaucer, this year, this semester."

He reached into a desk drawer and pulled a yellow cardboard-covered grade book. He thumbed through it, stopped, ran his eyes down a list, and said, "Yes, I have Miss Orchard in my Chaucer course."

Looking at the grade book upside down, I could see he had the student's last name and first initial. If he didn't know her name or whether she was in his class or not without looking her up in his grade book, how, looking at the listing ORCHARD, T., did he know it was Miss Orchard? Like Tabor, the zinnia head, no one seemed willing to know old Terry.

"Don't you know the names of your students, Dr. Hayden?" I asked, trying to say it neutrally, not as if I were critical. He took it as if it were critical.

"This is a very large university, Mr. Spenser." He had to check the card again to get my name. I hope he remembered Chaucer better. "I have an English survey course of sixty-eight students, for instance. I cannot keep track of the names, much as I try to do so. One of this university's serious problems is the absence of community. I am really able to remember only those students who respond to my efforts to personalize our relationship. Miss Orchard apparently is not one of those." He looked again at the open grade book. "Nor do her grades indicate that she has been unusually interested and attentive."

"How is she doing?" I asked, just to keep it going. I didn't know where I was going. I was fishing and I had to keep the conversation going.

"That is a matter concerning Miss Orchard and myself." Nice conversation primer, Spenser, you really know how to touch the right buttons.

"Sorry," I said. "I didn't mean to pry, but when you think about it, prying is more or less my business."

"Perhaps," Hayden said. "It is not, however, my business; nor is it, quite frankly, a business for which I have much respect."

"I know it's not important like Kittredge's marriage cycle, but it's better than enlisting, I suppose."

"I'm quite busy, Mr. Spenser." He didn't have to check this time. A quick study, I thought.

"I appreciate that, Dr. Hayden. Let me be brief. Terry Orchard is accused of the murder of her boyfriend, Dennis Powell." No reaction. "I am working to clear her of suspicion. Is there anything you can tell me that would help?"

"No, I'm sorry, there isn't."

"Do you know Dennis Powell?"

"No, I do not. I can check through my grade books, but I don't recall him."

"That's not necessary. The grade book won't tell me anything. There's nothing at all you can think of? About either?"

"Nothing. I'm sorry, but I don't know the people involved."

"Are you aware that the Godwulf Manuscript has been stolen?"

"Yes, I am."

"Do you have any idea what might have happened to it?"

"Mr. Spenser, this is absurd. I assume your interest relates to the fact that I am a medievalist. I am not, however, a thief."

"Well," I said, "thanks anyway." I got up.

"You're welcome. I'm sorry I wasn't more useful." His voice was remarkable. Deep and resonant, it seemed incongruous with his slight frame. "Thanks for coming by."

As I left the office, two students were waiting outside, sitting on the floor, coats and books in a pile beside them. They looked at me curiously as I entered the elevator. As it descended I could hear Hayden's voice booming. "Come in, Mr. Vale. What can I do for you?"

On the ground floor were two campus policemen, and they wanted me. I hadn't eluded Mary Masculine after all. She was hovering in the doorway to the English office. One of the cops was big and fat with a thick, pockmarked face and an enormous belly. The other was much smaller, a black man with a neat Sugar Ray mustache and a tailored uniform. They weren't wearing guns, but each had a nightstick stuck in his hip pocket. The fat one took my arm above the elbow in what he must have felt was an iron grip.

"Start walking, trooper," he said, barely moving his lips.

I was frustrated, and angry at Lowell Hayden and at Mary Masculine and the university. I said, "Let go of my arm or I'll put a dent in your face."

"You and who else?" he said. It broke my tension.

"Snappy," I said. "On your days off could you come over and be my dialogue coach?"

The black cop laughed. The fat one looked puzzled and let go of my arm.

"What do you mean?" he said.

"Never mind, Lloyd," the black cop said. "Come on, Jim, we got to walk you off campus."

I nodded. "Okay, but not arm in arm. I don't go for that kind of stuff."

"Me neither, Jim. We'll just stroll along."

And we did. The fat cop had his nightstick out and tapped it against his leg as we went out of the building and toward the street. His eyes never left me. Alert, I thought, vigilant. When we got to my car, the black cop opened the door for me with a small, graceful flourish.

The fat one said, "Don't come back. Next time you show up here you'll be arrested."

"For crissake," I said. "I'm working for the university. Your boss hired me."

"I don't know nothing about that, but we got our orders. Get out and stay out."

The black cop said, "I don't know, Jim, but I think maybe you been canceled." He closed the door and stepped back. I started the car and pulled away. They still stood there as I drove off, the fat one looking balefully after me, still slapping his nightstick against his leg.

CHAPTER TEN

IT WAS GETTING DARK, and the commuter traffic was starting to thicken the streets. I drove slowly back to my office, parked my car, and went in.

When I unlocked my office door the first thing I noticed was the smell of cigarette smoke. I hadn't smoked in ten years. I pushed it open hard and went in low with my gun out. There was someone sitting at my desk, and another man standing against the wall. In the half-light the tip of his cigarette glowed. Neither of them moved. I backed to the wall and felt for the light switch. I found it, and the room brightened.

The man against the wall laughed, a thin sound, without humor.

"Look at that, Phil. Maybe if we give him money he'll do that again."

The man at my desk said nothing. He was sitting with

his feet up, my chair tipped back, his hat still on, his overcoat still buttoned up, though it must have been ninety in there, wearing rose-colored gold-rimmed glasses. He looked at me without expression, a very tall man, narrow, with high shoulders, six foot four or five, probably. Behind the glasses one eye was blank and white and turned partly up. Along the right line of his jaw was a purple birthmark maybe two inches wide, running the whole length of the jaw from chin to ear. His hands were folded across his stomach. Big hands, long, square, thick fingers, the backs prominently veined, the knuckles lumpy. I could tell he was impressed with the gun in my hand. The only thing that would have scared him more would have been if I had threatened to flog him with a dandelion.

"Put that away," he said. "If he was going to push you I wouldn't have let Sonny smoke." His voice was a harsh whisper, as if he had an artificial throat.

Sonny gave me a moon-faced smile. He was thick and round, running to fat, with mutton-chop sideburns that came to the corners of his mouth. His coat was off and his collar open, the tie at half-mast. Sweat soaked the big half-moon circles around his armpits, and his face was shiny with it. I put the gun away.

"A man wants to see you," Phil said. I hadn't seen him move since I came in. His voice was entirely without inflection.

"Joe Broz?" I said.

Sonny said, "What makes you think so?"

Phil said, "He knows me."

"Yeah," I said, "you walk around behind Broz."

Phil said, "Let's go," and stood up. Six-five, at least. When he was standing you could see that his right shoulder was higher than his left.

I said, "What if I don't want to?"

Phil just looked at me. Sonny snickered, "What if he don't want to, Phil?"

Phil said, "Let's go."

We went. Outside, double-parked, was a Lincoln Continental. Sonny drove; Phil sat in back with me.

It had started to snow again, softly, big flakes, and the windshield wipers made the only sound in the car. I looked at the back of Sonny's neck as he drove. The hair was long and stylish and curled out over the collar of his white trench coat. Sonny seemed to be singing soundlessly to himself as he drove. His head bobbed, and he beat gentle time on the wheel with one suede-gloved hand. Phil was a silent and motionless shape in the corner of the back seat.

"Either of you guys seen *The Godfather?*" I asked.

Sonny snorted. Phil ignored me.

"Beat up any good candy store owners lately, Sonny?"

"Don't ride me, Peep; you'll find yourself looking up at the snow."

"I'm heavy work, Sonny. College kids are about your upper limit, I think."

"Goddammit," Sonny started, and Phil stopped him.

"Shut up," Phil said in his gear box voice, and we both knew he meant both of us.

"Just having a little snappy conversation, Phil, to pass the time," I said.

Phil just looked at me, and the menace was like a physical force. I could feel anxiety pulse up and down the long muscles of my arms and legs. Going to see Joe Broz was not normally a soothing experience anyway. Not many people looked forward to it.

The ride was short. Sonny pulled to a stop in front of a building on the lower end of State Street. Phil and I got out. I stuck my head back in before I closed the back door.

"If a tough meter maid puts the arm on you, Sonny, just scream and I'll come running."

Sonny swore at me and burned rubber away from the curb.

I followed Phil into the building. We took the self-service elevator to the eleventh floor. The corridor was silent and empty, with marble wainscoting and frosted glass doors. At the far end we went through one marked CONTINENTAL

CONSULTING CO. Inside was an empty stainless-steel and coral-vinyl reception room. There is little that is quieter than an office building after hours, and this one was no exception. The lights were all on, the receptionist's desk was geometrically neat. On one wall were staggered prints by Maurice Utrillo.

Phil said, "Gimme your gun."

I hesitated. I didn't like his manner, I didn't like his assumption that I'd do what I was told because he'd told me to, and I didn't like his assumption that if he had to he could make me. On the other hand, I'd come this far because I was curious. Something bothered Broz enough to have him send his top hand to bring me in. And Sonny looked a lot like one of the two hoods that Terry had described. Also, Phil didn't seem much to care whether I liked his assumptions or not.

I noticed that there was a gun in Phil's hand, and it was pointing at an area somewhere between my eyes. I'd never seen him move. I took my gun out of my hip holster and handed it to him, butt first. People were taking it away from me a lot lately. I didn't like that too much either. Phil stowed my gun away in an overcoat pocket, put away his own gun in the other, and stepped to one of the inner doors of the reception room. It was solid, no glass panel. I heard a buzz, and the door clicked open. I looked around and spotted the closed-circuit camera up high in one corner of the reception room. Phil pushed the door open and nodded me through it.

The room was bone white. The first thing I saw was my own reflection in the wide black picture window that stretched the width of the opposite wall. My reflection didn't look too aggressive. In front of the window was a broad black desk, neat, with a bank of phones on it. The room was carpeted with something thick and expensive, in a dark blue. There were several black leather chairs about. Along the side wall was an ebony bar with blue leather padding. Leaning against it was Joe Broz.

There was something theatrical about Broz, as if there was always a press photographer downstage left, kneeling to shoot a picture with his big Speed Graphic camera. He was a middle-size man who stood very straight with his chin up, as if squeezing every inch of height out of what God had given him. He had many teeth—a few too many for his mouth—and they were very prominent and white. His hair was slick black, combed straight back from a high forehead and gray at the temples. The sideburns were long and neatly trimmed. His nose was flat and thick with a slight ski-jump quality to the end that hinted at a break somewhere in the past. He wore a white suit, a white vest, a dark blue shirt, and a white tie. There was a gold chain across the vest, and presumably a gold watch tucked in the vest pocket. I would have bet against a Phi Beta key, but little is sure in life. He had one foot hooked on the brass rail of the bar, and a large diamond ring flashed from his little finger as he turned a thick highball glass in his hands.

"Do you always dress in blue and white?" I asked. "Or do you have the office redone to match your clothes every day?"

Broz sipped a little of his drink, put it down on the bar, and swung fully around toward me, both elbows resting on the bar.

"I have been told," he said in a deep voice that had the phony quality you hear in an announcer's voice when he's not on the air, "that you are a wise-ass punk. Apparently my information was correct. So let's get some ground rules. You are here because I sent for you. You will leave when I tell you to. You are of no consequence. You have no class. If you annoy me, I will have someone sprinkle roach powder on you. Do you understand that?"

"Yeah," I said. "I think so, but you better give me a drink. I feel faint."

Phil, who had drifted to a couch in the far corner and sprawled awkwardly on it, let out a soft sound that sounded almost like a sigh.

Broz moved to his desk, sat, and nodded at one of the leather chairs. "Sit down. I got things to say. Phil, make him a drink."

"Bourbon," I said, "with water, and some bitters."

Phil made the drink. He moved stiffly, and his hands

seemed like distorted work gloves. But they performed the task with a bare economy of motion that was incongruous. I'd have to be sure not to make any mistakes about Phil.

I leaned back in the black chair and took a sip of the bourbon. It was a little more expensive than the private label stuff I bought. There was too much bitters, but I decided not to call Phil on it. We'd probably have other issues. There was a knock on the door. Phil glanced at the monitor set in the wall by the door, opened the door, and let Sonny in. He had his trench coat folded over his arm, and his tie was neatly up. His neck spilled over slightly around his collar. He walked quietly over to a chair near the couch and sat down, holding the trench coat in his lap. Broz paid no attention to him. He stared at me with his yellowish eyes.

"You're working on a case." It wasn't really a question. I wasn't sure Broz ever asked questions.

I nodded.

"I want to hear about it," Broz said.

I shook my head.

Broz got a big curved-stem meerschaum pipe out of a rack on his desk and carefully began to pack it from a thick silver humidor.

"Spenser, this can be easy or hard. I'd just as soon it was easy, but the choice is yours."

"Look," I said, "one reason people employ me is because they want their business private. If I spill what I know every time anybody asks me, I am not likely to flourish."

"Your chances of flourishing are not very big right now, Spenser." Broz had the pipe packed to his satisfaction and spoke through a blue cloud of aromatic smoke. "I know you are looking for the Godwulf Manuscript. I know that you are working for Roland Orchard. What I want to know is what you've got. There's no breach of confidence in that."

"Why do you want to know?"

"Let's say I'm an interested party."

"Let's say more than that. Why be one way? You tell me what your interest is; I'll think about telling you what I know."

78

"Spenser, I'm hanging on to my patience. But it's slipping. I don't have to make swaps with you. I get what I ask for."

I didn't say anything.

From his place Sonny said, "Let me have him, Mr. Broz."

"What are you going to do, Sonny," I said, "sweat all over me till I beg for mercy?"

Phil made his little sighing sounds again. Sonny put his trench coat carefully on the arm of the couch and started toward me. I saw Phil look at Broz and saw Broz nod.

"You been crying for this, you sonova bitch," Sonny said.

I stood up. Sonny was probably thirty pounds heavier than I was, and a lot of it was muscle. But some of it was fat, and quickness didn't look to be Sonny's strong suit. He swung a big right hand at me. I rolled away from it and hit him in the middle of the face twice with left hooks, getting my shoulder nicely behind both of them, feeling the shock all the way up into my back. Sonny was tough. It rocked him, but he didn't go down. He grabbed at my shirtfront with his left hand and clubbed at me with his right. The punch glanced off my shoulder and caught me under the left eye. I broke his grip by bringing my clenched fists up under his forearm, and then drove my right forearm against the side of his jaw. He stumbled back two steps and sat down. But he got up. He was wary now. His hands up, he began to circle me. I turned as he did. He put his head down and lunged at me. I moved aside and tripped him and he sprawled against Broz's desk, knocking over the pipe rack. Broz never blinked. Sonny pushed himself up from the desk like a man doing his last pushup. He turned and came at me again. His nose was bleeding freely and his shirtfront was bloody. I feinted with my left hand at his stomach and then brought it up over his hands and jabbed him three times on that bloody nose, then crossed over with a right hand that caught him in the neck below the ear. He went down face first. This time he stayed. He got as far as his hands and knees and stayed, his head hanging, swaying slightly, with the blood dripping on the azure rug.

Broz spoke to Phil. "Get him out of here, he's messing on the rug." Phil got up, walked over, pulled Sonny to his feet by the back of his collar, and walked him, weaving and swaying, out through a side door.

Broz said, "Sonny seems to have exaggerated his ability."

"Maybe he just underestimated mine," I said.

"Either way," Broz said.

Phil came back in, wiping his hands on a handkerchief. "Ask him again, Joe," he rasped, "now that Sonny's got him softened." His face twisted in what was, I think, a momentary smile.

Broz looked disgusted. "I want you out of this business, Spenser."

"Which business?"

"The Godwulf Manuscript. I don't want you muddying up the water."

"What's in it for me if I pull out?"

"Health."

"You gonna unleash Sonny on me again?"

"I can put ten Sonnys on your back whenever I want to. Or Phil. Phil's not Sonny."

"I never thought he was," I said. "But I hired on to find the manuscript."

"Maybe the manuscript will turn up." Broz leaned back in the big leather executive swivel with the high back, and blew a lungful of pipe smoke at the ceiling. His eyes were squeezed down as he squinted through the smoke.

"If it does, I won't have to look for it anymore."

"Don't look for it anymore." Dramatically, Broz came forward in the swivel chair, his hands flat on the desk. "Stay out of it, or you'll end up looking at the trunk of your car from the inside. You've been warned. Now get the hell out of here." He swiveled the chair around to face the window, putting the high leather back between me and him. What a trouper, I thought.

Phil stood up. I followed him out through the door we'd entered. Broz never moved or said a word. In the anteroom a thin-faced Italian man with a goatee was cleaning his fingernails with the blade of a large pocket knife, his feet up on the desk, a Borsalino hat tipped forward over the bridge of his nose. He paid us no mind as we went through.

CHAPTER ELEVEN

I TOOK A CAB back from Broz's office to mine. When I got there, I sat in my chair in the dark and looked out the window. The snow was steady now and starting to screw up the traffic. Plows were out, and their noise added to the normal traffic sounds that drifted up through the closed window. "Sleigh bells ring," I thought, "are ya listening." The falling snow fuzzed out all the lights in the Combat Zone, giving them halos of neon red and street-light yellow. I was tired. My eye hurt. The knuckles of my left hand were sore and puffy from hitting Sonny in the face. I hadn't eaten for a long time and I was hungry, but I didn't seem to want to eat. I pulled a bottle of bourbon out of the desk drawer and opened it and drank some. It felt hot in my stomach.

Where was I? Somewhere along the line I had touched a nerve, and somebody had called Broz. Who? Could be anybody. Broz got around. But it was probably someone today. Broz would have no reason to wait once he knew I was trampling around on his lawn. I couldn't see Broz being tied into the Godwulf Manuscript. It wasn't worth any money. It was impossible to fence. But he'd implied he'd put it back if I dropped out. He knew a lot of people; maybe he could push the right button without being necessarily involved. Maybe he'd been lying. But something had stirred him up. Not only did he want me out of things, but he wanted to know what I knew. Maybe it was simply collateral interest. Maybe it was Powell's murder. Maybe he didn't want me digging into that. I liked that better. Terry's description of the two men included one like Sonny. The other one wasn't Phil. But Phil wouldn't do that kind of trench duty anyway. I was amazed he had done errand duty for me. But why would Broz care one way or the other about a loudmouth kid like Dennis Powell, care enough to send two employees to kill him and frame his girl? Yet somebody's employees did it. It wasn't an amateur job, by Terry's account. Came in, held them up, had her gun, the rubber gloves, the drug they'd brought, the whole thing. It didn't sound like it had been ad-libbed. Did they have inside help? How did they get hold of her gun? And what possible interest would Broz have in the university? He had a lot of interests—numbers, women, dope—but higher education didn't seem to be one of them. Of his line, dope would seem the best connection. It seemed the only place where college and Broz overlapped. Dennis Powell was reputed to be a channel for hard stuff: heroin, specifically. That meant, if it were true, that he had mob connections, direct or indirect. Now he was dead, in what looked like some kind of mob killing. And Joe Broz wanted me to keep my nose out of his business.

But what did that have to do with the manuscript? I didn't know. The best connection I had was the dope and the question of the gun. How did they know she'd have a gun there? She'd lived with another girl before she'd lived with Powell. I took another belt of the bourbon. Uncut by bitters or ice and cheap anyway, it grated down into my stomach. Catherine Connelly, Tower had told me. Let's try her. More bourbon. It wasn't really so bad, didn't taste bad at all, made you feel pretty nice in your stomach. Made you feel tough, too, and on top of it—whatever it was. The phone rang.

I picked it up and said, "Spenser industries, security division. We never sleep."

There was a pause, and then a woman spoke.

"Mr. Spenser?"

"Yeah."

"This is Marion Orchard, Terry's mother."

"Howya doing, sweets," I said, and took another pull on the bourbon.

"Mr. Spenser, she's gone."

"Me, too, sweets."

"No, really, she's gone, and I'm terribly worried."

I put the bottle down and said, "Oh, Christ!"

"Our lawyer called and said the police wished to speak with her again, and I went to her room and she wasn't there and she hasn't been home all day. There's two hundred thousand dollars bail money, and . . . I want her back. Can you find her, Mr. Spenser?"

"You got any ideas where I should look?"

"I . . . Mr. Spenser, we have hired you. You sound positively hostile, and I resent it."

"Yeah, you probably do," I said. "I been up a long time and have eaten little, and had a fight with a tough guinea and drank too much bourbon and was thinking about going and getting a sub sandwich and going to bed. I'll come out in a little while and we'll talk about it."

"Please, I'm very worried."

"Yeah, I'll be along." I hung up, put the cork in the bottle, put the bottle in the drawer. My head was light and my eyes focused badly and my mouth felt thick. I got my coat on, locked the office, and went down to my car. I parked in a taxi zone and got a submarine sandwich and a large black coffee to go. I ate the sandwich and drank the coffee as I headed out to Newton again. Eating a sub sandwich with one hand is sloppy work, and I got some tomato juice and oil on my shirtfront and some coffee stains on my pant leg. I stopped at a Dunkin' Donuts shop in West Newton Square, bought another black coffee, and sat in my car and drank it.

I felt terrible. The bourbon was wearing off, and I felt dull and sleepy and round-shouldered. I looked at my watch. It was a quarter to ten. The snow continued as I sat and forced the coffee down. I had read somewhere that black coffee won't sober you up, but I never believed it. After bourbon it tasted so awful it had to be doing some good.

The plows hadn't gotten to the Orchards' street; my wheels spun and my car skidded getting up their hill. I had my jacket unbuttoned, but the defrosters were going full blast. And, wrestling the car through the snow, I could feel the sweat in the hollow of my back, and my shirt collar was wet and limp. Sometimes I wondered if I was getting too old for this work. And sometimes I thought I had gotten too old last year. I jammed the car through a snowdrift into the Orchards' driveway and climbed out. There was no pathway, so I waded through the snow across the lawn and up to the front door. The same black maid answered the door. She remembered me, took my hat and coat, and led me to the same library we'd talked in before. A fire was still burning, but no one was in the room. I got a look at myself in the dark window: unshaven, sub sandwich stains on my shirt, collar open. There was a puffy mouse under one eye, courtesy of old Sonny. I looked like the leg man for a slumlord.

Marion Orchard came in. She was wearing an ankle-length blue housecoat that zipped up the front, a matching headband, and bare feet. I noticed her toenails were painted silver. She seemed as well groomed and together as before, but her face was flushed and I realized she had been drinking. Me, too. Who hadn't? The ride and the coffee had sobered me up and depressed me. My head ached, and my stomach felt like I'd been swallowing sand. Without a word Marion Orchard went to the sideboard, put ice in a glass from a silver bucket, added Scotch, and squirted soda in from a silver-laced dispenser. She drank half of it and turned toward me.

"You want some?"

"Yes, ma'am."

"Scotch or bourbon?"

"Bourbon, with bitters, if you've got it."

She turned and mixed me bourbon and soda with bitters in a big square-angled glass. I drank some and felt it begin to combat the coffee and the fatigue. I'd need more, though. From the looks of Marion Orchard, she would, too, and planned on getting it.

"Where's Mr. Orchard?" I asked.

"At the office. Sitting behind his big masculine desk, trying to feel like a man."

"Does he know Terry's gone?"

"Yes. That's why he went to the office. It makes him feel better about himself. All he can cope with is stocks and bonds. People, and daughters and wives, scare hell out of him." She finished the drink, took mine, which was still half-full, and made two fresh ones.

"Something scares hell out of everybody," I said. "Have you any thoughts on where I should look for Terry?"

"What scares hell out of you?" she asked.

The bourbon was making a lot of headway against the coffee. I felt a lot better than I had when I came in. The line of Marion Orchard's thigh was tight against the blue robe as she sat with her legs tucked up under her on the couch.

"The things people do to one another," I answered. "That scares hell out of me."

She drank some more. "Wrong," she said. "That engages your sympathy. It doesn't scare you. I'm an expert on what scares men. I've lived with a scared man for twenty-two years. I left college in my sophomore year to marry him, and I never finished. I was an English major. I wrote poetry. I don't anymore." I waited. She didn't really seem to be talking to me anymore.

"About Terry?" I prodded softly.

"Screw Terry," she said, and finished her drink. "When I was her age I was marrying her father and nobody with wide shoulders came around and got me out of that mess." She was busy making us two more drinks as she talked. Her voice was showing the liquor. She was talking with extra-careful enunciation—the way I was. She handed me the drink and then put her hand on my upper arm and squeezed it.

"How much do you weigh?" she asked.

"One ninety-five."

"You work out, don't you? How much can you lift?"

"I can bench press two-fifty ten times," I said.

"How'd you get the broken nose?" She bent over very carefully and examined my face from about two inches away. Her hair smelled like herbs.

"I fought a ranked heavyweight once."

She stayed bent over, her face two inches away, her fragrant hair tumbling forward, one hand still squeezing my arm, the other holding the drink. I put my left hand behind her head and kissed her. She folded up into my lap and kissed back. It wasn't eager. It was ferocious. She let the glass drop from her hand onto the floor, where I assume it tipped and spilled. Under the blue robe she was wearing nothing at all, and she was nowhere near as sinewy as she had looked to me the first time I saw her. Making love in a chair is heavy work. The only other time I'd attempted, I'd gotten a charley horse that damn near ruined the event. With one arm around her back I managed to slip the other one under her knees and pick her up, which is not easy from a sitting position in a soft chair. Her mouth never left mine, nor did the fierceness abate as I carried her to the couch. She bit me and scratched me, and at climax she pounded me on the back with her clenched fist as hard as she could. At the time I barely noticed. But when it was over, I felt as if I'd been in a fight, and maybe in some sense I had.

She had shed the robe during our encounter and now she walked naked over to the bar to make another drink for each of us. She had a fine body, tanned all over except for the stark whiteness of her buttocks and the thin line her bra strap had made. She returned with a drink in each hand. Gave one to me and then stroked my cheek once, quite gently. She drank half her drink, still standing naked in front of me, and lit a cigarette, took in a long lungful of smoke, let it out, picked up her robe, and slipped into it. There we were, all together again, neat, orderly, employee and employer. Here's to you, Mrs. Robinson.

"I think Terry is with a group in Cambridge that calls itself the Ceremony of Moloch. In the past, when she would get in trouble or be freaked out on drugs or have a fight with her father, she'd run off there, and they let her stay. One of her friends told me about it."

She'd known that when she'd called me. But she'd gotten me out here to tell me. She really didn't like her husband.

"Where in Cambridge is the Ceremony of Moloch?"

"I don't know. I don't even know if she's there, but it's all I could think of."

"Why did Terry take off?" I didn't use her name. After copulation on the couch, Mrs. Orchard sounded a little silly. On the other hand, we were not on a "Marion" basis.

"A fight with her father." She didn't use my name either.

"About what?"

"What's it ever about? He sees her as an extension of his career. She's supposed to adorn his success by being what he fantasizes a daughter is. She does everything the opposite to punish him for not being what she fantasizes a father is . . . and probably for sleeping with me. Ever read *Mourning Becomes Electra,* Spenser?"

That's how she solved her problem with names; she dropped the Mister. I wondered if I should call her Orchard. I decided not to. "Yeah, a long time ago. But is there anything you could tell me about Terry, or the Ceremony of Moloch, that might turn out useful? It is past midnight, and I've gotten a lot of exercise today."

I think she colored very slightly. "You are like a terrier after a rat. Nothing distracts your attention."

"Well," I said, "there are things, occasionally, Marion."

Her color got a little deeper and she smiled, but shook her head.

"I wonder," she said. "I wonder whether you might not have been thinking of a way to run down my dear daughter Terry, even then."

"Then," I said, "I wasn't thinking of anything."

She said, "Maybe."

I was silent. I was so tired it was an effort to move my mouth.

She shook her head again. "No, there's nothing. I can't

think of anything else to tell you that will help. But can you look? Can you find her?"

"I'll look," I said. "Did your lawyer tell you what the cops wanted?"

"No. He just said Lieutenant Quirk wanted her to come down tomorrow and talk with him some more."

I stood up. Partly to see if I could. Marion Orchard stood up with me.

"Thank you for coming. I know you'll do your best in finding Terry. I'm sorry to have kept you up so late." She put out her hand, and I took it. Christ, breeding. Here she was, upper crust, Boston society, yes'm. Thank you very much, ma'am, for the drink and the toss on the couch, ma'am, it's a pleasure to be of service to you and the master, ma'am. I gave her hand a squeeze. I was goddamned if I was going to shake it.

"I'll dig her up, Marion. When I do, I'll bring her home. It'll work out."

She nodded her head silently and her face got congested-looking and red around the eyes, and I realized she was going to cry in a minute. I said, "I'll find my way out. Try not to worry. It'll work out."

She nodded again, and as I left the library she touched my arm but said nothing. As I closed the door behind me I could hear the first stifled sob burst out. There were more before I got out of earshot. They would probably last most of the night. I went out the front door and into the dead, still white night, got in my car, and went back to town. Every fiber of my being felt awful.

CHAPTER TWELVE

IT WAS ABOUT ONE THIRTY when I got back to my apartment. I stripped off my clothes and took a long shower, slowly easing the water temperature down to cool. In the bedroom, putting on clean clothes, I looked at the bed with something approaching lust, but I kept myself away from it. Then I went to the living room in my socks and called a guy I knew who did night duty at the *Globe*. I asked him where I could find the Ceremony of Moloch. He gave me an address in Cambridge. I asked him what he knew about the group.

"Small," he said. "Freaky. Robes and statues and candlelight. That kind of crap. Moloch was some kind of Phoenician god that required human sacrifice. In *Paradise Lost,* Milton lumps him in with Satan and Beelzebub among the fallen angels. That's all I know about them. We did a feature once on the Cambridge-Boston subculture and they got about a paragraph."

I thanked him and hung up and went back into the bedroom for my shoes. I sat down on the bed to put them on, and that was where I lost it. As long as I was up I could move, but from sitting to lying was too short a distance. I lay back, just for a minute, and went to sleep.

I woke up, in the same position, nine hours later in broad daylight, with the morning gone. I went out to the kitchen, measured out the coffee, put the electric percolator on, went back, stripped down, shaved, showered, put on my shorts, and went out to the kitchen again. The coffee was ready and I drank it with cream and sugar while I sliced peppers and tomatoes for a Spanish omelet.

I felt good. The sleep had taken care of the exhaustion. The snow had stopped, and the sunlight, magnified by reflection, was pure white as it splashed about the kitchen. I greased the omelet pan and poured the eggs in. When the inside was right I put in the vegetables and flipped the omelet. I'm very good at flipping omelets. Finding out what was happening with Terry Orchard and the Godwulf Manuscript seemed to be something I wasn't very good at.

I ate the omelet with thick slices of fresh pumpernickel and drank three more cups of coffee while I looked at the morning *Globe*. I felt even better. Okay, Terry Orchard, here I come. You can run, but you can't hide. I considered stopping by to frighten Joe Broz some more but rejected the plan and headed for Cambridge.

The address I had for the Ceremony of Moloch was in North Cambridge in a neighborhood of brown and gray three-decker apartment buildings with open porches across the back of each floor where laundry hung stiff in the cold. I went up the unshoveled path without seeing the print of cloven hoofs. No smell of brimstone greeted me. No darkness visible, no moans of despair. For all I could tell the house was empty, and its inhabitants had gone to work or school. Every third person in Cambridge was a student.

In the front hall there were three mailboxes, each with a name plate. The one for the third floor apartment said simply MOLOCH. I went up the stairs without making more noise than I had to and stood outside the apartment door. No sound. I knocked. No answer. I tried the door. Locked. But it was an old door, with the frame warped. About thirty seconds with some thin plastic was all it took to open it.

The door opened onto a narrow hall that ran right and left from it. To the left I could see a kitchen, to the right the half-open door of a bathroom. Diagonally on the other wall an archway opened into a room I couldn't see. The wallpaper in the hall was faded brown fern leaves against a dirty beige background. There were large stains of a darker brown here and there, as if someone had splashed water against the walls. The floor was made of narrow hardwood painted dark

90

brown, and there was a threadbare red runner the length of the hall. The woodwork was white and had been repainted without being adequately scraped first, so that it looked lumpy and pocked. It had not been repainted recently, and there were many nicks and gouges in it. I could see part of the tub and part of the water closet in the bathroom. The tub had claw and ball feet, and the water closet had a pull chain from the storage tank mounted up by the ceiling. The place was dead still.

I walked through the arch into what must have been the living room. It no longer was. In the bay of the three-window bow along the right-hand wall there was an altar made out of packing crates and two-by-fours which reminded me of the fruit display racks in Faneuil Hall market. It was draped with velveteen hangings in black and crimson and at its highest reach was inverted a dime store crucifix. The crucifix was made of plastic, with the Sacred Heart redly exposed in the center of the flesh-tinted chest. On each side of the crucifix were human skulls. Beside them unmatched candelabra with assorted candles, partially burned. The walls were hung with more of the black velveteen, shabby and thin in the daylight. The floor had been painted black and scattered with cushions. The room smelled strongly of incense and faintly of marijuana and faintly also of unemptied Kitty Litter.

I went back down the corridor, through the kitchen with its oilcloth-covered table and its ancient black sink, and into a bedroom. There were no beds, but five bare mattresses covered the floor. Three of them had sleeping bags rolled neatly at the wall end. In the closet were two pairs of nearly white jeans, a work shirt, something that looked like a shift, and an olive drab undershirt. I couldn't tell if the owners were male or female. The two other bedrooms were much the same. In a pantry closet off the kitchen were maybe a dozen black robes, like graduation costumes. On the shelves were a five-pound bag of brown rice, some peanut butter, a loaf of Bone Bread, and a two-pound bag of granola. In the refrigerator there was a plastic pitcher of grape Kool-Aid, seven cans of Pepsi, and three cucumbers. Maybe they had a bundle in a numbered account in Switzerland, but on the surface it didn't look like the Ceremony of Moloch was a high-return venture.

I went back out, closed the door behind me, and went to my car. The noon sun was making the snow melt and heating the inside of my car. I sat in it, two doors up from the house of Moloch, and waited for someone to come there and do something. It was cold, and the snow had begun to crust over when someone finally showed up. Eight people, in a battered Volkswagen bus that had been hand-painted green. Three of the eight were girls, and one of them was Terry. They all went into what they probably called the temple. It occurred to me that I wasn't exactly sure what to do with Terry now that I'd found her. There wasn't much point in dragging her out by the hair and taking her home locked in the trunk. She'd just take off again and after a while I'd get sick of chasing and fetching.

It was dark now, and cold. A fifteen-year-old Oldsmobile sedan pulled up behind the Volkswagen bus and unloaded five more people. They went into the three-decker. I sat some more. The thing to do was to call Marion Orchard, tell her I'd located her daughter, have her notify the cops, and let them bring her in. I had no legal authority to go in and get her. No question. That was what I had to do. I looked at my watch. 7:15.

I slipped out of my coat, got out of the car, and went to the house of the Ceremony of Moloch. This time I was very quiet going up the stairs. At the door I stood silent and listened. I could hear music that sounded as if it were being played on one string of an Armenian banjo. The smell of incense and pot was very rich. At irregular intervals there were chimes like the ones rung during a Roman Catholic Mass. The thing to do was to call Terry's mother and have the cops come pick her up. I took out my plastic shim and opened the door. Inside the hallway the heat was tangible and stifling. There was no light.

From the living-room altar area came the twanging sound of the music, now quite loud, and the lesser sound of a man chanting. A flickering light fell into the hallway from the living room. Despite the heat I felt cold, and my throat was tight. The chimes sounded again. And I heard a kind of muffled whimper, like someone sobbing into a pillow. I looked carefully around the corner. Suspended by clothesline from the ceiling, in front of the altar I had seen earlier, was a full-sized cross, made of two-by-sixes. To it, in a parody of the Crucifixion, Terry Orchard was tied with more length of clothesline. She was naked, and her body had been marked with astrological and cabalistic signs in what looked to be, in the candlelight, several different colors of Magic Marker. She was gagged with a wide piece of gray tape.

Before her stood a tall, wiry man, naked too, wearing a black hood, his body covered with the same kind of Magic Marker design work. In a semicircle on the floor, in black robes, sat the rest of the people. The music was coming from a tape recorder behind the altar. In his hand the guy with the hood had a carved piece of black wood, about a foot and a half long, that looked like a nightstick. He was chanting in a monotonous singsong in a language I didn't understand and didn't recognize. And as he chanted he swayed in front of Terry in an approximation of the beat from the tape recorder. The seated audience rocked back and forth in the same tempo. Then he made a gesture with the nightstick, and I realized its function was phallic.

I took out my gun and put a bullet into the tape recorder. The explosion of the shot and the cessation of the music were simultaneous, and the silence that followed was paralyzing. I stepped into the room with my gun leveled at all of them, but especially the fruitcake with the hood. With my left hand I took a jackknife out of my pants pocket, and worked the blade open with one hand by holding it in my teeth. No one made a sound. I sidestepped around behind the cross and cut Terry loose without taking my eyes from the audience. When the ropes parted, she fell. I folded the knife shut against my leg and put it away. I reached down without looking and got her up with one hand under her arm. The guy with the hood and the funny nightstick never took his eyes off me, and the steady gaze through the Halloween pumpkin triangles cut in the hood made me very edgy. So did the fact that there was one of me and twelve of them.

My hand still hanging on to Terry's arm, I backed up out of the room, through the narrow hall, and out the still-open door. The cold air of the stairwell rushed up like the wind from an angel's wing in the doorway of Hell. "I'm going to close this door," I said, and my voice sounded like someone else's. "If it opens, I'll shoot at it."

No one said a word. No one moved. I let go of Terry's arm, closed the door, took hold of her arm again, and headed down the stairs. No one came after us. Out the front door and across to my car. We ran. In my mind I could see us from their third floor vantage, outlined sharp against the white snow in the streetlight. No one shot at us. I pushed Terry into the car first, came in behind her, and got it out of there. It was a full block before I looked at Terry. She huddled, still stark naked, still with the tape on her mouth, in the far corner of the seat. She must have been freezing. I reached into the back seat, took my coat from where I'd left it, and gave it to her. She pulled it around her.

"Maybe you ought to take the gag off," I said.

She peeled it carefully, and spit out what looked like a wadded paper towel that had been stuffed in her mouth. She didn't say anything. I didn't say anything. The heater had warmed up and was starting to warm the car. I turned on the radio. We went down along the Charles on Memorial Drive and across the Mass Ave bridge. Boston always looks great from there. Especially at night, with the lights and the sky-line against the starry sky and the sweep of the river in a graceful curve down toward the harbor. It probably didn't look too spiffy at the moment to Terry.

I turned off onto Marlborough Street and pulled up in front of my apartment. Terry waited in the car while I went around and opened the door. She was well brought up. She had to walk barefoot across the frozen pavement but showed no sign that she felt it. We went up in the elevator.

Inside my apartment she looked about curiously. As if we'd recently met at a cocktail party and I'd invited her home to see my carvings. I felt the urge to giggle hysterically, but stifled it. I went to the kitchen, got out some ice, and poured two big shots of bourbon over the ice. I gave her one. Then I went to the bathroom and started to run hot water in the tub. She stayed right behind me—like a dog I used to have when it was supper-time, or when he thought I might be about to go somewhere.

"Get in," I said. "Take a long, slow hot bath. Drink another drink. I'll make us some supper, and we'll eat it together. No candlelight, though. A lot of bright overheads."

I took her nearly empty glass, added more ice, and filled it again. I gave it to her, pushed her gently into the bathroom, and closed the door.

"There's some kind of bubble bath or whatever in the medicine cabinet," I said through the door. I waited till I heard her splash into the tub. Then I went to the kitchen. I put on a pot of rice to cook and got four boneless chicken breasts out of the meat keeper. I cooked them with wine and butter and cream and mushrooms. While they cooked I tossed a salad and made a dressing with lime juice and mint, olive oil, honey, and wine vinegar. There were two bottles of Rhine wine in the refrigerator for which I'd originally had other plans, but I could buy some more tomorrow.

By the time I'd gotten the table set in the living room, she was through, and came out of the bathroom wearing a towel with her hair tucked up and some color in her face. I handed her my bathrobe and she slipped into it, modestly closing it before she let the towel slip to the floor. It occurred to me that half the time we'd spent together she'd been without clothes.

I gave her a third drink and freshened up my own. She sat on a stool in the kitchen and sipped it while I put some baking powder biscuits in the oven.

She had not spoken since I'd found her. Now she said, "Do you have any cigarettes?"

I found some thin filter tips in a fancy feminine package that a friend had left in one of the kitchen drawers. I held a match for her as she lit one and inhaled deeply. She let the smoke slip slowly out of her nose as she sipped her drink, holding the glass in both hands. The smoke spread out on the surface of the bourbon and eddied gently back up around her face. I felt my stomach tighten; I had known someone a long time ago who used to do just that, in just that way.

I got out the corkscrew and opened one of the bottles of wine. I poured some into each glass, and then took the biscuits out and served the supper. She sat opposite me at the small table and ate. Her manners were terrific. One hand in the lap, small bites, delicate sips of wine. But she ate everything. So did I. Still no talk. I had the radio on in the kitchen. When I offered her more, she nodded yes. When I got up to get the second bottle of wine, I plugged in the coffee. Its steady perk made a pleasant counterpoint to the radio. When we'd finished eating, I poured the coffee and brought out some applejack and two pony glasses. I put them on the cobbler's bench coffee table in front of the sofa. She sat at one end and I sat at the other, and we drank our coffee and sipped our brandy and she smoked another cigarette, holding her hand primly over the gap in the front of the bathrobe as she leaned over to accept my light. I got out a cigar and we listened some more to the radio. She leaned back against the arm of the couch and closed her eyes.

I stood up and said, "You can sleep in my bed. I'll sleep out here." I walked to the bedroom door and opened it. She went in.

I said, "I'm sorry I don't have any pajamas. You could sleep in one of my dress shirts, I guess."

"No, thank you," she said. "I don't wear anything to bed anyway."

"Okay," I said. "Good night. We'll talk in the morning."

She went in and shut the door, then opened it a crack. I heard her get into the bed. I picked up the dishes and put them in the dishwasher. Then I went in and took a shower and shaved. I felt odd, like my father probably had when we were small and all home and in bed and he was the only one up in the house. I got a blanket out of the closet, shut out the lights, and lay on my back on the couch smoking the rest of my cigar, blowing the smoke across the glowing tip.

I heard the light click on in the bedroom. She called, "Spenser?"

"Yeah?"

"Would you come in here, please?"

I got up, put on a pair of pants, and went in, still smoking the cigar. She was lying on her back in bed with covers pulled up under her chin.

"Sit on the bed," she said.

I did.

"Did you ever work on a farm?" she asked me.

"Nope."

"My grandfather, my mother's father, had a farm in Illinois. He used to milk fifty cows a day, and he had forearms like yours. He wasn't as big as you, but he had muscles in his forearms like you do."

I nodded.

"You're not fat at all, are you?" she said. I shook my head.

"With your clothes on you look as if you might be a little fat, but with your shirt off you're not. It's all muscle, isn't it?"

I nodded.

"You look like . . . like a boxer, or like somebody in a Tarzan movie."

"Cheetah," I said.

"Do you know," she said, "do you know that I've only met you four times in my life, and you are the only person in the entire world I can trust?" As she got to the end of the sentence her eyes filled. I patted her leg and said, "Shhh." But she went on, her voice not quite steady but apparently under control.

"Dennis is dead. My mother and father use me to get even with each other. I thought I could join the Moloch people. They'd dropped out, they weren't hung up on all the crap my father is. I thought they just took you as you were. They don't." Her voice got shakier. "They initiate you."

I patted her thigh again. I had nothing to say. The stub of the cigar was too short. I put it in an ashtray on the night table.

"Do you know what the initiation is?"

"I figured out the first part," I said.

She sat up in bed and let the covers fall away.

"You are the only one in the world, in the whole god-damned sonova bitch world . . ." The tears started to come. I leaned toward her and put my arm around her and she caught hold of me and squeezed.

"Love me," she said in a choked voice. "Make love to me, make me feel, make love to me, make me feel." A fleeting part of my mind thought, "Jesus, first the mother, then the daughter," but the enduring majority of my mind said, Yes, Yes, Yes, as I bore her back onto the bed and turned the covers back from her.

CHAPTER THIRTEEN

IN THE MORNING I drove Terry home. Riding out to Newton we mentioned neither the Ceremony of Moloch nor the previous night. We ran through the events of the murder again; nothing new. I described Sonny for her in detail. Yes, that sounded like one of the men. They had brought the drug with them that she'd swallowed. They had brought her gun with them. Yes, she had shared that apartment with Cathy Connelly before Dennis had moved in. They had parted friends and still were, as far as Terry knew. Cathy lived on the Fenway, she said. On the museum side, near the end closest to the river. She didn't know the number. I stopped in front of her house and let her out. I didn't go in. Having slept with mother and daughter within the same twenty-four hours, I felt fussy about sitting around with both of them in the library and making small talk. She leaned back in through the open door of my car.

"Call me," she said.

"I will," I said.

She closed the door and I pulled away, watching her in the rearview mirror. She went in very slowly, turning once to wave at me. I tooted the horn in reply.

Back to Boston again. I seemed to be making this drive a lot. Turning off Storrow at the Charlesgate exit, I went up the ramp over Commonwealth Ave and looked down at the weeping willows underneath the arch—bare now, with slender branches crusted in snow and bending deep beneath winter weight. There was a Frost poem, but it was about birches, and then I was off the ramp and looking for a parking space. This was not a business for poets anyway.

I parked near the Westland Avenue entrance to the Fenway and walked across the street to a drugstore. There was no listing in the phone book for a Catherine Connelly on the Fenway. So I started at the north end and began looking at the mailboxes in apartment lobbies, working my way south toward the museum. In the third building I found it. Second floor. I rang. Nothing happened. I rang again and leaned on it. No soap. I rang some other buzzers at random. No one opened the door. A cagey lot. I rang all the buttons. No response. Then a mean, paunchy man in green twill shirt and pants came to the front door. He opened it about a foot and said, "Whaddya want?"

"You the super?" I said.

"Who do you think I am?" He was smoking a cigarette that looked as if he'd found it, and it waggled wetly in the corner of his mouth as he spoke.

"I thought you were one of Santa's helpers coming around to see if everything was set for Christmas."

"Huh?" he said.

"I'm looking for a young woman named Catherine Connelly. She doesn't answer her bell," I said.

"Then she ain't home."

"Mind if I check?"

"You better stop ringing them other buzzers too," he said, and shut the door. I resisted the temptation to ring all the buzzers again and run. "Childish," I thought. "Adolescent." I went back to my car, got in, and drove to the university. Maybe I'd be able to locate her there. I parked in a spot that was reserved for Dean Mersfelder and headed for the library basement.

Iris Milford was there in her NEWS office, behind her metal desk. There were several other members of the staff, obviously younger, doing journalistic things at their metal desks.

She recognized me when I came in.

"Nice eye you got," she said.

I'd forgotten the punch Sonny had landed. It looked worse than it felt, though it was still sore to touch.

"I bruise easily," I said.

"I'll bet," she said.

"Want to have lunch with me?" I asked.

"Absolutely," she said. She closed the folder she was looking at, picked up her purse, and came around the desk.

"Too bad about how you can't make up your mind," I said.

We walked out through the corridor. It was class-change time and the halls were crowded and hot and loud. A miasma of profanity and smoke and sweatiness under heavy winter coats. Ah, where are the white bucks of yesteryear? We wormed our way up to the first floor and finally out past the security apparatus that set off an alarm if someone smuggled out a book, past the scrutiny of a hard-faced librarian alert beside it, into the milling snow-crusted quadrangle. I got a cab and we rode to a restaurant I liked on top of an insurance building, where the city looked clean and patrician below, and the endless rows of red-brick town houses that had crumbled into slums looked geometric and orderly and a little European, stretching off to the south.

100

We had a drink and ordered lunch. Iris looked out at the orderly little brick houses.

"Get far enough away and it looks kinda pretty, don't it?" she said. "You only get order from a distance. Close up is always messy."

"Yeah," I said, "but your own life is always close up. You only see other people's lives at long range."

"You better believe it," she said. "I'll take another pop."

I ordered us two more drinks.

"Okay, Spenser, what is it? You not the type to feed drinks to a poor colored lady and take advantage of her body. Even one as irresistible as mine. What you want?"

I liked her. She'd been there and seen it done. A tough, wised-up, honest broad.

"Well, if you're not going to come across, I'll take second best. Tell me about Cathy Connelly."

"What you want to know?"

"I don't know, everything, anything. All I know is she was once Terry Orchard's roommate, that she moved out when the Powell kid moved in, that she now lives on the Fenway, and that she wasn't home when I called on her this morning."

"That's about as much as I know. She was in my Chaucer class, and I copied her notes a couple times. I don't know her much better than that."

"She belong to SCACE?"

"Not that I know. She seemed kind of a loner. Didn't belong to anything I know of. You never see her around campus, but that don't mean much because the goddamn campus is so big and crowded that you might not see a woolly rhinoceros around campus."

"Boyfriends?" I asked.

"None that I know. But I'm telling you, I don't hardly know her. What I'm saying could be wrong as hell."

"Where can I get a picture of her?"

"Student Personnel Office, I would guess. That's where we get ones we use in the paper for fast-breaking news stories, like who was elected captain of the girls' field hockey team. Campus security can probably get them for you."

"I don't think so, Iris. Last dealing I had with campus security was when they ejected me from the premises. I think they don't like me."

She widened her eyes. "I thought they hired you."

"They did, but I think they are in the process of making an agonizing reappraisal of that decision."

"You having a good week, Spenser. Someone plunks you in the eye, you get thrown off the campus, you gonna get fired, you can't find Cathy Connelly. I hope you don't depress easy."

"Like you were saying, it's always messy close up."

"What you want Connelly for, anyway?"

"She was Terry Orchard's roommate. She might know how Terry's gun got from her bedside table into a hood's pocket."

"Jesus, she don't look the type."

"There isn't any type, my love."

She nodded. "Ain't that the truth."

"Want dessert?" I said.

She nodded. "Do I look like someone who turns down dessert?"

I asked for a dessert menu.

Iris said, "I can get the picture for you. I'll go over to student personnel and tell them we need it for a feature we're doing. We do it all the time."

"Would you like two desserts?" I said.

After I paid the bill with some of Roland Orchard's retainer and drove her back to the university, she did what she said. I sat in the car with the heater on, and she strolled into the student center and returned twenty minutes later with a two-by-two ID photo of Cathy Connelly. I thanked her.

She said, "Two drinks and a lobster salad will get you almost anything, baby," and went to class.

I drove over to Mass Ave and had a technician I know at a photo lab blow the picture up to eight by ten. Service while I waited cost me twenty-five dollars more of Roland

Orchard's retainer, and I still hadn't got the tear fixed in my car top.

I took the picture back to my office and sat behind my desk looking at it. She looked like a pallid little girl. Small features, light hair, prominent teeth, serious eyes. While I was looking at her picture my door opened and in came Lieutenant Quirk. Hatless, wearing a glen plaid overcoat, shoes glossy, pocked face clean-shaven, ruddy from the cold, and glowing with health. He closed the door behind him, and stood looking at me with his hands in his overcoat pockets. He did not radiate cheer.

"Come in, Lieutenant," I said. "No need to knock, my door is always open to a public servant. You've come, no doubt, to ask my assistance in solving a particularly knotty puzzle . . ."

"Knock it off, Spenser. If I want to listen to bullshit, I'll go over to a City Council meeting."

"Okay, have a seat. Want a drink?"

Quirk ignored the chair I'd nodded at and stood in front of my desk.

"Yeah, I'll have a drink."

I poured two shots of bourbon into two paper cups. Quirk drank his off without expression and put the empty cup down. I sipped at mine a little and thought fondly of the stuff that Roland Orchard served.

"Terry Orchard is it, Spenser," he said.

"The hell she is."

"She's it. Captain Yates is taking personal charge of the case, and she's the one."

"Yates. That means you're off it?"

"That's right."

"What else does it mean?"

"It doesn't mean anything else."

I poured two more shots of bourbon. Quirk's hard face looked like he was concealing a toothache.

"Like hell it doesn't mean anything else, Quirk. You didn't make a special trip down here just to keep me informed on personnel shifts in the BPD. You don't like her for it, and you know it. Why is Yates on it?"

"He didn't say."

I sipped some more of my bourbon. Quirk walked over and looked out my window.

"What a really swell view you've got, Spenser."

I didn't say anything. Quirk came back to my desk, picked up the bottle, and poured himself another drink.

"Okay," he said. "I don't like the kid for the murder."

I said, "Me either."

"I got nothing. Everything I've got says she's guilty. Nice simple murder, nice simple solution. Why screw around with it?"

"That's right," I said. "Why screw around with it?"

"I've been on the force twenty-two years. You meet a lot of liars in twenty-two years. I don't think she was lying."

I said, "Me either."

Quirk was walking around the room as he talked, looking at it like he looked at everything, seeing it all, and if he ever had to, he'd remember it all.

"You went to see Joe Broz yesterday."

I nodded.

"Why?"

"So he could tell me to butt out of the Godwulf Manuscript–Terry Orchard affair."

"What did you say?"

"I said we'll see."

"Did you know the manuscript is back?"

I raised one eyebrow, something I'd perfected after years of practice and a score of old Brian Donlevy movies. Quirk appeared not to notice.

"Broz suggested that was possible," I said.

Quirk nodded. "Any idea why Broz wanted you to butt out?"

"No," I said. "Any idea why Yates wanted you to butt out?"

"No, but there's a lot of pressure from somewhere up the line."

104

"And Yates is responding."

Quirk's face seemed to shut down. "I don't know about what Yates is doing. I know he's in charge of the case and I'm not. He's the captain. He has the right to assign personnel."

"Yeah, sure. I know Yates a little. One of the things he does best is respond to pressure from somewhere up the line."

Quirk didn't say anything.

"Look, Lieutenant," I said, "does it seem odd to you that there are two guys looking into the Terry Orchard thing and both of us are told to butt out within the same day? Does that seem like any kind of coincidence to you?"

"Spenser, I am a cop. I have been a cop for twenty-two years, and I will keep on being one until they lock me out of the station house. One of the things that a cop has to have is discipline. He gets orders, he has to obey them—or the whole thing goes to hell. I don't have to like what's happening, but I do it. And I don't run around crying about it."

"Words to live by," I said. "It was the widely acclaimed Adolf Eichmann who popularized that 'I obey orders' routine, wasn't it?"

"That's a cheap shot, Spenser. You know goddamn well the cops are right more than they're wrong. We're not wiping out six million people. We're trying to keep the germs from taking over the world. To do that you got to have order, and if someone gets burned now and then so someone gets burned. If every cop started deciding which order to obey and which one not, then the germs would win. If the germs win, all the goddamn bleeding hearts will get their ass shot."

"Yeah, sure, the big picture. So some goddamn teen-aged kid gets fed to the fishes for something she didn't do. So you know she didn't do it and Joe Broz puts the squeeze on some politician who puts the squeeze on Captain Yates who takes you off the case. But you don't cry. It's good for society. Balls. Why don't you take what you got to the States?"

"Because I haven't got enough. The State cops would laugh and giggle if I came in with what I've got. And because, goddamn it, Spenser, because I can't. I'm a cop. It's what I do. I can't."

"I know," I said. "But I can. And I'm going to. I'm going to have Broz and Yates, and you, too, if I have to, and whoever else has got his thumb in whatever pie this is."

"Maybe you will," Quirk said. "I hear you were a pretty good cop before you got fired. What'd you get fired for?"

"Insubordination. It's one of my best things."

"And maybe Broz will have you shot in the back of the head."

I let that pass. We were silent.

"How much do I have to get for you before you go to the States?"

"I'm not asking you to get a damn thing for me," Quirk said.

"Yeah, I know. If I got you proof. Not suspicion, proof. Then what happens?"

"Then the pressure will go away. Yates is impressed with proof."

"I'll bet," I said.

More silence. Quirk didn't seem to want to leave, but he didn't have anything to say. Or at least he wasn't saying it.

"What do you know about Cathy Connelly, Lieutenant?"

"We checked her out routinely. No record, no evidence of drugs. Roomed with Orchard before her boyfriend moved in. Now lives somewhere over on the Fenway."

"Anybody interview her?"

"Couple of precinct boys in a radio car stopped by. She wasn't home. We saw no reason to press it. Do you?"

"Those two hoods had Terry Orchard's gun with them when they came to the apartment. How'd they get it?"

"If it's true."

"Of course, if it's true. I think it's true. Cathy Connelly seems like the best person to ask about how they got the gun. Terry doesn't know, Powell is dead. Who's left?"

"Why don't you go ask her then?" Quirk said. "Thanks for the drink."

He walked out leaving the door open behind him, and I listened to his footsteps going down the hall.

CHAPTER FOURTEEN

I WENT OVER to the university to call on Carl Tower. I hoped the campus cops weren't under orders to shoot on sight. Whether they were, the secretary with the ripe thighs was not. She was friendly. She had on a pants suit today, black, with a large red valentine heart over the left breast. Red platform heels, red enamel pendant earrings. Bright red lipstick. She obviously remembered me. I was probably haunting her dreams.

She said, "May I help you?"

"Don't pull that sweet talk on me," I said.

"I beg your pardon."

"I know what you're thinking, and I'm sorry, but I'm on duty."

"Of all the outer offices in all the towns in all the world," she said, "you had to walk into mine." There was no change in her expression.

I started to say something about, "If you want anything, just whistle," but at that moment Carl Tower appeared at his office door and saw me. I was obviously not haunting his dreams.

"Spenser," he said, "get the hell in my office."

I took off my wristwatch and gave it to the secretary. "If I don't come out alive," I said, "I want you to have this."

She giggled. I went into Tower's office.

Tower picked up a tabloid-size newspaper from his desk and tossed it across at me. It was the university newspaper. Across the top was the headline ADMINISTRATION AGENT SPIES ON STUDENT, and in a smaller drop head, PRIVATE EYE HIRED BY

ADMINISTRATION QUESTIONS ENGLISH PROFESSOR. I didn't bother to read the story, though I noticed they spelled my name wrong in the lead paragraph.

"It's with an *s*, not a *c*," I said. "Like the English poet. S-p-e-n-s-e-r."

Tower was biting down so hard on his back teeth that the muscles of his jaw bulged at the hinge.

"We won't ask for a return on the retainer, Spenser," he said. "But if you are on this campus again, ever, we'll arrest you for trespassing and use every influence we have to have your license lifted."

"I hear you got the manuscript back," I said.

"That's right. No thanks to you. Now beat it."

"Who returned it?"

"It just showed up yesterday in a cardboard box, on the library steps."

"Ever wonder why it came back?"

Tower stood up. "You're through, Spenser. As of this minute. You are no longer in the employ of this university. You have no business here. You're trespassing. Either you leave or I call some people to take you out of here."

"How many you going to call?"

Tower's face got quite red. He said, "You sonova bitch," and put his hand on the phone.

I said, "Never mind. If I whipped your entire force it would embarrass both of us."

On the way out I stopped by the secretary's desk. She handed me back my watch.

"I'm glad you made it," she said.

On the inside of the watch strap in red ink she had written "Brenda Loring, 555-3676."

I looked up at her. "I am, too," I said, and strapped the watch back on.

She went back to typing and I went back to leaving the university in disgrace. Administration agent, I thought as I went furtively down the corridor. Zowie!

CHAPTER FIFTEEN

BACK TO THE FENWAY to Cathy Connelly's apartment. I rang the bell; no answer. I didn't feel like swapping compliments with Charlie Charm the super, so I strolled around the building looking for an alternate solution. Behind the apartment was an asphalt courtyard with lines for parking spaces and a line of trash barrels, dented and bent, against the wall, behind low trapezoidal concrete barriers to keep the cars from denting and bending them more. Despite the ill-fitting covers on them, some of the trash had spilled out and littered the ground along the foundation. The cellar entrance door was open, but the screen door was closed and fastened with a hook and eye arrangement. It was plastic screening. I took out my jackknife and cut through the screen at the hook. I put my hand through and unhooked it. Tight security, I thought. Straight ahead and two steps down stretched the cellar. To my left rose the stairs. I went up them. Cathy Connelly was apartment 13. I guessed second floor, given the size of the building. I was wrong. It was third floor. Close observation is my business.

Down the corridor ran a frayed, faded rose runner. The doors were dark-veneer wood with the numbers in shiny silver decals asymmetrically pasted on. The knob on each door was fluted glass. The corridor was weakly lit by a bare bulb in a wall sconce at the end. In front of number 13 a faint apron of light spread out under the door. I looked at my watch; I knocked again. Same result. I put my ear against the door panel. The television was on, or the radio. I heard no other sound. That didn't prove anything. Lots of people left the TV running when they went out. Some to discourage burglars. Some because they forgot to turn them off. Some so it wouldn't seem so empty when they came home. I tried the knob. No soap. The door was locked. That was a problem about as serious as the screen door in the cellar. I kicked it open—which would probably irritate the super, since when I did, the jamb splintered. I stepped in and felt the muscles begin to tighten behind my shoulders. The apartment was hot and stuffy, and there was a smell I'd smelled before.

The real estate broker had probably described it as a studio apartment—which meant one room with kitchenette and bath. The bath was to my left, door slightly ajar. The kitchenette was directly before me, separated from the rest of the room by a plastic curtain. To my right were a day bed, the covers folded back as if someone were about to get in, an armchair with a faded pink and beige shawl draped over it as a slipcover, a bureau, a steamer trunk apparently used as a coffee table, and a wooden kitchen table, painted blue, which seemed to double as a desk. On it the television maundered in black and white. In front of the kitchen table was a straight chair. A woman's white blouse and faded denim skirt were folded over the back of it, underwear and socks tangled on the seat. A saddle shoe lay on its side beneath the chair and another stood flat-footed under the table. There was no one in the room. There was no one behind the plastic curtain. I turned into the bathroom and found her.

She was in the tub, face down, her head under water, her body beginning to bloat. The smell was stronger in here. I forced myself to look. There was a clotted tangle of blood in the hair at the back of one ear. I touched the water; it was room temperature. Her body was the same. I wanted to turn her over, but I couldn't make myself do it. On the floor by the tub, looking as if she'd just stepped out of them, were a pair of flowered baby doll pajamas. She'd been there awhile. Couple of days, anyway. While I'd been ringing her bell and asking the super if he'd seen her, she'd been right here floating motionless in the tepid water. How do you do, Miss Connelly, my name is Spenser, very sorry I didn't get to meet you sooner.

Hell of a way to meet now. I looked at her for two, maybe three minutes, feeling the nausea bubble inside me. Nothing happened, so I began to look at the bathroom. It was crummy. Plastic tiles, worn linoleum buckling up from the floor. The sink was dirty and the faucet dripped steadily. There was no shower. Big patches of paint had peeled off the ceiling. I thought of a line from a poem: "Even the dreadful martyrdom must run its course/Anyhow in a corner, some untidy spot." I forget who wrote it.

There were no telltale cigar butts, no torn halves of claim checks, no traces of lint from an imported cashmere cloth sold only by J. Press. No footprints, no thumb prints, no clues. Just a drowned kid swelling with death in a shabby bathroom in a crummy apartment in a lousy building run by a grumpy janitor. And me.

I went back out into the living room. No phone. God is my copilot. I went out to the hall and down the stairs to the cellar. The super had an office partitioned off with chicken wire from the rest of the cellar. In it were a rolltop desk, an antique television set, and a swivel chair, in which sat the super. The smell of bad wine oozed out of the place. He looked at me with no sign of recognition or welcome.

I said, "I want to use your phone."

He said, "There's a pay phone at the drugstore across the street. I ain't running no charity here."

I said, "There is a dead person in room thirteen, and I am going to call the police and tell them. If you say anything to me but yes, sir, I will hit you at least six times in the face."

He said, "Yes, sir." Pushing an old wino around always enlivens your spirits. I picked up the phone and called Quirk. Then I went back upstairs and waited for him to arrive with his troops. It wasn't as long a wait as it seemed. When they arrived Captain Yates was along.

He and Quirk went in to look at the remains. I sat on the day bed and didn't look at anything. Sergeant Belson sat on the edge of the table smoking a short cigar butt that looked like he'd stepped on it.

"Do you buy those things secondhand?" I asked.

Belson took the cigar butt out of his mouth and looked at it. "If I smoked the big fifty cent jobs in the cedar wrappers, you'd figure I was on the take."

"Not the way you dress," I said.

"You ever think of another line of work, Spenser? So far all you've detected is two stiffs. Maybe a crossing guard, say, or . . ."

Quirk and Yates came out of the bathroom with a man from the coroner's. The lines in Quirk's face looked very deep, and the medic was finishing a shrug. Yates came over to me. He was a tall man with narrow shoulders and a hard-looking pot belly. He wore glasses with translucent plastic rims like they used to hand out in the army. His mouth was wide and loose.

He looked at me very hard and said, "Someone's going to have to pay for that door."

Belson gave him a startled look; Quirk was expressionless. I couldn't think of anything to say, so I didn't say anything. It was a technique I ought to work on.

Yates said, "What's your story, Jack? What the hell are you doing here?"

"Spenser," I said, "with an *s* like the English poet. I was selling Girl Scout cookies door to door and they told us to be persistent. . . ."

"Don't get smart with me, Jack; we got you for breaking and entering. If the lieutenant here hadn't said he knew you, I'da run you in already. The janitor says you threatened him, too."

I looked at Belson. He was concentrating mightily on getting his cigar butt relit, turning it carefully over the flame of a kitchen match to make sure it fired evenly. He didn't look at me.

"What's the coroner's man say about the kid?" I asked Quirk.

Yates answered, "Accidental death. She slipped getting in the tub, hit her head, and drowned." Belson made a noise that sounded like a cough. Yates spun toward him. "You got something to say, Sergeant?"

112

Belson looked up. "Not me, Captain, no, sir, just inhaled some smoke wrong. Fell right on her head, all right, yes, sir."

Yates stared at Belson for about fifteen seconds. Belson puffed on his cigar. His face showed nothing. Quirk was looking carefully at the light fixture on the ceiling.

"Captain," I said, "does it bother you that her bed is turned back, her clothes are on the chair, and her pajamas are on the bathroom floor? Does it seem funny to you that someone would take off her clothes, put on her pajamas, and get in the bathtub?"

"She brought them in to put on when she got through," Yates said very quickly. His mouth moved erratically as he talked. It was like watching a movie with the soundtrack out of sync. Peculiar.

"And dropped them carefully in a pile on the floor where the tub would splash them and she'd drip on them when she got out because she loved putting on wet pajamas," I said.

"Accidental death by drowning. Open and shut." Yates said it hard and loud with a lot of lip motion. Fascinating to watch. "Quirk, let's go. Belson, get this guy's statement. And you, Jack"—he gave me the hard look again—"be where I can reach you. And when I call, you better come running."

"How about I come over and sleep on your back step," I said, but Yates was already on his way out.

Quirk looked at Belson. Belson said, "Right on her head she fell, Marty."

Quirk said, "Yeah," and went out after Yates.

Belson whistled "The Battle Hymn of the Republic" between his teeth as he got out his notebook and looked at me. "Shoot," he said.

"For crissake, Frank, this is really raw."

"Captain don't want an editorial," Belson said, "just what happened."

"Even if you aren't bothered by the pajamas and all, isn't it worth more than routine when the ex-roommate of a murder suspect dies violently?"

113

Belson said, "I spent six years rattling doorknobs under the MTA tracks in Charlestown. Now ride in a car and wear a tie. Captain just wants what happened."

I told him.

CHAPTER SIXTEEN

I SAT IN MY CAR on the dark Fenway. The super had, grumbling, installed a padlock on the splintered door to the Connelly apartment while a prowl car cop watched. Belson had departed with my statement, and everything was neat and orderly again. The corpse gone. The mob, the cops, the university had all told me to mind my own business. Not a bad trio; I was waiting for a threat from organized religion. In a few weeks Terry Orchard would be gone, to the women's reformatory in Framingham; twenty years probably, a crime of passion by a young woman. She'd be out when she was forty, ready to start anew. You meet such interesting people in jail.

I got a flashlight and some tape out of the glove compartment and a pinch bar out of my trunk and went back over to the apartment house. The super hadn't fixed the screen on the back door, but he had shut and locked the inside door. I went to a cellar window. It was locked. On my hands and knees I looked through the frost patterns of grime. Inside was darkness. I flashed the light through. Inside was what looked like a coal bin, no longer used for coal. There were barrels and boxes and a couple of bicycles. I taped a tic-tac-toe pattern on one of the windowpanes and tapped the glass out with the pinch bar. The tape kept the noise down. When the opening was big enough I reached my hand through and unlatched the window. It was not a very big window, but I managed to slide

114

through it and drop to the cellar floor. I scraped both shins in the process.

The cellar was a maze of plastic trash bags, old wooden barrels, steamer trunks, cardboard boxes, clumsily tied piles of newspaper. A rat scuttled out of the beam from my flashlight as I worked my way through the junk. At the far end a door, slightly ajar, opened onto the furnace room, and to the left were the stairway and the super's cage. I could hear canned laughter from the television. I went very quietly along the wall toward the stairs. I was in luck; when I peered around the corner of the super's office he was in his swivel chair, asleep in the rich fumes of port wine and furnace heat, the TV blaring before him. I went up the same stairs to the third floor. No hesitation on the second floor—I learn quickly. The padlock on Cathy Connelly's door was cheap and badly installed. I got the pinch bar under the hasp and pulled it loose with very little noise. Once inside I put a chair against the door to keep it closed and turned on the lights. The place hadn't changed much in the past two hours. The bloated corpse was gone, but otherwise there was nothing different. It wasn't a very big apartment. I could search it in a couple of hours probably. I didn't know what I was looking for, of course, which would slow me down, because I couldn't eliminate things on an "is-it-bigger-than-a-bread-box" basis.

I started in the bathroom, because it was on the left. If you are going to get something searched you have to do it orderly. Start at a point and go section by section through the place, not where things are most likely, or least likely, or anything else, just section by section until you've looked at everything. The bathroom didn't take long. There was in the medicine cabinet some toothpaste, some aspirin, some nose drops prescribed by a doctor in New Rochelle, New York, a bottle of Cope, some lipstick, some liquid make-up, a safety razor, an eyebrow pencil. I emptied out the make-up bottle; there was nothing in it but make-up. The aspirin tasted like aspirin, the Cope appeared to be Cope, the nose drops smelled like nose drops. There was nothing in the lipstick tube but lipstick. There was nothing in the toilet tank, nothing taped

115

underneath the sink, no sign that anything had been slipped under the buckling linoleum. I stood on the toilet seat and unscrewed the ceiling fixture with a jackknife blade—nothing inside but dusty wiring that looked like it wouldn't pass the city's electrical code. I screwed the fixture back in place.

I went over the kitchen next. I emptied the flour, sugar, dry cereal, salt, and pepper into the sink one by one and sifted through them. Other than some little black insects I found nothing. The stove was an old gas stove. I took up the grillwork over the burners, looked carefully at the oven. The stove couldn't be moved without disconnecting the gas pipe. I was willing to bet Cathy Connelly never had. I took all the pans out of the under sink cabinet and wormed under the sink on my back, using my flashlight to examine it all. A cockroach. There was little food in the old gas refrigerator. I emptied it. A couple of TV dinners. I melted them under the hot water in the sink and found nothing. I took the panel off of the bottom and looked carefully in. The motor was thick with dust kitties, and the drip pan was gummy with God knows what.

The living room was of course the one that took time. It was about two in the morning when I found something. In the bottom bureau drawer was a cigar box containing letters, bills, canceled checks. I took it over to the daybed, sat down, and began to read through them. There were two letters from her mother full of aimless amenities that made my throat tighten. The dog got on the school bus and her father had gotten a call from the school and had to leave the store and go get it, younger brother was in a junior high school pageant, momma had lost three pounds, she hoped Cathy was watching what she ate, daddy sent his love.

The third letter was different. It was on the stationery of a Peabody motel. It said:

> Darling,
> You are beautiful when you are asleep. As I write this I am looking at you and the covers are half off you so I can see your breasts. They are beautiful. I want to

climb back into bed with you, but I must leave. You can cut my eight o'clock class, but I can't. I won't mark you absent though and I'll be thinking about last night all the time. The room is paid for and you have to leave by noon, they said. I love you.

There was no date, no signature. It was written in a distinctive cursive script.

For crissake! A clue. A goddamned clue. I folded the note up and put it in my inside coat pocket. So far I was guilty of breaking and entering, possession of burglar's tools, and destruction of property. I figured tampering with evidence would round things out nicely. I wanted to run right out and track down my clue, but I didn't. I searched the rest of the room. There were no other clues.

I turned off the lights, moved the chair, and went out. The door wouldn't stay shut because of the broken padlock. I went out the front way this time, as if I belonged. When I reached my car I put the pinch bar back in the trunk, got in the car, and sat for a bit. Now that I had a clue, what exactly was I supposed to do with it? I looked at my watch. 3 A.M. Searching apartments is slow business. I turned on the interior light in my car, took out my clue, and read it again. It said the same thing it said the first time. I folded it up again and tapped my front teeth with it for about fifteen seconds. Then I put it back in my pocket, turned off the interior light, started up the car, and went home. When I decide something I don't hesitate.

I went to bed and dreamed I was a miner and the tunnel was collapsing and everyone else had left. I woke up with the dream unfinished and my clock said ten minutes of seven. I looked at the bureau. My clue was up there where I'd left it, partly unfolded, along with my loose change and my jackknife and my wallet. Maybe I'd catch somebody today. Maybe I'd detect something. Maybe I'd solve a crime. There are such days. I'd even had some. I climbed out of bed and plodded to the shower. I hadn't worked out in four days and felt it. If I solved something this morning, maybe I could take the afternoon off and go over to the Y.

I took a shower and shaved and dressed and went out. It was only 7:45 and cold. The snow was hard-crusted and the sun glistened off it very brightly. I put on my sunglasses. Even through their dark lenses it was a bright and lovely day. I stopped at a diner and had two cups of coffee and three plain doughnuts. I looked at my watch. 8:15. The trouble with being up and at 'em bright and early was once you were up most of the 'em that you wanted to be at weren't out yet.

I bought a paper and cruised over to the university. There was room to park in a tow zone near the gymnasium. I parked there and read the paper for half an hour. Nowhere was there mention of the fact that I'd found a clue. In fact, nowhere was anyone even predicting that I would. At nine o'clock I got out and went looking for Iris Milford.

She wasn't in the newspaper office. The kid cropping photos at the next desk told me she never came in until the afternoon, and showed me her class schedule pasted on the corner of her desk. With his help I figured out that from nine to ten she had a sociology course in room 218 of the chemistry building. He told me how to get there. I had a half-hour wait in the corridor, where I entertained myself examining the girl students who went by. During class time they were sparse and I had nothing else to do but marvel at the consistency with which the university architects had designed their buildings. Cinder block and vinyl tile seem to suffice for all seasons. At ten minutes to ten the bell rang and the kids poured into the corridor. Iris saw me as she came out of the classroom. She said, "Hell, Spenser. How'd you know where to find me?"

I said, "I'm a trained detective. Want some coffee?"

We went to the cafeteria in the student union. Above the cafeteria entrance someone had scrawled in purple magic marker, "Abandon All Hope Ye Who Enter Here."

I said, "Isn't that from Dante?"

She said, "Very good. It's written over the entrance to hell in book three of 'The Inferno.'"

118

I said, "Aw, I bet you looked that up."

The cafeteria was modernistic as far as cinder block and vinyl tile will permit. The service area along one side was low-ceilinged and close. The dining area was three stories high, with one wall of windows that reached the ceiling and opened on a parking lot. The cluttered tables were a spectrum of bright pastels, and the floor was red quarry tile in squares. It was somewhere between an aviary and Penn Station. It was noisy and hot. The smoke of thousands of cigarettes drifted through the shafts of winter sunlight that fused in through the windows. Abandon All Hope Ye Who Enter Here.

I said, "Many campus romances start here?"

She laughed and shook her head. "Not hardly," she said. "You want to scuff hand and hand through fallen leaves, you don't go here."

We stood in line for our coffee. The service was cardboard, by Dixie. I paid, and we found a table. It was cluttered with paper plates, plastic forks, and cardboard beverage trays and napkins. I crumpled them together and deposited them in a trash can.

"How long you had this neatness fetish?" Iris asked.

I grinned, took a sip of coffee.

"You find Cathy Connelly?" she asked.

"Yeah," I said, "but she was dead."

Iris's mouth pulled back in a grimace and she said, "Shit."

"She'd been drowned in her bathtub, by someone who tried to make it look accidental."

Iris sipped her coffee and said nothing.

I took the letter from my inside pocket and gave it to her. "I found this in her room," I said.

Iris read it slowly.

"Well, she didn't die a virgin," Iris said.

"There's that," I said.

"She was sleeping with some professor," Iris said.

"Yep."

"If you can find out what eight o'clock classes she had, you'll know who."

"Yep."

"But you can't get that information because you've been banished from the campus."

"Yep."

"Which leaves old Iris to do it, right?"

"Right."

"Why do you want to know?"

"Because I don't know. It's a clue. There's a professor in here someplace. The missing manuscript would suggest a professor. Terry says she heard Powell talking to a professor before he was killed, now Cathy Connelly appears to have been sleeping with a professor, and she's dead. I want to know who he is. He could be the same professor. Can you get her class schedule?"

"This year?"

"All years, there's no date on the note."

"Okay, I got a friend in the registrar's office. She'll check it for me."

"How soon?"

"As soon as she can. Probably know tomorrow."

"I'm betting on Hayden," I said.

"As a secret lover?"

"Yep. The manuscript is medieval. He's a medieval specialist. He teaches Chaucer, which is an early class. Terry Orchard was up early for her Chaucer course the day that Powell threatened some professor on the phone. The conversation implied that the professor on the phone had an early class. Hayden pretended not to know Terry Orchard when in fact he did know her. He's a raging radical according to a very reliable witness. There's enough coincidence for me to wager on. Why don't you get in touch with your friend and find out if I'm right?"

She said, "Soon as I finish my coffee. I'll call you when I know."

I left her and headed back for my car.

CHAPTER SEVENTEEN

I WAS RIGHT. Iris called me at eleven thirty the next morning to report that Cathy Connelly had taken Chaucer this year with Lowell Hayden at eight o'clock Monday, Wednesday, and Friday. The only other eight o'clock class she'd had in her three years at the university had been a course in Western civilization taught by a woman.

"Unless she was gay," Iris said, "it looks like Dr. Hayden."

"You took the same course, right?" I asked.

"Yeah."

"Got any term papers or exams, or something with a sample of his writing?"

"I think so. Come on over to the newspaper office. I'll dig some up."

"Don't you ever go to class?"

"Not while I'm tracking down a criminal, I don't."

"I'll be over," I said.

When I got there Iris had a typewritten paper bound in red plastic lying on her desk. It was twenty-two pages long and titled "The Radix Trait: A Study of Chaucer's Technique of Characterization in *The Canterbury Tales*." Underneath it said "Iris Milford," and in the upper right-hand corner it said "En 308, Dr. Hayden, 10/28." Above the title in red pencil with a circle around it was the grade A minus.

"Inside back page," she said. "That's where he comments."

I opened the manuscript. In the same red pencil Hayden had written, "Good study, perhaps a bit too dependent on

121

secondary sources, but well stated and judicious. I wish you had not eschewed the political and class implications of the *Tales,* however."

I took the note out of my coat pocket and put it down beside the paper. It was the same fancy hand.

"Can I have this paper?" I asked Iris.

"Sure—why, want to read it in bed?"

"No, I'm housebreaking a puppy."

She laughed. "Take it away," she said.

Near my office there was a Xerox copy center. I went in and made a copy of the note and the comment page in Iris's paper. I took the original up to my office and locked it in the top drawer of my desk. I put the copies in my pocket and drove over to see Lowell Hayden.

He wasn't in his office, and the schedule card posted on his door indicated that he had no more classes until Monday. Across the street at a drugstore I looked for his name in the directory. He wasn't listed in the Boston books. I looked up the English Department and called them.

"Hi," I said, "this is Dr. Porter. I'm lecturing over here at Tufts this evening and I'm trying to locate Lowell Hayden. We were grad students together. Do you have his home address?"

They did, and they gave it to me. He lived in Marblehead. I looked at my watch. 11:10. I could get there for lunch.

Marblehead is north, through the Callahan Tunnel and along Route 1A. An ocean town, yachting center, summer home, and old downtown district that reeked of tar and salt and quaint. Hayden had an apartment in a converted warehouse that fronted on the harbor. First floor, front.

A big hatchet-faced woman in her midthirties answered my ring. She was taller than I was and her blond hair was pulled back in a tight bun. She wore no make-up, and the only thing that ornamented her face were huge Gloria Steinem glasses with gold rims and pink lenses. Her lips were thin, her face very pale. She wore a man's green pullover sweater, Levi's, and penny loafers without socks. Big as she

122

was, there was no extra weight. She was as lean and hard as a canoe paddle, and nearly as sexy.

"Mrs. Hayden?" I asked.

"Yes."

"Is Dr. Hayden in?"

"He's in his study. What do you want?"

"I'd like to speak with him, please."

"He always spends two hours a day in his study. I don't permit him to be bothered during that time. Tell me what you want."

"You're beautiful when you're angry," I said.

"What do you want?"

I offered her my card. "If you'll give that to Dr. Hayden, perhaps he'll break his rules just once."

"I will do nothing of the kind," she said without taking the card.

"Okay, but if you'll give him this card when he is through his meditations I'll be waiting out in my car, looking at the ocean, thinking long thoughts." I wrote on the back of the card, "Cathy Connelly?" and put the card down on the edge of the umbrella stand by the door. She didn't slam it, but she closed it firmly. I had the feeling she did everything firmly.

I went back to my car and watched the sun glint on the water. There weren't many boats in the harbor in winter, mostly sea gulls bobbing on the cold water and swooping in the bright sky. A lobster boat came slowly into the harbor mouth past the lighthouse on the point of Marblehead Neck. Behind me, the seafood restaurant on the wharf was filling with lunchtime customers, and ahead of me two tourists were taking pictures of the wharf building. I watched the Hayden apartment. Hatchet face never so much as peeked out a window at me. Her husband as far as I could tell continued to meditate. The waves hit the wharf regularly; the interval between waves was about three seconds. After two hours and twenty minutes Lowell Hayden appeared at the front door and looked hard at me. I waved. He shut the door and I sat some more. Another half hour and Hayden appeared again, this time wearing a tan poplin jacket with a fur-lined hood. Other than that he seemed to be dressed just as he had been the last time I saw him. His wife loomed behind him, much taller. She stood in the open door while he came to the car. Making sure I wouldn't mug him, I guess. He opened the door and got in. I smiled pleasingly.

He said, "Spenser, you'd better leave me alone." His little pale face was clenched and there was a flush on each cheekbone. He looked a bit like Raggedy Andy.

"Why is that?" I said.

"Because you'll get hurt."

"No," I said. "You're not saying it right. Keep the lips almost motionless, and squinch your eyes up."

"I'm warning you now, Spenser. You stay away from me. I have friends who know how to deal with people like you."

"You gonna call in some hard cases from the Modern Language Association?"

"I mean people who will kill you if I say so."

"Oh, Mrs. Hayden, you mean."

"You leave her out of this. You've upset her enough." He looked nervously at the motionless and implacable figure in the doorway.

"She asking you funny questions about Cathy Connelly?"

"I don't know anything about Cathy Connelly."

"Yeah, you do," I said. "You know about spending the night with her in a motel in romantic Peabody. You know that she's dead, and you know how she died."

"I do not." His resonant voice was up about three octaves; for the first time it matched his appearance. He glanced back at the woman in the doorway. "I'll have you killed, you bastard. I don't know anything about this. You leave me alone or you'll be so sorry—you can't imagine."

"You don't really think Joe Broz will kill me on your say-so, do you?"

His pale face went chalk white. The flush left his cheeks and his left eyelid began to flutter. My right hand was resting on the steering wheel and he suddenly dug his finger-nails into it. I yanked my hand away and Hayden jumped out of the car and walked very fast to the house.

"You'll see," he shouted back to me. "You'll see, you bastard. You'll see."

He went in past his wife, who closed the door. Firmly.

There were four red scratches on the back of my hand. Lucky it wasn't the wife; they would have been on my throat. I leaned back in the car and took a big lungful of air and let it out slowly. I knew something. I knew that Hayden was it, or at least part of it. He'd overreacted. And he'd made a big mistake threatening me with tough-guy connections. It had to be Broz, and his reaction to the name made it certain. English professors don't know hired muscle unless there's something funny. Here there was something very funny. But exactly what? What was Lowell Hayden's connection with Joe Broz? What did either one have that the other would want? Hayden didn't have money, which was all Broz would want. The connection had to be dope somewhere. Powell was reputed to be a contact for heroin. Powell might be connected with Hayden. Hayden was connected to Cathy Connelly, who was connected to Terry Orchard, who was connected to Powell.

My head began to feel like a mare's nest. I could connect Hayden to Cathy Connelly for sure. The rest was just speculation, and what I knew in my gut wasn't going to get Terry Orchard out of jail. My best hope was Hayden's hysteria. He panicked pretty easily, and if I kept pushing at him, who knows what else might boil to the surface? But first I needed another point of view, a third party, you might say. It was time to go call on old Mark Tabor again. And this time maybe I'd stay longer and lean a little heavier.

CHAPTER EIGHTEEN

MARK TABOR WAS NOT HOME when I got to Westland Avenue. I had to walk up four flights of stairs to find that out. I walked back down and sat outside in my car. I spent a lot of time doing that. It was getting dark and colder; I kept the motor running and the heater going. My stomach was making great cavernous noises at six thirty when Tabor showed up. He came down from Mass Ave with his hands deep in the pockets of a pea jacket, the collar up, and his red corona of hair blossoming about the dark coat like an eruption. He turned in at his building and I came up behind him, reaching his door as he was closing it. I hit it hard with my shoulder and it flew open, propelling Tabor across the room. He tripped over the bed as he staggered backward and fell on it. I shut the door hard behind me, for effect. I wanted him scared.

"Hey, man, what the hell," he said.

"The hell is this, stupid," I said. "If you don't answer what I ask I'm going to pound you into an omelet."

"Who the Christ are you, man?"

"My name's Spenser. I was here before, and you proved too tough for me to break. I'm back for another try, boy, only this time I'll try harder."

"I don't know nothing you care about, man."

"Oh, yeah, you do. You know about Lowell Hayden. Tell me. Tell me everything you know about Lowell Hayden."

"Hey, man, all I know is he's a professor, you know. That's all I know."

"No, you know more than that. You know he's in

SCACE with you, don't you?" I moved toward him and he scrambled off the bed and backed toward the wall.

"No, man, honest. . . ."

"Yeah, you know that. And you'll tell me. But there's something else."

I was on his side of the bed now and close to him. He tried to jump onto the bed and away from me. I grabbed him by the shirtfront and slammed him back up against the wall.

"Before you tell me about Hayden, I want to speak to you about the manner in which you address me."

I had my face very close to his and was holding him very tight up against the wall. "I want you to address me as Mr. Spenser. I do not want you to address me as 'man.' Do you understand that?"

"Aw, man . . ." he began, and I slapped him in the face.

"Mr. Spenser, boy," I said.

"Lemme go, Mr. Spenser. You got no right to come in here and hassle me."

I jerked him away from the wall and slammed him back up against it.

"We're not here to discuss my rights, stupid, we're here to talk about Lowell Hayden. Is he in SCACE?"

"No, man . . . Mr. Spenser."

I slapped him across the face again, a little harder, twice.

"I'll kill you if I have to, stupid," I said.

"Okay, okay, yeah, he was in SCACE, but he was like a secret member, you know? Dennis Powell brought him in; he said this dude would be like a faculty contact only under cover, you dig? And me and Dennis would be like the only ones to know." He was beginning to sniffle a little as he talked.

"And the manuscript, what about that?" I twisted a little more shirtfront up in my hand and lifted him up on tiptoe for emphasis.

"I didn't have nothing to do with that; that was Dennis and Hayden. Hayden arranged it. I never even saw it."

"Okay, one more: Was Powell dealing hard drugs on campus?"

"Yeah."

"What?"

"Skag, mostly."

"Where did he get it?"

"I don't know."

I slammed him against the wall again.

"Honest to God, Mr. Spenser, I don't know. Ask Hayden, him and Dennis were close as a bastard. He might know. I don't know."

"How did Dennis get killed?"

"I don't know."

"How did Cathy Connelly get killed?"

"I don't know, honest to Christ, I don't know about any of that."

He was shaking and his teeth chattered.

I believed him. But I had some hard facts for the first time. I had Hayden connected with Powell. I had Powell connected with heroin, which meant mob connections. If Powell and Hayden were that close, I had Hayden connected to the mob. I had Hayden and Powell both connected to the Godwulf Manuscript, and I had the Godwulf Manuscript connected to Broz. More than that, I had Cathy Connelly connected to both Hayden and Terry Orchard. In fact, I had Hayden connected with two murders.

"Let me go, Mr. Spenser. I don't know anything else."

I realized I was still holding Tabor half off the ground. I let him go. He sank onto the bed and began to cry.

I said, "Everyone gets scared when they are overmatched in the dark; it's not something to be ashamed of, kid."

He didn't stop crying, and I couldn't think of anything else to say. So I left. I had a lot of information, but I had an unpleasant taste in my mouth. Maybe on the way home I could stop and rough up a Girl Scout.

It was raining when I came out, a cold rain about a degree above snow, and in the dark the wetness made the city look better than it was. The light diffused and reflected off things that in the daylight were dull and ugly.

It was nearly eight o'clock. I hadn't eaten since breakfast. I went to a steak house and ate. Halfway through my steak I caught sight of myself in the mirror behind the bar. I looked like someone who ought to eat alone. I didn't look in the mirror again.

It was twenty minutes of ten as I parked in front of my apartment. In front of me was parked an aggressively nondescript car made noticeable by the big whip antenna folded forward over the roof and clipped down. It was Quirk.

When I got out of the car he was waiting for me, and I said, "What the hell do you want, Lieutenant?"

"I want to talk with you. Let's go inside."

Quirk was great for small talk. When we got to my apartment I offered him a drink. He said, "Thanks."

"Okay, Lieutenant, what do you want to talk about? How poor Cathy Connelly fell in the bathtub and hit her little head?"

"What have you got?" Quirk said.

"What do you mean what have I got? You taking a survey for H.E.W.?"

"What have you got on the Connelly thing and on Lowell Hayden and the Powell murder?"

"Say, you must be some kind of investigator; you know all about what I'm up to."

Quirk stood up, walked across the room, and looked out my window. He took a long pull at the bourbon and water in his hand and turned around and looked at me.

"I'm trying, Spenser, I'm trying to ask you polite, and treat you like you weren't a wise-ass sonova bitch, because I owe you. Because maybe I need you to do some stuff for me. Why don't you try to help me through this by trying out your nightclub act on someone else? What have you got for me?"

Quirk was right. I felt lousy about Mark Tabor, and I was taking it out on Quirk. "I got three categories of things," I said. "What I know and can prove; what I know and can't prove; and what I don't know."

Quirk sat in my armchair and looked at me and listened.

"Here's what I know and can prove. Lowell Hayden and Cathy Connelly were lovers. They spent at least one night together in a Holiday Inn in Peabody—Peabody, what a romantic!—and I've got a note he wrote that locks him up on that one. Lowell Hayden and Dennis Powell were in on the theft of the Godwulf Manuscript. Hayden was an anonymous member of a student radical group called SCACE. Powell was dealing heroin. I've got a witness that will confirm that. I told Joe Broz I'd stop messing around with the case if the manuscript were returned. The next day it was returned."

"But you're still messing around," Quirk said.

"Yeah," I said. "I lied."

"Broz probably won't like that."

"Probably won't," I said.

"What else can you prove?"

"Nothing. But here's what I know anyway. Hayden is tied to Broz. It was after I talked to him the first time that Broz warned me off. This afternoon when I talked to him he said he had people who would kill me if he said so. You and I know where to find people like that, but your average teacher of medieval lit doesn't. If Powell was dealing heroin, he was tied to the mob too. That's too big a coincidence—that Powell and Hayden should both be mob connected and connected to each other and not have it mean something. Hayden had to have something to do with drug pushing. That's the only thing that Broz would have in common with a university community. More connection: Hayden's girl friend was a roommate of Powell's girl friend, Cathy Connelly and Terry Orchard, and if Terry's story is true, it would be Cathy Connelly who would have known that Terry had a gun, and where she kept it, and how to get it. If Terry's story is true, the killing of Powell was not amateur work. Now who would have both professional connections and access to knowledge of Terry's gun?"

Quirk said, "Hayden."

"And," I said, "the killing of Cathy Connelly was an

amateur production, even though Yates seemed to like it. Powell was dead and Terry was in Charles Street at the time. Of this interlocking quartet who does that leave?"

"Hayden."

"Clues must be your game, Lieutenant," I said. "You're two for two."

"Got some more?"

"Yeah, here's the hard stuff. Why did Powell get killed? Why did Terry get framed? Why did Cathy Connelly get killed? One point—Hayden is not playing with fifty-two cards. I talked to him today, there're pieces missing. Kidnaping that manuscript sounds just about right for him. So if he's it in this game, it may be harder to explain because he is not normal. The reasons he would do things are not predictable reasons."

"You got a nice assortment of possibilities," Quirk said. "So far you're into organized crime, dope pushing, theft, radical politics, adultery, and murder. I'm not saying I agree with you. But if I did, Hayden would look good to me. He would be the handle, and I'd keep turning it until something opened." Quirk stood up. "If you're messing with Joe Broz, you might turn up dead some morning. I'd better know the name of this witness in case you do."

"Tabor," I said. "Mark Tabor, seventy-seven Westland Ave, apartment forty-one."

"Thanks," Quirk said. "Thanks for the drink, too. See you."

I let him out. He was clearly sick with worry about me getting killed.

CHAPTER NINETEEN

THE NEXT MORNING I went over to the university and put a tail on Hayden. I couldn't think of anything else to do. I knew he was involved in two killings and that Terry was involved in none, but I couldn't prove it. I could nail him for manuscript-naping or whatever, but I was willing to bet that the university wouldn't press charges, and even if they did, with a good lawyer and a first offense what would happen to him? I could threaten to tell his wife about Cathy Connelly, but he wasn't likely to confess to murder to placate his wife. But he knew I knew, and it had to bother him. He might do something stupid, and if I kept after him I might catch him doing it.

So in the fresh of morning when Hayden showed up for his nine o'clock class in pre-Shakespearean drama I was lurking about the north end of the corridor, and when he came out fifty minutes later, I was at the south end of the corridor getting a drink from the bubbler. While he conferred with students in his office about image patterns in *The Play of the Weather* and *Gammer Gurton's Needle,* I studied the announcements and grad school advertisements on the bulletin board down the corridor.

Surveillance on a guy that knows you is hard, and it's much harder when you're trying to do it alone. In the long run it's not possible. Eventually Hayden would catch me and there was nothing to do about it. On the other hand, before he did I might catch him, and anyway, I didn't know what else to do.

Hayden ate lunch in his office from a brown paper bag and a thermos. I didn't. By three o'clock that afternoon I was pretty sure how Hayden would spot me. He'd hear my stomach rolling. At four Hayden went to his *Beowulf* class. As soon as he was safely into his lecture I ducked out and bought half a dozen hamburgers at McDonald's. On the way back I bought a pint of Wild Turkey bourbon at a package store and was back in time to pick Hayden up after class and follow him to the parking lot.

Following him through the rush hour traffic was two-handed work, and I didn't get to my supper until we were through the Callahan Tunnel and into East Boston. By the time we got to Lynn Shore Drive I'd eaten three cold hamburgers and swallowed about two inches of the pint. A cold McDonald's hamburger is halfway between a jelly doughnut and a hockey puck, but the nine-dollar bourbon helped.

I sat at the head of Hayden's street with the motor idling and the heater on until nine o'clock, when I ran low on gas and had to shut off the motor. By ten fifteen I was cold. The hamburgers were long gone, though the memory lingered on the back of my throat, and I was almost through the bourbon. During that time Hayden had not come to me and confessed. He had not had a visit from Joe Broz or Phil, or the Ghost of Christmas Future. The Ceremony of Moloch had not shown up and sung "The Sweetheart of Sigma Chi" under his window. At eleven o'clock the lights in his living room went out and I went home—stiff, sore, tired, crabby, dyspeptic, cold, and about five-eighths drunk.

The next day we did it all again. This time I brought along a satchel of sandwiches and a large thermos of coffee. At the end of the day my stomach felt better, but I didn't know anything more, and I had discovered new dimensions of boredom.

On the third day things picked up. It was raining again. Hard and steady. Everything was frosted with slush. Hayden had a class from four to five, and it was dark when I stood in a doorway across the street and watched him get in his car in the parking lot. He was turning over the engine when two guys got in with him. One in front, one in back. The windshield wipers went on, then the headlights. The car began to back out of its space. My car was parked on a hydrant one hundred feet from the doorway and I was in it with the motor running when Hayden's car turned out of the parking lot. I stayed close behind him. Too close really, but it was dark and wet and I was worried. The two guys that got in his car didn't look like poets to me, and I didn't want to lose Hayden. He was all I had, and if something became of him, nothing much good would become of Terry Orchard.

We turned south on Huntington Avenue, past the new high-rise apartments, a hospital, another college, and out onto the Jamaicaway. Big houses, mostly brick, set well back and sumptuous, lined the road. Elms that had survived the Dutch disease arched over it, and to the right in an extended hollow was Jamaica Pond, wooded and grassy under the gray slush. Hayden's car pulled off the road and parked on the shoulder. I drove on by, turned left into a side street beyond, and parked.

I cut through the backyard of a large brick Dutch colonial house on the corner and came out opposite where Hayden's car was parked on the shoulder across the street. I didn't see any of them. The hard rain and warm weather were causing the wet slush to steam and a fog to rise from the rotting ice on the pond. I ran across the street and came up behind Hayden's car. It was empty. I realized that I had my gun in my hand though I didn't recall taking it from the hip holster. I stopped and listened. No sound but the rain and the cars on the Jamaicaway whooshing past on their way to Dedham and Milton. My stomach buzzed with tension.

There were tracks in the slush leading down toward the pond. I followed them into the mist. Closer to the pond it was so dense I could only see a few feet ahead.

I half expected to see Beowulf jump out of the bog and rip the arm off something. . . . "My God, Holmes, those are the footprints of a gigantic hound. . . ." I was wearing a hip-length wool jacket, and the rain was soaking through along my shoulders. The wet wool smelled like a grammar school coatroom. Ahead of me I heard a kind of low wail. I stopped still in the dark. In front of me there were indistinct figures. I looked at them obliquely as I'd learned to do a long time ago in Korea, and they came into sharper focus. Hayden was the one making the mournful noise. He seemed to be having trouble standing, and one of the other men had him under the arms. He stepped away and Hayden slumped to his knees and began to wail louder. The man who hadn't been holding him brought a long-barreled pistol from his side and placed it against the back of Hayden's head. I turned sideways as you do on the pistol range, and yelled, "Freeze!"

The guy with the gun snapped around and I felt the thump in my side simultaneous to the muzzle flash and before I heard the shot. It felt like I'd been hit in the ribs with a brick. I staggered, steadied myself, let out my breath, and brought my gun down on the middle of his chest . . . slack . . . squeeze . . . and my own shot exploded. He fell over backward. His buddy was shooting now, and a bullet thunked into a tree beside me. Out of the edge of my vision I saw Hayden crawling for some bushes. I ducked behind the tree. There was no pain yet, but my whole left side was numb and I felt a little dizzy. It was quiet again. Up on the Jamaicaway the headlights were fuzzy in the fog and the whoosh of their passage was cottony. The rain droned down. I slid down the tree and stretched out, belly down in the slush, and peered around the edge of the tree. I couldn't see anyone. Still on my belly I began to inch backward.

About ten feet in back of the tree was a big old blue spruce whose bottom boughs skirted out six or eight feet around the bottom. I inched backward under them and lay still. Nothing moved. I was feeling dizzier, and the first twitches of hurt were cutting through the numbness in my side. The slush was cold, and underneath the tree the earth had started to thaw and turn to mud. Inching backward for ten feet had scraped a lot of it up under my coat.

I wondered if I'd die here. Face down under a spruce tree in the mud trying to keep a double murderer from getting shot by two hired thugs. I felt like I wanted to throw up. The noise would locate me. I swallowed it back. More silence while I fought the nausea and the cold.

After what seemed to be the duration of the Christian epoch, I saw him. He had circled the tree where I'd first hidden and stepped out so that had I still been there he'd have been behind me. He was good; it took him maybe a second to realize I wasn't there and where I probably was. He spun and I put three shots into his chest, holding the gun in both hands to keep it steady. His gun bounced out of his hand and plopped softly into the slush. He fell more slowly sideways and joined it. I crawled out from under the tree and over to him. I felt in his neck for the big pulse. There wasn't any. I crawled on over to his buddy. Same thing. I got up and looked around for Hayden. I didn't see him, and getting up was an error. My head spun and I sat down backward. The jar of it set the pain in my side to moving.

"Hayden," I yelled. No sound.

"Hayden, you dumb sonova bitch, it's Spenser. You're all right. They're dead. Come on out."

I got hunched over on one hip and put my gun back in the holster. Then I got both hands onto the trunk of a sapling and pulled myself up.

"Hayden!"

He appeared from behind the bushes. His glasses were gone, and his wet lank hair was plastered down over his small skull.

"They were going to kill me," he said. "They were going to kill me. They . . . they had no right . . ."

Hayden looked at me blankly. His eyes were red and swollen and his face, without glasses, looked naked.

"They were supposed to kill you," he said.

"Yeah, we'll talk about that, but gimme a hand."

The numbness was about gone now, and the blood was a warm and sticky layer over the pain.

"We were allies. We were working together. And they were going to kill me."

He backed away from me, up toward the road. I let go of the tree and took a step toward him. He backed up faster.

"They were supposed to kill you."

I took another step toward him and fell down. He was

136

now backing up so fast he was running. Like a cornerback trying to stay with a wide receiver.

"Hayden!" I yelled.

He turned and ran up toward his car. Sonova bitch. At least he didn't kick me when I fell. I heard his car start but I didn't see him pull away. I was busy with other things. Two more tries convinced me that I'd have trouble walking up the hill, so I crawled. It was getting harder as the dizziness and the nausea progressed.

CHAPTER TWENTY

I DON'T KNOW how long it took me to get up that hill to the street. Every few feet I had to rest, and the last hundred feet or so I had to drag myself along on my stomach. I pulled myself over the curb and rested with my cheek in the gutter of the road and the rain drumming on my back. The pain drummed even harder in my side, and there was a kind of counterpoint throb in my head. Then, suddenly, there was a big red-faced MDC cop standing over me in the glare of headlights and the steady pulse of the blue light. I didn't know how long I'd been out or where I was exactly.

"Just lay there, Jack. Don't move around."

"I'm not drunk," I said.

"I can tell that, Jack. The left side of your coat is soaked with blood."

"I'm not drunk," I said again. It seemed very important to keep saying it. At the same time I knew he knew I wasn't drunk. He'd just said that he knew that. "I'm not," I said. The cop nodded. His face was red and healthy looking. He had a thick lower lip and a fine gray stubble on his chin.

His partner brought the folding stretcher and they inched me onto it.

"Jesus Christ," I said.

Then I was looking up at the funny big light that diffuses the glare and the tubes and apparatus and a woman in a white coat, and I realized my coat and shirt were off. "I been shot," I said.

"That was my diagnosis too." She was bending over and looking at my side closely.

"Bullet went right through, banged off a rib, probably cracked it—I don't think it's broken—and went on out. Tore up the latissimus dorsi a bit, caused a lot of blood loss and some shock. You'll live. This will sting." She swabbed something on the wound.

"Jesus Christ," I said.

A nurse wheeled me on the table down to have the rib X-rayed. Then she wheeled me back. The same ruddy-faced MDC cop that had picked me up was sitting on one of the other treatment tables in the cubicle off the emergency room. His partner leaned against the door jamb. He was skinny with pimples.

"I'll need a statement," ruddy-face said.

"Yeah, I imagine. Look, you know Quirk, homicide commander?"

He nodded.

"Call him, tell him I'm here and need to see him. He'll come down and I'll give the statement to both of you. You been through my wallet yet?"

"Yep."

"Okay, you know my name and my line of work. It's important that Quirk gets what I have to say. A guy might get killed, and he's the key to a couple of murders."

The doctor returned with my X rays and pushed past Pimples into the room. "As I said, rib cracked. I'll tape it and bandage the wound, then we'll put you to bed. In two or three days you'll be back on your feet."

Ruddy-face said to his partner, "Go call the lieutenant, Pooler."

138

Pooler said, "How come he gets special treatment? I say we get his statement and let Quirk know through channels."

"That's what you say, huh." Ruddy-face took out a big wooden kitchen match and stuck it in his mouth and chewed on it.

"Yeah, how come because the guy's got a private license we have to kiss his ass. Quirk'll get to his statement when he's ready."

Ruddy-face took the match out of his mouth and examined the chewed end.

"You be sure and call the lieutenant by his last name when you see him, Pooler. He'll like that. Makes him feel he's popular with the men."

"Jesus Christ . . ."

Ruddy-face got a very hard sound into his voice. "Goddammit, Pooler, will you call the lieutenant? This guy got shot, two other people got killed. Lieutenant's going to see him anyway. If he knows him maybe he'll want to see him sooner. Why would this guy make up the story? 'Cause he's queer for the lieutenant? If the guy's right and we don't call we'll be directing traffic in South Dorchester Christmas morning."

Pooler went. The doctor was busy wrapping my rib cage and ignored them both.

"Where am I?" I asked her. "Boston City?"

"Yep."

When the doctor got through a nurse wheeled me up to a ward bed. The ruddy-faced cop came with me. His partner stayed down to wait for Quirk. The ward was half-empty and depressing.

"It'll be full by morning," the nurse said. She cranked up the bed and she and the cop slid me onto it.

"Doctor says give you a shot to help you sleep," she said.

"Not yet," I said. "Wait until I've talked with the cops."

Ruddy-face nodded at her that he agreed.

"Okay," she said to ruddy-face. "Tell the floor nurse

139

when you're through and we'll come in and give him his shot then." She left. Ruddy-face sat down beside the bed.

"How you feel?" he asked.

"Like I been kicked in the side by a giraffe," I said.

He fumbled inside his coat and brought out a pint of Old Overholt.

"Want a shot before the nurse gets back?" he said.

I took the bottle.

"Crank me up," I said. He raised the head end of the bed so I was half-sitting, and I inhaled half his bottle.

I handed him back the bottle. He wiped the top off with his hand in an unconscious gesture of long practice, and took a long pull. He handed it back to me.

"Finish it," he said. "I got another one in the car."

The liquor burned hot in my stomach, and the pain was a little duller. Quirk arrived; Belson was with him. Quirk looked at the bottle and then at ruddy-face. I put the bottle down empty on the night stand away from ruddy-face.

"Where'd he get the bottle, Kenneally?"

Ruddy-face shrugged. "Musta had it with him, Lieutenant. How ya doing, Frank?"

Quirk said, "I'll bet." Belson nodded at ruddy-face.

"Okay"—Quirk turned to me—"lemme have it."

Belson had a notebook out. Ruddy-face got up and moved to the end of the ward, where he broke out a new match and began to chew on it.

"I'm fine, thanks, Lieutenant. Just a little old bullet wound."

"Yeah, good, let's hear it all. There's two carcasses downstairs right now that the MDC people brought in from Jamaica Pond. I want to hear."

I told him. He listened without interruption. When I got through he turned to Belson. "You see the two, Frank?"

"Yeah. One of them is a gofer for Joe Broz, Sully Roselli. I don't know the other one. His driver's license says Albert J. Brooks. Mean anything to you?"

Quirk shook his head and looked at me. I shook mine too.

140

"CID is looking into him," Belson said.

"Right, now see what you can do about getting a leash on Hayden. Pick up and hold."

"Yates will be disappointed," I said.

"Can't be helped," Quirk said. "Hayden's a witness to attempted murder and two homicides. Got to bring him in."

Quirk looked back at me thoughtfully.

"Two of them in the dark," he said. "Not bad."

He nodded at Belson and they left. As they went out Quirk said to Kenneally, "Tell the nurse we're through. And don't give him any more booze."

By the time the nurse got there I was halfway under again and barely felt the needle jab.

CHAPTER TWENTY-ONE

I WOKE UP in bright daylight, confused, to the sound of a monotonous deep cough from the other end of the room. I shifted in the bed and felt the pain in my side and remembered where I was. The coughing went on down the ward. I creaked myself around on the bed, dropped my legs over the side, and got myself sitting up. All the beds were full. I had a hospital johnny and an adhesive sash around my torso. Very natty. I stood up. My legs felt spongy, and I braced myself with one hand against the bed. Steady. I walked the length of the bed. Not bad. I walked back to the head. Better. I U-turned, back toward the foot. Then I started down the length of the ward. Slow, shaky, but halfway down I didn't have to hold on. An old man with no teeth mumbled to me from one of the beds.

"You get hell if they catch you out of bed," he said.

"Watch," I said.

I kept going. All the way to the end of the ward, then back, then down the ward again. I was feeling balanced and ambulatory when the floor nurse came in. She had a cheerful Irish face and a broad beam. She looked at me as if I'd messed on the floor.

"Oh, no," she said. "Right back in the bed, there. We're not supposed to be strolling around. Come on."

"Cookie," I said, "we are doing more than strolling. We are getting the hell out of here as soon as we can find our pants."

"Nonsense, I want you to hop right back in that bed. This minute." She clapped her hands sharply for emphasis.

"Don't do that," I said. "I may faint, and you'll have to give me mouth-to-mouth resuscitation." I kept on walking.

She glanced at the name card at the foot of my empty bed. "Mr. Spenser, must I call the resident?"

In the middle of the ward was a large double door. I pushed it open. It was a walk-in closet with baskets on shelves. My clothes were in one of them. I put on my pants, still soggy with the mud half-dried on them.

"Mr. Spenser." She stood in semiparalysis in the doorway. I dropped the johnny and slipped my jacket on over the bandaged body. Shirt and underwear were so bloodsoaked and mud-drenched that I didn't bother. I jammed my feet into my loafers. They had been my favorites, tassles over the instep. One tassle was now missing and there were two inches of mud caked all over them. My gun and wallet were missing. I'd worry about that later.

I pushed past the nurse, whose face had turned very red.

"Don't fret, cookie," I said. "You've done what you could, but I've got stuff I have to do and promises to keep. And for a guy with my virility what's a bullet wound or so?"

I kept going. She came behind me and at the desk outside by the elevator a second nurse joined her in protest. I ignored them and went down the elevator.

When I got outside onto Harrison Ave it was a very nice day—sunny, pleasant—and it occurred to me that I

142

didn't have a car or money or a ride home. I didn't have my watch either, but it was early. There was little traffic on the streets. I turned back toward the hospital and my Irish nurse came out.

"Mr. Spenser, you're not in condition to walk out like this. You've lost blood; you've suffered shock."

"Listen to me now, lovey," I said. "You're probably right. But I'm leaving anyway. And we both know you can't prevent it. But what you can do is lend me cab fare home."

She looked at me, startled for a minute, and then laughed. "Okay," she said. "You deserve something for sheer balls. Let me get my purse." I waited, and she was back in a minute with a five-dollar bill.

"I'll return it," I said.

She just shook her head.

I walked over to Mass Avenue and waited till a cab cruised by. When I got in the cabby said, "You got money?"

I showed him the five. He nodded. I gave him the address and we went home.

When he let me out I gave him the five and told him to keep it.

I got a look at my reflection in the glass door of my apartment building and I knew why he'd asked me for money first. My coat was black with mud, blood, and rain. The same for my pants. My ankles showed naked above the mud-crusted shoes. I had a forty-six-hour beard stubble and a big bruise on my forehead I must have gotten when I crawled over the curbstone the night before.

I realized I didn't have a key. I rang for the super. When he came he made no comment.

"I've lost my key," I said. "Can you let me into my apartment?"

"Yep," he said, and headed up the stairs to my place. I followed. He opened my door and I went in "Thanks," I said.

"Yep," he said. I closed the door.

I wondered if he'd noticed that I looked different. Maybe he thought it an improvement.

Despite the palpable silence of the place I was glad to

be home. I looked at my pine Indian still on the sideboard in the living room. I hadn't gotten to the horse yet, and he seemed to flow into a block of wood. I went into the kitchen, took off the coat, pants, and shoes, and stuffed them into the wastebasket. Then I went in and took a shower. I kept the wounded side away from the water as much as I could. I shaved with the shower still running and stepped back in to rinse off the shave cream. I toweled dry and dressed. Gray, hard-finished slacks with a medium flare, blue paisley flowered shirt with short sleeves, blue wool socks, mahogany-colored buckle boots with a side zipper, broad mahogany belt with a brass buckle. I liked getting dressed, feeling the clean cloth on my clean body. I paid special attention to it all. It was good not to be dead in the mud under a blue spruce tree.

In the kitchen I made coffee and put six homemade German sausages in the fry pan. They were big fat ones I had to go up to the North Shore to buy from a guy who made them in the back of the store. You should always start them on low in a cold fry pan. When they began to sizzle I cored a big green apple and peeled it. I sliced it thick, dipped the slices in flour, and fried them in the sausage fat. The coffee had perked, and I had a cup with heavy cream and two sugars. The smell of the sausage and apple cooking began to make my throat ache. I slipped a spatula under the apples and turned them. I took the sausages out with tongs and let them drain on a paper towel. When the apple rings were done, I drained them with the sausages and ate both with two big slices of coarse rye bread and wild strawberry jam in a crock that you can buy up at the Mass Ave end of Newbury Street.

I listened to the morning news on the radio while I drank the last of my coffee. They mentioned the shooting in the Jamaicaway but gave no names. I was referred to as a Boston private detective. When it was over I switched off the radio, left the dishes where they were, and went to my bedroom. I got a spare gun out of the drawer and put it in an extra hip holster. The hip holster had slots for six extra bullets and I slipped them in and clipped it to my belt with the barrel end in my right back pocket.

144

I got five ten-dollar bills and a spare set of keys out of my top bureau drawer and slipped them into my pocket. Went to the front closet and got my other jacket. It was my week-end-in-the-country jacket, cream-colored canvas, with a sherpa lining that spilled out over the collar. I was saving it in case I was ever invited down to the Myopia Hunt Club for cocktails and a polo match. But since someone had shot a hole in my other coat, I'd have to wear it now. It was 8:10 when I left my apartment. Smart, clean, well fed, and alive as a son-ova bitch.

CHAPTER TWENTY-TWO

I TOOK A CAB back out to Jamaica Pond. My car was where I'd left it, keys still in the ignition, sunglasses still up on the dashboard. Hubcaps still on the wheels. Ah, law and order. I got in, started it up, and drove on back into town to my office. I opened all the windows to air the place out and checked my mail. Called the answering service to find that Marion Orchard had called three times and Roland Orchard once. I called Quirk to see if they'd found Hayden. They hadn't. I hung up and started to lean back in my chair and put my feet up. My side hurt and I froze in midmotion, remembering the wound, and eased my feet back to the ground. I sat very still for about thirty seconds, breathing in small shallow breaths till things subsided. Then I got up quite carefully and closed the window. No sudden moves.

It was time to start looking for Hayden. I looked down at Stuart Street; he wasn't there. I felt a good deal like going home and lying down on my bed, but Hayden probably wasn't there either. The best I could think of was go out and talk to

Mrs. Hayden. As I was driving out to Marblehead again, the pain in my side began to be tiresome. At first it was almost a pleasant reminder that I was alive and hadn't bled to death in Jamaica Pond. But by now I was used to being alive and was again accepting it as my due, the common course of things; and the pain now served no other purpose than to remind me of my mortality. Also, the drive to Marblehead is among the worst in Massachusetts. It is only barely possible to reach Marblehead from anywhere, and the drive from Boston through the Callahan Tunnel, out Route 1A through East Boston, Revere, and Lynn is narrow, cluttered, ugly, and long. Particularly if you've recently been shot in the side.

There was a sea gull perched on the ridgepole of Hayden's gray weather duplex when I pulled in to the driveway. There was a larger number of people on the wharf than there had been last time, and I realized it was Saturday.

The shades of Hayden's place were drawn, but there was a stir of motion at the edge of one by the front door. I rang the bell and waited. No answer. No sound. I rang again. Same thing. I leaned on the bell and stayed there watching the ocean chop and flutter in the harbor and the bigger waves break against the causeway at the east end of the harbor. Inside I could hear the steady bleat of the bell. It sounded like a Bronx cheer. I felt it was directed at me—or was I getting paranoiac? She was tough; she hung in there for maybe five minutes. Then the door opened about two inches on a chain and she said, "Get out of here."

I said, "We've got to talk, Mrs. Hayden."

She said, "The police have been here already. I don't know where Lowell is. Get out of here."

I said, "Lowell's got one chance to stay alive, and I'm it. You shut the door on me and you'll be slamming the lid on your husband's casket."

The door slammed. Persuasive, that's me. Old silver tongue. I leaned on the bell some more. Another four or five minutes and she cracked. People who can endure bamboo slivers under the fingernails begin to weaken after ten minutes of doorbell ringing. She opened up again. Two inches, on the chain.

I said real quick, "Look. I saved your husband's life last night and got shot in the chest for my troubles and damn near bled to death because your husband ran off and left me. He owes me. You owe me. Let me save his life again. You won't get another chance." The door shut, but this time only for about thirty seconds. As I started to lean on the bell again I heard the chain bolt slide off and the door opened.

"Come in," she said.

She was as sumptuously dressed as she had been on my previous visit. This time it was brown corduroy pants that tapered at the ankles, brown leather sandals with a loop over the big toe, and a gray sweat shirt. Her hair was in the same tight bun, her face as empty of make-up as it had been. Her eyes behind the big pinkish eyeglasses were as warm and as deep as the end of a pool cue.

The apartment smelled of cat food. The front door opened into the living room. Beyond that I could see the kitchen and to the right of it a closed door, which I assumed led to another room. Maybe the master's study. In front of me, opposite the door and along the right-hand wall, rose a staircase.

The living room was big and sunny and looked like the display window at Sid and Mabel's furniture outlet. There were four canvas director's chairs, two blue ones and two orange ones, more or less grouped around a clear plastic cube with an empty vase on it. On the far wall was a blond bookcase with a brilliant coat of shellac on it, which held an assortment of textbook-looking books, mostly paperbacks, and a pile on the bottom shelf of record albums and coarse-paper magazines without covers, which were probably academic journals. On top of it were a McIntosh amplifier and a Garrard turntable. On each side, standing three feet high on the floor, were two Fisher speakers. The whole rig probably had cost more than my car, and surely more than the furniture. On the floor were two rugs, fake fur in the shape they would have had were they real and skinned out to dry. One was a zebra, one a tiger. House beautiful.

"Sit down," she said, and her thin lips barely moved as she talked. "Coffee?"

"Yes, please." I eased into one of the director's chairs. A fat Angora cat looked at me from the chair opposite, its yellow eyes as blank as doorknobs, its fur snarled and burry. It was the first time I could recall sitting in a director's chair. I had missed little, I decided. Mrs. Hayden appeared with the coffee in a white plastic mug, insulated, the kind you get with ten gallons of gas at an Exxon station. I took it black and sipped. It was instant.

"You say my husband needs your help. Why?"

"He's involved in one larceny and two murders. There is obviously a contract out on him. And if I don't find him before the contractors do, he's going to have all his troubles solved for him with a neat lead injection."

"I don't know what you're talking about."

"I bet you do. But I'm not going to argue with you. I'm telling you that if he doesn't come in under cover, he's dead."

"What makes you think you can help him?"

"That's my line of work. I helped him last night. I can do it again. There's a homicide cop named Quirk who'll help too."

"Why should I trust you?"

"Because I got a hole in the left side of my body to prove it. Because you could trust me last night a hell of a lot more than I could trust your husband."

"Why do you care what happens to him?"

"I don't. But I care what happens to a twenty-year-old kid who'll end up in the women's reformatory unless I can find out the truth from your husband."

"And what happens to him when you find out whatever you think the truth is?"

"He'll live. I can't promise much else, but it's better than what he'll get if Broz gets there first. The Supreme Court has outlawed the death penalty, but Broz hasn't."

"This is ridiculous," she said in her flat thin voice. "I do not know anyone named Broz. I do not know anything about any killings or any girls going to jail. My husband is away for a few days on professional business."

She had her hands in her lap and was twisting the gold wedding ring round and round on her finger. I didn't say anything. Her voice went up half a note.

"It's absurd. You're absurd. It's an absurd fairy tale. My husband is a respected scholar. He is known all over America in his field. You wouldn't know that. You wouldn't know anything about us. You're nothing but a . . . a . . ."

"Cheap gumshoe?" I suggested.

"A snoop! A sneaky snoop! Nothing will happen to my husband. He's fine. He'll be back in a few days. He's just traveling professionally. I told you that. Why do you keep asking me?" Her voice went up another half note. "You bastard. Why are you hounding him? Why does everyone hound him? He's a scholar, but you won't leave him alone. None of you. You, the police, those men, that girl . . ." Tears began to run down her face; her voice thickened.

"What girl?"

She wailed then. Her face got red and contorted and her mouth pulled back from her lips so that her gums were exposed. Her nose ran a little, and she cried with her whole considerable frame—huge, gasping sobs mixed with a high eerie sound like locusts. She drooled a bit too. I sipped on my coffee and said it again.

"What girl?"

Had she buried her face in her hands, or turned away, or fled the room it would have been tolerable. But she didn't. She sat, looking at me full face, and cried harder and harder till I began to think she would hurt herself. I couldn't keep looking. I got up and walked around the room. I looked out at the harbor. There was dust in random patterns on the windowpane. I put my hands in my pockets and walked back across the room and looked out the other window. She continued to howl. My side hurt and my head throbbed and I felt a little sick.

I looked at her sideways. She was trying to pick up her

coffee cup but her hand shook so violently that the coffee sloshed out onto the coffee table and formed a brown puddle on the clear plastic. She kept trying, even though most of the coffee had sloshed out, and finally threw it frantically on the floor. The cat jumped off the chair and went into the kitchen.

She was screaming now steadily, except for the wrenching gasp when she had to breathe. I went over and put one hand on her shoulder. She jerked away and scrambled out of the chair. Both her hands were pushed out in front of her as she backed away from me, across the room. She stopped in the far corner and screamed with her hands straight out before her, palms up, as if pushing against something.

She swore at me now, the curses bubbling out through the screams as if her saliva were viscous, repetitious obscenities, including one I hadn't heard before. Then she stopped. The gasping breaths became more frequent, the screaming interludes shorter. Then she was whimpering. Then she was breathing as if she'd just run three miles, her chest heaving under the sweat shirt, her face wet with tears and sweat and saliva and nasal mucus. The effect of her hysteria had loosened her hair in strands, and it stuck to the wetness on her cheek and forehead. She let her hands drop and straightened up in the corner. Her breathing slowed a little and the air ceased to rasp as it went to and from her lungs.

I said, "What girl?"

She shook her head without speaking. Then she went to the kitchen. I stepped to the kitchen door to make sure she didn't guillotine herself on the electric can opener, but her plan was better than that. She took a bottle of Scotch out of one of the cabinets—they kept it in with the Wheaties—removed the cap, and poured about half a cup into a water glass. She didn't offer me any. She drank it as if it were a nighttime cold medicine. All of it. And poured another. This she carried back out into the living room and placed before her on the glass cube as she sat back down. She wiped her face with the sleeve of her sweat shirt, and pushed her hair back off her face. From one pocket of the corduroy Levi's she took a bent packet of Kents. It took her two matches to get a cigarette going. But she did it and dragged a big lungful through the filter. The cigarette was old and dry and the big drag consumed nearly half of it, leaving a big glowing end which faded into ash and dropped on the floor. She paid it no attention. What looked like a descendant of the shaggy cat I'd seen earlier appeared from the kitchen and mewed at the front door. Mrs. Hayden seemed not to hear it. The cat mewed again, and I got up and let it out.

I turned back from the door and leaned against it with my arms folded. My side didn't seem to hurt quite as much if I stood that way.

"What about the girl?" I asked.

She shook her head.

"Look, Mrs. Hayden, you're in a box. You've got trouble you can't handle. There are people trying to kill your husband, the cops can't help because your husband is involved in a criminal act, you don't know what to do, and you just had hysterics to prove it. I'm all you've got. That may not make you happy, but there isn't any way around it. Asking your husband to go one-on-one with Joe Broz is like putting a guppy in the piranha pool. If we don't find him before Broz does, he'll be eaten alive."

Maybe it was the "we." Maybe it was my impeccable logic. Maybe it was desperation. But she said, "I'll take you to him."

Like that. No preamble.

I said, "Okay."

She went to the hall closet and put on a red quilted ski parka with a hood and brown knitted woolen gloves with imitation leather palms. She stepped out of the sandals and stuck her bare feet into green rubber boots with yellow laces. They were all laced and ready to go. She put on a white and brown knitted ski cap with a yellow tassle on the top and we went.

In my car I said, "Where?"

She said, "Boston, the Copley Plaza." And she didn't say another thing all the way back into town.

CHAPTER TWENTY-THREE

THE COPLEY PLAZA FRONTS on Copley Square, as do the Boston Public Library and Trinity Church. In the center of the square is a sunken brick piazza where in the summer a fountain plays. It is very nice there and a classy area to hide out in. The hotel itself is high ceilinged and deep carpeted. At four each afternoon they serve tea in the lobby. And if you want a drink you can go to the Merry-Go-Round Room and sit at a bar that revolves slowly. There is a good deal of gilt and there are a good many Grecian Revival columns, and the bell-boys are very dignified in green uniforms with gold piping. I always felt I should lower my voice in the Copley Plaza, although my line of work didn't take me there with any regularity.

We went in the elevator, got off with another couple at the fourth floor, and walked down a corridor rather elegantly papered in pale beige. She knocked on the door of 411. The other couple passed us and went around the corner. They looked as if they might be on a honeymoon, or maybe they just worked in the same office and were on their lunch hour. Mrs. Hayden knocked again twice and then twice more. Christ, a secret code. Made you wish Ian Fleming had taken up music or something.

The door opened an inch on the chain. Hayden's voice emerged.

"What is it, Judy?" Judy? The name was bad; Mrs. Hayden wasn't a Judy. A Ruth, maybe, or an Elsie, but Judy?

"Let us in, Lowell."

"What's he doing here? Has he forced you, Judy? I told you never to bring anyone—"

Judy's voice got sharper. "Let us in, Lowell." And then more gently. "It's all right."

The door closed. The chain came off, and it opened again. In we went. It was a nice room with a big double bed, unmade now, and a window that looked out onto Dartmouth Street. The television was tuned to a game show. *The Boston Globe* was scattered around the room.

Hayden shut the door, put the chain lock back on, and put the bed between me and him.

"What do you want?" he said.

The game show host introduced their defending champion, "Mrs. Tyler Moorehouse from Grand Island, Nebraska." The audience cheered. I reached over and shut it off.

I said, "You owe me a favor."

Judy Hayden went over around the bed and stood beside her husband. She was at least three inches taller.

"I don't owe you anything, Spenser. You just stay away from me."

He was a consistent sonova bitch.

"If I hadn't happened along last night, Hayden, you would now be enriching the soil in the area of Jamaica Pond. And if you don't help me now, that time will come again."

"They were supposed to kill you." He seemed to be repeating some kind of litany—by rote, as if, like ritual, the repetition of it, if done just right, would save him.

"They are not going to kill me, Hayden. They are going to kill you. Here's why. They want this case closed and forgotten. I keep nosing around in it, and it is you that I've nosed up into the light. If they kill me that'll cause some more nosing around, by other people who know I'm nosing around you. You're the key, Hayden. You're the one who knows the stuff that Broz doesn't want known. If they kill me you are still the one who knows and you are still around and someone, like say a homicide cop named Quirk, might take hold of you and begin to shake you until what you know falls out. But"—Mrs. Hayden had put an arm around her husband's shoulder,

153

maternal—"but if they kill you there isn't anyone around who knows what Broz doesn't want known and Quirk and I can shake each other till we turn to butter and no information is going to fall out because we don't have it. How's that sound to you?"

Hayden just looked at me. I plowed ahead.

"I figure that you and Powell were involved in pushing dope at the university. Maybe for money, maybe because you wanted to turn on the sons of the middle class, maybe because you're a screwball and Tim Leary is your idol. Why doesn't matter so much for now; you can tell us that later. Broz supplied you. For him the university was a nice new market for some goods he had on hand, and as long as you could deliver the market he could use you. But you and Powell had to get fancy. You stole that manuscript and held it for ransom. That was dumb, because that got the university police and me involved. No big threat, maybe, but there's no advantage to having legal types sniffing around. But what was dumber was that you and Powell had a falling out. About what, I don't know. You can tell me that, too. But it was you he was arguing with on the phone, and it was you who set him up for the mob hit. It had to be you because you're the only one around who could have supplied Terry Orchard's gun. You got it through Cathy Connelly."

Judy Hayden's arm tightened around Hayden's shoulder. He seemed to be resisting her, pulling against the arm pressure, like maybe he didn't want to be hugged as much as she wanted to hug him.

"She'd been Terry's roommate, and she knew about the gun. She was also your girl friend, and it had to be she who told you about it. So it was done and you were clean and all was well and then I showed up. And I talked to you about it, and you panicked. You must have called Broz the minute I left your office that day because he sent his people out to talk to me right after that. And the manuscript was returned the next day. But I kept it up and you panicked worse. Cathy Connelly could tie you to the murder. What if you broke up? What if your wife heard about her and blew the whistle on your girl friend and your girl friend talked for spite? She was the only one who knew about you and Broz. Other people maybe could tie you to SCACE, but the worst that would mean is a no decision at tenure time. The university wasn't pressing charges on the Godwulf Manuscript. If you could get rid of Cathy Connelly, you and Broz could recruit a new pusher to replace Dennis Powell and things would be going just as swell and nice as they had before. So you went and killed her. That was maybe the dumbest thing of all, because it's not your line of work and you did a terrible job. If Broz hadn't put a lot of pressure on someone you'd be sitting around in a small room at Walpole right now. And when I kept after you and you called Broz about it again, Broz must have had enough. So you thought he'd kill me, but he thought he'd kill you. And he will. You got one chance and that is to take away his reason. Tell me, tell the cops, maybe we can get Broz, but whether or not we do we can keep him from getting you . . . I think."

"She helped me," he said.

Judy Hayden said, "Lowell . . ." in a choked voice.

"It was her idea to kill Cathy. She went with me; she held Cathy when I hit her on the head. She said to make it look as if Cathy drowned in the tub."

Her arm dropped away from his shoulder and hung straight down by her side. She didn't look at him, or me.

Hayden went on with no animation, like a recording. "I don't use drugs, but many people need them to liberate their consciousness, to elevate their perceptions and free them from the bondage of American hypocrisy. A drug culture is the first step to an open society. I was the man who got them from Joseph Broz. Dennis supplied them to the community. He didn't know where I got them, and I didn't know where he sold them. It was just right." He had a dreamy little half smile on his face now as he talked, and his eyes were concentrating on a point somewhere left of my shoulder.

"Then he spoiled it. He complained about the quality. Said the heroin was cut too much. I said I'd speak to my supplier. Joseph Broz said that the quality was fine and was going to remain the way it was. Dennis threatened to tell the police on me. He threatened to bring down everything we'd worked for, everything that SCACE stood for. Simply because he wanted the heroin stronger. He sacrificed his every ideal. He betrayed the movement. He had to be executed. Miss Connelly and I discussed it and she suggested the gun. I discussed it with a representative of Joseph Broz and he said if we would give him the gun, he would manage the rest. Miss Connelly went there to visit and took the gun. It is too bad Miss Orchard has to suffer; she is a member of the movement and we bear her no ill will."

He paused. Still looking past my shoulder. The smile was a full smile now and his eyes were shiny. In a minute he'd start addressing me as "my fellow Americans."

The smile faded. "So now you know," he said.

"Will you tell it all to the police?" I said.

He shook his head. "I'll die without speaking," he said. Ronald Colman, Major André, Nathan Hale, the Christian martyrs.

"You're not going to die," I said. "The death penalty is not legal at the moment. You will merely go to jail, unless you don't tell the cops. Then you will die without speaking like you almost did last night. Remember last night. You didn't seem so eager for silent martyrdom last night."

Judy Hayden put her hand on his shoulder. "Tell them, Lowell," she said. He shrugged his shoulder away from her touch. "I've told him, and that's all I'm telling anyone. You brought him here. I wouldn't have had to tell him anything if you'd not brought him here. I trusted you and you betrayed me too. Can I trust no one? You've never cared about the movement. Dennis never cared about the movement. Cathy never cared about the movement."

"I care about you," she said. She was standing very stiff and very still. The palms of her hands appeared to press hard against her thighs.

"I am the movement," he said, and the dreamy smile was back and the eyes positively glistened. He was listening

156

to the sound of a different drummer all right, and it was playing "God Save the King."

No one said anything. I didn't want to look at Mrs. Hayden. In the silence I heard a click like a key turning in the lock. I turned toward the door behind me, but I was wrong. It was the connecting door to the next room. It swung open suddenly and Phil stepped through it. In his hand was a gun with a silencer. He pointed it at me, and said in his rusty voice, "Time's up."

CHAPTER TWENTY-FOUR

PHIL CLOSED THE DOOR.

"The couple in the elevator with us," I said. Phil nodded.

"You had Mrs. Hayden staked out," I said. Phil nodded again.

"I am a horse's ass," I said.

"We used five people," Phil said. "It's hard to spot."

The gun in his hand was an Army issue .45 automatic. It fired a slug about the size of a baseball and at close range would knock down a sex-crazed rhinoceros. Most people didn't use them because they were big and clumsy and uncomfortable to wear and they jumped in your hand a lot when you fired. In Phil's hand it looked natural and just right.

Hayden said, "Thank God you're here."

Phil made a movement with his lower jaw that might have been a smile. "Get over beside Spenser," he said. Hayden stared at him.

Phil's voice grated without inflection. "Move."

Hayden moved. Mrs. Hayden moved with him. Fred

Astaire and Ginger Rogers. What the hell made me think of that?

"Take your gun out with two fingers of your left hand, Spenser, and drop it on the floor."

I did as he said. Since the gun was on my right hip I had to twist my body some, and that made my side hurt more. In a little while it wouldn't matter.

I felt shaky, like I'd had too much coffee, and apprehension tingled along my arms. I fumbled the gun out and dropped it on the floor.

"Kick it under the bed," Phil said. Every time he talked you wanted to clear your throat. I kicked the gun.

"You can't harm me," Hayden said. "If you do and Joseph Broz hears of it, you will be in very serious trouble."

Jesus, Alice in Wonderland. I was studying Phil. He was a puzzle, and that opaque white walleye didn't help any. It was hard to tell what he was looking at. He was dressed as he had been before—the coat buttoned up the neck, the pink-tinted glasses. I watched his hand on the gun; maybe at the instant I saw the finger tighten on the trigger, I could jump him. The hammer wasn't back. Phil probably always carried a round in the chamber. That would give me an extra hundredth of a second. I wished my side weren't sore and bandaged. I felt weak, and diving across the bed and taking the gun away from Phil was not the kind of work that the weak do well. It wasn't a very big chance, but standing still while he shot me in the face was an even smaller chance. He'd shoot me first, figuring I'd be the one to give him trouble.

Hayden kept talking in a singsong voice that rose in pitch as he spoke. "Do you have any idea whom you're dealing with? Do you know how many people are in the movement? If anything happens to me they'll never rest till I'm avenged. They'll track you down and harry you out, however well hidden you may think you are. And Joseph Broz will be very angry with you."

Phil seemed interested. He'd probably never seen anything like Hayden before.

"And you know how angry Joseph Broz can be. I'm on

your side. I want to change all of this. I want a world where you won't have to work outside the law. I'm not your enemy. Shoot them. He's your enemy and she is, too, she betrayed me. She led him here. She led you here. Kill her. Don't kill me. Please don't. Please don't."

His legs went out from beneath him, and he dropped to his knees and back onto his heels. "Please don't. Please don't. Please don't."

Phil liked it. He cackled to himself.

"What are you going to do to my husband?" Mrs. Hayden asked.

Phil cackled again. "I'm going to shoot him."

Mrs. Hayden jumped at him. The gun made a muffled thud as Phil fired. It must have hit her, but it didn't stop her. She got hold of his gun arm with both hands and bit into his wrist. She was making a sound that was somewhere between a moan and a growl. The gun thudded again. I went over the bed at Phil. With his left forearm he cuffed me across the face. It was like running into a tree branch. I sprawled on the bed, rolled onto the floor, and came up for him again. Mrs. Hayden had her teeth sunk in his arm. He was pounding the side of her head with his left hand, and trying to get his right loose to use the gun. I got on his back this time and got my right arm around his neck. He moved away from the bed and I rode his back like a kid, wrapping my legs around his middle. I was trying to get my left hand against the back of his head and lock my right hand against my left forearm. If I could do that, I could strangle him.

It was not easy to do. Phil kept his chin tucked down and I couldn't get my forearm against his windpipe. He reached backward with his left hand and got hold of my hair. He bowed his back and tried to flip me over forward. He couldn't, because I had my legs scissored around his middle. But the effort tumbled him forward and all three of us went down in a pile. Mrs. Hayden was beneath us, her teeth still sunk into Phil's forearm, her hands still clutching the gun. Phil let go of my hair with his left hand and his thumb felt for my eye. I pressed my face against his back to protect it. He had a sweaty, rancid smell. I got the fingers of my left hand hooked under his nostrils and pulled. He grunted and his chin came up an inch. It was enough. My right forearm slipped in against his Adam's apple. I put the right hand on the left forearm and made a pivot of it, bringing my left hand up behind his head. Then I squeezed.

I could feel the muscles in his neck bulge. It was like trying to strangle a hydrant. He gurgled, and I squeezed harder. He was incredibly strong. He heaved himself up, carrying me on his back and dragging Mrs. Hayden up too. The gun thudded three more times. He tried to break the hold by lunging back against the wall and knocking me loose, but he couldn't. He clawed left-handed at my forearm, then with his fingernails. The gun thudded again and again until all eight rounds were gone. I had no idea what they were hitting. I was concentrating everything I had on strangling Phil. My whole life was invested in the pressure of my forearm on his throat.

He gurgled again, and I could feel his chest heaving in the struggle to breathe. He was scratching at my forearm like he was digging for the bone. I squeezed. The blood pounded in my ears from the effort and I couldn't see anything but a dance of dust motes where my face stayed pressed against his shoulder. Phil made a noise like a crow cawing, turned very slowly in a complete turn, and fell over backward on top of me. He stopped clawing at my arm. He made no noise. He was inert. Mrs. Hayden was inert on top of both of us, her teeth still in his arm. I kept squeezing, unable to see with his back pressed against my face, unable to feel anything but the strain of my arm against his neck. I squeezed. I don't know how long I squeezed, but it was surely for a long time after it made any difference.

When I let go I could barely open my hand. I was slippery with sweat and too tired to move right away. I lay there panting with the weight of Phil and Judy Hayden on me. When the dancing motes began to dissipate I dragged myself out from under the body.

Phil was dead. I realized that Phil and the floor and my leg were sticky with blood—Mrs. Hayden's blood. I touched her and she didn't move. I felt for her pulse. She had none. She'd bled to death hanging on to Phil's arm. Her teeth were still bitten into it. Phil had emptied his gun in desperation. There was no way to tell how many had hit her. I didn't want to know. I stood up. The room was a shambles. Blood was smeared everywhere. The night stand was tipped over. So was the television set. The bed was broken. I was aware that my side hurt. There was some blood staining my shirt. The wound had opened again.

I remembered Hayden. I looked around. I didn't see him. He was going to get few merit badges for *semper fidelis.* I started for the door. The chain lock was still on it. The door that Phil had come through locked from the other side. I went over to the bathroom. It was locked.

I said, "Hayden."

No answer. I banged on the door. Nothing. I felt crazy and hot. I backed up three steps and ran right through the door. It was thin and tore from its hinges. No Hayden. I pulled the shower curtain aside and there he was. In the tub, sitting down with his knees drawn up to his chest.

He looked at me and said, "Please don't."

I reached down, took the front of his shirt in both hands, and yanked him up out of the tub. There was a peculiar smell about him and I realized he'd wet himself. I was revolted. I swung him around, the way a trackman throws the hammer, and slung him into the bedroom. He stumbled, almost fell, and stopped, looking down at his wife. I came beside him. I took his chin in my hand and raised his head. I put my face up against his, so that our noses touched. I could barely speak, and my body was shivering. I said, "I have killed three people to save your miserable goddamn ass. Your wife took about six slugs in the stomach and bled to death in great agony to save your miserable goddamn ass. I will call up Martin Quirk in a minute, and he will come here to arrest you. You will tell him everything that you know and everything that I want you to tell him and everything that he asks you. If you do not, I will get Quirk to put us alone together in a cell in the cellar, and I will beat you to death. I promise you that I will."

He said, "Yes, sir." When I let him go he didn't move—just stood there looking down at his wife with his hands clasped behind his back. I went to the phone and dialed a number I knew too well.

CHAPTER TWENTY-FIVE

THE ROOM WAS BUSY. The people from the coroner's office had come and taken Phil away, and Mrs. Hayden. The hotel doctor had come and rebandaged my side and told me to go in to outpatient this afternoon and have some new stitches in the wound. Beside the broken TV set Frank Belson stood in front of Lowell Hayden, who sat in the only chair in the room. Hayden was talking and Belson was writing things down as he talked. Quirk was there and three uniformed cops and a couple of plainclothes types were standing around looking shrewd and keeping an eye out for clues. The occupant of the next room had been whacked on the head and locked in a closet and was now planning to sue the hotel. The house man was trying to persuade him not to.

Quirk was as immaculate and dapper as ever. He had on a belted tweed topcoat, pale pigskin gloves.

"Not bad," he said. "He had a gun and you didn't and you took him? Not bad at all. Sometimes you amaze me, Spenser."

"We took him," I said. "Me and Mrs. Hayden."

"Either way," Quirk said.

"How about the kid?" I said.

"Orchard? I already called. They're processing her out now. She'll be on the street by the time we get through here."

"Yates?"

Quirk smiled with his mouth shut. "Captain Yates is at this moment telling the people in the pressroom about another triumph for truth, justice, and the American way."

"He's got all the moves, hasn't he?" I said.

One of the plainclothes dicks snickered, and Quirk looked at him hard enough to hurt.

"How about Joe Broz?"

Quirk shrugged. "We got a pickup order out on him. How long we can keep him when we get him, you can guess as well as I can. In the last fifteen years we've arrested him eight times and made one charge stick—loitering. It will help if Hayden sticks to his story."

I looked at Hayden, sitting in the chair. He was talking now in his deep, phony voice. Lecturing Belson. Explaining in detail every aspect of the case and explaining its connection with the movement, drawing inference, elaborating implications, demonstrating significance, and suggesting symbolic meaning. Belson looked as if he had a headache. Hayden was enjoying himself very much.

"He'll stick," I said. "Imagine him lecturing a jury. Your only problem will be getting him to stop."

The phone rang. One of the plainclothes cops answered and held it out to Quirk.

"For you, Lieutenant."

Quirk answered, listened, said "Okay," and hung up.

"Orchard's parents can't be located, Spenser. She says she wants you to come down and pick her up. How's your side?"

"It only hurts when I laugh."

"Okay, beat it. We'll be in touch about the coroner's inquest."

I looked at Hayden again. He was still talking to Belson, his rich voice rolling out and filling the room. For him, a big, homely, masculine woman had taken six .45 slugs in the stomach. The press arrived and a photographer in what looked like a leather trench coat was snapping Hayden's picture. Hayden looked positively triumphant. *Le mouvement, c'est moi.* Jesus!

Outside the room the corridor was crowded with people. Two uniformed cops kept them at bay. As I shoved through, someone asked what had happened in there.

"It was a lover's quarrel," I said, "with the world."

I wondered what I meant. I didn't even remember where I got the phrase. Downstairs the lobby was as refined and ornate as ever. I went through it into the midafternoon sunshine. The hotel was dwarfed by the enormous insurance building that rose behind it. The sides of the skyscraper were reflecting glass, and the sun off the glass was dazzling. Tallest building in Boston. Excelsior, I thought. Tower of Babel, I thought. My car was parked in front of the library. I got in and drove the short block to police headquarters. I parked out front by the yellow curb on Berkeley Street. It's the only place in the area where there are always parking spaces.

I got out of the car arthritically. When I straightened up she was outside the building, on the top step. Squinting against the light, she was wearing a dapple gray suede coat with white fur trim at collar, cuffs, hem, and down the front where it buttoned. Her hands were thrust deep in her pockets and a shoulder purse hung against her left side. She was wearing black boots with three-inch heels, and looking up at her from street level, she looked a lot taller than I knew she was. Her hair was loose and dark against the high white fur collar.

Neither of us moved for a minute. We stood in silence in the bright afternoon and looked at each other. Then she came down the steps.

I said, "Hi."

She said, "Hi."

I went around and opened the door to my car on her side. She got in, tucking the skirt of her long coat modestly under as she slid in. I went around and got in my side.

She said, "Do you have a cigarette?"

I said, "No. But I can stop and pick some up. There's a Liggett's on the corner."

She said, "If you would. I'd like to buy some make-up too."

I pulled over and parked in the alley between the parking garage and the drugstore at the corner of Berkeley and Boylston streets. As we got out she said, "I don't have any money, can you lend me some?"

I nodded. We went into the drugstore. It was a big one —a soda fountain down one side, bottles of almost everything on the other three walls, three wide aisles with shelves selling heating pads and baby strollers, paperback books and candy and Christmas lights. Terry bought a package of Eve cigarettes, opened it, took one out, lit it, and inhaled half of it. She let the smoke out slowly through her nose. I paid. Then we went to the make-up counter. She bought eye liner, eye shadow, make-up base, rouge, lipstick, and face powder. I paid.

I said, "Would you like an ice cream cone?"

She nodded and I bought us two ice cream cones. Vanilla for me, butter pecan for her. Two scoops. We went back out to my car and got in.

"Could we drive around for a little while?" she asked.

"Sure."

I drove on down Berkeley Street and onto Storrow Drive. At Leverett Circle I went over the dam to the Cambridge side and drove back up along the river on Memorial Drive. When we got to Magazine Beach we parked. She used the rearview mirror to put on some of the make-up. I looked across the gray river at the railroad yards. Behind them, half-hidden by the elevated extension of the Mass Turnpike, was Boston University Field, with high-rise dorms built up around the stadium. When I was a kid it had been Braves Field until the Braves moved to Milwaukee and B.U. bought the field. I remembered going there with my father, the excitement building as we went past the ticket taker and up from the dark under stands into the bright green presence of the diamond. The Dodgers and the Giants used to come here then. Dixie Walker, Clint Hartung, Sibbi Sisti, and Tommy Holmes. I wondered if they were still alive.

Terry Orchard finished her make-up and stowed it all away in her shoulder purse.

"Spenser?"

"Yeah?"

"What can I say? Thank you seems pretty silly."

"Don't say anything, kid. You know and I know. Let it be."

She leaned forward and held my face in her hands and kissed me hard on the mouth and held it for a long time. The fresh make-up was sweet smelling. When she finished, her lipstick was badly smeared.

"Gotcha," I said. "Let's go home."

We drove on out Soldier's Field Road toward Newton. She slid over in the seat beside me and put her head against my shoulder while I drove, and smoked another cigarette. There was a maroon car in the driveway of her house when we got there.

"My father," she said. "The police must have reached him." As I pulled up to the curb the front door opened and Terry's mother and father appeared on the porch.

"Shit," she said.

"I'll let you out here and keep going, love," I said. "This is family business."

"Spenser, when am I going to see you again?"

"I don't know. We don't live in the same neighborhood, love. But I'm around. Maybe I'll come by sometime and take you to lunch."

"Or buy me an ice cream," she said.

"Yeah, that too."

She stared at me and her eyes filled up.

She said, "Thank you," and got out of the car and walked up toward her house. I drove back to town, got my side stitched at Boston City by the same doctor, and went home.

It was dark when I got there, and I sat down in my living room and drank bourbon from the bottle without turning on the lights. They'd given me two pills at the hospital and combined with the bourbon they seemed to kill the pain pretty well.

I looked at the luminous dial of my wristwatch. 6:45.

I felt as if I'd wrung out, and was drip-drying. I also felt that spending the night alone would have me screaming incoherently by 3 A.M.

I looked at my watch again. 6:55.

I turned the light on and took off the watch. Inside, it still said Brenda Loring, 555-3676.

I dialed the number. She answered.

I said, "Hello, my name is Spenser; do you remember me?"

She laughed, a terrific laugh, a high-class laugh. "With the shoulders, and the nice eyes, yeah, I remember." And she laughed again. A good laugh, full of promise. A hell of a laugh when you thought about it.

MORTAL STAKES

This too is for Joan, David, and Daniel

Only where love and need are one,
And the work is play for mortal stakes,
Is the deed ever really done
For Heaven and the future's sakes.

ROBERT FROST

CHAPTER ONE

IT WAS SUMMERTIME, and the living was easy for the Red Sox because Marty Rabb was throwing the ball past the New York Yankees in a style to which he'd become accustomed. I was there. In the skyview seats, drinking Miller High Life from a big paper cup, eating peanuts and having a very nice time. I wasn't supposed to be having a nice time. I was supposed to be working. But now and then you can do both.

For serious looking at baseball there are few places better than Fenway Park. The stands are close to the playing field, the fences are a hopeful green, and the young men in their white uniforms are working on real grass, the authentic natural article; under the actual sky in the temperature as it really is. No Tartan Turf. No Astrodome. No air conditioning. Not too many pennants over the years, but no Texans either. Life is adjustment. And I loved the beer.

The best pitcher I ever saw was Sandy Koufax, and the next best was Marty Rabb. Rabb was left-handed like Koufax, but bigger, and he had a hard slider that waited for you to commit yourself before it broke. While I shelled the last peanut in the bag he laid the slider vigorously on Thurman Munson and the Yankees were out in the eighth. While the sides changed I went for another bag of peanuts and another beer.

The skyviews were originally built in 1946, when the Red Sox had won their next-to-last pennant and had to have additional press facilities for the World Series. They were built on the roof of the grandstand between first and third. Since the World Series was not an annual ritual in Boston the press facilities were converted to box seats. You reached them over boardwalks laid on the tar and gravel roof of the grandstand, and there was a booth up there for peanuts, beer, hot dogs, and programs and another for toilet facilities. All connected with boardwalks. Leisurely, no crowds. I got back to my seat just as the Sox were coming to bat and settled back with my feet up on the railing. Late June, sun, warmth, baseball, beer, and peanuts. Ah, wilderness. The only flaw was that the gun on my right hip kept digging into my back. I adjusted.

Looking at a ball game is like looking through a stereopticon. Everything seems heightened. The grass is greener. The uniform whites are brighter than they should be. Maybe it's the containment. The narrowing of focus. On the other hand, maybe it's the tendency to drink six or eight beers in the early innings. Whatever—Alex Montoya, the Red Sox center fielder, hit a home run in the last of the eighth. Rabb fell upon the Yankee hitters in the ninth like a cleaver upon a lamb chop, and the game was over.

It was a Wednesday, and the crowd was moderate. No pushing and trampling. I strolled on down past them under the stands to the lower level. Down there it was dark and littered. A hundred programs rolled and dropped on the floor. The guys in the concession booths were already rolling down the steel curtains that closed them off like a bunch of rolltop desks. There were a lot of fathers and kids going out. And a lot of old guys with short cigars and plowed Irish faces that seemed in no hurry to leave. Peanut shells crunched underfoot.

Out on Jersey Street I turned right. Next door to the park is an office building with an advance sale ticket office behind plate glass and a small door that says BOSTON AMERICAN LEAGUE BASEBALL CLUB. I went in. There was a flight of stairs, dark wood, the walls a pale green latex. At the top another door. Inside a foyer in the same green latex with a dark green carpet and a receptionist with stiff blue hair. I said to the receptionist, "My name is Spenser. To see Harold Erskine." I tried to look like a short-relief prospect just in from Pawtucket. I don't think I fooled her.

She said, "Do you have an appointment?"

I said, "Yes."

She spoke into the intercom, listened to the answer, and said, "Go in."

Harold Erskine's office was small and plain. There were two green file cabinets side by side in a corner, a yellow deal desk opposite the door, a small conference table, two straight chairs, and a window that looked out on Brookline Ave. Erskine was as unpretentious as his office. He was a small plump man, bald on top. The gray that remained was cut close to his head. His face was round and red-cheeked, his hands pudgy. I'd read somewhere that he'd been a minor-league shortstop and hit .327 one year at Pueblo. That had been a while ago; now he looked like a defrocked Santa.

"Come in, Mr. Spenser, enjoy the game?"

"Yeah, thanks for the pass." I sat in one of the straight chairs.

"My pleasure. Marty's something else, isn't he?"

I nodded. Erskine leaned back in his chair and cleaned the corners of his mouth with the thumb and forefinger of his left hand, drawing them together along his lower lip. "My attorney says I can trust you."

I nodded again. I didn't know his attorney.

Erskine rubbed his lip again. "Can I?"

"Depends on what you want to trust me to do."

"Can you guarantee that what we say will be confidential, no matter what you decide?"

"Yes." Erskine kept working on his lower lip. It looked clean enough to me.

"What did my lawyer tell you when he called?"

"He said you'd like to see me after today's game and

177

there'd be a pass waiting for me at the press entrance on Jersey Street if I wanted to watch the game first."

"What do you charge?"

"A hundred a day and expenses. But I'm running a special this week; at no extra charge I teach you how to wave a blackjack."

Erskine said, "I heard you were a wit." I wasn't sure he believed it.

"Your lawyer tell you that too?" I asked.

"Yes. He discussed you with a state police detective named Healy. I think Healy's sister married my lawyer's wife's brother."

"Well, hell, Erskine. You know all you really can know about me. The only way you can find out if you can trust me is to try it. I'm a licensed private detective. I've never been to jail. And I have an open, honest face. I'm willing to sit here and let you look at me for a while, I owe you for the free ball game, but eventually you'll have to tell me what you want or ask me to leave."

Erskine stared at me some more. His cheeks seemed a little redder, and he was beginning to develop callus tissue on his lower lip. He brought his left hand down flat on the top of the desk. "Okay," he said. "You're right. I got no choice."

"It's nice to be wanted," I said.

"I want you to see if Marty Rabb's got gambling connections."

"Rabb," I said. Snappy comebacks are one of my specialities.

"That's right, Rabb. There's a rumor, no, not even that, a whisper, a faint, pale hint, that Rabb might be shading a game now and then."

"Marty Rabb?" I said. When I've got a good line, I like to stick with it.

"I know. It's hard to believe. I don't believe it, in fact. But it's possible and it's got to be checked. You know what even the rumor of a fix means to baseball."

I nodded. "If you did have Rabb in your teacup, you could make a buck, couldn't you?"

Just hearing me say it made Erskine swallow hard. He leaned forward over the desk. "That's right," he said. "You can get good odds against the Sox anytime Marty pitches. If you could get that extra percentage by having Rabb on your end of the bet, you could make a lot of money."

"He doesn't lose much," I said. "What was he last year, twenty-five and six?"

"Yeah, but when he does lose, you could make a bundle. And even if he doesn't lose, what if you've got money bet on the biggest inning? Marty could ease up a little at the right time. We don't score much. We're all pitching and defense and speed. Marty wouldn't have to give up many runs to lose, or many runs to make a big inning. If you bet right he wouldn't have to do it very often."

"Okay, I agree, it would be a wise investment for someone to get Rabb's cooperation. But what makes you think someone has?"

"I don't quite know. You hear things that don't mean anything by themselves. You see stuff that doesn't mean anything by itself. You know, Marty grooving one to Reggie Jackson at the wrong time. Could happen to anyone. Cy Young probably did it too. But after a while you get that funny feeling. And I've got it. I'm probably wrong. I got nothing hard. But I have to know. It's not just the club, it's Marty. He's a terrific kid. If other people started to get the funny feeling it would destroy him. He'd be gone and no one would even have to prove it. He wouldn't be able to pitch for the Yokohama Giants."

"Hiring a private cop to investigate him isn't the best way to keep it quiet," I said.

"I know, you've got to work undercover. Even if you proved him innocent the damage would be done."

"There's another question there too. What if he's guilty?"

"If he's guilty I'll hound him out of baseball. The minute people don't trust the integrity of the final score, the whole system goes right down the tube. But I've got to know first, and I'm betting there's nothing to it. I've got to have absolute proof. And it's got to be confidential."

"I've got to talk to people. I've got to be around the club. I can't find out the truth without asking questions and watching."

"I know. We'll have to come up with a story to cover that. I don't suppose you play ball?"

"I was the second leading hitter on the Vine Street Hawks in nineteen forty-six."

"Yeah, you ever stood up at the plate and had someone throw you a major-league curve ball?"

I shook my head.

"I have. Nineteen fifty-two I went to spring training with the Dodgers and Clem Labine threw about ten of them at me the first intersquad game. It helped get me into the front office. Besides you're too old."

"I didn't think it showed," I said.

"Well, I mean, for a ballplayer, starting out."

"How about a writer?" I said.

"The guys know all the writers."

"Not a sports reporter, a writer. A guy doing a book on baseball—you know, *The Boys of Summer, The Summer Game,* that stuff."

Erskine thought about it. "Not bad," he said. "Not bad. You don't look much like a writer, but hell, what's a writer look like? Right? Why not? I'll take you down, tell them you're doing a book and you're going to be hanging around the club and asking questions. It's perfect. You know anything about writing?"

"I've read some," I said.

"I mean, can you sound like a writer? You look like the bouncer at a health club."

"I can keep from sounding as stupid as I look," I said.

"Yeah, okay, it sounds good to me. I see no problem. But you gotta be, for crissake, discreet. I mean dis-goddamn-creet. Right?"

"I am, as we writers say, the very soul of discretion. I'll need a press pass or whatever credentials you people issue.

And it is probably smart if you take me down and introduce me around."

"Yeah, I'll take care of that." He looked at me and started working on his lip again. "This is between you and me," he said. "No one else knows. Not the manager, not the owners, not the players, nobody."

"How about your lawyer?" I asked.

"He is my own lawyer, not the club's. He thinks I wanted you for personal business."

"Okay, when do I meet the team?"

Erskine looked at his watch. "Too late today, half of them are showered and gone. How about tomorrow? We'll go in before the game and I'll introduce you around."

"I'll show up here about noon tomorrow then."

"Yeah," he said. "That'll be good. You got a title for this book you're supposed to be writing?"

"I'm looking for sales appeal," I said. "How about *The Sensuous Baseball*?"

Erskine said he didn't like that title. I went home to think of another one.

CHAPTER TWO

I GOT UP early the next morning and jogged along the river. There were sparrows and grackles mixed in among the pigeons on the esplanade, and I saw two chickadees in the sandpit of one of the play areas. A couple of rowers were on the river, a girl in jeans tucked into high brown boots was walking two Welsh corgis, and there were some other joggers.

Near the lagoon, past the concert shell, a bum in an old blue sharkskin suit was sleeping on a newspaper, and along Storrow Drive the commuter traffic was just beginning. I was still living at the bottom of Marlborough Street and the run up to the BU footbridge took about ten minutes. I crossed the footbridge over Storrow Drive and went in the side door of the BU gym. I knew a guy in the athletic department and they let me use the weight room. I spent forty-five minutes on the irons and another half hour on the heavy bag. By that time some coeds were passing by on their way to class and I finished up with a big flourish on the speed bag. They didn't seem impressed.

I jogged back downriver with the sun much warmer now and the dew gone from the grass and the commuter traffic in full cry. I was back in my apartment at five of nine, glistening with sweat, and reeking of good circulation, and throbbing with appetite.

I squeezed some orange juice and drank it, plugged in the coffee, and went for a shower. At quarter past nine I was back in the kitchen again in my red and white terry-cloth robe that Susan Silverman had given me on my last birthday. It had short sleeves and a golf umbrella on the breast pocket and the label said JACK NICKLAUS. Every time I put it on I wanted to yell "Fore."

I drank my first cup of coffee while I made a mushroom omelet with sherry, and my second cup of coffee while I ate the omelet, along with a warm loaf of unleavened Arab bread, and read the morning *Globe*. When I finished, I put the dishes in the dishwasher, made the bed, and got dressed. Gray socks, gray slacks, black loafers, and an eggshell-colored stretch knit shirt with small red hexagons all over it. I clipped my holster on over the belt on my right hip. The blue steel revolver was nicely color-coordinated with the black holster and the gray slacks. It clashed badly when I wore brown. To cover the gun I wore a gray denim jacket with red stitching along the pockets and lapels. I checked myself in the mirror. Adorable. Lucky it wasn't ladies' day. I'd get molested at the park.

The temperature was in the mid-eighties and the sun was bright when I got out onto Marlborough Street. I walked a block over to Commonwealth and strolled up the mall toward Fenway Park. It was still too early for the crowd to start gathering, but the early signs of a game were there. The old guy that sells peanuts from a pushcart was pushing it along toward Kenmore Square, an old canvas over the peanuts. A middle-aged couple had parked a maroon Chevy by a hydrant near Kenmore Square and were setting up to sell balloons from the trunk. The trunk lid was up, an air tank leaned against the rear bumper, and the husband, wearing a blue and red tennis visor, was opening a large cardboard box in the trunk. Near the corner of Brookline Ave, outside the subway kiosk, a young man with shoulder-length blond hair was selling small pennants that said RED SOX in red script against a blue background. I looked at my watch: 11:40. You couldn't see the park from Kenmore Square, but the light standards loomed up over the buildings and you knew it was close. As I turned down Brookline Ave toward the park I felt the old feeling. My father and I used to go this early to watch the teams take infield.

I walked the two blocks down Brookline Ave, turned the corner at Jersey Street, and went up the stairs to Erskine's office. He was in, reading what looked like a legal document, his chair tilted back and one foot on the open bottom drawer. I closed the door.

"You think of a new title for that book yet, Spenser?" he said.

An air conditioner set in one of the side windows was humming.

"How about *Valley of the Bat Boys*?"

"Goddamn it, Spenser, this isn't funny. You gotta have some kind of answer if someone asks you."

"The Balls of Summer?"

Erskine took a deep breath, let it out, shook his head, as if there were a horsefly on it, kicked the drawer shut, and stood up. "Never mind," he said. "Let's go."

As we went down the stairs, he handed me a press pass. "Keep it in your wallet," he said. "It'll let you in anywhere."

A blue-capped usher at Gate A said, "How's it going, Harold?" as we went past him. Vendors were starting to set up. A man in a green twill work uniform was unloading cases of beer onto a dolly. We went into the locker room.

My first reaction was disappointment. It looked like most other locker rooms. Open lockers with a shelf at the top, stools in front of them, nameplates above. To the right the training area with whirlpool, rubbing table, medical-looking cabinet with an assortment of tape and liniment behind the glass doors at the top. A man in a white T-shirt and white cotton pants was taping the left ankle of a burly black man who sat on the table in his shorts, smoking a cigar.

The players were dressing. One of them, a squat red-haired kid, was yelling to someone out of sight behind the lockers.

"Hey, Ray, can I be in the pen again today? There's a broad out there gives me a beaver shot every time we're home."

A voice from behind the lockers said, "Were you looking for her in Detroit last week when you dropped that foul?"

"Ah come on, Ray, Bill Dickey used to drop them once in a while. I seen you drop one once when I was a little kid and you was my idol."

A tall, lean man came around the lockers with his hands in his back pockets. He was maybe forty-five, with black hair cut short and parted on the left. There were no sideburns, and you knew he went to a barber who did most of his work with the electric clippers. His face was dark-tanned, and a sprinkle of gray showed in his hair. He wore no sweat shirt under his uniform blouse, and the veins were prominent in his arms. Erskine gestured him toward us. "Ray," he said, "I want you to meet Mr. Spenser. Spenser, Ray Farrell, the manager." We shook hands. "Spenser's a writer, doing a book on baseball, and I've arranged for him to be around the club for a while, interview some players, that sort of thing."

Farrell nodded. "What's the name of the book, Spenser?" he said.

"The Summer Season," I said. Erskine looked relieved.

"That's nice." Farrell turned toward the locker room. "Okay, listen up. This guy's name is Spenser. He's writing a book and he'll be around talking with you and probably taking some notes. I want everyone to cooperate." He turned back toward me. "Nice meeting you, Spenser. You want me to have someone introduce you around?"

"No, that's okay, I'll introduce myself as we go," I said.

"Okay, nice meeting you. Anything I can do, feel free." He walked away.

Erskine said, "Well, you're on your own now. Keep in touch," and left me.

The black man on the training table yelled over to the redhead, "Hey, Billy, you better start watching your mouth about beaver. This guy'll be writing you up in a book, and Sally will have your ass when she reads it." His voice was high and squeaky.

"Naw, she wouldn't believe it anyway." The redhead came over and put out his hand. "Billy Carter," he said. "I catch when Fats has got a hangover." He nodded at the black man who had climbed off the table and started toward us. He was short and very wide and the smooth tan coating of fat over his body didn't conceal the thick elastic muscles underneath.

I shook hands with Carter. "Collect all your bubblegum cards," I said. I turned toward the black man. "You're West, aren't you?"

He nodded. "You seen me play?" he said.

"No," I said, "I remember you from a Brut commercial."

He laughed, a high giggle. "Never without, man, put it on between innings." He did a small Flip Wilson impression and snapped his fingers.

From down the line of lockers a voice said, "Hey, Holly, everybody in the league says you smell like a fairy."

"Not to my face," West squeaked.

Most of the players were dressed and heading out to the field. A short, thin man in a pale blue seersucker suit and dark horn-rimmed glasses came into the locker room. He

185

spotted me and came over. "Spenser?" he said. I nodded. "Jack Little," he said. "I do PR for the Sox. Hal Erskine told me I'd find you here."

I said, "Glad to meet you."

He said, "Anything I can do to help, I'd be delighted. That's my job."

"Do you have biog sheets on the players?" I said.

"You bet. I've got a press book on every player. Stop by my office and I'll have my gal give you the whole packet."

"How old is your gal?" I said.

"Millie? Oh, Christ, I don't know. She's been with the club a long time. I don't ask a lady her age, Spenser. Get in trouble that way. Am I right?"

"Right," I said. "You're right."

"C'mon," he said, "I'll take you out to the dugout, point out some of the players, get you what you might call acclimated, okay?"

I nodded. "Acclimated," I said.

CHAPTER THREE

I SAT IN THE DUGOUT and watched the players take batting practice. Little sat beside me and chain-smoked Chesterfield Kings.

"That's Montoya," he said. "Alex Montoya was the player of the year at Pawtucket in 'sixty-eight. Hit two ninety-three last year, twenty-five homers."

I nodded. Marty Rabb was shagging in the outfield. Catching fly balls vest-pocket style like Willie Mays and lobbing the ball back to the infield underhanded.

"That's Johnny Tabor. He switch-hits. Look at the size

of him, huh? Doesn't look like he could get the bat around. Am I right or wrong?"

"Thin," I said. "Doesn't look like he could get the bat around."

"Well, you know. We pay him for his glove. Strong up the middle, that's what Ray's always said. And Tabor's got the leather. Right?"

"Right."

The crowd was beginning to fill the stands and the noise level rose. The Yankees came out and took infield in their gray road uniforms. Most of them were kids. Long hair under the caps, bubble gum. Much younger than I was. Whatever happened to Johnny Lindell?

Rabb came into the dugout, wearing his warm-up jacket.

"That's Marty Rabb, with the clipboard," Little said. "He pitched yesterday, so today he charts the pitches."

I nodded. "He's a great one," Little said. "Nicest kid you ever want to see. No temperament, you know, no ego. Loves the game. I mean a lot of these kids nowadays are in it for the big buck, you know, but not Marty. Nicest kid you ever want to meet. Loves the game."

A man with several chins came out of the alleyway to the clubhouse and stood on the top step of the dugout, looking over the diamond. His fading blond hair was long and very contemporary. It showed the touch of a ten-dollar barber. He was fat, with a sharp, beaked nose jutting from the red dumpling face. A red-checked shirt, the top two buttons open, hung over the mass of his stomach like the flag of his appetite. His slacks were textured navy blue with a wide flare, and he had on shiny white shoes with brass buckles on them.

"Who's that?" I asked Little.

"Don't you know him? Hell, that's Bucky Maynard. Only the best play by play in the business, that's all. Don't let him know you didn't recognize him. Man, he'll crucify you."

"I gather he doesn't work out a lot with the team," I said. Maynard took out a pale green cigar and lit it carefully, turning it as he puffed to get it burning evenly.

187

"Jesus, don't comment on his weight either," Little said. "He'll eat you alive."

"Is it okay if I clear my throat while he's in the park?"

"You can kid around, but if Bucky Maynard doesn't like you, you got a lot of trouble. I mean, he can destroy you on the air. And he will."

"I thought he worked for the club," I said.

"He does. But he's so popular that we couldn't get rid of him if we wanted. God knows there have been times." Little stopped. His eyes shifted up and down the dugout. I wondered if he was worried about a bug. "Don't get me wrong, now. Buck's a great guy; he's just got a lot of pride, and it don't help to get on the wrong side of him. Course it don't pay to get on the wrong side of anybody. Am I right or wrong?"

"Right as rain," I said. Little liked the phrase. I bet he'd use it within the day. I'm really into language.

Maynard came toward us, and Little stood up. "Hey, Buck, how's it going?"

Maynard looked at Little without speaking. Little swallowed and said, "Like to have you say hello to Mr. Spenser here, doing a book about the Sox."

Maynard nodded at me. "Spenser," he said. His southern accent stretched out the last syllable and dropped the r.

"Nice to meet you," I said. I hoped he wasn't offended.

"He'll be wanting to talk to you, Buck, I know. No book about the Sox would be worth much if Old Buck wasn't in it. Am I right, Spenser, or am I right?"

"Right," I said. Little lit a new Chesterfield King from the butt of the old one.

Maynard said, "Why don't y'all come on up the booth later on and watch some of the game? Get a chance to see how a broadcast team works."

"Thanks," I said, "I'd like to."

"Just remember you're not going to get any predigested Pablum up there. In mah booth by God we call the game the way it is played. No press release bullshit; if a guy's doggin' it, by God we say he's doggin' it. You follow?"

"I can follow that okay."

Maynard's eyes narrowed as he looked at me. They were pale and small and flat, like two Necco wafers. "You better believe it 'cause anyone who knows me knows it's true. Isn't that right, Jack?"

Little answered before Maynard finished asking. "Absolutely, Buck, anybody knows that. Bucky tells it like it is, Spenser. That's why the fans love him."

"C'mon up, Spenser, anytime. Jack'll show you the way." Maynard rolled the green cigar about in the center of his mouth, winked, and moved out onto the field toward the Yankee dugout.

Billy Carter from the end of the dugout yelled, "Whale, ho," and then stared out toward the right-field stands as Maynard whirled and looked into the dugout. Ray Farrell had come out of the dressing room and was posting the lineup at the far end of the dugout. He ignored Carter and Maynard. Maynard looked for maybe a minute into the dugout while Carter observed the right-field foul line from under the brim of his cap, his feet cocked up against one of the dugout supports. He was whistling "Turkey in the Straw." Maynard turned and continued toward the Yankee dugout.

Little blew out his breath. "That goddamned Carter is going to get in real trouble someday. Always the wisecracks. Always the goddamned hot dog. He ain't that good. I mean, he catches maybe thirty games a year. You'd think he'd be a little humble, but always the big mouth." Little spilled some ashes onto his shirtfront and brushed them off vigorously.

"I was thinking about some Moby Dick humor myself when Maynard was standing there blotting out the sun."

"You screw around with Bucky and you'll never get your book written, I'll tell you that straight out, Spenser. That's no shit." Little looked as if he was in pain, his small-featured face contorted with sincerity. Farrell went up the steps of the dugout and out toward home plate with his lineup card. The Yankee manager came out toward home plate from the other side, and, for the first time, I saw the umpires. Older than the players, and bulkier.

"I think I'll go up in the broadcast booth," I said. "If

Maynard turns on me and truths me to death, I want you to write my mom."

Little didn't even want to talk about it. He brought me up to the press entry, along the catwalk, under the roof toward Maynardville.

The broadcast booth was a warren of cable lash-up, television monitors, microphone cords, and one big color TV camera set up to point at a blank wall to the rear of the booth. For live commercials, I assumed. Give Bucky Maynard a chance to tell it like it is about somebody's bottled beer. There were two men in the booth already. One I recognized. Doc Wilson, who used to play first base for the Minnesota Twins and now did color commentary for the Sox games. He was a tall, angular man, with rimless glasses and short, wavy brown hair. He was sitting at the broadcast table, running through the stat book and drinking black coffee from a paper cup. The other man was young, maybe twenty-two, middle height and willowy with Dutch boy blond hair and an Oakland A's mustache. He had on a white safari hat with a wide leopard-skin band, pilot's sunglasses, a white silk shirt open to the waist, like Herb Jeffries, and white jeans tucked into the top of rust-colored Frye boots. There was a brass-studded rust-colored woven leather belt around his waist and a copper bracelet on his right wrist. He was slouched in a red canvas director's chair with his feet up on the broadcast counter, reading a copy of the *National Star* and chewing gum.

Wilson looked up as we came in. "Hey, Jack, howsa kid?"

"Doc, say hello to Spenser, here. He's a writer, doing a book on the Sox, and Bucky invited him up to the booth for a look-see."

Wilson reached around, and we shook hands. "Good deal," he said. "If Buck says go, it's go. Anything I can help with, just give a holler." The kid in the safari hat never looked up. He licked his thumb, turned a page of the *Star,* his jaws working smoothly, the muscles at the hinge swelling regularly as he chewed.

Little said, "This here's Lester Floyd. Lester, this is Mr. Spenser."

Lester gave a single upward jerk of his head, raised one finger without releasing the magazine, and kept reading. I said, "What's he do, sing 'Flamingo' at the station breaks?"

The kid looked up then. I couldn't see his eyes behind the amber lenses of his aviator shades. He blew a large pink bubble, popped it with his teeth, and slowly chewed it back into his mouth.

Little said, "Lester is Bucky's driver, Spenser. Spenser's going to be doing a book on the Sox and on Bucky, Lester."

Lester blew another big bubble and chewed it back in. "He's gonna be looking up his own asshole if he gets smart with me," he said. There was a red flush on his cheekbones.

"Guess he doesn't sing 'Flamingo,'" I said to Wilson.

"Aw now, Lester, Mr. Spenser's just kidding around." Little did a small nervous shuffle step. Wilson was staring out at the diamond. Lester was working harder on the gum.

"And I'm telling him not to," Lester said.

"Never mind, Lester." The voice came from behind me. It was Maynard. "Ah invited Mr. Spenser up here to listen to mah broadcast. He's mah guest."

"He said something smart about me singing, Bucky. I don't like that sorta talk."

"Ah know, Lester, ah don't blame you. Mr. Spenser, Ah'd appreciate it if you was to apologize to Lester here. He's a good boy, but he's very emotional. He's also got a black belt in tae kwon do. And ah wouldn't want to get your writing hand all messed up before you even start."

Waltzing with Lester in the broadcast booth wasn't going to tell me anything about Marty Rabb. If he was any good, it might tell me something about me, but that wasn't what I was getting paid for. Besides, I knew about me. And if I was a writer, I wasn't supposed to be roughing it up with black belts. Maybe box with José Torres on a talk show, but brawling at a ball game . . . ? "I'm sorry, Lester," I said. "Sometimes I try too hard to be funny."

Lester popped his gum at me again and went back to the *National Star.* Maynard smiled with his mouth only and moved to a big upholstered swivel chair at the broadcast table. He sat down, put on big padded earphones, and spoke into the mike. The small monitor built into the table to his right had flickered into life and displayed a picture of the batter's box below. There was a long mimeographed list in front of him on a clipboard, and he checked off the first two items as he spoke.

"Burt, ah want to open on Stabile warming up. Doc and me will do some business about the knuckler and how it flutters. Right? . . . Yup, soon's you run the opening cartridge."

Wilson looked over and said to me, "He's talking to the people outside in the truck." I nodded. Lester licked his thumb again and turned another page.

Little leaned over and whispered to me. "Gotta run, anything you need just let me know." I nodded again, and Little tiptoed out like a man leaving church early.

Maynard said to the people in the truck, "Ah got nothing to do live up here, right? . . . well, ah don't see nothing on the sheet . . . no, goddamn it, ah taped that yesterday afternoon . . . okay, well get it straight, boy."

A cartoon picture of a slightly loutish-looking baseball player in a Red Sox uniform appeared on the monitor. Maynard said, "Twenty seconds," to Wilson. Below and to our right along the first-base line a portly right-handed pitcher named Rick Stabile was warming up. He threw without effort, lobbing the ball toward the catcher.

Wilson said into his mike, "Good afternoon, everyone, from Fenway Park in Boston, where today the Red Sox go against the Yankees in the rubber game of a three-game series. This is Doc Wilson along with Bucky Maynard standing by to bring you all the action."

A beer commercial appeared on the monitor screen, and Wilson leaned back. "You gonna pick it up on Stabile, Buck?"

Maynard said, "Check." Wilson handed him the stat

sheet and leaned forward as the beer company logo filled the monitor screen. Lester was finished with the tabloid and settled down into his chair and apparently went to sleep. He looked like a peaceful serpent. Tae kwon do? Never tried somebody that did that. I gave him a hard look. He was motionless; the breath from his nostrils ruffled his mustache gently. He was probably paralyzed with fear. Maynard said, "Howdy, all you Red Soxers, this is the old Buckaroo and you're looking at Rick Stabile's butterfly . . ."

By the sixth inning the game was gone for Boston. Stabile's knuckler had apparently deked when it should have dived, and the Yankees led 11 to 1. I made two trips, one for beer and hot dogs and one for peanuts. Lester slept, and Maynard and Wilson tried to talk some excitement into a laugher.

"Stabile's got to get some of the lard off from around his middle, Doc."

"Well, he's a fine boy, Bucky, but he's been playing a little heavy this year."

"Tell it like it is, Doc. He came into spring training hog fat and he hasn't lost it. He's got the tools, but he's gotta learn to back off from the table or he'll eat himself right out of the league." Maynard checked off an item on his log sheet.

"Here's Graig Nettles, two for two today, including the downtowner in the first with Gotham on all the corners."

I got up and headed out of the booth. Wilson winked at me as I left.

I stopped by at Little's office to pick up the press kit on Marty Rabb and four others. Little's gal had dentures.

CHAPTER FOUR

STEAM FROM THE SHOWERS drifted into the locker room and made the air moist. The final score was 14 to 3 and no one was pouring champagne on anyone. I sat down beside Marty Rabb. He was bent over, unlacing his spikes. When he straightened, I said, "My name's Spenser, I'm writing a book about the Sox, and I guess I oughta start with you."

Rabb smiled and put out his hand. "Hi, glad to help. How about you don't mention today, though, huh?" He shook his head. He was well above my six feet one—all flat planes and sharp angles. His short brown hair grew down over his forehead in a wedge. His head was square and long, like a square-bladed garden spade. His cheekbones were high and prominent, making the cheeks slightly hollow beneath them.

I said, "Bucky Maynard tells me Stabile's too fat and that's why he's having trouble."

"You ever see Lolich or Wilbur Wood?" Rabb said.

"Yeah," I said. "I've seen Maynard too."

Rabb smiled. "Ricky doesn't pitch with his stomach. The ball wasn't moving for him today, that's all."

"It was moving for you yesterday."

"Yeah, I had it grooved yesterday." Rabb undressed as he talked. He was long-muscled and bony, his body pale in contrast to the dark tan on his face, neck, and arms.

"Well," I said, "I'm really more interested in the human side of the game, Marty. Could we get together tonight and talk a little?"

Rabb was naked now, standing with a towel over his

shoulder. In fact, most of the people in the dressing room were naked. I felt like a streaker in a nudist colony.

"Yeah, sure. Ah, lemme see, no, we're not doing anything tonight that I know of. Why don't you come over to the apartment, meet my wife, maybe have a drink? That okay with you?"

"Fine, what time?"

"Well, the kid goes to bed about seven—about seven thirty. Wanna do that?"

"Yes. Where?"

"Church Park. You know where that is?"

"Yeah."

"Apartment six twelve."

I looked at my watch: 4:35. "That's fine. I'll be there. Thanks very much."

"See you." Rabb headed for the showers. His body high and narrow, the left trapezius muscle overdeveloped, swelling out along the left side of his spine.

I left. Outside the dressing room there were two people sweeping. Other than that the place was empty. I walked up the ramp under the stands and looked out at the field. It was empty. I went down and hopped the railing of the box seats. There was no sound. I walked over to home plate. The wall in left seemed an arm's length away and 300 cubits high. The sun was still bright and at that time of day slanted in over the third-base stands, and the shadows of the light towers looked like giant renderings by Dali. A pigeon flew down from the center-field bleachers and pecked at the warning track. I walked out to the pitcher's mound and stood with my right foot on the rubber, looking down into home plate. Traffic sounds drifted in from the city, but muffled. I put my right hand behind me and let it rest against my butt. Left hand relaxed on my left thigh. I squinted in toward the plate. Last of the ninth, two out, three on, Spenser checks the sign. One of the men who'd been sweeping came out of the passageway and yelled, "Hey, what the hell are you doing out there?"

"Striking out Tommy Henrich, you dumb bastard. Don't you know anything?"

"You ain't supposed to be out there."

"I know," I said. "I never was."

I walked back in through the stands and on out of the ball park. I looked at my watch. It was nearly five. I walked back down the Commonwealth Avenue mall to Massachusetts Avenue. If Commonwealth Ave is yin, then Mass Ave is yang. Steak houses that no one you knew had gone to, office buildings with dirty windows, fast food, a palm reader, a massage parlor. I crossed Mass Ave and went into the Yorktown Tavern. It had plate glass windows and brown linoleum, a high tin ceiling painted white, booths along the left, a bar along the right. In the back corner was a color TV carrying a bowling game called *Duckpins for Dollars*. No one was watching. All the barstools were taken, and most of the booths. No one was wearing a tie. No one was drinking a Harvey Wallbanger. The house special was a shot and a beer.

In the last booth on the left, alone, was a guy named Seltzer who always reminded me of a seal. He was sleek and plumpish, thin through the chest, thicker through the hips. His hair was shiny black, parted in the middle and slicked tight against his head. He had a thin mustache, a pointed nose, and a dark pinstriped suit that cost at least $300. His white shirt gleamed in contrast to the darkness of the suit and the dinginess of the bar. He was reading the *Herald American*. As I slid in opposite him, he turned the page and folded it neatly back. I could see the big diamond ring on his little finger and the diamond chips set in the massive silver cuff links. He smelled of cologne, and when he looked up at me and smiled, his white teeth were even, cap perfect in his small mouth.

I said, "Evening, Lennie."

He said, "You know, Spenser, little things break your balls. You ever notice that? I mean I used to read the *Record American,* right? Nice little tabloid size, easy to handle. Then they buy up the *Herald* and go the big format and it's like reading a freakin' road map. Now that busts my nuts, trying to fold this thing right. That kinda stuff bother you ever?"

"On slow days," I said.

"Want a drink?"

"Yeah, I'll have a brandy Alexander," I said.

Seltzer laughed. "Hey, Frank." He raised a finger at the bartender. "A shot and a beer, okay?"

The bartender brought them over, put the beer on a little paper coaster, and went back behind the bar. I drank the shot.

"Well," I said, "if I had worms, I guess they're taken care of."

"Yeah, Frank don't age that stuff all that long, does he?"

I sipped the beer. It was better than the whiskey. "Lennie, I need to know something without letting it get around that I'm asking." His skin was remarkable. Smooth and pale and unlined. The sun had rarely shone upon it. It made him look a lot younger than I knew he was.

"Yeah," he said. "Sure, kid. I never saw any advantage talking about things for no good reason. What do you want to know?" He sipped some beer, holding the glass in the tips of his fingers with the little finger sticking out. When he put the glass down, he took the handkerchief from his breast pocket and wiped his mouth carefully.

"I want to know if you've heard anything about Marty Rabb."

Seltzer was very careful putting the handkerchief back in his pocket. He got the three points arranged and stood half up in the booth to look across the bar into the mirror and make sure they were right.

"Like what?" he said.

"Like anything at all."

"You mean, does he occasionally place a wager? That kind of thing?"

"That, or anything else."

"Well, he never placed a bet with me," Seltzer said, "but I heard something peculiar about him. The odds seem to shift a little when he pitches. I mean, there's some funny money placed when he's scheduled to go. Nothing big, nothing

I'd even think about if somebody like you didn't come around and ask about him."

"You think he's in the satchel?"

"Rabb? Hell, no, Spenser. Nothing that strong. There's just a whisper, just a ruffle, that not everything is entirely jake. I wouldn't hesitate taking money when Rabb's pitching. I don't know anyone that would. It's just . . ." He shrugged and spread his hands out palms up. "Want another drink?"

I shook my head. "The last one took the enamel off my front teeth," I said.

"Aw, Spenser." Seltzer shook his head. "You're going soft. I remember twenty years ago you was fighting prelims in the Arena, you thought that stuff was imported from France."

"In those days I don't remember you dressing like George Brent either," I said.

Seltzer nodded. "Yeah," he said, "things change. Now instead of a newspaper, they give you a freaking road map. You know?"

I left him refolding his paper and went to get something to eat. The bar whiskey was thrashing about in my stomach, and I thought maybe I could smother it with something.

CHAPTER FIVE

I HAD TWO CHEESEBURGERS and a chocolate shake at an antique brick McDonald's on Huntington, just down from Symphony Hall. The food throttled the whiskey okay, but I was furtive coming out. If anyone saw me, I could never eat at Locke-Ober's again. The guilty part was I liked the cheeseburgers.

It was a little after six and I had some time to kill.

There seemed to be more of it and harder to kill as I got older. I strolled back down Mass Ave toward the river. The college kids were out on the esplanade in large numbers, and the air was colorful with Frisbees and sweet with the smell of grass. I sat on a bench near the Mass Ave Bridge and looked at the river and watched a boy and girl share a bottle of Ripple. Sailboats veered and drifted on the river, and an occasional powerboat left a rolling wake upstream. Across the river MIT loomed like a concrete temple to the Great God Brown. A six-foot black girl with red hot pants and platform sandals went by with a Lhasa apso on a short leash. I watched her out of sight around the bend westbound.

At seven fifteen I strolled back up Mass Ave toward Church Park. Church Park is a large, gray, cement urban development associated with the Christian Science church complex across the street. It replaced a large number of shabby brick buildings with a very long twelve-story cement one that had stores on the bottom floor and apartments above. The doorman made me wait while he called up.

When I came out of the elevator, Marty Rabb was at his door, looking down the corridor at me. There was something surrealistic about the way his head appeared to violate the fearful symmetry of the hall.

"Down this way, Spenser," he said. "Glad to see you."

The front door opened into the living room. To the right a bedroom, straight ahead a small kitchen. To the left the living room opened out toward the street and looked out at the dome of the Mother Church of Christ Scientist across the street. Traffic sound drifted up through the open windows. The living room was done in wall-to-wall beige carpet; the walls were eggshell white. There were framed mementos of Rabb's career scattered on the walls. The furniture was in browns and beiges, and the tone was modern. On the glass-topped coffee table near the couch were a tray of raw vegetables and a bowl of sour cream dip.

"Honey, this is Mr. Spenser that's writing the book," Rabb said. "Spenser, this is my wife, Linda."

We shook hands. She was small and black-haired. Her

199

features were small and close together, and her eyes domi-
nated her face. They were very round and dark, with long
lashes. Her black hair was long down her back and pulled
back at the nape of her neck with a dark wooden clip. She had
on a salmon pink sleeveless shell and white jeans. Her
makeup was so understated that at first I thought she wore
none.

"Nice to meet you, Mr. Spenser. Why don't you have a
seat here on the couch? It's closest to the dip." She smiled,
and her teeth were small and rather sharp.

I said, "Thank you."

"Would you like a hard drink, Mr. Spenser, or beer?"
Rabb said. "I got some nice ale from Canada, Labatt Fifty,
you ever try it?"

"Tried and approved," I said. "I'll take the ale."

"Honey?"

"You know what I'd love, that we haven't had in a
while, a Margarita. Have we got the stuff to make a Margarita, Marty?"

"Yeah, sure. We got about everything."

"Okay, and put a lot of salt on the rim," she said.

She sat on one of the big armchairs opposite the couch,
kicked her sandals off, and tucked her feet up under her. "Tell
me about this book you're writing, Mr. Spenser."

"Well, Mrs. Rabb—"

"Linda."

"Okay, Linda. I suppose you'd say it's along the lines of
several others, looking at baseball as the institutionalized expression of human personality." She nodded and I wondered
why. I didn't know what the hell I'd just said.

"Isn't that interesting," she said.

"I like to see sports as a kind of metaphor for human
life, contained by rules, patterned by tradition." I was hot
now, and rolling. Rabb came back with the Margarita in a
lowball glass and the ale in Tiffany-designed goblets that said
COCA-COLA. I thought Linda Rabb looked relieved. Maybe I
wouldn't switch to the talk show circuit yet. Rabb passed out
the drinks.

200

"What's patterned by tradition, Mr. Spenser?" he said.

"Sports. It's a way of imposing order on disorder."

Rabb nodded. "Yeah, right, that's certainly true," he said. He didn't know what the hell I had just said either. He drank some of the ale and put some dry-roasted cashews in his mouth, holding a handful and popping them in serially.

"But I'm here to talk about you, Marty, and Linda too. What is your feeling about the game?"

Rabb said, "I love it," at the same time that Linda said, "Marty loves it." They laughed.

"I'd play it for nothing," Rabb said. "Since I could walk, I been playing, and I want to do it all my life."

"Why?" I said.

"I don't know," Rabb said. "I never gave it any thought. When I was about five my father bought me a Frankie Gustine autograph glove. I can still remember it. It was too big for me and he had to buy me one of those little cheap ones made in Taiwan, you know, with a couple of little laces for webbing? And I used to oil that damn Frankie Gustine glove and bang my fist in the pocket and rub some more oil until I was about ten and I was big enough to play with it. I still got it somewhere."

"Play other sports?" I didn't know where I was going, but I was used to that.

"Oh yeah, matter of fact, I went to college on a basketball scholarship. Got drafted by the Lakers in the fifth round, but I never thought about doing anything else but baseball when I got out."

"Did you meet Linda in college?"

"No."

"How about you, Linda, how do you feel about baseball?"

"I never cared about it till I met Marty. I don't like the traveling part of it. Marty's away about eighty games a season. But other than that I think it's fine. Marty loves it. It makes him happy."

"Where'd you two meet?" I asked.

"It's there in the biog sheet, isn't it?" Rabb said.

"Yeah, I suppose so. But we both know about PR material."

Rabb said, "Yeah."

"Well, let's do this. Let's run through the press kit and maybe elaborate a little." Linda Rabb nodded.

Rabb said, "It's all in there."

"You were born in Lafayette, Indiana, in nineteen forty-four." Rabb nodded. "Went to Marquette, graduated nineteen sixty-five. Signed with the Sox that year, pitched a year in Charleston and a year at Pawtucket. Came up in nineteen sixty-eight. Been here ever since."

Rabb said, "That's about it."

I said, "Where'd you meet Linda?"

"Chicago," Rabb said. "At a White Sox game. She asked for my autograph, and I said, yeah, but she had to go out with me. She did. And bingo."

I look at my biog sheet. "That would have been in nineteen seventy?"

"Right." My glass was empty, and Rabb got up to refill it. I noticed his was less than half gone.

"We were married about six months later in Chicago." Linda Rabb smiled. "In the off-season."

"Best thing I ever did," Rabb said, and gave me a new bottle of ale. I poured it into the glass, ate some peanuts, and drank some ale.

"You from Chicago, Linda?"

"No, Arlington Heights, a little bit away from Chicago."

"What was your maiden name?"

Rabb said, "Oh for crissake, Spenser, why do you want to know that?"

"I don't know," I said. "You ever see one of those machines that grades apples, or oranges, or eggs, that sort of thing, by size? They dump all sizes in the hopper and the machine lets the various sizes drop into the right holes as it works down. That's how I am. I just ask questions and let it all go into the hopper and then sort it out later."

"Well, you're not sorting eggs now, for crissake."

"Oh, Marty, let him do his job. My maiden name was Hawkins, Mr. Spenser."

"Okay, Marty, let's go back to why you love baseball," I said. "I mean, think about it a little. Isn't it a game for kids? I mean, who finally cares whether a team beats another team?" It sounded like the kind of thing a writer would ask, and I wanted to get them talking. Much of what I do depends on knowing who I'm doing it with.

"Oh, Christ, I don't know, Spenser. I mean, what isn't a game for kids, you know? How about writing stories, is that something for grown-ups? It's something to do. I'm good at it, I like it, and I know the rules. You're one of twenty-five guys all working for something bigger than they are, and at the end of the year you know whether or not you got it. If you didn't get it, then you can start over next year. If you did, then you got a chance to do it again. Some old-timey ballplayer said something about you have to have a lot of little boy in you to play this game, but you gotta be a man too."

"Roy Campanella," I said.

"Yeah, right, Campanella. Anyway, it's a nice clean kind of work. You're important to a lot of kids. You got a chance to influence kids' lives maybe, by being an example to them. It's a lot better than selling cigarettes or making napalm. It's what I do, you know?"

"What about when you get too old?"

"Maybe I can coach. I'd be a good pitching coach. Maybe manage. Maybe do color. I'll stay around the game one way or another."

"What if you can't?"

"I'll still have Linda and the boy."

"And when the boy grows up?"

"I'll still have Linda."

I was getting caught up in the part. I'd started to lose track. I was interested. Maybe some of the questions were about me.

"Maybe I better finish up my Labatt Fifty and go home," I said. "I've taken enough of your time."

Linda Rabb said, "Oh no, don't go yet. Marty, get him another beer. We were just getting started."

I shook my head, drained my glass, and stood up. "No, thank you very much, Linda. We'll talk again."

"Marty, make him stay."

"Linda, for crissake, if he wants to go, let him go. She does this every time we have company, Spenser."

They both walked with me to the door. I left them standing together. He towered over her in the doorway. His right arm was around her shoulder, and she rested her left hand on it. I took a cab home and went to bed. I was working my way through Samuel Eliot Morison's *The Oxford History of the American People,* and I spent two hours on it before I went to sleep.

CHAPTER SIX

IT WAS DEAD quiet in my bedroom when I woke up in the morning. The sun vibrated in the room and the hum of my air conditioner underlined the silence. I lay on my back with my hands behind my head for a while and thought about what was bothering me about Linda Rabb.

What was bothering me was that she'd said she knew nothing about baseball till she met Marty but that she'd met Marty at a ball game when she'd asked for his autograph. The two didn't go together. Nothing much, but it didn't fit. It was the only thing that didn't. The rest was whole cloth. Middle American jock-ethic-kid and his loving wife. In the off-season I bet he hunted and fished and took his little boy sliding. Would he be going into the tank? "It's what I do," he'd said. "I know the rules." I could understand that. I knew about the need for rules. I didn't believe he'd dump one. I never believed Nixon would be President either. I got up, did 100 push-ups, 100 sit-ups, took a shower, got dressed, and made the bed.

There's a restaurant in Portsmouth, New Hampshire, which makes whipped cream biscuits, and I got the recipe once while I was up there having dinner with Brenda Loring. I made some while the coffee perked, and while they baked I squeezed a pint of orange juice and drank it. I had the biscuits with fresh strawberries and sour cream and three cups of coffee.

It was nearly ten o'clock when I got out onto the street. There was a bright smell of summer outside my apartment house. Across Arlington Street the Public Garden was a sunny pleasure. I strolled on past the enormous Thomas Ball statue of Washington on horseback. The flower beds were rich with petunias and redolent of pansies against a flourish of scarlet snapdragons. The swan boats had begun to cruise the pond, pedaled by college kids in yachting caps and trailed by an orderly assemblage of hungry ducks that broke formation to dart at the peanuts the tourists threw. I crossed the bridge over the swan boat lake and headed toward the Common on the other side of Charles Street. At the crossing there was a guy selling popcorn from a pushcart and another selling ice cream and another selling balloons and little monkeys dangling from thin sticks and blue pennants that said BOSTON, MASS., in yellow script. I turned right, walked up Charles toward Boylston. At the corner was the old guy that takes candids with a big tripod camera; faded tan samples were displayed in a case on the tripod. I turned up Boylston toward Tremont and down Tremont toward Stuart. My office was on Stuart Street. It wasn't much of an office, but it suited the location. It would have been an ideal spot for a VD clinic or a public exterminator.

I opened the window as soon as I got in. I'd have to remember not to do push-ups on the days I had to open that window. I hung up my blue blazer, sat down at my desk, got my yellow pad out, and pulled the phone over. By one thirty I had pretty well confirmed Marty Rabb's biography as stated.

The town clerk's office in Lafayette, Indiana, established that Marty Rabb had in fact lived there and that his parents still did. The office of the registrar at Marquette confirmed his attendance and graduation in 1965. I called a cop I knew in Providence and asked him if they had anything on Rabb when he was at Pawtucket. He called me back in forty minutes to say no. He promised me he'd keep his mouth shut about my question, and I half thought he would. He was as trustworthy as I was likely to find.

Linda Rabb was more of a problem. There was no record of her marriage to Rabb at the Chicago Hall of Records. As far as they knew, Marty Rabb hadn't married Linda Hawkins or anyone else in Chicago in 1970 or any other time. Maybe they got married by some JP in a suburb. I called Arlington Heights and talked with the city clerk himself. No record. How about any record of Linda Hawkins or Linda Rabb? None, no birth certificate, no marriage license. If I'd wait a minute, he'd check motor vehicles. I waited. It was more like ten minutes. The air blowing in from Stuart Street was hot and gritty. The sweat had soaked through my polo shirt and made it stick to my back. I looked at my watch: 3:15. I hadn't had lunch yet. I sniffed at the hot breeze. If the wind was right, I could catch the scent of sauerbraten wafting across the street from Jake Wirth's. It wasn't right. All I could smell was the uncontrolled emission of the traffic.

The Arlington Heights city clerk came back on the phone.

"Still there?"

"Yep."

"Got no record of a driver's license. No auto registration. There's four Hawkinses in the city directory but no Linda. Want the phone numbers?"

"Yes, and can you give me the number of the school administration department?"

"Yeah, one minute, I'll check it here."

He did and gave it to me. I called them. They had no record of Linda Rabb or Linda Hawkins. There had been eight children named Hawkins in the school system since 1960. Six were boys. The other two were named Doris and Olive.

I hung up. Very cooperative.

I called the first Hawkins number in Arlington Heights. No soap. Nor was there any soap at the next two. The fourth number didn't answer. But unless they were the ones when I finally got them, I was going to have to wonder about old Linda. I looked at my watch: 4:30. Three thirty in Illinois. I hadn't eaten since breakfast. I went over to Jake Wirth's, had some sauerbraten and dark beer, came back to the office at five forty-five, and called the fourth Hawkins again. A woman answered who had never heard of Linda Hawkins.

I swung my chair around and propped my feet on the windowsill and looked out at the top floor of the garment loft across the street. It was empty. Everyone had gone home. There are a lot of reasons why someone doesn't check out right off quick when you begin to look into her background. But most of them have to do with deceit, and most deceit is based on having something to hide. Two pigeons settled down onto the window ledge of the loft and looked at me looking at them. I looked at my watch: 6:10. After supper on a summer evening. Twilight softball leagues were getting under way at this hour. Kids were going out to hang out on the corner till dark. Men were watering their lawns, their wives sitting nearby in lawn chairs. I was looking at two pigeons.

Linda Rabb was not what she was supposed to be, and that bothered me, like it bothered me that she met Rabb at a ball game even though she wasn't interested in baseball till she married him. Little things, but they weren't right. The pigeons flew off. The traffic sounds were dwindling. I'd have to find out about Linda Rabb. The Sox had a night game tonight, which meant Rabb wouldn't be home. But Linda Rabb probably would be because of the kid. I called. She was.

"I wonder if I could drop by just for a minute," I said. "Just want to get the wife's angle on things. You know, what it's like to be home while the game's on, that sort of thing."

207

What a writer I'd make, get the wife's angle. Slick. Probably should have said "little woman's angle."

"That's okay, Mr. Spenser, I'm just giving the baby his bath. If you drop around in an hour or so, I'll be watching the game on television, but we can talk."

I thanked her and hung up. I looked at the window ledge on the garment loft some more. My office door opened behind me. I swiveled the chair around. A short fat man in a Hawaiian shirt and a panama hat came in and left the door open behind him. The shirt hung outside his maroon double knit pants. He wore wraparound black-rimmed sunglasses and smoked a cigar. He looked around my office without saying anything. I put my feet up on my desk and looked at him. He stepped aside, and another man came in and sat down in front of my desk. He was wearing a tan suit, dark brown shirt, and a wide red-striped tie in browns, whites, and yellows. His tan loafers were gleaming; his hands were manicured; his face was tanned. His hair was bright gray and expensively barbered, curling over his collar in the back, falling in a single ringlet over his forehead. Despite the gray hair, his face was young and unlined. I knew him. His name was Frank Doerr.

"I'd like to talk with you, Spenser."

"Oh golly," I said, "you heard about my whipped cream biscuits and you were hoping I'd give you the recipe."

The fat guy in the panama hat had closed the door behind Doerr and was leaning against it with his arms folded. Akim Tamiroff.

Doerr said, "You know who I am, Spenser?"

"Aren't you Julia Child?" I said.

"My name's Doerr. I want to know what business you're doing with the Red Sox."

A master of disguise, the man of 1,000 faces. "Red Sox?" I said.

"Red Sox," he said.

"Jesus, I didn't think the word would get out that quickly. How'd you find out?"

"Never mind how I found out, I want answers."

"Sure, sure thing, Mr. Doerr. You any relation to Bobby?"

"Don't irritate me, Spenser. I am used to getting answers."

"Yeah, well, I didn't know you had anything against Bobby Doerr, I thought he was a hell of a second baseman."

Doerr said, "Wally," without looking around, and the fat man at the door brought a gun out from under his flowered shirt. "Now knock off the bullshit, Spenser. I haven't got a lot of time to spend in this roach hole."

I thought "roach hole" was a little unkind, but I thought the gun in Wally's hand was a little unkind too. "Okay," I said, "no need to get sore. I was a regional winner in the Leon Culberson look-alike contest, and the Sox wanted to talk to me about being a designated hitter."

Doerr and Wally looked at me. The silence got to be quite long. "You don't think I look like Leon Culberson?" I said.

Doerr leaned forward. "I asked around a little about you, Spenser. I heard you think you're a riot. I think you're a roach in a roach hole. I think you're a thirty-five-cent piece of hamburg, and I think you need to learn some manners."

The building was quiet; the traffic sounds were less frequent through the open window. Wally's gun pointed at me without moving. Wally sucked on one of his canine teeth. My stomach hurt a little.

Doerr went on. "You are hanging around Fenway Park, hanging around the broadcast booth, talking with people, pretending you're a writer, and not telling anyone at all that you're only a goddamned egg-sucking snoop, a nickel-and-dime cheapie. I want to know why, and I want to know right now or Wally will make you wish you'd never been born."

I took my feet off the desk, slowly, and put them on the floor. I put my hands, slowly, on the desk and stood up. When I was on my feet, I said, "Frank, baby, you're a gambling man, and I'll make a bet with you. In fact, I'll make two. First one is that you won't shoot because you want to know what's happening and what I'm into and it's lousy percentage to shoot a guy without being sure why. Second bet is that if your pet pork chop tries to hassle me, I can take away his piece and clean his teeth with it. Even money."

As far as Wally showed anything, I might have been talking about Sam Yorty or the Aga Khan. He didn't move. Neither did the gun. Doerr's sun-lamp face seemed to have gotten whiter. The lines from his nostrils to the corners of his mouth had gotten deeper, and his right eyelid tremored. My stomachache continued.

Another silence. If I weren't so tough, I would have thought maybe I was scared. Wally's gun was a Walther P.38. Nine-millimeter. Seven shots in the clip. Nice gun, the grip on a Walther was very comfortable, and the balance was good. Wally seemed happy with his. Below on Stuart Street somebody with a trick horn blew shave-and-a-haircut-two-bits. And some brakes squealed.

Doerr got up suddenly, turned on his heels, and walked out. Wally put the gun away, followed him out, and closed the door. I breathed in most of the air in the office through my nose and let it out again very slowly. My fingertips tingled. I sat down again, opened the bottom desk drawer, took out a bottle of bourbon, and drank from the neck. I coughed. I'd have to stop buying the house brand at Vito's Superette.

I looked around at the empty office. Green file cabinet, three Vermeer prints that Susan Silverman had given me for Christmas, the chair that Doerr had sat in. Didn't look so goddamned roachie to me.

CHAPTER SEVEN

I TOOK A POLAROID camera with me when I visited Linda Rabb.

"I want to think about graphics, maybe a coffee table book," I told her. "Maybe a big format."

She was in blue jeans, barefoot, a ribbon in her hair, her makeup fresh. On a twenty-five-inch color console in the living room, Buck Maynard was calling the play by play. "Ah want to tell ya, Holly West could throw a lamb chop past a wolf pack, Doc. He gunned Amos Otis down by twenty feet."

"Great arm, Buck," Wilson said, "a real cannon back there."

I snapped some pictures of Linda and the living room from different angles.

"Do you get nervous watching Marty pitch, Linda?" I lay on the floor to get an exotic angle, shooting up through the glass top of the coffee table.

"No, not so much anymore. He's so good, you know— it's more, I'm surprised when he loses. But I don't worry."

"Does he bring it home or leave it at the park?"

"When he loses? He leaves it there. Unless you've been watching the game, you don't know if he won or lost when he comes in the door. He doesn't talk about it at all. Little Marty barely knows what his father does."

I placed the five color shots on the coffee table in front of Linda Rabb.

"Which one do you like best?" I said. "They're only idea shots; if the publishers decide to go to the big picture format, we'll use a pro." I sounded like Arthur Author—it pays to listen to the Carson show.

She picked up the last one on the left and held it at an angle to the light.

"This is an interesting shot," she said. It was the one I'd taken from floor level. It was interesting. Casey Crime Photographer.

"Yeah, that's good," I said. "I like that one too." I took it from her and put it in an envelope. "How about the others?"

She looked at several more. "They're okay, but the one I gave you first is my favorite."

"Okay," I said. "We agree." I scooped the other four into a second envelope.

Bucky Maynard said, "We got us a real barn burner here, Doc. Both pitchers are hummin' it in there pretty good."

"You're absolutely right, Bucky. A couple of real fine arms out there tonight."

I stood up. "Thank you, Linda. I'm sorry to have barged in on you like this."

"That's okay. I enjoyed it. The only thing is, I don't know about pictures of me, or of the baby. Marty doesn't like to have his family brought into things. I mean, we're very private people. Marty may not want you to do pictures."

"I can understand that, Linda. Don't worry. There are lots of people on the team, and if we decide to go to visuals, we can use some of them if Marty objects."

She shook my hand at the door. It was a bony hand and cold.

Outside, it was dark now, and the traffic was infrequent. I walked up Mass Ave toward the river, crossing before I got to Boylston Street to look at the Spanish melons in the window of a gourmet food shop. Mingled with the smell of automobiles and commerce were the thin, damp smell of the river and the memory of trees and soil that the city supplanted. At Marlborough I turned right and strolled down toward my apartment. The small trees and the flowering shrubs in front of the brick and brownstone buildings enhanced the river smell.

It was nine fifteen when I got in my apartment. I called the Essex County DA's office on the chance that someone might be there late. Someone was, probably an assistant DA working up a loan proposal so he could open an office and go into private practice.

"Lieutenant Healy around?" I asked.

"Nope, he's working out of ten-ten Commonwealth, temporary duty, probably be there a couple of months. Can I do anything for you?"

I said no and hung up.

I called state police headquarters at 1010 Commonwealth Ave in Boston. Healy wasn't in. Call back in the morning. I hung up and turned on the TV. Boston had a two-run lead over Kansas City. I opened a bottle of Amstel beer, lay down on my couch, and watched the ball game. John Mayberry tied the game with a one-on home run in the top of the ninth, and I went through three more Amstels before Johnny Tabor scored from third on a Holly West sacrifice fly in the eleventh inning. While the news was on, I made a Westphalian ham sandwich on pumpernickel, ate it, and drank another bottle of Amstel. A man needs sustenance before bed. I might have an exciting dream. I didn't.

Next morning I drove over to 1010 Commonwealth. Healy was in his office, his coat off, the cuffs of his white shirt turned back, but the narrow black knit tie neat and tight around the short, pointed collar. He was medium height, slim, with a gray crew cut and pale blue eyes like Paul Newman. He looked like a career man in a discount shirt store. Five years ago he had gone into a candy store unarmed and rescued two hostages from a nervous junkie with a shotgun. The only person hurt was the junkie.

He said, "What do you want, Spenser?" I was always one of his favorites.

I said, "I'm selling copies of the *Police Gazette* and thought you might wish to keep abreast of the professional developments in your field."

"Knock off the horse crap, Spenser, what do you want?"

I took out the envelope containing my Polaroid picture of Marty Rabb's coffee table.

"There's a photograph in here with two sets of prints on it. One set is mine. I want to know who the other one belongs to. Can you run it through the FBI for me?"

"Why?"

"Would you buy, I'm getting married and want to run a credit check on my bride-to-be?"

"No."

"I didn't think so. Okay. It's confidential. I don't want to tell you if I don't have to. But I gotta know, and I'll give you the reasons if you insist."

"Where do you buy your clothes, Spenser?"

"Aha, bribery. You want the name of my tailor, because I'm your clothing idol."

"You dress like a goddamned hippie. Don't you own a tie?"

"One," I said. "So I can eat in the main dining room at the Ritz."

"Gimme the photo," Healy said. "I'll let you know what comes back."

I gave him the envelope. "Tell your people to try and not get grape jelly and marshmallow fluff all over the photo, okay?"

Healy ignored me. I left.

Going out, I got a look at myself in the glass doors. I had on a red and black paisley sport coat, a black polo shirt, black slacks, and shiny black loafers with a crinkle finish and gold buckles. Hippie? Healy's idea of aggressive fashion was French cuffs. I put on my sunglasses, got in my car, and headed down Commonwealth toward Kenmore Square. The top was down and the seat was quite hot. Not a single girl turned to stare at me as I went by.

CHAPTER EIGHT

I WENT OVER to Fenway and watched the Sox get ready for an afternoon game. I talked for a half hour with Holly West and a half hour with Alex Montoya to keep up my investigative-writer image, but I wondered how long that would last. Doerr knew I was there, which meant probably that someone there knew I was not a writer. Which also meant that there was a connection between Doerr and the Sox, a connection Doerr wanted to protect. He'd made an error coming to see me. But it's the kind of error guys like Doerr are always making. They get so used to having everyone say yes to them that they forget about the chance that someone will say no. People with a lot of power get like that. They think they're omnipotent. They screw up. Doerr was so surprised that I told him and Wally to take a walk that he didn't know what else to do, so he took a walk. But the cat was now out of the valise. I had a feeling I might hear from Doerr again. It was not a soothing feeling.

I was leaning against the railing of the box seats by the Red Sox dugout, watching batting practice, when Billy Carter said, "Hey, Spenser, want to take a few cuts?"

I did, but I couldn't take my coat off and show the gun. And I didn't want to swing with my coat on. I didn't need any handicaps. I shook my head.

"Why not? Sully's just lobbing them up," Carter said.

"I promised my mom when I took up the violin I'd never play baseball again."

"Violin? Are you shitting? You don't look like no violinist to me. How much you weigh?"

"One ninety-five, one ninety-seven, around there."

"Yeah? You work out or anything?"

"I lift a little. Run some."

"Yeah. I thought you did something. You didn't get that neck from playing no fiddle. What can you bench?"

"Two fifty."

"How many reps?"

"Fifteen."

"Hey, man, we oughta set up an arm wrestle between you and Holly. Wouldn't that be hot shit if you beat him? Man, Holly would turn blue if a goddamned writer beat him arm wrestling."

"Who's pitching today?" I asked.

"Marty," Carter said. "Who busted up your nose?"

"It's a long list," I said. "I used to fight once. How's Marty to catch?"

"A tit," Carter said. One of the coaches was hitting fungoes to the outfield from a circle to the right of the batting cage. The ball parabolaed out in what seemed slow motion against the high tangible sky. "A real tit. You just sit back there and put your glove on the back of the plate and Marty hits it. And you can call the game. You give a sign, Marty nods, and the pitch comes right there. He never shakes you off."

"Everything works, huh?"

"Yeah, I mean he's got the fast ball, slider, a big curve, and a change off all of them. And he can put them all up a gnat's ass at sixty feet six, you know. I mean, he's a tit to catch. If I could catch him every day, and the other guys didn't throw curves, I could be Hall of Fame, baby. Cooperstown."

"When do you think you'll catch a game, Billy?"

"Soon as Holly gets so he can't walk. Around there. Whoops . . . here comes the song of the South, old hush puppy."

Bucky Maynard had come out from under the stands and was behind the batting cage. With him was Lester, resplendent in a buckskin hunting shirt and a black cowboy hat with big silver conches on the band around the crown. Maynard had swapped his red-checked shirt for a white one with green ferns on it. His arms in the short sleeves were pink with sunburn. He had the look of someone who didn't tan.

"You don't seem too fond of Maynard," I said.

"Me? I love every ounce of his cuddly little lard-assed self."

"Okay to quote you?" I wanted to see Carter's reaction.

"Jesus, no. If sowbelly gets on your ass, you'll find yourself warming up relievers in the Sally League. No shit, Spenser, I think he's got more influence around here than Farrell."

"How come?"

"I don't know. I mean, the freakin' fans love him. They think he's giving them the real scoop, you know, all the hot gossip about the big-league stars, facts you don't get on the bubble-gum card."

"Is he?"

"No, not really. He's just nasty. If he hears any gossip, he spreads it. The goddamned yahoos eat it up. Tell-it-like-it-is Bucky. Shit."

"What's the real story on the lizard that trails behind him?"

"Lester?"

"Yeah."

Carter shrugged. "I dunno, he drives Bucky around. He keeps people away from him. He's some kind of karate freak or whatever."

"Tae kwon do," I said. "It's Korean karate."

"Yeah, whatever. I wouldn't mess much with him either. I guess he's a real bastard. I hear he did a real tune on some guy out in Anaheim. The guy was giving Maynard some crap in the hotel bar out there and Lester the Fester damn near killed him. Hey, I gotta take some swings. Catch you later."

Carter headed for the batting cage. Clyde Sullivan, the pitching coach, was pitching batting practice, and when Carter stepped in, he turned and waved the outfielders in.

"Up yours, Sully," Carter said. Maynard left the batting cage and strolled over toward me. Lester moved along bonelessly behind him.

"How you doing, Mr. Spenser?" Maynard said.

"Fine," I said. "And yourself?"

"Oh, passable, for an older gentleman. That Carter's funny as a crutch, ain't he?"

I nodded.

"Ah just wish his arm was as good as his mouth," Maynard said. "He can't throw past the pitcher's mound."

"How's his bat?"

Maynard smiled. It was not a radiant smile; the lips pulled down over the teeth so that the smile was a toothless crescent in his red face with neither warmth nor humor suggested. "He's all right if the ball comes straight. Except the ball don't never come straight a course."

"Nice kid, though," I said. Lester had hooked both elbows over the railings and was standing with one booted foot against the wall and one foot flat on the ground. Gary Cooper. He spit a large amount of brown saliva toward the batter's cage, and I realized he was chewing tobacco. When he got into an outfit, he went all the way.

"Maybe," Maynard said, "but ah wouldn't pay much mind to what he says. He likes to run his mouth."

"Don't we all," I said. "Hell, writers and broadcasters get paid for it."

"Ah get paid for reporting what happens, Carter tends to make stuff up. There's a difference."

Maynard looked quite steadily at me, and I had the feeling we were talking about serious stuff. Lester spit another dollop of tobacco juice.

"Okay by me," I said. "I'm just here listening and thinking. I'm not making any judgments yet."

"What might you be making judgments about, Spenser?"

"What to include, what to leave out, what seems to be the truth, what seems to be fertilizer. Why do you ask?"

"Just interested. Ah like to know a man, and one way

is to know how he does his job. Ah'm just lookin' into how you do yours."

"Fair enough," I said. "I'll be looking into how you do yours in a bit." Veiled innuendo, that's the ticket, Spenser. Subtle.

"Long as you don't interfere, ah'll be happy to help. Who'd you say was your publisher?"

"Subsidy," I said. "Subsidy Press, in New York."

Maynard looked at his watch. It was one of those that you press a button and the time is given as a digital readout. "Well, time for the Old Buckaroo to get on up to the booth. Nice talking to you, Spenser."

He waddled off, his feet splayed, the toes pointing out at forty-five-degree angles. Lester unhinged and slouched after him, eyes alert under the hatbrim for lurking rustlers. There never was a man like Shane. Tomorrow he'd probably be D'Artagnan.

There'd been some fencing going on there, more than there should have been. It was nearly one. I went down into the locker room and used the phone on Farrell's desk to call Brenda Loring at work.

"I have for you, my dear, a proposition," I said.

"I know," she said. "You make it every time I see you."

"Not that proposition," I said. "I have an additional one, though that previously referred to above should not be considered thereby inoperative."

"I beg your pardon?"

"I didn't understand that either," I said. "Look, here's my plan. If you can get the afternoon off, I will escort you to the baseball game, buy you some peanuts and Cracker Jacks, and you won't care if you ever come back."

"Do I get dinner afterwards?"

"Certainly and afterwards we can go to an all-night movie and neck. What do you say?"

"Oh, be still my heart," she said. "Shall I meet you at the park?"

"Yeah, Jersey Street entrance. You'll recognize me at

once by the cluster of teenyboppers trying to get me to autograph their bras."

"I'll hurry," she said.

CHAPTER NINE

WHEN BRENDA LORING GOT OUT of a brown and white Boston cab, I was brushing off an old man in an army shirt and a flowered tie who wanted me to give him a quarter.

"Did you autograph his bra, sweetie?" she said.

"They were here," I said, "but I warned them about your jealous passion and they fled at your approach."

"Fled? That is quite fancy talk for a professional thug."

"That's another thing. Around here I'm supposed to be writing a book. My true identity must remain concealed. Reveal it to no one."

"A writer?"

"Yeah. I'm supposed to be doing a book on the Red Sox and baseball."

"Was that your agent you were talking with when I drove up?"

"No, a reader."

She shook her head. Her blond hair was cut short and shaped around her head. Her eyes were green. Her makeup was expert. She was wearing a short green dress with a small floral print and long sleeves. She was darkly tanned, and a small gold locket gleamed on a thin chain against her chest where the neckline of the dress formed a V. Across Jersey Street a guy selling souvenirs was staring at her. I was staring at her too. I always did. She was ten pounds on the right side of plump. "Voluptuous," I said.

220

"I beg your pardon."

"That's how we writers would describe you. Voluptuous with a saucy hint of deviltry lurking in the sparkling of the eyes and the impertinent cast of the mouth."

"Spenser, I want a hot dog and some beer and peanuts and a ball game. Could you please, please, please, pretty please, please with sugar on it knock off the writer bullshit and escort me through the gate?"

I shook my head. "Writers aren't understood much," I said, and we went in.

I was showing off for Brenda and took her up to the broadcast booth to watch the game. My presence didn't seem to be a spur to the Red Sox. They lost to Kansas City 5-2, with Freddie Patek driving in three runs on a bases-loaded fly ball that Alex Montoya played into a triple. Maynard ignored us, Wilson studied Brenda closely between innings, and Lester boned up on the *National Enquirer* through the whole afternoon. Thoughtful.

It was four ten when we got out onto Jersey Street again. Brenda said, "Who was the cute thing in the cowboy suit?"

"Never mind about him," I said. "I suppose you're not going to settle for the two hot dogs I bought you."

"For dinner? I'll wait right here for the cowboy."

"Where would you like to go? It's early, but we could stop for a drink."

We decided on a drink at the outdoor café by City Hall. I had draft beer, and Brenda a stinger on the rocks, under the colorful umbrellas across from the open brick piazza. The area was new, reclaimed from the miasma of Scollay Square where Winnie Garrett the Flaming Redhead used to take it all off on the first show Monday before the city censor decreed the G-string. Pinball parlors, and tattoo shops, the Old Howard and the Casino, winos, whores, sailors, barrooms, and novelty shops: an adolescent vision of Sodom and Gomorrah, all gone now, giving way to fountains and arcades and a sweep of open plaza.

"You know, it never really was Sodom and Gomorrah anyway," I said.

"What wasn't?"

"Scollay Square. It was pre-Vietnam sin. Burlesque dancers and barrooms where bleached blondes danced in G-strings and net stockings. Places that sold plastic dog turds and whoopee cushions."

"I never came here," she said. "My mother had me convinced that to step into Scollay Square was to be molested instantly."

"Naw. There were ten college kids here for every dirty old man. Compared to the Combat Zone, Scollay Square was the Goosie Gander Nursery School."

I ordered two more drinks. The tables were glass-topped and the café was carpeted in Astroturf. The waitress was attentive. Brenda Loring's nails were done in a bright red. Dark was still a long way off.

Brenda went to the ladies' room, and I called my answering service. There was a message to call Healy. He'd be in his office till six. I looked at my watch: 5:40. I called.

"This is Spenser, what have you got?"

"Prints belong to Donna Burlington." He spelled it. "Busted in Redford, Illinois, three-eighteen-sixty-six, for possession of a prohibited substance. That's when the prints got logged into the bureau files. No other arrests recorded."

"Thanks, Lieutenant."

"You owe me," Healy said and hung up. Mr. Warmth.

I was back at the table before Brenda.

At seven fifteen we strolled up Tremont Street to a French restaurant in the old City Hall and had rack of lamb for two and a chilled bottle of Traminer and strawberry tarts for dessert. It was nearly nine thirty when we finished and walked back up School Street to Tremont. It was dark now but still warm, a soft night, midsummer, and the Common seemed very gentle as we strolled across it. Brenda Loring held my hand as we walked. No one attempted to mug us all the way to Marlborough Street.

In my apartment I said to Brenda, "Want some brandy or would you like to get right to the necking?"

"Actually, cookie, I would like first to take a shower."

"A shower?"

"Uh-huh. You pour us two big snifters of brandy and hop into bed, and I'll come along in a few minutes."

"A shower?"

"Go on," she said. "I won't take long."

I went to the kitchen and got a bottle of Rémy Martin out of the kitchen cabinet. Did David Niven keep cognac in the kitchen? Not likely. I got two brandy snifters out and filled them half full and headed back toward the bedroom. I could hear the shower running. I put the two glasses down on the bureau and got undressed. The shower was still running. I went to the bathroom door. My bare feet made no noise at all on the wall-to-wall carpeting. I turned the handle and it opened. The room was steamy. Brenda's clothes were in a small pile on the floor under the sink. I noticed her lingerie matched her dress. Class. The steam was billowing up over the drawn shower curtain. I looked in. Brenda had her eyes closed, her head arched back, the water running down over her shiny brown body. Her buttocks were in white contrast to the rest of her. She was humming an old Billy Eckstine song. I got in behind her and put my arms around her.

"Jesus Christ, Spenser," she said. "What are you doing?"

"Cleanliness is next to godliness," I said. "Want me to wash your back?"

She handed me the soap and I lathered her back. When I was finished, she turned to rinse it off, and her breasts, as she faced me, were the same startling white that her buttocks had been.

"Want me to wash your front?" I said.

She laughed and put her arms around me. Her body was slick and wet. I kissed her. There is excitement in a new kiss, but there is a quality of memory and intimacy in kissing

223

someone you've kissed often before. I liked the quality. Maybe continuity is better than change. With the shower still running we went towelless to bed.

CHAPTER TEN

TEN HOURS LATER I was in the coach section, window seat, aft of the wing, in an American Airlines 747, sipping coffee and chewing with little pleasure a preheated bun that tasted vaguely of adhesive tape. We were passing over Buffalo, which was a good idea, and heading for Chicago.

Beside me was a kid, maybe fifteen, and his brother, maybe eleven. They were discussing somebody named Ben, who might have been a dog, laughing like hell about it. Their mother and father across the aisle took turns giving them occasional warning glances when the laughter got raucous. Their mother looked like she might be a fashion designer or a lady lawyer; the old man looked like a stevedore, uncomfortable in a shirt and tie. Beauty and the beast.

We got into Chicago at eleven. I rented a car, got a road map from the girl at the rental agency counter, and drove southwest from Chicago toward Redford, Illinois. It took six and a half hours, and the great heartland of America was hot as hell. My green rental Dodge had air conditioning and I kept it at full blast all the way. About two thirty I stopped at a diner and had two cheeseburgers and a black coffee. There was a blackberry pie which the counterman claimed his wife made, and I ate two pieces. He had married well. About four thirty the highway bent south and I saw the river. I'd seen it before, but each time I felt the same tug. The Mississippi, Cartier and La Salle, Grant at Vicksburg and "it's lovely to live on a raft." A mile wide and "just keeps rolling." I pulled up onto the shoulder of the highway and looked at it for maybe five minutes. It was brown and placid.

I got to Redford at twenty of seven and checked into a two-story Holiday Inn just north of town that offered a view of the river and a swimming pool. The dining room was open and more than half empty. I ordered a draft beer and looked at the menu. The beer came in an enormous schooner. I ordered Wiener schnitzel and fresh garden vegetables and was startled to find when it came that it was excellent. I had finished two of the enormous schooners by then and perhaps my palate was insensitive to nuance. My compliments to the chef. Three stars for the Holiday Inn in Redford, Illinois. I signed the check and went to bed.

The next morning I went into town. Outside the air-conditioned motel the air was hot with a strong river smell. Cicadas hummed. The Holiday Inn and the Mississippi River were obviously Redford's high spots. It was a very small town, barely more than a cluster of shabby frame houses along the river. The yards were mostly bare dirt with an occasional clump of coarse and ratty-looking grass. The town's single main street contained a hardware and feed store, a Woolworth's five-and-ten, Scooter's Lunch, Bill and Betty's Market with two Phillips 66 pumps out front, and, fronting on a small square of dandelion-spattered grass, the yellow clapboard two-story town hall. There were two Greek Revival columns holding up the overhanging second floor and a bell tower that extended up perhaps two more stories to a thin spire with a weathervane at the tip. In the small square were a nineteenth-century cannon and a pyramid of cannonballs. Two kids were sitting astride the cannon as I pulled up in front of the town hall. In the parking area to the right of the town hall was a black and white Chevy with a whip antenna and POLICE lettered on the side. I went around to that side and down along the building. In the back was a screen door with a small blue light over it. I went in.

There was a head-high standing floor fan at the long end of a narrow room, and it blew a steady stream of hot air at me. To my right was a low mahogany dividing rail, and behind it a gray steel desk and matching swivel chair, a radio receiver-transmitter and a table mike on a maple table with claw and ball feet, a white round-edged refrigerator with gold trim, and some wanted posters fixed to the door with magnets. And a gray steel file cabinet.

A gray-haired man with rimless glasses and a screaming eagle emblem tattooed on his right forearm was sitting at the desk with his arms folded across his chest and his feet up. He had on a khaki uniform, obviously starched, and his black engineer boots gleamed with polish. A buff-colored campaign hat lay on the desk beside an open can of Dr Pepper. On a wheel-around stand next to the radio equipment a portable black-and-white television was showing *Hollywood Squares.* A nameplate on the desk said T. P. DONALDSON. A big silver star on his shirt said SHERIFF. A brown cardboard bakery box on the desk contained what looked like some lemon-filled doughnuts.

"My name's Spenser," I said, and showed the photostat of my license in its clear plastic coating. Germ-free. "I'm trying to backtrack a woman named Donna Burlington. According to the FBI records she was arrested here in nineteen sixty-six."

"Sheriff Donaldson," the gray-haired man said, and stood up to shake hands. He was tall and in shape with healthy color to his tan face, and oversize hands with prominent knuckles. His shirt was ironed in a military press and had been tailored down so that it was skintight.

"Hundred and First?" I said.

"The tattoo? Yeah. I was a kid then, you know. Fulla piss and vinegar, drunk in London, and three of us got it done. My wife's always telling me to get rid of it but . . ." He shrugged. "You airborne?"

"Nope, infantry and a different war. But I remember the Hundred and First. Were you at Bastogne?"

"Yep. Had a bad case of boils on my back. The medics said I ought to eat better food and wash more often." His face was solemn. "Krauts took care of it, though. I got a back full of shrapnel and the boils were gone."

"Medical science," I said.

He shook his head. "Christ, that was thirty years ago."

"It's one of the things you don't forget," I said.

"You don't for sure," he said. "Who was that you were after?"

"Burlington, Donna Burlington. A.k.a. Linda Hawkins, about twenty-six years old, five feet four, black hair, FBI records show she was fingerprinted here in nineteen sixty-six, at which time she would have been about eighteen. You here then?"

He nodded. "Yep, I been here since nineteen forty-six." He turned toward the file cabinet. A pair of handcuffs draped over his belt in the small of his back, and he wore an army .45 in a government-issue flap holster on his right hip. He rustled through the third file drawer down and came up with a manila folder. He opened it, his back still to me, and read through the contents, closed it, turned around, put the folder facedown on the desk, and sat down. "You want a Dr Pepper?" he said.

"No, thanks. You have Donna Burlington?"

"Could I see your license again, and maybe some other ID?"

I gave him the license and my driver's license. He looked at them carefully and turned them back to me. "Why do you want to know about Donna Burlington?"

"I don't want to tell you. I'm looking into something that might hurt a lot of people, who could turn out to be innocent, if the word got out."

"What's Donna Burlington got to do with it?"

"She lied to me about her name, where she lived, how she got married. I want to know why."

"You think she's committed a crime?"

"Not that I know of. I don't want her for anything. I just ran across a lie and I want to run it down. You know how it goes, people lie to you, you want to know why."

Donaldson nodded. He took a swig from his Dr Pepper, swallowed it, and began to suck on his upper lip.

"I don't want to stir up old troubles," I said. "She was

eighteen when you busted her. Everyone is entitled to screw up when they're eighteen. I just want to know about her."

Donaldson kept sucking on his upper lip and looking at me.

"It'll be worse if I start asking around and get people wondering why some dick from the East is asking about Donna Burlington. I'll find out anyway. This isn't that big a place."

"I might not let you ask around," Donaldson said.

"Aw come on, Hondo," I said. "If you give me trouble, I'll go get the state cops and a court order and come on back and ask around and more people will notice and a bigger puff of smoke will go up and you'll be worse off than you are now. I'm making what you call your legitimate inquiry."

"Persistent sonovabitch, aren't you? Okay, I'll go along. I just don't like telling people's business to others without a pretty good reason."

"Me either," I said.

"Okay." He opened the folder and looked at it. "I arrested Donna Burlington for possession of three marijuana cigarettes. She was smoking with two boys from Buckston in a pickup truck back of Scooter's Lunch. It was a first offense, but we were a little jumpier about reefers around here in 'sixty-six than we are now. I booked her; she went to court and got a suspended sentence and a year's probation. Six weeks later she broke probation and went off to New York City with a local hellion. She never came back."

"What was the hellion's name?"

"Tony Reece. He was about seven or eight years older than Donna."

"What kind of kid was she?"

"It was a while ago," Donaldson said. "But kind of restless, not really happy, you know—nothing bad, but she had a reputation, hung out with the older hotshots. The first girl in class to smoke, the first to drink, the first one to try pot, the one the boys took out as soon as they dared while the other girls were still going to dancing school at the grange hall and blushing if someone talked dirty."

"Family still live in town?"

"Yeah, but they don't know where she is. After she took off, they were after me to locate her. But there's only me and two deputies, and one of them's part-time. When nothing came of that, they wrote her off. In a way they were probably glad she took off. They didn't know what to do with her. She was a late baby, you know? The Burlingtons never had any kids, and then, when Mrs. Burlington was going through the change, there came Donna. That's what my wife says anyway. Embarrassed hell out of both of them."

"How about Reece? He ever show up again?"

Donaldson shook his head. "Nope. I heard he got in some kind of jam in New York and he might be doing time. But he hasn't shown up around here anyway."

"Okay, any last known address?"

"Just the house here."

"Can you give me that? I'd like to talk to the parents."

"I'll drive you over. They'll be a little easier if I'm there. They're old and they get nervous."

"I'm not going to give them the third degree, Donaldson, I'm just going to talk to them and ask them if they know anything more than you do about Donna Burlington."

"I'll go along. They're sorta shiftless and crummy, but they're my people, you know? I like to look out for them."

I nodded. "Okay, let's go."

We got into Donaldson's black and white and drove back up the main street past the row of storefronts and the sparse yards. At the end of the street we turned left, down toward the river, and pulled up in front of a big shanty. Originally it had probably been a four-room bungalow backing onto the river. Over the years lean-tos and sagging additions had been scabbed onto it so that it was difficult to say how many rooms there were now. The area in front of the house was mud, and several dirty white chickens pecked in it. A brown and white pig had rooted itself out a hollow against the foundation and was sleeping in it. To the right of the front door, two big gas bottles of dull gray-green metal stood upright, and to the left the remnants of a vine were so bedraggled I couldn't recognize what kind it was. The land to the side and rear of the house sloped in a kind of eroded gully down to the river. There was a stack of old tires at the corner of one of the lean-tos, and beyond that the rusted frame of a forty-year-old pickup truck, a stack of empty vegetable crates, and on the flat mud margin where the river lapped at the land a bedspring, mossy and slick with river scum.

I thought of Linda Rabb in her Church Park apartment with the fresh jeans and her black hair gleaming.

"Come to where the flavor is," I said.

"Yeah, it's not much, is it? Don't much wonder that Donna took off as soon as she could." We got up and walked to the front door. There were the brown remains of a wreath hanging from a galvanized nail. The ghost of Christmas past. Maybe of a Christmas future for the Burlingtons.

An old woman answered Donaldson's knock. She was fat and lumpy in a yellow housedress. Her legs were bare and mottled, her feet thrust into scuffed men's loafers. Her gray hair was short and straight around her head, the ends uneven, cut at home probably, with dull scissors. Her face was nearly without features, fat puffing around her eyes, making them seem small and squinty.

"Morning, Mrs. Burlington," Donaldson said. "Got a man here from Boston wants to talk with you about Donna."

She looked at me. "You seen Donna?" she said.

"May we come in?" I said.

She stood aside. "I guess so," she said. Her voice wasn't very old, but it was without variation, a tired monotone, as if there were nothing worth saying.

Donaldson took off his hat and went in. I followed. The room smelled of kerosene and dogs and things I didn't recognize. The clutter was dense. Donaldson and I found room on an old daybed and sat. Mrs. Burlington shuffled off down a corridor and returned in a moment with her husband. He was pallid and bald, a tall old man in a sleeveless undershirt and black worsted trousers with the fly open. His face had gray stubble on it, and some egg was dried in the corner of his mouth. The skin was loose on his thin white arms and

230

wrinkled in the fold at the armpit. He poured a handful of Bond Street pipe tobacco from a can into the palm of his hand and slurped it into his mouth.

He nodded at Donaldson, who said, "Morning, Mr. Burlington." Mrs. Burlington stood, and they both looked at Donaldson and me without moving or speaking. American Gothic.

I said, "I'm a detective. I can't tell you where your daughter is, except that she's well and happy. But I need to learn a little about her background. I mean her no harm, and I'm trying to help her, but the whole situation is very confidential."

"What do you want to know?" Mrs. Burlington said.

"When is the last time you heard from her?"

Mrs. Burlington said, "We ain't. Not since she run off."

"No letter, no call, nothing. Not a word?"

Mrs. Burlington shook her head. The old man made no move, changed his expression not at all.

"Do you know where she went when she left here?"

"Left us a note saying she was going to New York with a fellow we never met, never heard nothing more."

"Didn't you look for her?"

Mrs. Burlington nodded at Donaldson, "Told T.P. here. He looked. Couldn't find her." A bony mongrel dog with short yellow fur and mismatched ears appeared behind Mr. Burlington. He growled at us, and Burlington turned and kicked him hard in the ribs. The dog yelped and disappeared.

"You ever hear from Tony Reece?" It was like talking to a postoperative lobotomy case. And compared to the old man, she was animated.

She shook her head. "Never seen him," she said. The old man squirted a long stream of tobacco juice at a cardboard box of sand behind the door. He missed.

And that was it. They didn't know anything about anything, and they didn't care. The old man never spoke while I was there and just nodded when Donaldson said good-bye.

In the car Donaldson said, "Where to now?"

"Let's just sit here a minute until I catch my breath."

"They been poor all their life," Donaldson said. "It tends to wear you out." I nodded.

"Okay, how about Tony Reece? He got any family here?"

"Nope. Folks are both dead." Donaldson started the engine and turned the car back toward the town hall. When we got there, he offered me his hand. "If I was you, Spenser, I'd try New York next."

"Fun City," I said.

CHAPTER ELEVEN

IT WAS SUNSET when the plane swung in over the water and landed at La Guardia Airport. I took the bus into the East Side terminal at Thirty-eighth Street and a cab from there to the Holiday Inn at West Fifty-seventh Street. The Wiener schnitzel had been so good in Redford, I thought I might as well stay with a winner.

The West Side hadn't gotten any more fashionable since I had been there last and the hotel looked as if it belonged where it was. The lobby was so discouraging that I didn't bother to check the dining room for Wiener schnitzel. Instead, I walked over to a Scandinavian restaurant on Fifty-eighth Street and ravaged its smorgasbord.

The next morning I made some phone calls to the New York Department of Social Services while I drank coffee in my room. When I finished I walked along Fifty-seventh Street to Fifth Avenue and headed downtown. I always walk in New York. In the window of F.A.O. Schwarz was an enormous stuffed giraffe, and Brentano's had a display of ethnic cookbooks in the window. I thought about going in and asking

them if they were a branch of the Boston store but decided not
to. They probably lacked my zesty sense of humor.

It was about nine forty-five when I reached Thirty-
fourth Street and turned left. Four blocks east, between Third
and Second avenues, was a three-story beige brick building
that looked like a modified fire station. The brown metal entrance doors, up four stairs, were flanked with flagpoles at
right angles to the building. A plaque under the right-hand
flagpole said CITY OF NEW YORK, DEPARTMENT OF SOCIAL SERVICES,
YORKVILLE INCOME MAINTENANCE CENTER. I went in.

It was a big open room, the color a predictable green;
molded plastic chairs in red, green, and blue stood three rows
deep to the right of the entrance. To the left a low counter.
Behind the counter a big black woman with blue-framed
glasses on a chain around her neck was telling an old woman
in an ankle-length dress that her check would come next
week and would not come sooner. The woman protested in
broken English, and the woman behind the desk said it again,
louder. At the end of the counter, sitting in a folding chair,
was a New York City cop, a slim black woman with badge,
gun, short hair, and enormous high platform shoes. Beyond
the counter the room L'd to the left, and I could see office
space partitioned off. There was no one else on the floor.

Behind me, to the right of the entry, a stair led up. A
handprinted sign said FACE TO FACE UPSTAIRS with an arrow. I
went up. The second floor had been warrened off into cubicles
where face to face could go on in privacy. The first cubicle was
busy; the second was not. I knocked on the frame of the open
door and went in. It was little bigger than a confessional, just
a desk, a file cabinet, and a chair for the face to face. The
woman at the desk was lean and young, not long out of Vassar
or Bennington. She had a tanned outdoor face, with small
lines around the eyes that she wasn't supposed to get yet. She
had on a white sleeveless blouse open at the neck. Her brown
hair was cut short and she wore no makeup. Her face pre-
sented an expression of no-nonsense compassion that I suspected she was still working on. The sign on her desk said MS.
HARRIS.

"Come in," she said, her hands resting on the neat desk in front of her. A pencil in the right one. I was dressed for New York in my wheat-colored summer suit, dark blue shirt, and a white tie with blue and gold stripes. Would she invite me to her apartment? Maybe she thought I was another welfare case. If so, I'd have to speak with my tailor. I gave her a card; she frowned down at it for about thirty seconds and then looked up and said, "Yes?"

"Do you think I ought to have a motto on it?" I said.

"I beg your pardon?"

"A motto," I said. "On the card. You know, like 'We never sleep' or maybe 'Trouble is my business.' Something like that."

"Mr."—she checked the card—"Spenser, I assume you're joking and there's nothing wrong with that, but I have a good deal to do and I wonder if you might tell me what you want directly?"

"Yes, ma'am. May I sit?"

"Please do."

"Okay, I'm looking for a young woman who might have showed up here and gone on welfare about eight years ago."

"Why do you want to find her?"

I shook my head. "It's a reasonable question, but I can't tell you."

She frowned at me the way she had frowned at my card. "Why do you think we'd have information about something that far back?"

"Because you are a government agency. Government agencies never throw anything away because someone someday might need something to cover himself in case a question of responsibility was raised. You got welfare records for Peter Stuyvesant."

The frown got more severe, making a groove between her eyebrows. "Why do you think this young woman was on welfare?"

"You shouldn't frown like that," I said. "You'll get little premature wrinkles in the corners of your eyes."

"I would prefer it, Mr. Spenser, if you did not attempt

to personalize this contact. The condition of my eyes is not relevant to this discussion."

"Ah, but how they sparkle when you're angry," I said.

She almost smiled, caught herself, and got the frown back in place. "Answer my question, please."

"She was about eighteen; she ran away from a small midwestern town with the local bad kid, who probably ditched her after they got here. She's a good bet to have ended up on welfare or prostitution or both. I figured that you'd have better records than Diamond Nell's Parlor of Delight."

The pencil in her right hand went tap-tap-tap on the desk. Maybe six taps before she heard it and stopped. "The fact of someone's presence on welfare rolls has sometimes been used against them. Cruel as that may seem, it is a fact of life, and I hope you can understand my reticence in this matter."

"I'm on the girl's side," I said.

"But I have no way to know that."

"Just my word," I said.

"But I don't know if your word is good."

"That's true," I said. "You don't."

The pencil went tap-tap-tap again. She looked at the phone. Pass the buck? She looked away. Good for her. "What is the girl's name?"

"Donna Burlington." I could hear a typewriter in one of the other cubicles and footsteps down another corridor. "Go ahead," I said. "Do it. It will get done by someone. It's only a matter of who. Me? Cops? Courts? Your boss? His boss? Why not you? Less fuss."

She nodded her head. "Yes. You are probably right. Very well." She got up and left the room. She had very nice legs.

It took a while. I stood in the window of the cubicle and looked down on Thirty-fourth Street and watched the people coming and going from the welfare office. It wasn't as busy as I'd thought it would be. Nor were the people as shabby. Down the corridor a man swore rapidly in Spanish. The typewriter had stopped. The rest was silence.

Ms. Harris returned with a file folder. She sat, opened it on the desk, and read the papers in it. "Donna Burlington was on income maintenance at this office from August to November nineteen sixty-six. At the time her address was One Sixteen East Thirteenth Street. Her relationship with this office ended on November thirteenth, nineteen sixty-six, and I have no further knowledge of her." She closed the folder and folded her hands on top of it.

I said, "Thank you very much."

She said, "You're welcome."

I looked at my watch: 10:50. "Would you like to join me for an early lunch?" I said.

"No, thank you," she said. So much for the operator down from Boston.

"Would you like to see me do a one-hand push-up?" I said.

"Certainly not," she said. "If you have nothing more, Mr. Spenser, I have a good deal of work to do."

"Oh, sure, okay. Thanks very much for your trouble." She stood as I left the room. From the corridor I stuck my head back into the office and said, "Not everyone can do a one-hand push-up, you know?"

She seemed unimpressed and I left.

CHAPTER TWELVE

THIRTEENTH STREET WAS a twenty-five-minute walk downtown and 116 was in the East Village between Second and Third. There was a group of men outside 116, leaning against the parked cars with their shirts unbuttoned, smoking cigarettes and drinking beer from quart bottles. They were speaking

Spanish. One Sixteen was a four-story brick house, which had long ago been painted yellow and from which the paint peeled in myriad patches. Next to it was a six-story four-unit apartment building newly done in light gray paint with the door and window frames and the fire escapes and the railing along the front steps a bright red. The beer drinkers had a portable radio that played Spanish music very loudly.

I went up the four steps to number 116 and rang the bell marked CUSTODIAN. Nothing happened, and I rang it again.

One of the beer drinkers said, "Don't work, man. Who you want?"

"I want the manager."

"Inside, knock on the first door."

"Thanks."

In the entry was an empty bottle of Boone's Farm apple wine and a sneaker without laces. Stairs led up against the left wall ahead of me, and a brief corridor went back into the building to the right of the stairs. I knocked on the first door and a woman answered the first knock.

She was tall and strongly built, olive skin and short black hair. A gray streak ran through her hair from the forehead back. She had on a man's white shirt and cutoff jeans. Her feet were bare, and her toenails were painted a dark plum color. She looked about forty-five.

I said, "My name is Spenser. I'm a private detective from Boston, and I'm looking for a girl who lived here once about eight years ago."

She smiled and her teeth were very white and even. "Come in," she said. The room was large and square, and a lot of light came in through the high windows that faced out onto the street. The walls and ceiling were white, and there were red drapes at the windows and a red rug on the floor. In the middle of the room stood a big, square, thick-legged wooden table with a red linoleum top, a large bowl of fruit in the center and a high-backed wooden chair at either end. She gestured toward one of the chairs. "Coffee?" she said.

"Yes, thank you."

I sat at the table and looked about the room while she

disappeared through a bead-curtained archway to make the coffee. There was a red plush round-back Victorian sofa with mahogany arms in front of the windows and an assortment of Velázquez prints on the wall. She came back in with a carafe of coffee and two white china mugs on a round red tray.

"Cream or sugar?"

I shook my head. She poured the coffee into the cups, gave me one, and sat down at the other end of the table.

"The coffee is wonderful," I said.

"I grind it myself," she said. "My name is Rose Estrada. How can I help you?" There was a very small trace of another language in her speech.

I took out the picture of Linda Rabb that I'd taken at her apartment. "This is a recent picture of a girl named Donna Burlington. In nineteen sixty-six, from August to November, she lived at this address. Can you tell me anything about her?"

She thought aloud as she looked at the picture. "Nineteen sixty-six, my youngest would have been ten. . . . Yes, I remember her, Donna Burlington. She came from somewhere in the Midwest. She seemed very young to be alone in New York, far from home. She was with a boy for a little while, but he didn't stay."

"What happened to her when she left you, do you know?"

"No."

"No forwarding address?"

"None. I remember she had no money and was behind in her rent, and I sent her down to the welfare people on Thirty-fourth Street. And then one day she gave me all the back room rent in cash and moved out."

"Any idea where she got the money?"

"I think she was hustling."

"Prostitute?"

She nodded. "I can't be sure, but I know she was out often and she brought men home often and she used to spend time with a pimp named Violet."

"Is he still around?"

"Oh sure. People like Violet are around forever."

"Where do I find him?"

"He's usually on Third Avenue, in front of the Casa Grande near Fifteenth."

"What's his full name?"

She shrugged. "Just Violet," she said. "More coffee?"

"Thank you." I held my cup out, and she poured from the carafe. Her hands were strong and clean, the fingernails the same plum color as her toenails. No rings. Outside I could hear the portable radio playing and occasionally the voices of the men drinking beer.

"She was a very small, thin, little girl," Rose Estrada said. "Very scared. She didn't want to be here, but she didn't want to go home. She didn't know anything about makeup or clothes. She didn't know what to say to people. If she was turning tricks, it must have been very hard on her."

I finished my coffee and stood. "Thank you for the coffee and for the information," I said.

"Is she in trouble?"

"No, I don't think so," I said. "Nothing I can't get her out of."

We shook hands and I left. The street seemed hot and noisy after Rose Estrada's apartment. I walked the half block to Third Ave and turned uptown. At the corner of Fourteenth Street a man in a covert cloth overcoat was urinating against the brick wall of a variety store. He was having trouble standing and lurched against the wall, holding his coat around him with one hand. Modesty, I thought, if you're going to whiz on a wall, do it with modesty. A few feet downstream another man was lying on the sidewalk, knees bent, eyes closed. Drinking buddies. I looked at my watch, it was two thirty in the afternoon.

At the corner of Fifteenth Street was a bar with a fake fieldstone front below a plate glass window. The entry to the left of the window was imitation oak. A small neon sign said CASA GRANDE, BEER ON DRAFT. At the curb in front of the Casa Grande were a white Continental and a maroon Coupe de Ville with a white vinyl roof. Leaning against the Coupe de

Ville was a man who'd seen too many *Superfly* movies. He was a black man probably six-three in his socks and about six-seven in the open-toed red platform shoes he was wearing. He was also wearing red-and-black argyle socks, black knickers, and a chain mail vest. A black Three Musketeers' hat with an enormous red plume was tipped forward over his eyes. Subtle. All he lacked was a sign saying THE PIMP IS IN.

"Excuse me," I said, "I'm looking for Violet."

The pimp looked down at me from on top of his shoes and said, "Why?"

"I was told he could give me information about a girl."

"Someone's talking shit to you, man. I don't know nothing about no girl."

"You Violet?"

He shrugged and looked down Third Avenue.

"I'm looking for information about a girl named Donna Burlington," I said.

The Lincoln started up, backed away from the curb, U-turned, and drove away.

"You federal?" Violet said. "I ain't seen you around."

"I'm not anything," I said. "Just a guy looking to buy some information."

"Well, I hope you got a license for that piece on your right hip then."

Violet paid attention to detail. "Okay." I took a card from my breast pocket and gave it to him. "I'm a private cop. From Boston. But I'm still buying information."

"Baaahston." Violet laughed. "Shit. What Donna do, steal some beans?"

"No, she stole some teenybopper clothes from a ladies' dress shop and I think you're wearing some of them."

Violet laughed again. "Hey, man, you want me to dress like one of you tight-assed honkies?" He slapped one hand down on the hood of the Cadillac and whooped with laughter. "Look at that little mother-loving Buster Brown suit. Shit." Tears were forming in his eyes.

"Look, Violet," I said. "I didn't come down here to write

a sonnet about your Easter bonnet. How about I buy you a beer and we talk a little?"

"Yeah, why not, man? You said something about buying information?"

We went in the Casa Grande and sat at the bar. There was a Mets game on television down the bar. The bartender, a middle-aged man in a clean white shirt who looked like Gilbert Roland, came down and wiped the bar off in front of us.

"What'll it be, gentlemen?" he asked, looking carefully at a spot between my head and Violet's.

"Two drafts," I said.

Violet said, "Be cool, Hec, he's okay. We just talking a little business."

The bartender looked at me then. "Okay, Violet," he said and drew the beers.

Violet took his hat off. His head was stark bald and smooth. "Hec figured you for fuzz too. I hope you don't think you working in disguise, man."

I shook my head. "You either," I said. Violet whooped again.

"What you want to know, man?"

I took out my picture of Donna Burlington and showed it to Violet. "Know her eight years younger?"

"You mentioned buying. How much you buying for?"

"Fifty bucks."

"That's not much bread, man."

"You don't have to work very hard for it," I said. "It'll cover your next tankful in that brontosaurus out front."

Violet nodded, drank half his beer, and said, "Yeah, I remember Donna. Remembered her when you said her name."

"Tell me about her."

"A shit kicker," Violet said. "Come from somewhere out in the woods. Real young when she worked for me. Worked for me maybe six months."

"How'd you meet her?"

"Her boyfriend was pimping her on my turf, man. I chased him off and she stayed with me."

"She have any choice?"

Violet grinned. "Not in this neighborhood, man."

"How come you remember her so well?"

"She was white, man. Most of my chicks are black."

"What happened to her?"

Violet shrugged. "Moved uptown, fancy stuff, appointment only." He finished the beer. The bartender brought us two more without being asked.

"She work on her own?"

"Naw, she work for another broad, a madame, baby. Very classy. Probably screwed only Baaahston dudes, dig?" And again the whooping laugh.

"Can you give me the name?"

"I can get it, but that's extra."

"Another fifty?"

"That's cool." Violet got up and went to a pay phone by the door. He was back in five minutes. "Patricia Utley," he said. "Fifty-seven East Thirty-seventh Street."

"Thanks, Violet," I took a $100 bill out of my wallet and handed it to him. "If you're ever in Boston . . ."

Violet laughed again. "Yeah, baby, if I ever want some beans . . ."

I finished the beer and got up. Violet turned and leaned his elbows on the bar. "Hey, Spenser," he said. "Utley works for very heavy people, dig?"

"That's okay," I said. "I don't mind heavy work."

"Well, you built for it, I give you that. But you walk around Utley careful, baby, this ain't Boston."

"Violet," I said, "I'm not sure this is even earth."

CHAPTER THIRTEEN

MIDTOWN EAST SIDE in Manhattan is the New York they show in the movies. Elegant, charming, clean, "I bought you violets for your furs." Patricia Utley occupied a four-story town house on East Thirty-seventh, west of Lexington. The building was stone, painted a Colonial gray with a wrought-iron filigree on the glass door and the windows faced in white. Two small dormers protruded from the slate mansard roof, and a tiny terrace to the right of the front door bloomed with flowers against the green of several miniature trees. Red geraniums and white patient Lucys in black iron pots lined the three granite steps that led up to the front door.

A well-built man with gray hair and a white mess jacket answered my ring. I gave him my card. "For Patricia Utley," I said.

"Come in, please," he said and stepped aside. I entered a center hall with a polished flagstone floor and a mahogany staircase with white risers opposite the door. The black man opened a door on the right-hand wall, and I went into a small sitting room that looked out over Thirty-seventh Street and the miniature garden. The walls were white-paneled, and there was a Tiffany lamp in green, red, and gold hanging in the center of the room. The rugs were Oriental, and the furniture was Edwardian.

The butler said, "Wait here, please," and left. He closed the door behind him.

There was a mahogany highboy on the wall opposite the windows with four cut-glass decanters and a collection of small crystal glasses. I took the stoppers out of the decanters and sniffed. Sherry, cognac, port, Calvados. I poured myself a glass of the Calvados. On the wall opposite the door was a black marble fireplace, and on either side floor-to-ceiling bookcases. I looked at the titles: *The Complete Works of Charles Dickens, A History of the English-Speaking Peoples* by Winston Churchill, *Longfellow: Complete Poetical and Prose Works,* H. G. Wells's *The Outline of History,* Chaucer's *The Canterbury Tales,* with illustrations by Rockwell Kent. The door opened behind me, and a woman entered. The butler closed it softly behind her.

"Mr. Spenser," she said, "I'm Patricia Utley," and put out her hand. I shook it. She looked as if she might have read all the books and understood them. She was fortyish, small and blond with good bones and big black-rimmed round glasses. Her hair was pulled back tight against her head with a bun in the back. She was wearing an off-white sleeveless linen dress with blue and green piping at the hem and along the neckline. Her legs were bare and tanned.

"Please sit down," she said. "I see you have a drink. Good. How may I help you?" I sat on the sofa. She sat opposite me on an ottoman. Her knees together, ankles crossed, hands folded in her lap.

"I'm looking for information about a girl named Donna Burlington who you probably knew about eight years ago." I showed her the picture.

"And why would you think I know anything about her, Mr. Spenser?"

"One of your colleagues suggested that she had left his employ and joined your firm."

"I'm sorry, I don't understand." Her blue eyes were direct and steady as she looked at me. Her face without lines.

"Well, ma'am, I don't mean to be coarse, but an East Village pimp named Violet told me she moved uptown and went to work for you in the late fall of nineteen sixty-six."

"I'm afraid I don't know anyone named Violet," she said.

"Tall, thin guy, aggressive dresser, but small-time. No

reason for you to know him. The Pinkerton Agency has never heard of me either."

"Oh, I'm sure you're well known in your field, Mr. Spenser." She smiled, and a dimple appeared in each cheek. "But I really don't see how I can help you. This Violet person has misled you, I suppose for money. New York is a very grasping city."

The room was cool and silent, central air conditioning. I sipped the Calvados, and it reminded me that I hadn't eaten since about seven thirty. It was now almost four thirty. "Ms. Utley," I said, "I don't wish to rock your boat and I don't want anything bad to happen to Donna Burlington, I just need to know about her."

"Ms. Utley," she said. "That's charming, but it's Mrs., thank you."

"Okay, Mrs. Utley, but what I said stands. I need to know about Donna Burlington. Confidential. No harm to anyone, and I can't tell you why. But I need to know." I finished the brandy. She stood, took my glass, filled it, and set it down on the marble-topped coffee table in front of me. Her movements were precise and graceful and stylish. So was she.

"I have no quarrel with that, Mr. Spenser, but I can't help you. I don't know the young lady, nor can I imagine how anyone could think that I might."

"Mrs. Utley, I know we've only met, but would you join me for dinner?"

"Is that part of your technique, Mr. Spenser? Candle-light and wine and perhaps I'll remember something about the young lady?"

"Well, there's that," I said. "But I hate to eat alone. The only people I know in the city are you and Violet, and Violet already had a date."

"Well, I don't know about being second choice to—what was it you said—an East Village pimp?"

"I'll tell you about my most exciting cases," I said. "Why, I remember one I call the howling dog caper . . ."

The dimple reappeared.

"And I'll do a one-hand push-up for you, and sing a

dozen popular songs, pronouncing the lyrics so clearly that you can hear every word."

"And if I still refuse?"

"Then I go down to Foley Square and see if I can find someone in the DA's office that knows you and might put in a word for me."

"I do not like to be threatened, Mr. Spenser."

"Desperation," I said. "Loneliness and desire make a man crazy. Here, look at the kind of treat ahead of you." I put my glass on the end table, got down on the rug, and did a one-hand push-up. I looked up at her from the push-up position, my left hand behind my back. "Want to see another one?" I said.

She was laughing. Silently at first with her face serious but her stomach jiggling and giving her away, and then aloud, with her head back and the dimples big enough to hold a ripe olive.

"I'll go," she said. "Let me change, and we'll go. Now, for God sakes, get off the floor, you damn fool."

I got up. "The old one-hand push-up," I said. "Gets them almost every time."

She didn't take long. I had time to sip one more brandy before she reappeared in a backless white dress that tied around the neck and had a royal blue sash around the middle. Her shoes matched the sash, and so did her earrings.

I said, "Hubba, hubba."

"Hub-ba, hub-ba? What on earth does that mean?"

"You look very nice," I said. "Where would you like to go?"

"There's a lovely restaurant uptown a little ways we could try, if you'd like."

"I'm in your hands," I said. "This is your city."

"You are not, I would guess, ever in anyone's hands, Spenser, but I think you'll like this place."

"Cab?" I said.

"No, Steven will drive us."

When we went out the front door, there was the same

well-built black man, sitting at the wheel of a Mercedes sedan. He'd swapped his mess jacket for a blue blazer.

We drove uptown.

The restaurant was at Sixty-fifth Street on the East
Side and was called The Wings of the Dove.

"Do you suppose they serve the food in a golden bowl?"
I said.

"I don't believe so. Why do you ask?"

"Henry James," I said. "It's a book joke."

"I guess I haven't read it."

It was only five thirty when we went in. Too early for
most people to go to dinner, but most people had probably
eaten lunch. I hadn't. It was a small restaurant, with a lavish
dessert table in the foyer and two rooms separated by an
archway. The ceiling was frosted glass that opened out, like a
greenhouse, and the walls were used brick, some from the
original building, some quite artfully integrated with the
original. The tablecloths were pink, and there were flowers
and green plants everywhere, many of them in hanging pots.

The maître d' in a tuxedo said, "Good evening, Mrs.
Utley. We have your table."

She smiled and followed him. I followed her. One wall
of the restaurant was mirrored, and it gave the illusion of a
good deal more space than there was. I checked myself as we
filed in. The suit was holding up, I'd had a haircut just last
week, if only a talent scout from *Playgirl* spotted me.

"Would you care for cocktails?"

Patricia Utley said, "Campari on the rocks with a
twist, please, John."

I said, "Do you have any draft beer?"

The maître d' said, "No."

I said, "Do you have any Amstel in bottles?"

He said, "No."

I said to Patricia Utley, "Is Nedick's still open?"

She said to the maître d', "Bring him a bottle of
Heineken, John."

The maître d' said, "Certainly, Mrs. Utley," and
stalked toward the kitchen.

She looked at me and shook her head slowly. "Are you ever serious, Spenser?"

"Yes, I am," I said. "I am serious, for instance, about discussing Donna Burlington with you."

"And I am serious when I say to you, why should you think I'd know her?"

"Because you are in charge of a high-priced prostitution operation and are bankrolled with what my source refers to as heavy money. Now I know it, and you know it, and why not stop the pretense? The truth, Mrs. Utley, will set us free."

"All right," she said, "say you are correct. Why should I discuss it with you?"

A waiter brought our drinks and I waited while he put them down. Mine rather disdainfully, I thought.

"Because I can cause you aggravation—cops, newspapers, maybe the feds—maybe I could cause you trouble, I don't know. Depends on how heavy the bankrollers really are. If you talk with me, then it's confidential, there's no aggravation at all. And I might do another one-arm push-up for you."

"What if my bankrollers decided to cause you aggravation?"

"I have a very high aggravation tolerance."

She sipped her Campari. "It's funny, or maybe it's not funny at all, but you're the second person who's come asking about Donna."

"Who else?"

"He never said, but he was quite odd. He was, oh, what, in costume, I guess you'd say. Dressed all in white, white suit and shirt, white tie, white shoes and a big white straw hat like a South American planter."

"Tall and slim? Chewed gum?"

"Yes."

I said, "Aha."

"Aha?"

"Yeah, like Aha I see a connection, or Aha I have discovered a clue. It's detective talk."

"You know who he is then."

"Yes, I do. What did he want?"

She sipped some more Campari. I drank some Heineken. "Among my enterprises," she said, "is a film business. This gentleman had apparently seen Donna in one of our films and wanted the master print."

"Aha, aha!" I said. "Corporate diversification." The waiter came for our order. When he was gone, I said, "Start from the beginning. When did you meet Donna, what did she do for you, what kind of film was she in, tell me all."

"Very well, if you promise not to keep saying Aha."

"Agreed."

"Donna came to me through a client. He'd picked her up down in the East Village when he was drunk." She grimaced. "She was working for Violet then; her boyfriend had pimped for her before but had run from Violet. I don't know what happened to the boyfriend. The client thought she was too nice a girl to be hustling out of the back of a car with a two-dollar pimp like Violet. He put her in touch with me."

The waiter came with our soup. I had gazpacho; Patricia Utley had vichyssoise.

"I run a very first-rate operation, Spenser."

"I can tell that," I said.

"Of course, I would deny this to anyone if it ever came up."

"It won't. I don't care about your operation. I only care about Donna Burlington."

"But you disapprove."

"I don't approve or disapprove. To tell you the truth, Mrs. Utley, I don't give a damn. I think about one thing at a time. Right now I'm thinking about Donna Burlington."

"It's a volunteer business," she said. "It exists because men have needs." She said it as if the needs had a foul odor.

"Now who's disapproving?"

"You don't know," she said. "You've never seen what I've seen."

"About Donna Burlington," I said.

"She was eighteen when I took her. She didn't know anything. She didn't know how to dress, how to do her hair, how to wear makeup. She hadn't read anything, been anyplace, talked to anyone. I had her two years and taught her everything. How to walk, how to sit, how to talk with people. I gave her books to read, showed her how to make up, how to dress."

The waiter brought the fish. Sole in a saffron sauce for her. Scallops St. Jacques for me.

"You and Rex Harrison," I said.

"Yes," she said. "It was rather like that. I liked Donna, she was a very unsophisticated little thing. It was like having a, oh not a daughter, but a niece perhaps. Then one day she left. To get married."

"Who'd she marry?"

"She wouldn't tell me—a client, I gathered, but she wouldn't say whom, and I never saw her again."

"When was this?"

Patricia Utley thought for a moment. "It was the same year as the Cambodian raids and the great protest, nineteen seventy. She left me in winter nineteen seventy. I remember it was winter because I watched her walk away in a lovely fur-collared tweed coat she had."

The waiter cleared the fish and put down the salad, spinach leaves with raw mushrooms in a lemon and oil dressing. I took a bite. So-so. "I assume the films were what I used to call dirty movies when I was a kid."

She smiled. "It is getting awfully hard to decide, isn't it? They were erotic films. But of good quality, sold by subscription."

"Black socks, garter belts, two girls and a guy? That kind of stuff?"

"No, as I said, tasteful, high quality, good color and sound. No sadism, no homosexuality, no group sex."

"And Donna was in some?"

"She was in one, shortly before she left me. The pay was good, and while it was a lot of work, it was a bit of a change for her. Her film was called *Suburban Fancy*. She was quite believable in it."

"What did you tell the man who came asking?"

"I told him that he was under some kind of false

impression. That I knew nothing about the films or the young lady involved. He became somewhat abusive, and I had to call for Steven to show him out."

"I heard this guy was pretty tough," I said.

"Steven was armed," she said.

"Oh," I said. "How come you didn't have Steven show me out?"

"You did not become abusive."

The entrée came. Duck in a fig and brandy sauce for me, striped bass in cucumber and crabmeat sauce for her. The duck was wonderful.

I said, "You sell these films by subscription." She nodded. "How's chances on a look at the subscription list?"

"None," she said.

"No chance?"

"No chance at all. Obviously you can see my situation. Such material must remain confidential to protect our clients."

"People do sell mailing lists," I said.

"I do not," she said. "I have no need for money, Mr. Spenser."

"No, I guess you don't. Okay, how about I name a couple of people and you tell me if they're on your list? That doesn't compromise any but those I suspect anyway."

There were carrots in brown sauce with fresh dill and zucchini in butter with the entrée, and Patricia Utley ate some of each before she answered. "Perhaps we can go back to my home for brandy after dinner and I'll have someone check."

For dessert we had *clafoutis,* which still tastes like blueberry pancakes to me, and coffee. The coffee was weak. The bill was $119 including tip.

CHAPTER FOURTEEN

AT PATRICIA UTLEY'S HOME I returned to the Calvados. Patricia Utley had some sherry.

"Would you care to see the film, Spenser?" she said.

"No, thank you."

"Why not? I never met a man that didn't care for eroticism."

"Oh, I'm all for eroticism." I was thinking of Linda Rabb in her Church Park apartment in her clean white jeans. "It's movies I don't like."

"As you wish." She sipped some sherry. "You were going to mention some names to me."

"Yeah, Bucky Maynard—I don't know the real first name, maybe that's it—and Lester Floyd." I was gambling she'd never followed sports and had never heard of Maynard. I didn't want to tie Donna Burlington to the Red Sox, but I needed to know. If she'd ever heard of Bucky Maynard, she gave no sign. Lester didn't look like a self-starter. If he was in on this, it was a good bet he represented Maynard.

"I'll see," she said. She picked up a phone on the end table near the couch and dialed a three-digit number. "Would you please check the subscription list, specifically on *Suburban Fancy,* and see if we have either a Bucky Maynard or a Lester Floyd, and the address and date? Thank you. Yes, call me right back, I'm in the library."

"How many copies of that film are there?" I asked.

"I won't tell you," she said. "That's confidential."

"Okay, it doesn't matter anyway. The real question is can I get all the copies?"

"No, I offered to show you the film and you didn't want to."

"That's not the point."

The phone rang and Patricia Utley answered, listened a moment, wrote on a note pad, and hung up.

"There is a Lester Floyd on our subscription list. There is no Bucky Maynard."

"What's the address on Floyd?"

"Harbor Towers, Atlantic Avenue, Boston, Mass. Do you need the street number?"

"No, thank you, that's fine." I finished my brandy and she poured me another.

"The point I was making before is that I don't want the films to look at. I want them to destroy. Donna Burlington has a nice life now. Married, kid, shiny oak floors in her living room, all-electric kitchen. Her husband loves her. That kind of stuff. These films could destroy her."

"That is hardly my problem, Spenser. The odds are very good that no one who saw these films would know Donna or connect her with them. And this is not eighteen seventy-five. Queen Victoria is dead. Aren't you being a little dramatic that someone who acted once in an erotic movie would be destroyed?"

"Not in her circles. In her circles it would be murder."

"Well, even if you are right, as I said, it is not my problem. I am in business, not social work. Destroying those films is not profitable."

"Even if purchased at what us collectors like to call fair market value?"

"Not the master. That would be like killing the goose. You can have all the prints you want, at fair market value, but not the master."

I got up and walked across the room and looked out the windows at Thirty-seventh Street. The streetlights had come on, and while it wasn't full dark yet, there was a softening bronze tinge to everything. The traffic was light, and the people who strolled by looked like extras in a Fred Astaire

253

movie. Well dressed and good-looking. Brilliant red flowers the size of a trumpet bell bloomed in the little garden.

"Mrs. Utley," I said, "I think that Donna's being black-mailed and that the blackmailer will eventually ruin her life and her husband's and he's using your films."

Silence behind me. I turned around and put my hands in my hip pocket. "If I can get those films, I can take away his leverage." She sat quietly with her knees together and her ankles crossed as she had before and took a delicate sip of sherry. "You remember Donna, don't you? Like a niece almost. You taught her everything. Pygmalion. Remember her? She started out in life caught in a mudhole. And she's climbed out. She has gotten out of the bog and onto solid ground, and now she's getting dragged back in. You don't need money. You told me that."

"I'm a businesswoman," she said. "I do not follow bad business practices."

"Is that how you stay out of the bog?" I said.

"I beg your pardon?"

"You climbed out of the mudhole a bit too, is that how? You keep telling yourself you're a businesswoman and that's the code you live by. So that you don't have to deal with the fact that you are also a pimp. Like Violet."

There was no change in her expression. "You lousy no-dick son of a bitch," she said.

I laughed. "Now, baby, now we are getting it together. You got a lot of style and great manners, but you and I are from the same neighborhood, darling, and now that we both know it maybe we can do business. I want those goddamned films, and I'll do what I have to to get them."

Her face was whiter now than it had been. I could see the makeup more clearly.

"You want her back in the mudhole?" I said. "She got out, and you helped her. Now she's got style and manners, and there's a man that wants to dirty her up and rub her nose in what she was. It'll destroy her. You want to destroy her? For business? When I said you were like Violet, you got mad.

Think how mad it would make Violet." She reached over and picked up the phone and pressed the intercom button.

"Steven," she said, "I need you."

By the time the phone was back in the cradle, Steven was in the room. He had a nice springy step when he walked. Vigorous. He also had a .38 caliber Ruger Black Hawk.

Patricia Utley said, "I believe he has a gun, Steven."

Steven said, "Yeah, right hip, I spotted it when he came in. Shall I take it away from him?" Steven was holding the Ruger at his side, the barrel pointing at the floor. As he spoke, he slapped it absentmindedly against his thigh.

"No," Patricia Utley said, "just show him to the street, please."

Steven gestured with his head toward the door. "Move it," he said.

I looked at Patricia Utley. Her color had returned. She was poised, still controlled, handsome. I couldn't think of anything to say. So I moved it.

Outside, it was a warm summer night. Dark now, the bronze glow gone. And on the East Side, midtown, quiet. I walked over to Fifth Avenue and caught a cab uptown to my motel. The West Side was a little noisier but nowhere near as suave. When I got into my room, I turned up the air conditioner, turned on the television, and took a shower. When I came out, there was a Yankee game on and I lay on the bed and watched it.

Was it Lester? Was it Maynard with Lester as the straw? It had to be something like that. The coincidence would have been too big. The rumor that Rabb is shading games, the wife's past, Marty knew something about it. He lied about the marriage circumstances, and Lester Floyd showing up asking about the wife and Lester Floyd's name being on the mailing list. It had to be. Lester or Maynard had spotted Linda Rabb in the film and put the screws on her husband. I couldn't prove it, but I didn't have to. I could report back to Erskine that it looked probable Rabb was in somebody's pocket and he could go to the DA and they could take it from there. I could get a print of the film and show

Erskine and we could brace Rabb and talk about the integrity of the game and what he ought to do for the good of baseball and the kids of America. Then I could throw up.

I wasn't going to do any of those things, and I knew it when I started thinking about it. The Yankee game went into extra innings and was won by John Briggs in the tenth inning, when he singled Don Money in from third. Milwaukee was doing better in New York than I was.

CHAPTER FIFTEEN

I SPENT A GOOD DEAL of time thinking about how to get the master print of *Suburban Fancy* from Patricia Utley and consequently spent not very much time sleeping till about 4:00 A.M. I didn't think of anything before I fell asleep, and when I woke up, it was almost 10 and I hadn't thought of anything while I slept. I was shaving at 10:20 when there was a knock at the door. I opened it with a towel around my middle, and there was a porter with a neat square package.

"Mr. Spenser?"

"Yeah."

"Gentleman asked me to give this to you."

I took it, went to the bureau, found two quarters, and gave them to the porter. He said thank you and went away. I closed the door and sat on the bed and opened the package. It was a canister of film. In the package was a note typed on white parchment paper.

Spenser,

This is the master print of *Suburban Fancy*. I have destroyed the remaining two copies in my posses-

256

sion. My records show a copy sold to the gentleman we discussed last night. There are ten other copies outstanding, but I can find no pattern in their distribution. You will have to deal with the gentleman mentioned above. I wish you success in that.

Doing this violates good business practice and has cost me a good deal more than the money involved. Violet would not have done it.

Yours,
Patricia C. Utley

She had signed it with a black felt-tipped pen in handwriting so neat it looked like type. I'd wasted a sleepless night.

I got out the Manhattan Yellow Pages from the bedside table and looked under "Photographic Equipment" till I found a store in my area that rented projectors. I was going to have to look at the film. If it turned out to be a film on traffic safety, or VD prevention, I would look like an awful goober. Patricia Utley had no reason particularly to lie to me but I was premising too much on the film's authenticity to proceed without looking.

I had mediocre eggs Benedict in the hotel coffee shop and went out and got my projector. Walking back up Fifty-seventh Street with it, I felt furtive, as if the watch and ward society had a tail on me. Going up in the elevator, I tried to look like an executive going to a sales conference. Back in my room I set up the projector on the luggage rack, pulled the drapes, shut off the lights, and sat on one of the beds to watch the movie. Wasteful practice giving me a room with two beds. Motels did that to me often. Alone in a two-bed room. A great song title, maybe I'd get me a funny suit and a guitar and record it. The projector whirred. The movie showed up on the bare wall.

Patricia Utley was right, it was a high-class operation. The color was good, even on the beige wall. I hadn't bothered with sound. The titles were professional, and the set was well lit and realistic-looking. The plot, as I got it without the sound, was about a housewife, frustrated by her church, children, and kitchen existence, who relieves her sense of limitation in the time-honored manner of skin flicks immemorial. The housewife was, in fact, Linda Rabb.

Watching in the darkened motel room, I felt nasty. A middle-aged man alone in a motel watching a dirty movie. When I got through here, I could go down to Forty-second Street and feed quarters into the peep show Movieolas. After the first sexual contact had established for sure what I was looking at, I shut off the projector and rewound the film. I went into the bathroom and stripped the film off the reel into the tub. I got the package of complimentary matches from the bedside table and lit the film. When it had burned up, I turned on the shower and washed the remnants down the drain. It was close to noon when I checked out of the hotel. Before I caught the shuttle back to Boston, I wanted to visit the Metropolitan Museum. On the way uptown in a cab, I stopped at a flower shop and had a dozen roses delivered to Patricia Utley. I checked my overnight bag at the museum, spent the afternoon walking about and throwing my head back and squinting at paintings, had lunch in the fountain room, took a cab to La Guardia, and caught the six o'clock shuttle to Boston. At seven forty-five I was home.

My apartment was as empty as it had been when I left, but stuffier. I opened all the windows, got a bottle of Amstel out of the refrigerator, and sat by the front window to drink it. After a while I got hungry and went to the kitchen. There was nothing to eat. I drank another beer and looked again, and found half a loaf of whole wheat bread behind the beer in the back of the refrigerator and an unopened jar of peanut butter in the cupboard. I made two peanut butter sandwiches and put them on a plate, opened another bottle of beer and went and sat by the window and looked out and ate the sandwiches and drank the beer. *Bas cuisine.*

At nine thirty I got into bed and read another chapter in Morison's *History* and went to sleep. I dreamed something strange about the colonists playing baseball with the British and I was playing third for the colonists and struck out with the bases loaded. In the morning I woke up depressed.

I hadn't worked out during my travels, and my body craved exercise. I jogged along the river and worked out in the BU gym. When I was through and showered and dressed, I didn't feel depressed anymore. So what's a strikeout? Ty Cobb must have struck out once in a while.

It was about ten when I went into the Yorktown Tavern. Already there were drinkers, sitting separate from each other smoking cigarettes, drinking a shot and a beer, watching *The Price Is Right* on TV or looking into the beer glass. In his booth in the back, Lennie Seltzer had set up for the day. He was reading the *Globe*. The *Herald American* and the New York *Daily News* were folded neatly on the table in front of him. A glass of beer stood by his right hand. He was wearing a light tan glen plaid three-piece suit today, and he smelled of bay rum.

He said, "How's business, kid?" as I slid in opposite him.

"The poor are always with us," I said. He started to gesture at the bartender, and I shook my head. "Not at ten in the morning, Len."

"Why not, tastes just as good then as any other time. Better, in fact, I think."

"That's what I'm afraid of. I got enough trouble staying sober now."

"It's pacing, kid, all pacing, ya know. I mean, I just sip a little beer and let it rest and sip a little more and let it rest and I do it all day and it don't bother me. I go home to my old lady, and I'm sober as a freaking nun, ya know." He took an illustrative sip of beer and set the glass down precisely in the ring it had left on the tabletop. "Find out if Marty Rabb's going into el tanko yet?"

I shook my head. "I need some information on some betting habits, though."

"Uh-huh?"

"Guy named Lester Floyd. Ever hear of him?"

Seltzer shook his head. "How about Bucky Maynard?"

"The announcer?"

"Yeah. Floyd is his batman."

"His what?"

"Batman, like in the British army, each officer had a batman, a personal servant."

"You spend too much time reading, Spenser. You know more stuff that don't make you money than anybody I know."

"'Tis better to know than not to know," I said.

"Aw bullshit, what is it you want to know about Maynard and what's'isname?"

"Lester Floyd. I want to know if they bet on baseball and, if they do, what games they bet on. I want the dates. And I need an idea of how much they're betting. Either one or both."

Seltzer nodded. "Okay, I'll let you know."

CHAPTER SIXTEEN

LENNIE SELTZER CALLED me two days later at my office. "Neither Maynard nor Floyd does any betting at all I can find out about," he said.

"Sonovabitch," I said.

"Screw up a theory?"

"Yeah. How sure are you?"

"Pretty sure. Can't be positive, but I been in business here a long time."

"Goddamn," I said.

"I hear that Maynard used to bet a lot, and he got into the hole with a guy and couldn't pay up and the guy sold the paper to a shylock. Pretty good deal, the guy said. Shylock gave him seventy cents on the dollar."

I said, "Aha."

Seltzer said, "Huh?"

I said, "Never mind, just thinking out loud. What's the shylock's name?"

"Wally Hogg. Real name's Walter Hogarth. Works for Frank Doerr."

"Short, fat person, smokes cigars?"

"Yeah, know him?"

"I've seen him around," I said. "Does he always work for Doerr, or does he free-lance?"

"I don't know of him free-lancing. I also don't know many guys like me ever made a profit talking about Frank Doerr."

"Yeah, I know, Lennie. Okay, thanks."

He hung up. I held the phone for a minute and looked up at the ceiling. Seventy cents on the dollar. That was a good rate. Doerr must have had some confidence in Maynard's ability to pay. I looked at my watch: 11:45. I was supposed to meet Brenda Loring in the Public Garden for a picnic lunch. Her treat. I put on my jacket, locked the office, and headed out.

She was already there when I arrived, sitting on the grass beside the swan boat pond with a big wicker basket beside her.

"A hamper?" I said. "A genuine wicker picnic hamper like in Abercrombie and Fitch?"

"I think you're supposed to admire me first," she said, "then the food basket. I've always been suspicious of your value system."

"You look good enough to eat," I said.

"I think I won't pursue that line," she said. She was wearing a pale blue linen suit and an enormous white straw hat. All the young executive types looked at her as they strolled by with their lunches hidden in attaché cases. "Tell me about your travels."

"I had a terrific blackberry pie in Illinois and a wonderful roast duck in New York."

"Oh, I'm glad for you. Did you also encounter any

clues?" She opened the hamper as she talked and took out a red-and-white-checked tablecloth and spread it between us. The day was warm and still, and the cloth lay quiet on the ground.

"Yeah. I found out a lot of things and all of them are bad. I think. It's kind of complicated at the moment."

She took dark blue glossy-finish paper plates out of the hamper and set them out on the cloth. "Tell me about it. Maybe it'll help you sort out the complicated parts."

I was looking into the hamper. "Is that wine in there?" I said. She took my nose and turned my head away.

"Be patient," she said. "I went to a lot of trouble to arrange this and bring it out one item at a time and impress the hell out of you, and I'll not have it spoiled."

"Instinct," I said. "Remember I'm a trained sleuth."

"Tell me about your trip." She put out two sets of what looked like real silver.

"Okay, Rabb's got reason to be dumping a game or two."

"Oh, that's too bad."

"Yeah. Mrs. Rabb isn't who she's supposed to be. She's a kid from lower-middle America who smoked a little dope early and ran off with a local hotshot when she was eighteen. She went to New York, was a whore for a while, and went into acting. Her acting was done with her clothes off in films distributed by mail. She started out turning tricks in one-night cheap hotels. Then she graduated to a high-class call girl operation run, or at least fronted, by a very swish woman out of a fancy town house on the East Side. That's when I think she met her husband."

Brenda placed two big wine goblets in front of us and handed me a bottle of rosé and a corkscrew. "You mean, he was a—what should I call him—a customer?"

"Yeah, I think so. How can I talk and open the wine at the same time? You know my powers of concentration."

"I've heard," she said, "that you can't walk and whistle at the same time. Just open the wine and then talk while I pour."

I opened the wine and handed it to her. "Now," I said, "where was I?"

"Oh, giant intellect," she said, and poured some wine into my glass. "You were saying that Marty Rabb had met his wife when she was—as we sociologists would put it—screwing him professionally."

"Words," I said, "what a magic web you weave with them. Yeah, that's what I think."

"How do you know?" She poured herself a half glass of wine.

"Well, he's covering up her past. He lied about how he met her and where they were married. I don't know what he knows, but he knows something."

Brenda brought out an unsliced loaf of bread and took off the transparent wrapping.

"Sourdough?" I said.

She nodded and put the loaf on one of the paper plates. "Is there more?" she said.

"Yeah. A print of the film she made was sold to Lester Floyd." She looked puzzled. "Lester Floyd," I said, "is Bucky Maynard's gofer, and Bucky Maynard is, in case you forgot, the play by play man for the Sox."

"What's a gofer?"

"A lackey. Someone to go-for coffee and go-for cigarettes and go-for whatever he's told."

"And you think Maynard told him to go-for the film?"

"Yeah, maybe, anyway, say Bucky got a look at the film and recognized Mrs. Rabb. Is that smoked turkey?"

Brenda nodded and put a cranshaw melon out beside it, and four nectarines.

"Oh, I hope she doesn't know," she said.

"Yeah, but I think she does know. And I think Marty knows."

"Some kind of blackmail?"

"Yeah. First I thought it was maybe Maynard or Lester of the costumes getting Rabb to shave a game here and there and cleaning up from the bookies. But they don't seem to bet any these days, and I found out that Maynard owes money to a shylock."

"Is that like a loan shark?"

"Just like a loan shark," I said.

A large wedge of Monterey Jack cheese came out of the hamper, and a small crystal vase with a single red rose in it, which Brenda placed in the middle of the tablecloth.

"That hamper is like the clown car at the circus. I'm waiting for the sommelier to jump out with his gold key and ask if Monsieur is pleased with the wine."

"Eat," she said.

While I was breaking a chunk off the sourdough bread, Brenda said, "So what does the loan shark mean?"

I said, "Phnumph."

She said, "Don't talk with your mouth full. I'll wait till you've eaten a little and gotten control of yourself."

I drank some wine and said, "My compliments to the chef."

She said, "The chef is Bert Heidemann at Bert's Deli on Newbury Street. I'll tell him you were pleased."

"The shylock means that maybe Maynard can't pay up and they've put the squeeze on him and he gave them Rabb."

"What do you mean, gave them Rabb?"

"Well, say Maynard owes a lot of bread to the shylock and he can't pay, and he can't pay the vig, and—"

"The what?"

"The vig, vigorish, interest. A good shylock can keep you paying interest the rest of your life and never dent the principal . . . like a revolving charge. . . . Anyway, say Maynard can't make the payments. Shylocks like Wally Hogg are quite scary. They threaten broken bones, or propane torches on the bottoms of feet, or maybe cut off a finger each time you miss a payment."

Brenda shivered and made a face.

"Yeah, I know, okay, say that's the case and along comes this piece of luck. Mrs. Rabb in the skin flick. He tells the shylock he can control the games that Marty Rabb pitches, and Rabb, being probably the best pitcher now active,

264

if he's under control can make the shylock and his employers a good many tax-free muffins."

"But would he go for it?" Brenda asked. "I mean it would be embarrassing, but the sexual revolution has been won. No one, surely, would stone her to death."

"Maybe so if she were married to someone in a different line of work, but baseball is more conservative than the entire city of Buffalo. And Rabb is part of a whole ethic: Man protects the family, no matter what."

"Even if he has to throw games? What about the jock ethic? You know winning isn't everything, it's the only thing. Wouldn't that be a problem?"

"That's not the real jock ethic, that's the jock ethic that people who don't know a hell of a lot about jocks believe. The real jock ethic's a lot more complicated."

"My, we're a little touchy about the jock ethic, aren't we?"

"I didn't mean you," I said.

"Maybe you haven't outgrown the jock ethic yourself."

"Maybe it's not something to outgrow," I said. "Anyway, some other time I'll give my widely acclaimed lecture on the real jock ethic. The thing is that unless I misjudged Rabb a lot, he's in an awful bind. Because his ethic is violated whichever way he turns. He feels commitment to play the game as best he can and to protect his wife and family as best he can. Both those commitments are probably absolute, and the point when they conflict must be sharp."

Brenda sipped some wine and looked at me without saying anything.

"A quarter for your thoughts if you accept Diners Club?"

She smiled. "You sound sort of caught up in all this. Maybe you're talking some about yourself too. I think maybe you are."

I leered at her. "Want me to tell you about the movie Mrs. Rabb was in and what they did?"

"You think I need pointers?" Brenda said.

"When we stop learning, we stop growing," I said.

265

"And you got us off that subject nicely, didn't you?"

I had once again qualified for membership in the clean plate club by then, and we had begun a second bottle of wine. "You have to get back to work?" I said.

"No, I took the afternoon off. I had the feeling lunch would stretch out."

"That's good," I said, and filled my wineglass again.

CHAPTER SEVENTEEN

IT WAS A CLASSIC summer morning when I dropped Brenda Loring off at her Charles River Park apartment. The river was a vigorous and optimistic blue, and the MDC cop at Leverett Circle was whistling "Buttons and Bows" as he directed traffic. Across the river Cambridge looked clean and bright in sharp relief against the sky. I went around Leverett Circle and headed back westbound on Storrow Drive. The last hurrah of the rush-hour traffic was still to be heard, and it took me twenty minutes to get to Church Park. I parked at a hydrant and took the elevator to the sixth floor. I'd called before I left that morning, so Linda Rabb was expecting me. Marty wasn't home; he was with the club in Oakland.

"Coffee, Mr. Spenser?" she said when I came in.

"Yeah, I'd love some," I said. It was already perked and on the coffee table with a plate of assorted muffins: corn, cranberry, and blueberry; all among my favorites. She was wearing pale blue jeans and a blue-and-pink-striped man-tailored shirt, open at the neck with a pink scarf knotted at the throat. On her feet were cork-soled blue suede slip-on shoes. The engagement ring on her right hand had a heart-shaped diamond in it big enough to make her arm weary. The wedding ring on her left was a wide gold band, unadorned. A small boy who looked like his father hung around the coffee table, eyeing the muffins but hesitant about snatching one from so close to me. I picked up the plate and offered him one, and he retreated quickly back behind his mother's leg.

"Marty's shy, Mr. Spenser," she said. And to the boy: "Do you want cranberry or blueberry, Marty?" The boy turned his head toward her leg and mumbled something I couldn't hear. He looked about three. Linda Rabb picked up a blueberry muffin and gave it to him. "Why don't you get your crayons," she said, "and bring them in here and draw here on the floor while I talk with Mr. Spenser?" The kid mumbled something again that I couldn't hear. Linda Rabb took a deep breath and said, "Okay, Marty, come on, I'll go with you to get them." And to me: "Excuse me, Mr. Spenser."

They went out, the kid hanging onto Linda Rabb's pants leg as they went. No wonder so many housewives ended up drinking Boone's Farm in the morning. They were back in maybe two minutes with a lined yellow legal-sized pad of paper and a box of crayons. The kid got down on the floor by his mother's chair and began to draw stick-figured people in various colors, with orange predominant.

"Now, what can I do for you, Mr. Spenser?" she asked.

I hadn't counted on the kid. "Well, it's kind of complicated, Mrs. Rabb, maybe I ought to come back when the boy isn't . . ." I left it hanging. I didn't know how much the kid would understand, and I didn't want him to think I didn't want him around.

"Oh, that's all right, Mr. Spenser, Marty's fine. He doesn't mind what we talk about."

"Well, I don't know, this is kind of ticklish."

"For heaven's sake, Mr. Spenser, say what's on your mind. Believe me, it is all right."

I drank some coffee. "Okay, I'll tell you two things; then you decide whether we should go on. First, I'm not a writer, I'm a private detective. Second, I've seen a film called *Suburban Fancy*."

She put her hand down on the boy's head; otherwise she didn't move. But her face got white and crowded.

"Who hired you?" she said.

"Erskine, but that doesn't matter. I won't hurt you."

"Why?" she said.

"Why did Erskine hire me? He wanted to find out if your husband was involved in fixing baseball games."

"O my God Jesus," she said, and the kid looked up at her. She smiled. "Oh, isn't that a nice family you're drawing. There's the momma and the daddy and the baby."

"Would it be better if I came back?" I said.

"There's nothing to come back for," Linda Rabb said. "I don't know anything about it. There's nothing to talk about."

"Mrs. Rabb, you know there is," I said. "You're panicky now and you don't know what to say, so you just say no, and hope if you keep saying it, it'll be true. But there's a lot to talk about."

"No."

"Yeah, there is. I can't help you if I don't know."

"Erskine didn't hire you to help us."

"I'm not sure if he did or not. I can always give him his money back."

"There's nothing to help. We don't need any help."

"Yeah, you do."

The kid tugged at his mother's pants leg again and held up his drawing. "That's lovely, Marty," she said. "Is that a doggie?" The kid turned and held the picture so I could see it.

I said, "I like that very much. Do you want to tell me about it?"

The kid shook his head. "No," I said, "I don't blame you. I don't like to talk about my work all that much either."

"Marty," Linda Rabb said, "draw a house for the doggie." The boy bent back to the task. I noticed that he stuck his tongue out as he worked.

"Even if we did need help, what could you do?" Linda Rabb said.

268

"Depends on what exactly is going on. But this is my kind of work. I'm pretty sure to be better at it than you are."

My coffee cup was empty, and Linda Rabb got up and refilled it. I took a corn muffin, my third. I hoped she didn't notice.

"I've got to talk with Marty," she said.

I bit off one side of my corn muffin. Probably should have broken it first. Susan Silverman was always telling me about taking small bites and such. Linda Rabb didn't notice. She was looking at her watch. "Little Marty goes to nursery school for a couple of hours in the afternoon." She looked at the telephone and then at the kid and then at her watch again. Then she looked at me. "Why don't you come back a little after one?"

"Okay."

I got up and went to the door. Linda Rabb came with me. The kid came right behind her, close to her leg but no longer hanging on. As I left, I pointed my finger at him, from the hip, and brought my thumb down like the hammer of a pistol. He looked at me silently and made no response. On the other hand, he didn't run and hide. Always had a way with kids. The Dr. Spock of the gumshoes.

Outside on Mass Ave, I looked at my watch: 11:35. An hour and a half to kill. I went around the corner to the Y on Huntington Ave where I am a member and got in a full workout on the Universal, including an extra set of bench presses and two extra sets of wrist rolls. By the time I got showered and dressed my pulse rate was back down under 100 and my breathing was almost under control. At 1:15 I was back at Linda Rabb's door. She answered the first ring.

"Marty's at school, Mr. Spenser. We can talk openly," she said.

CHAPTER EIGHTEEN

THE COFFEE AND MUFFINS were gone. Linda Rabb said, "Has it been raining somewhere? Your hair's wet."

"Shower," I said. "I went over to the Y and worked out."

"Oh, how nice."

"Sound mind in a healthy body and all that."

"Could you show me some identification, Mr. Spenser?"

I got out the photostat of my license in its little plastic case and handed it to her. Also my driver's license. She looked at them both and gave them back.

"I guess you really are a detective."

"Thanks," I said, "I need reassurance sometimes."

"Just what do you know, Mr. Spenser?"

"I've been to Redford, Illinois, I've talked with Sheriff Donaldson and with your mother and father. I know you got busted there in 'sixty-six for possession of marijuana. I know you ran away with a guy named Tony Reece and that you haven't been back. I know you went to New York, that you lived in a rooming house on Thirteenth Street in the East Village, that you were hustling for a living first for old Tony, then for a pimp named Violet. I know you moved uptown, went to work for Patricia Utley, made one pornographic movie, fell in love with one of your customers, and left to get married in the winter of nineteen seventy, wearing a lovely fur-collared tweed coat. I've been to New York, I've talked with Violet and with Patricia Utley, I preferred Mrs. Utley."

"Yes," Linda Rabb said without any expression, "I did too. Did you see me in the movie?"

"Yeah."

She was looking past me out the window. "Did you enjoy it?"

"I think you're very pretty."

She kept staring out the window. There wasn't anything to see except the dome of the Christian Science Mother Church. I was quiet.

"What do you want?" she said finally.

"I don't know yet. I told you what I know; now I'll tell you what I think. I think the client you married was Marty. I think someone got hold of *Suburban Fancy* that knows you and is blackmailing you and Marty, and that Marty is modifying some of the games he pitches so that whoever is blackmailing you can bet right and make a bundle."

Again silence and the stare. I thought about moving in front of the window to intercept it.

"If I hadn't made the film," she said. "It was just a break, in a way, from turning tricks with strangers. I mean there was every kind of sex in it, but it was just acting. It was always just acting, but in the movie it was supposed to be acting and the guy was acting and there were people you knew around. You didn't have to go alone to a strange hotel room and make conversation with someone you didn't know and wonder if he might be freaky, you know? I mean, some of them are freaky. Christ, you don't know." She shifted her stare from the window to me. I wanted to look out the window.

"One film," she said. "One goddamned film for good money under first-class conditions and no S and M or group sex, and right after that I met Marty."

"In New York?"

"Yes, they were in town to play the Yankees, and one of the other players set it up. Mrs. Utley sent three of us over to the hotel. It was Marty's first time with a whore." The word came out harsh and her stare was heavy on me. "He was always very straight."

271

More silence.

"He was a little drunk and laughing and making suggestive remarks, but as soon as we were alone, he got embarrassed. I had to lead him through it. And afterward we had some food sent up and ate a late supper and watched an old movie on TV. I still remember it. It was a Jimmy Stewart western called *Broken Arrow*. He kissed me good-bye when I left, and he was embarrassed to death to pay me."

"And you saw him again?"

"Yes, I called him at his hotel the next day. It was raining and the game with the Yankees was canceled. So we went to the Museum of Natural History."

"How about the other two players that night? Didn't they recognize you?"

"No, I had on a blond wig and different makeup. They didn't pay much attention to me anyway. Nobody looks at a whore. When I met Marty the next day, he didn't even recognize me at first."

"When did you get married?"

"When we said, except that we changed it. Marty and I worked out the story about me being from Arlington Heights and meeting in Chicago and all. I'd been to Chicago a couple of times and knew my way around okay if anyone wanted to ask about it. And Marty and I went out there before we were married and went to Comiskey Park, or whatever it's called now, and around Chicago so my story would sound okay."

"Where'd you get Arlington Heights?"

"Picked it out on a map."

We looked at each other. I could hear the faint hum of the refrigerator in the kitchen. And somewhere down the corridor a door opened and closed.

"That goddamned movie," she said. "When the letter came, I wanted to confess, but Marty wouldn't let me."

"What letter?"

"The first blackmail letter."

"Do you know who sent it?"

"No."

"I assume you don't have it."

"No."

"What did it say?"

"It said—I can remember it almost exactly—it was to Marty and it said, 'I have a copy of a movie called *Suburban Fancy*. If you don't lose your next ball game, I'll release it to the media.'"

"That's all?"

"That's all. No name or return address or anything."

"And did he?"

Linda Rabb looked blank. "Did he what?"

"Did Marty lose his next game?"

"Yes, he hung a curve in the seventh inning with the bases loaded against the Tigers, on purpose. I woke up in the middle of the night, that night, and he wasn't in bed, he was out in the living room, looking out the window and crying."

Her face was very white, and her eyes were puffy.

"And you wanted to confess it again."

"Yes. But he said no. And I said, 'It will kill you to throw games.' And he said a man looked out for his wife and his kid, and I said, 'But it will kill you.' And he wouldn't talk about it again. He said it was done and maybe there wouldn't be another letter, but we both knew there would."

"And there was."

She nodded.

"And they kept coming?"

She nodded.

"And Marty kept doing what they said to do?"

She nodded again.

"How often?" I said.

"The letters? Not often. Marty gets about thirty-five starts a year. There were maybe five or six letters last year, three so far this year."

"Smart," I said. "Didn't get greedy. Do you have any idea who it is?"

"No."

"It's a hell of a hustle," I said. "Blackmail is dangerous if the victim knows you or at the point when the money is exchanged. This is perfect. There is no money exchanged. You render a service, and he gets the money elsewhere. He never has to reveal himself. There are probably one hundred thousand people who've seen that film, and you can't know who they are. He mails his instructions, bets his money, and who's to know?"

"Yes."

"And furthermore, the act of payment is itself a blackmailable offense so that the more you comply with his requests, the more he's got to blackmail you for."

"I know that too," she said. "If there was a hint of gambling influence, Marty would be out of baseball forever."

"If you look at it by itself, it's almost beautiful."

"I've never looked at it by itself."

"Yeah, I guess not." I said, "Is it killing Marty?"

"A little, I think. He says you get used to anything— maybe he's right."

"How are you?"

"It's not me that has to cheat at my job."

"It's you that has to feel guilty about it," I said. "He can say he's doing it for you. What do you say?"

Tears formed in her eyes and began to run down her face. "I say it's what he gets for marrying a whore."

"See what I mean?" I said. "Wouldn't you rather be him?"

She didn't answer me. She sat still with her hands clenched in her lap, and the tears ran down her face without sound.

I got up and walked around the living room with my hands in my hip pockets. I'd found out what I was supposed to find out, and I'd earned the pay I'd hired on at.

"Did you call your husband?" I said.

She shook her head. "He's pitching today," she said, and her voice was steady but without inflection. "I don't like to bother him on the days he's pitching. I don't want to break his concentration. He should be thinking about the Oakland hitters."

"Mrs. Rabb, it's not a goddamned religion," I said.

"He's not out there in Oakland building a temple to the Lord or a stairway to paradise. He's throwing a ball and the other guys are trying to hit it. Kids do it every day in schoolyards all over the land."

"It's Marty's religion," she said. "It's what he does."

"How about you?"

"We're part of it too, me and the boy—the game and the family. It's all he cares about. That's why it's killing him because he has to screw us or screw the game. Which is like screwing himself."

I should be gone. I should be in Harold Erskine's office, laying it all out for him and getting a bonus and maybe a plaque: OFFICIAL MAJOR LEAGUE PRIVATE EYE. Gumshoe of the stars. But I knew I wasn't going to be gone. I knew that I was here, and I probably knew it back in Redford, Illinois, when I went to her house and met her mom and dad.

"I'm going to get you out of this," I said.

She didn't look at me.

"I know who's blackmailing you."

This time she looked.

CHAPTER NINETEEN

I TOLD HER what I knew and what I thought.

"Maybe you can scare him off," she said. "Maybe when he realizes you know who he is, he'll stop."

"If he's wearing Frank Doerr's harness, I'd say no."

"Why?"

"Because he's got to be more scared of Frank Doerr than I can make him of me."

"Are you sure he's working for Frank What's'isname?"

"I'm not sure of anything. I'm guessing. Right after I started looking around the ball club, Doerr came to my office with one of his gunbearers and told me I might become an endangered species if I kept at it. That's suggestive, but it ain't definitive."

"Can you find out?"

"Maybe."

"Marty makes a lot of money. We could pay you. How much do you charge?"

"My normal retainer is two corn muffins and a black coffee. I bill the rest upon completion."

"I'm serious. We can pay a lot."

"Like Jack Webb would say, you already have, ma'am."

"Thank you."

"You're welcome."

"But I don't want you to start until we get Marty's approval."

"Un-unh. Your retainer doesn't buy that. I'm still also working for Erskine, and I'm still looking into the situation. I'm now looking with an eye to getting you unhooked, but you can't call me off."

"But you won't say anything about us?" Her eyes were wide and her face was pale and tight again and she was scared.

"No," I said.

"Not unless Marty says okay."

"Not until I've checked with you and Marty."

"That's not quite the same thing," she said.

"I know."

"But, Spenser, it's our life. It's us you're frigging around with."

"I know that too. I'll be as careful as I can be."

"Then, damn it, you have got to promise."

"No. I won't promise because I may not be able to deliver. Or maybe it will turn out different. Maybe I'll have to blow the whistle on you for reasons I can't see yet. But if I do, I'll tell you first."

"But you won't promise."

"I can't promise."

"Why not, goddamn you?"

"I already told you."

She shook her head once, as if there were a horsefly on it. "That's bullshit," she said. "I want a better reason than that for you to ruin us."

"I can't give you a better reason. I care about promises, and I don't want to make one I can't be sure I'll keep. It's important to me."

"Bullshit, bullshit, bullshit." She was leaning forward, and her nostrils seemed to flare wider as she did.

"My game has rules too, Mrs. Rabb."

"You sound like Marty," she said.

I didn't say anything.

She was looking at the Christian Science dome again. "Children," she said to it. "Goddamned adolescent children."

My stomach felt a little funny, and I was uncomfortable as hell.

"Mrs. Rabb," I said, "I will try to help. And I am good at this. I'll try."

She kept looking at the dome. "You and Marty and all the goddamned game-playing children. You're all good at all the games." She turned around and looked at me. "Screw," she said, and jerked her head at the door.

I couldn't think of much to say to that, so I screwed. She slammed the door behind me, and I went down in the elevator feeling like a horse's ass and not sure why.

It was almost three o'clock. There was a public phone outside the drugstore next to the apartment building entrance. I went in and called Martin Quirk.

"Spenser," he said. "Thank God you called. I've got this murder took place in a locked room. It's got us all stumped and the chief said; 'Quirk,' he said, 'only one man can solve this.'"

"Can I buy you lunch or a drink or something?"

"Lunch? A drink? Christ, you must be in deep trouble."

I did not feel jolly. "Yes or no," I said. "If I wanted humor, I'd have called Dial-A-Joke."

"Yeah, okay. I'll meet you at the Red Coach on Stanhope Street."

I hung up. There was a parking ticket neatly tucked under the wiper blade on the driver's side. The string looped around the base. A conscientious meter maid. A lot of them just jam it under the wiper without looping the string, and sometimes on the passenger side where you can't even see it. It was nice to see samples of professional pride. I put the ticket in a public trash receptacle attached to a lamppost.

I drove down Boylston Street past the Prudential Center and the new public library wing and through Copley Square. The fountain in the square was in full spray, and college kids and construction workers mingled on the wall around it, eating lunch, drinking beer, taking the sun. A lot of them were shirtless. Beyond the fountain was the Copley Plaza with two enormous gilded lions flanking the entrance. And at the Clarendon Street end of the square, Trinity Church gleamed, recently sandblasted, its brown stones fresh-looking, its spires reflecting brightly in the windows of the Hancock Building. A quart of beer, I thought, and a cutlet sub. Shirt off, catch some rays, maybe strike up a conversation with a coed. Would you believe, my dear, I could be your father? Oh, you would.

I turned right on Clarendon and left onto Stanhope, where I parked in a loading zone. Stanhope Street is barely more than an alley and tucked into it between an electrical supply store and a garage is the Red Coach Grill, looking very old world with red tile roof and leaded windows. It was right back of police headquarters, and a lot of cops hung out there. Also a lot of insurance types and ad men. Despite that, it wasn't a bad place. Quiet lighting, oaken beams, and such. Quirk was at the bar. He looked like I always figured a cop ought to. Bigger than I am and thick. Short, thick black hair, thick hands and fingers, thick neck, thick features, a pockmarked face, and dressed like he'd just come from a summit meeting. Today he had on a light gray three-piece suit with a pale red plaid pattern, a white shirt, and a silk-finish wide red tie. His shoes were patent leather loafers with a gold trim. I slipped onto a barstool beside him.

"You gotta be on the take," I said. "Fuzz don't get paid enough to dress like that."

"They do if they don't do anything else. I haven't been on vacation in fifteen years. What are you spending your dough on?"

"Lunch for cops," I said. "Want to sit in a booth?"

Quirk picked up his drink, and we sat down across from the bar in one of the high-backed walnut booths that run parallel to the bar front to back and separate it from the dining room.

I ordered a bourbon on the rocks from the waitress. "Shot of bitters and a twist," I said, "and another for my date." The waitress was young with a short skirt and very short blond hair. Quirk and I watched her lean over the bar to pick up the drinks.

"You are a dirty lecherous old man," I said. "I may speak to the vice squad about you."

"What were you doing, looking for clues?"

"Just checking for concealed weapons, Lieutenant."

She brought the drinks. Quirk had Scotch and soda.

We drank. I took a lot of mine in the first swallow. Quirk said, "I thought you were a beer drinker."

"Yeah, but I got a bad taste I want to get rid of and the bourbon is quicker."

"You must be used to a bad taste in your line of business."

I finished the drink and nodded at the waitress. She looked at Quirk. He shook his head. "I'll nurse this," he said.

"I thought you guys weren't supposed to drink on duty," I said.

"That's right," he said. "What do you want?"

"I just thought maybe we could rap a little about law enforcement theory and prison reform, and swap detective techniques, stuff like that."

"Spenser, I got eighteen unsolved homicides in my left-hand desk drawer at this moment. You want to knock off the bullshit and get to it."

"Frank Doerr," I said. "I want to know about him."

"Why?"

"I think he owns some paper on a guy who is squeezing a client."

"And the guy is squeezing the client because of the paper?"

"Yes."

"Doerr's probably free-lance. Got his own organization, operates around the fringe of the mob's territory. Gambling, mostly, used to be a gambler. Vegas, Reno, Cuba in the old days. Does loan sharking too. Successful, but I hear he's a little crazy, things don't go right, he gets bananas and starts shooting everybody. And he's too greedy. He's going to bite off too big a piece of somebody else's pie and the company will have him dusted. He's looking flashy now, but he's not going to last."

"Where do I find him?"

"If you're screwing around in this operation, he'll find you."

"But say I want to find him before he does, where?"

"I don't know, exactly. Runs a funeral parlor, somewhere in Charlestown. I get back to the station I'll check for you."

"Has he got a handle I can shake him with?"

"You? Scare him off? You try scaring Doerr and they'll be tying a tag on your big toe down at Boston City."

"Well, what's he like best? Women? Booze? Performing seals? There must be a way to him."

"Money," Quirk said. "He likes money. Far as I know he doesn't like anything else."

"How do you know he doesn't like me?" I said.

"I surmise it," Quirk said. "You met him?"

"Once."

"Who was with him?"

"Wally Hogg."

Quirk shook his head. "Get out of this, Spenser. You're

in with people that will waste you like a popsicle on a warm day." The waitress brought us another round. She was wearing fishnet stockings. Could it be Ms. Right? I drank some bourbon.

"I wish I could get out of this, Marty. I can't."

"You're in trouble yourself?" Quirk asked.

"No, but I gotta do this, and it's not making anyone too happy."

"Wally Hogg," Quirk said, "will kill anyone Doerr tells him to. He doesn't like it or not like it. Slow or fast, one or a hundred, whatever. Doerr points him and he goes bang. He's a piece with feet."

"Well, if he goes bang at me," I said, "he'll be Wally Sausage."

"You're not as good as you think you are, Spenser. But neither is Captain Marvel. I've seen people worse than you, and maybe you got a chance. But sober. Don't go up against any of Doerr's group half-gassed. Go bright and early in the morning after eight hours' sleep and a good breakfast." He stirred the ice in his new drink. I noticed he hadn't finished the old one.

"Slow," I said. "Always knew you were a slow drinker." I reached over and picked up his old drink and finished it. "I can drink you right out of your orthopedic shoes, Quirk."

"Christ, this thing really is bugging you, isn't it?" Quirk said. He stood up. "I'm going back to work before you start to slobber."

"Quirk," I said.

He stopped and looked at me.

"Thanks for not asking for names."

"I knew you wouldn't tell me," Quirk said. "And watch your ass on this, Spenser. There must be someone who'd miss you."

I gave him a thumbs-up gesture, like in the old RAF movies, and he walked off. I drank Quirk's new drink and gestured to the waitress. There'll always be an England.

By five thirty in the afternoon I was sitting at the desk in my office, drinking bourbon from the bottle neck. Brenda

Loring had a date, Susan Silverman didn't answer her phone. The afternoon sun slanted in at my window and made the room hot. I had the sash up, but there wasn't much breeze and the sweat was collecting where my back pressed against the chair.

Maybe I should get out of this thing. Maybe it bothered me too much. Why? I'd been told to screw before. Why did this time bother me? "Goddamned adolescent children." I'd heard worse than that before. "Goddamned game-playing children." I'd heard worse than that too. I drank some bourbon. My nose felt sort of numb and the surface of my face felt insulated. Dumb broad. Promises. Shit, I can't promise what I don't know. World ain't that simple, for crissake. I said I'd try. What the hell she want, for crissake? By God, I would get her out of it. I held the bottle up toward the window and looked at how much was left. Half. Good. Even if I finished it, there was another one in the file cabinet. Warm feeling having another one in the file cabinet. I winked at the file cabinet and grinned with one side of my mouth like Clark Gable used to. He never did it at file cabinets, though, far as I could remember. I drank some more and rinsed it around in my mouth. Maybe my teeth will get drunk. I giggled. Goddamned sure Clark Gable never giggled. Drink up, teeth. Hot damn. She was right, though, it was a kind of game. I mean, you played ball or something and whatever you did there had to be some kind of rules for it, for crissake. Otherwise you ended up getting bombed and winking at file cabinets. And your teeth got drunk. I giggled again. I was going to have Frank Doerr's ass. But sober, Quirk was right, sober, and in shape. "I'm coming, Doerr, you sonovabitch." Tongue wasn't drunk yet. I could still talk. Have a drink, tongue, baby. I drank. "Only where love and need are one," I said out loud. My voice sounded even stranger. Detached and over in the other corner of the room. "And the work is play for goddamned mortal stakes/Is the deed ever really done." My throat felt hot, and I inhaled a lot of air to cool it. "Mortal goddamned stakes," I said. "You got that, Linda Rabb/Donna Burlington, baby?" I had unclipped my holster, and it lay with my .38 detective special in it on the desk beside the bourbon bottle. I drank a little more bourbon, put down the bottle, picked up the gun still in its holster, and pointed it at one of the Vermeer prints, the one of the Dutch girl with a milk pitcher. "How do you like them goddamned games, Frank?" Then I made a plonking sound with my tongue.

It was quiet then for a while. I sipped a little. And listened to the street sounds a little and then I heard someone snoring and it was me.

CHAPTER TWENTY

THE NEXT DAY it took me five miles of jogging and an hour and a half in the weight room to get the swelling out of my tongue and my vital signs functioning. I had breakfast in a diner, nothing could be finer, took two aspirin, and set out after Frank Doerr. A funeral parlor in Charlestown, Quirk had said. I brought all my sleuthing wiles to bear on the problem of how to locate it and looked in the Yellow Pages. Elementary, my dear Holmes. There it was, under "Funeral Directors": Francis X. Doerr, 228 Main Street, Charlestown. There's no escape Doerr.

With the top down I drove my eight-year-old Chevy across the bridge into City Square. Charlestown is a section of Boston. Bunker Hill is there, and *Old Ironsides,* but the dominant quality of Charlestown is the convergence of elevated transportation. The Mystic River Bridge, Route 93, and the Fitzgerald Expressway all interchange in Charlestown. Through the maze run the tracks of the elevated MBTA. Steel and concrete stanchions have flourished in the City Square area as nowhere else. If the British wanted to attack Bunker Hill now, they wouldn't be able to find it.

From City Square I drove out Main Street under the elevated tracks. Doerr was maybe a half mile out from City Square toward Everett. Parking in that area of Charlestown was no problem. Most of the stores along that stretch of Main Street are boarded up. And urban renewal had not yet brought economic renewal. My car looked just right in the neighborhood.

Doerr's Funeral Parlor was a two-story brick house with a slate roof. It was wedged in between an unoccupied grocery store with plywood nailed over the windows and a discount shoe store called Ronny's Rejects. Across the street a vacant lot, not yet renewed, supported a flourishing crop of chicory and Queen Anne's lace. Nature never betrayed the heart that loved her.

I brushed my hand over the gun on my hip for security and rang the bell at the front door. Inside, it made a very gentle chime. Full of solicitude. The door was opened almost at once by a plump man with a perfectly bald head. Striped pants, white shirt, dark coat, black tie. The undertaker's undertaker.

"May I help you," he said. Soft. Solicitous. May I take your wallet, may I have all your money? Leave everything to us.

"Yes," I said. "I'd like to speak with Mr. Doerr." Mr. Doerr? He had me talking like him. I felt the scared feeling in my stomach.

"Concerning what, sir?"

I gave Baldy my card, the one with just my name on it, and said, "Tell Doerr I'd like to continue the discussion we began the other night." Dropping the "Mr." made me feel more aggressive.

"Certainly, sir, won't you sit down for a moment?"

I sat in a straight-back chair with a velvet seat, and the bald man left the room. I thought he might genuflect before he left but he didn't, just left with a dignified and reverent nod. It didn't help my stomach. Getting the hell out would have helped my stomach but would have done little for my self-image. Doerr probably wasn't that tough anyway. And Big Wally looked out of shape. Course you don't have to be in really great shape to squeeze off, say, two rounds from a nine-millimeter Walther.

The building was absolutely silent and had a churchy smell. The entry hall where I sat was papered in a dim beige with palm fronds on it. Very understated and elderly. The rug on the floor was Oriental, with dull maroon the dominant color, and the ceiling fixture was wreathed in molded plaster fruit.

The bald man came back. "This way, please, sir," he said, and stood aside to let me precede him through the door. Well, Spenser, I said, it's your funeral. Sometimes I'm uncontrollably droll.

Doerr's office was on the second floor front and looked out at the elevated tracks. Just right if you wanted to make eye contact with commuters. Apparently Doerr didn't because he sat behind a mahogany desk with his back to the window. His desk was cluttered with manila file folders. There were two phones, and a big vase of snapdragons flourished on a small stand beside the window.

"What do you want?" Doerr said.

I sat in one of the two straight chairs in front of the desk. Doerr didn't waste a lot of bread on decor.

"Why don't you get right to the point, Frank?" I said. "Don't hide behind evasive pleasantries."

"What do you want?"

"I want to answer some of the questions you asked me the other day."

"Why?"

"Openness and candor," I said. "The very hallmark of my profession."

Doerr was sitting straight, hands resting on the arms of his swivel chair. He looked at me without expression. Without comment. A train clattered by outside the window, headed for Sullivan Square. Doerr ignored it.

285

"Okay," I said. "You asked me what I was doing out at the ball park besides playing pepper."

Doerr continued to look at me.

"I was hired to see if someone was going into the tank out there."

Doerr said, "And?"

"And someone is."

"Who?"

"I think we both know."

"Why do you think that?"

"Several things, including the fact you came calling with your gunslinger right after I was out there."

"So?"

"So you heard from someone. I know who's dumping the games, I know who's blackmailing him into it, and I know what shylock the blackmailer owes. And that brings us right back here to you. Okay if I call you Shy for short? We get on so well and all."

"Names, Spenser. I'm not interested in a lot of bullshit about who you know and what anonymous whosis is doing what. Gimme a name and maybe I'm interested."

"Marty Rabb, Bucky Maynard, and you, Blue Eyes."

"Those are serious allegations, you got proof?"

"Serious allegations." I whistled. "That's very good for a guy whose lips move when he reads the funnies."

"Look, you piece of turd, don't get smart with me. I can have you blown away before you can scratch your ass. You understand? Now gimme what you got or you're going to get hurt."

"That's better," I said, "that's the old glib Frankie. Yeah, I got some proof, and I can get some more. What I haven't got for proof yet is the tie between you and Maynard, but I can get it. I'll bet Maynard might begin to ooze under pressure."

"Saying you're right, saying that's the way it is, and you can get some proof out of Maynard. Why don't I just waste Maynard or, maybe better, waste you?"

"You won't waste Maynard, because I'll bet you don't

286

know what he's got on Rabb and I'll bet even more that he's got it stashed somewhere so if something happens to him, you'll never know. You won't waste me because I'm so god-damned lovable. And because there's a homicide cop named Quirk that knows I'm here. Besides, I'm not sure you got the manpower."

"You're doing a lot of guessing."

As far as you could tell from Doerr's face, I might have been in there arranging a low-budget funeral. And maybe I was.

"I'm licensed to," I said. "The state of Massachusetts says I'm permitted to make guesses and investigate them."

"So what do you want?"

"I want it to stop. I want Maynard to give me the item he's using for blackmail, and I want everyone to leave the Rabbs alone."

"Or what?"

"I don't suppose you'd accept 'or else.' "

"I'm getting sick of you, Spenser. I'm sick of the way you look, and the way you dress, and the way you get your hair cut, and the way you keep shoving your face into my work. I'm sick of you being alive and making wise remarks. You understand what I'm saying to you, turd?"

"What's wrong with the way I dress?"

"Shut up." Doerr's face had gotten a little red under the health club tan. He swung his chair sideways and stared out the window. And he had begun to fiddle with a pencil. Tapping it against his thigh until it had slid through his fingers and then reversing it and tapping it again. Tap-tap-tap. Reverse. Tap-tap-tap. Reverse. Lead end. Erasure end. Tap-tap-tap. Another train went by, almost empty, heading this time from Everett Station toward City Square. I slid my gun out of the hip holster and held it between my legs under my thighs with my hands clasped over it so it looked like I was leaning forward in concealed anxiety. I had no trouble at all simulating the anxiety.

Doerr swung his chair back around, still holding the pencil. He pointed it at me.

"Okay," he said. "I'm going to let you walk out of here. But before you go, I'm going to give you an idea of what happens when I get sick of someone."

There must have been a button under the desk that he could hit with his knee, or maybe the room was bugged. Either way a door to the left of the desk opened and Wally Hogg came in. He had on another flowered shirt, hanging outside the double knit pants, and the same wraparound sunglasses. In his right hand was one of those rubber truncheons that French cops use for riot control. He reminded me of one of the nasty trolls that used to lurk under bridges.

"Wally," Doerr said, looking at me while he said it, "show him what hurts."

Wally came around the desk. "You want it sitting down or standing up," he said. "It don't make no difference to me." He stood directly in front of me, looking down as I leaned over in even greater anxiety. I brought the gun up from between my thighs, thumbed the hammer back while I was doing that, and put the muzzle against the underside of his jaw, behind the jawbone, where it's soft. And I pressed up a little.

"Wally," I said, "have you ever thought of renting out as a goblin for Halloween parties?"

Wally's body was between Doerr and me, and Doerr couldn't see the gun. "What the hell are you waiting for, Wally? I want to hear him yelling."

I stood up and Wally inched back. The pressure of the gun muzzle made him rise slightly on the balls of his feet.

"Overconfidence," I said. "Overconfidence again, Frankie. That's twice you said ugly things to me and then couldn't back them up. Now I am thinking about whether I should shoot Wally in the tongue or not. Put the baton in my left hand, porklet," I said to Wally. He did. Our faces were about an inch apart, and his was as blank as it had been when he'd walked into the room. Without looking, I tossed it into the corner behind me.

"Of course, you could try me, Frank. You could rummage around in your desk maybe and come up with a weapon and have a go at me. Pretty good odds, Frankie. I have to shoot the Hog first before I can get you. Why not? It's quicker than scaring me to death." I kept the pressure of the gun barrel up under Wally's chin and looked past his shoulder at Doerr. Doerr had his hands, palms down, on the desk in front of him. His face was quite red and his lips were trembling. But he didn't move. He stared at me and the lines from his nostrils to the corners of his mouth were deep and there was a very small tic in his left eyelid. With my left hand I patted Wally down and found the P .38 in its shoulder holster under his belt. All the time I watched Doerr. His mouth was open maybe an inch, and a small bubble of saliva had formed in the right-hand corner. I could see the tip of his tongue and it seemed to tremble, like the tic in his eye and in counterpoint to the movement of his lips. It was kind of interesting. But I was getting sick of standing that close to Wally.

"Turn around, Wall," I said. "Rest your hands on the desk and back away with your feet apart till all your weight is on your arms. You probably know the routine." I stepped away from him around the desk closer to Doerr, and Wally did as he was told.

"Okay, Frank," I said. "So much for what hurts. Are you going to climb down from Marty Rabb's back, or am I going to have to take you off?"

Doerr's mouth had opened wider and his tongue was quivering against his lower lip much more violently than it had been. The small bubble had popped and a small trickle of saliva had replaced it. His head had dropped, and as he began to look at me, he had to roll his eyes up toward his eyebrows. His mouth was moving too, but he wasn't making any noise.

"How about it, Frank? I like standing around watching you drool, but I got things to do."

Doerr opened his middle drawer and came out with a gun. I slammed my gun down on the back of his wrist, and it cracked against the edge of the desk. The gun rattled across the desk top and fell on the floor. Wally Hogg raised his head and I turned the gun at him. Doerr doubled up over his hand and made a repetitive grunting noise. Rocking back and forth in the swivel chair, grunting and drooling and making a sound that was very much like crying.

"Am I to interpret this as a rejection, Frank?"

He kept rocking and moaning and crying. "Aw balls," I said. I picked up Doerr's little automatic and stuck it in my pocket and said to Wally, "If you try to stop me, I'll kill you," and walked out the door. No one was downstairs. No one let me out. No one pursued me as I drove off.

CHAPTER TWENTY-ONE

THERE'S A BIRD I read about that lives around rhinos and feeds on the insects that the rhinos stir up when they walk. I'd always figured that my work was like that. If the rhinos were moving, things would happen. This time, though, the rhino had started to cry and I wasn't too sure how to deal with that. I had a feeling, though, how Doerr would deal with that once he stopped crying. I didn't like the feeling. Maybe the technique only worked with real birds and real rhinos. Maybe I was doing more harm than good. Maybe I should get back on the cops and do what the watch commander said. I could get rid of a lot of maybes that way. I drove out Main Street, past the candy factory and around the circle at Sullivan Square, and back in toward Boston on Rutherford Ave. The sweet smell from the factory masked the smoke that billowed out of the skyscraper chimneys at the Edison plant across the Mystic River. Past the community college I turned right over the Prison Point Bridge, which had been torn down and rebuilt and called the Somebody T. Gilmore Bridge. The traffic reporters called it the Gilmore Bridge, but I remembered when it led to the old prison in Charlestown, where the walls were red brick like the rest of the city, and on execution nights people used to gather in the streets to watch the lights dim when they turned on the current in the chair. Now state prison was in Walpole and electrocutions were accidental. Ah sweet bird of youth.

It was before lunchtime still and traffic was light. In five minutes I was at my office and sliding into a handy tow zone to park. I bought a copy of the *Globe* at a cigar store and went up to my office to read it. The Sox had an off day today and opened at home against Cleveland tomorrow. Marty Rabb had beaten Oakland 2 to 0 yesterday on the coast, and the team had flown into Logan this morning early.

I called Harold Erskine and got Bucky Maynard's home address. It was what I thought it would be.

"Why do you want to know?" Erskine asked.

"Because it's there," I said.

"I don't want you screwing around with Maynard. That's the surest way to have this whole thing blow wide open."

"Don't worry, I am a model of circumspection."

"Yeah," Erskine said, "sure. You find out anything yet?"

"Nothing I can report on yet, I need to put some things together."

"Well, for crissake, what have you found out? Is Marty or isn't he?"

"It's not that simple, Mr. Erskine. You'll have to give me a little more time."

"How much more? You're costing me a hundred a day. What do your expenses look like?"

"High," I said. "I been to Illinois and New York City and spent a hundred and nineteen bucks buying dinner for a witness."

"Jesus Galloping Christ, Spenser. I got a goddamned budget to work with, and I don't want you appearing in it. How the Christ am I going to bury that kind of dough? God-damn it, I want you to check with me before you go spending my money like that."

"I don't work that way, Mr. Erskine, but I think I won't run up much more expense money." I needed to stay on this thing. I couldn't afford to get fired and shut off from the Sox. Also I needed the money. My charger needed feed and my armor needed polish. "I'm closing in on the truth."

"Yeah, well, close in on it quick," Erskine said, and hung up.

The old phrasemaker, Closing In on the Truth. I should have been a poet. If I went back on the cops, I wouldn't need to worry about charger feed and armor polish.

Harbor Towers is new, a complex of highrise apartments that looks out over Boston Bay. It represents a substantial monument to the renaissance of the waterfront, and the smell of new concrete still lingers in the lobbies. The central artery cuts them off from the rest of the city, penning them against the ocean, and they form a small peninsula of recent affluence where once the wharves rotted.

I parked in the permanent shade under the artery, on Atlantic Ave, near Maynard's apartment. It was hot enough for the asphalt to soften and the air conditioning in the lobby felt nice. I gave my name to the houseman, who called it up, then nodded at me. "Top floor, sir, number eight." The elevator was lined with mirrors and I was trying to see how I looked in profile when we got to the top floor and the doors opened. I looked quickly ahead, but no one was there. It's always embarrassing to get caught admiring yourself. Number 8 was opposite the elevator and Lester Floyd opened it on my first ring.

He had on white denim shorts, white sandals, a white headband, and sunglasses with big white plastic frames and black lenses. His upper body was as smooth and shiny as a snake's, tight-muscled and flexible. Instead of a belt, there was what looked like a black silk scarf passed through the belt loops and knotted over his left hip. He was chewing bubble gum. He held the door open and nodded his head toward the living room. I went in. He shut the door behind me. The living room looked to be thirty feet long, with the far wall a bank of glass that opened onto a balcony. Beyond the balcony, the Atlantic, blue and steady and more than my eye could fully register. Lester slid open one of the glass doors, went out, slid it shut behind him, settled down on a chaise made from filigreed white iron, rubbed some lotion on his chest, and chewed his gum at the sun. Mr. Warm.

I sat in a big red leather chair. The room was full of pictures, mostly eight-by-ten framed glossy prints of Maynard and various celebrities. Ballplayers, politicians, a couple of movie types. I didn't see any private eyes. Discriminatory bastard. Or maybe just discriminating. The sound of a portable radio drifted in faintly from Lester's sun deck. The top forty. Music with the enchantment and soul of a penny gum machine. Ah when you and I were young, Sarah.

Bucky Maynard came into the living room from a door in the far right-hand wall. He was wearing bright yellow pajamas under a maroon silk bathrobe with a big velvet belt. He needed a shave and his eyes were puffy. He hadn't been awake long.

"Y'all keep some early hours, Spenser. Ah didn't get to bed till four A.M."

"Early to bed," I said, "early to rise. I wanted to ask you what Lester was doing down in New York talking with Patricia Utley."

The collar of Maynard's robe was turned up on one side. He smoothed it down carefully. "Ah can't say ah know what you mean, Spenser. Ah can ask him."

"As us kids say out in the bleachers, don't jive me, Bucko. Lester was down there on your business. I've talked with Utley. I've talked with Frank Doerr and Wally the bone breaker. I've seen a film called *Suburban Fancy* and I've talked with Linda Rabb. Actually I guess I asked the wrong question. I know what Lester was doing down there. What I want to know is what we do now that I know."

"Lester." Maynard showed no change in expression. Lester left the radio playing and came into the living room and blew a pink bubble that nearly obscured his face.

"Criminentlies, Lester," I said. "That's a really heavy bubble. I think you're my bubble-blowing idol. Zowie." Lester chewed the bubble back into his mouth without even a trace sticking to his lips. "Hours," I said. "It must take hours of practice."

Lester looked at Maynard. "Spenser and ah are going to talk, and ah want you to be around and to listen, Lester." Lester leaned against the edge of the sliding door and crossed his arms and looked at me. Maynard sat in one of the leather chairs and said, "Now what exactly is the point of your question, Spenser?"

"I figure that we've got a mutual problem and maybe we could conspire to solve it. Conspire, Lester. That means get together."

"Get to the point, Spenser. Lester gonna get mad at you."

"You owe Frank Doerr money and you can't pay, so you're blackmailing Marty Rabb into going into the tank for you and you're feeding the information to Doerr so he won't hurt you."

"Frank Doerr gotta deal with me before he hurts anybody," Lester said.

"Yeah, that's a big problem for him," I said. "Flex at him next time he and the Hog come calling. See if he faints."

"I'm getting goddamned sick of you, you wise bastard." Lester unfolded his arms and moved a step toward me.

"Lester," Maynard said, "we're talking." Lester refolded, stepped back, and leaned on the door again. Like reversing a film sequence.

"Ah don't know why you think all that stuff, Spenser. But say y'all was right. What business would that be of yours? You being a writer and all?"

"You know and I know that I'm not a writer."

"Ah do? Ah don't know any such thing. You told me you was a writer." The cornpone accent had gotten thicker. I didn't know if it was the real one coming through under duress or a fake one getting faker. Actually I couldn't see that it mattered much.

"Yeah, and you hollered to Doerr and he looked me up and we both know I'm a private cop."

"How about that?" Maynard raised both eyebrows. "A private detective. That still leaves the question, though, Spenser. What is your interest?"

"I would like you to stop blackmailing the Rabbs."

"And if ah was blackmailing them, and ah stopped, what would ah get out of that?"

"Well, I'd be grateful."

From his post by the sliding door, Lester said, "Shit," drawing it out into a two-syllable word.

"Anything besides that?" Maynard said.

"I'll help you with Frank Doerr."

Lester said, "Shit," again. This time in three syllables.

"Well, Spenser, that's awful kind of you, but there's some things wrong with it all. One, ah don't much give a rat's ass for your gratitude, you know? And number two, ah don't figure, even if ah was having trouble with Frank Doerr, that you'd be the one ah'd ask to help me. And of course, number three, ah'm not blackmailing anybody. Am I, Lester?"

Lester shook his head no.

"So, ah guess you wasted some time coming up here. Interesting to know about you being a detective, though. Isn't that interesting, Lester?"

Lester nodded his head yes. From the radio on the sun deck the disk jockey was yelling about a "rock classic."

I said, "Y'all seem to be takin' the short view." Christ, now he had me doing it.

"Why do you say so?"

"Because you have only a short-term solution. How long will Marty Rabb pitch? Five more years. You think that when he's through with baseball, Doerr will be through with you? Doerr will feed on you till you die."

"I can handle Doerr," Lester said. He didn't get too much variety into the conversation.

"Lester," I said, "you can't handle Doerr. Handling Doerr is different from beating up some tourist in a bar or breaking bricks with your bare hand. Wally Hogg is a professional tough guy. You are an amateur. He would blow you away like a midsummer dandelion."

295

Lester said, "Shit." You find a line that works for you, I suppose you ought to stick with it.

Maynard said, "If these people are so tough, Spenser, what makes you think you can help?"

"Because I'm a professional too, Bucko, and that means I know what I can do and also what I can't do. It means I don't walk around thinking I can go up against the likes of Frank Doerr, head-on, without getting my body creased. It means I know how to even things up a bit. It means I know what I'm doing and you two clowns don't."

"You don't look so frigging tough to me," Lester said.

"That's the difference between you and me, Lester. Aside from our taste in music. I don't worry about how things look. You do. I don't have to prove whether I'm tough. You do. You'll say something like that to Wally the Hog and he'll shoot you three times or so in your nose, while you're posing and blowing bubbles."

Lester had gone into the stance, legs bent, left fist forward, right drawn back, clenched palms up, a little like the old pictures of the great John L. "Why don't you try me, you mother?"

I stood up. "Lester, let me show you something," I said. And brought my gun out and aimed it at his forehead. "This is a thirty-eight caliber Colt detective special. If I pull the trigger, your mastery of the martial arts will be of very little use to you."

Maynard said, "Now, Spenser . . ."

Lester looked at the gun.

"Now put that thing down, Spenser," Maynard said. "Lester. Y'all just relax over there."

Lester said, "If you didn't have that gun."

"But that's the point, Les, baby, I do have the gun. Wally Hogg has a gun. You don't have a gun. Professionals are the people with the guns who get them out first."

"Now relax, y'all, just relax," Maynard said.

"You won't always have that gun, Spenser."

"See, boy, see what a baby you are," I said. "You're wrong again. I will always have the gun. You'd forget the gun, you wouldn't have it where you could get at it, but I will always have it."

"Lester," Maynard said again. This time loud. "Y'all just settle down. You hear me. Now you settle down. Ah don't want no more of this."

Lester eased out of his attack stance and leaned back against the doorjamb, but he kept his eyes on me and one of the eyelids seemed to flicker as he stared. I put the gun away.

I said to Maynard, "You keep him away from me or I will hurt him badly."

"Now, Spenser," Maynard said. "Lester excites kind of prompt, but he's not a fool. Right, Lester?"

Lester didn't speak. I noticed that there was a glisten of sweat on Maynard's upper lip. "Suppose ah was interested in joining forces with you," Maynard said. "What would be your plan? How would you keep Doerr from coming around and killing me?"

"I'd tell him that right now we call off the scheme and end the blackmail and he's out some bread, but no one's incriminated. If he causes trouble, it'll mean the cops, and then someone will be incriminated. And it'll be him, because we've stashed evidence where the cops will find it if anything happens to you."

"What about the money I owe him, Ah mean hypothetically?"

"You've paid that off long ago if Doerr got any bread down at all on Rabb's pitching."

"But maybe Doerr will want more, and ah don't have it."

"It'll be my job to convince him not to want more."

"That's it. That's the part ah want to know," Maynard said, and his face looked very moist. "How you going to convince him of anything?"

"I don't know. Appeal to his business sense. Dropping the scheme is a lot less trouble than sticking to it. He can pick up dough a lot of other ways. You and Rabb aren't the only goobers in the patch."

Maynard took a deep breath. The top forty played on

outside on the deck. Lester glared at me from the doorjamb. Whitecaps continued to pattern the bay. Maynard shook his head. "Not good enough, Spenser. What you say may be so, but right now ah'm not getting hurt. And what you say makes getting hurt more likely."

"I can handle Doerr, Bucky." Lester sounded almost plaintive from the doorjamb.

"Maybe yes, maybe no, Lester. You couldn't have handled Spenser here, if it had been for real. Ah'm saying right now, no. Ah'm not going to take the chance. Things have worked out so far."

"But it's different now, Buck," I said. "I'm in it now. And I'm going to poke around and aggravate the hornets. It's not safe anymore to go along with the program."

"Maybe that's true too," Maynard said. "But ah got a choice between you and Frank Doerr, and right now ah'm betting on Frank Doerr. But ah'll tell you this. If you come up with something better than you have, ah'm willing to listen."

He had me. Maybe if I were he, I'd go that way too.

"Lester," Maynard said, "show Mr. Spenser out."

I shook my head. "I'll show myself out. I want Lester to stay there. Mad, like he is, he might slam the door on my foot."

Maynard nodded. There was a little drip of sweat at the tip of his beaky little canary nose. It was the last thing I saw as I backed out.

CHAPTER TWENTY-TWO

THE AQUARIUM IS NEAR Harbor Towers, and I walked to it. Inside, it was nearly empty at midday, dark and cool and unconnected with the city outside. I went up the spiral walkway around it and watched the fish glide in silent pattern around and around the tank, swimming at different strata, sharks and groupers and turtles and fish I didn't know in the clear water. They were oblivious of me and seemed oblivious of each other as they swam in a kind of implacable order around and around the tank. The spiral walk was open and the rest of the aquarium was spacious. Below the flat pool, bottom lit and cool green, silhouetted other, smaller fish, black and quick in the bright water.

A small group of children, perhaps a second-grade class on a field trip, came in, shepherded by a plump little nun with horn-rimmed glasses. After a fast inspection of the fish, the children ignored them and began to enjoy the building and the space as if the real occasion for the visit was not the fish but the feel of the aquarium. The kids ran up and down the spiral and looked over the balcony and yelled at each other from above and below. The nun made no serious attempt to shush them, and the open space and the darkness seemed to absorb the noise. It was still nearly quiet.

I stood and stared in through the six-inch-thick glass windows of the tank and watched the sharks, small, well fed, and without threat, as they glided in their endless circle. I had screwed up the situation. I knew that. I had made Frank Doerr mad and Doerr was a cuckoo. Maynard was right not to buy what I was selling. Doerr wouldn't let Maynard off the hook and he wouldn't bargain with me. Maybe he never would have, but his honor was at stake now and he'd die before he let me talk him into, or scare him into, doing anything.

A small boy pushed in front of me to stare through the glass. His belt was too long, I noticed, and the surplus had been tucked through his belt loops halfway around his body. Another kid joined him and I found myself being moved away from the fish tank. Kids already know how to block out, I thought. I walked off the spiral and looked at the penguins on the first balcony. They were the false note in the place. There was no glass wall, no separation between us except six feet of space. The smell of fish and, I supposed, penguin was rank and uninsulated. I didn't like it. The silent fish in the lucid water were fantasy. The smelly penguins were real.

I went on back down the spiral and out into the bright hot day that met me with a clang as I came out of the aquarium. I could put Doerr and Maynard away by going to the cops. But that would humiliate Linda Rabb and probably get Marty Rabb barred from baseball. I could disarm Doerr and Maynard by getting Linda to make a public confession. But that would have the same results. The top was down on my car and the seats were hot and uncomfortable when I got in. I couldn't shake Maynard loose from Doerr. Doerr was the key and I had handled him wrong. If I got near him again, he'd try to kill me. It made negotiations difficult.

Back to the Rabbs. The lobby attendant called up, and Marty Rabb was waiting for me at the apartment door. His face was white, and the hinge muscles of his jaw were bunched.

"You sonovabitch," he said. His voice was hoarse.

"Maybe," I said, "but that won't help."

"What do you want now, plant a bug in our bedroom maybe?"

"I don't want to talk about it out in the corridor."

"I don't give a shit what you don't want. I don't want you in my goddamned house, stinking up the place."

"Look, kid, I feel lousy and I understand how you feel,

300

and I don't blame you, but I need to talk and I can't do it out here in the hall with you yelling at me."

"You're lucky I'm yelling, you bastard. You're lucky I don't knock you on your ass."

Linda Rabb came to the door beside her husband. "Let him in, Marty," she said. "We're in trouble. Yelling won't change that. Neither will hitting him."

"The sonovabitch caused it. We were doing all right till he came sticking his goddamned nose into things."

"I caused it as much as he did, Marty. I'm the whore, not Spenser."

Rabb turned at her. "I don't want to hear you say that again," he said. "Not again. I won't have any talk like that in my house. I don't want my son hearing that kind of talk."

Linda Rabb's voice sounded as if she were tired. "Your son's not home, Marty; he's at nursery. You know that. Come in, Spenser." She pulled Rabb away from the door, holding his right arm in both her hands. I went in.

I sat on the edge of the sofa. Rabb didn't sit. He stood looking at me with his hands clenched. "Be goddamned careful what you say, Spenser. I want to belt you so bad I can feel it in my guts, and if you make one smart remark, I'm going to level you."

"Marty, you are the third person this morning who has offered to disassemble my body. You are also third in order of probable success. I can't throw a baseball like you can, but the odds are very good that I could put you in the hospital before you ever got a hand on me." I was getting sick of people yelling at me.

"You think so."

I was proud of myself. I didn't say, "I know so."

Linda Rabb let go of his arm and came around in front of him and put both her arms around his waist. "Stop it, Marty. Both of you, grow up. This isn't a playground where you little boys can prove to each other how tough you are. This is our home and our future and little Marty and our life. You can't handle every problem as if it were an arm-wrestling contest." Her voice was getting thicker and she pressed her face against Rabb's chest. I knew she was crying, and I bet it wasn't the first time today.

"But, Jesus Christ, Linda, a man's gotta—"

She screamed at him, the voice muffled against his chest. "Shut up. Just shut up about a man's gotta."

I wished I smoked. It would have given me something to do with my hands. Rabb put his arms around his wife and rubbed the top of her head with his chin.

"I don't know," he said. "I don't know what in hell to do."

"Me either," I said. "But if you'd sit down, maybe we could figure something out."

Linda Rabb said, "Sit down, Marty," and pushed him away from her with both hands against his chest. He sat. She sat beside him, her head turned away, and wiped her eyes with a Kleenex.

"I don't know," Rabb said again. He was sitting on the edge of the couch, his elbows on his thighs, his hands clasped together between his knees, staring at his thumbnails. Then he looked up at me.

"How much does Erskine know?" he said.

"Nothing. He had heard just the hint that something might not be square. He hired me to prove it was square. He wants to believe it's square and you're square."

"Yeah," Rabb said, "I'm square okay. You got any good ideas?"

"Your wife's told you what I said yesterday?" He nodded. "I've talked with Doerr and I've talked with Maynard. Doerr won't let go of Maynard and Maynard won't let go of you. He's too scared."

"Maynard really is in debt to a loan shark?"

"Yes."

"I can't see anything else to do but keep on the way we have been," Rabb said.

"If you can stand it," I said.

"You can stand what you can't change," Rabb said. "You got a better idea?"

"You could blow the whistle."

Linda Rabb had finished with her Kleenex and was looking at us again.

"Yes," she said.

"No," Rabb said.

"Marty," she said.

"No."

"Marty," she said again, "we can't stand it. I can't stand it. I can't stand the guilt and watching how you feel every time you lose a game so they can make money."

"I don't always have to lose," he said. "Sometimes I give up a run or two for the inning pools."

"Don't quibble, Marty. You're in a funk for a week after every letter. You have lived too long believing in do-or-die for dear old Siwash. It's killing you and it's killing me."

"I'm not having your name blabbed all over the country. You want your kid to hear that kind of talk about his mother. Maybe we should show him the movie."

"It will pass, Marty. He's only three."

"And it'll make nice talk in the bullpen, you know. You want me to listen to those bastards laughing in the dugout when I go out to pitch? Or maybe that doesn't matter either because if it gets out that I been dumping games I won't be pitching anyway. You want that?"

"No, but I don't want this either, Marty."

"Yeah, well maybe you should have thought of that when you were spreading your legs in New York."

I felt a jangle of shock in my solar plexus. Linda Rabb never flinched. She looked at her husband steadily. The silence hung between them. It was Rabb who broke it. "Jesus, honey, I'm sorry," he said and put his arms around her. She didn't pull away, but her body was as stiff and remote as a wire coat hanger and her eyes were focused on something far beyond the room as he held her.

"Jesus," he said again, "Jesus Christ, what is going to happen to us? What are we going to do?"

CHAPTER TWENTY-THREE

"WHAT WOULD YOU DO if you didn't play ball?" I said.

"Coach."

"And if you didn't coach?"

"Scout, maybe."

"And if you couldn't scout and couldn't coach? If you were out of baseball altogether?"

Rabb was looking at his thumbnails again. "I don't know," he said.

"What did you major in in college?"

"Phys ed."

"Well, what would you like to do?"

"Play ball and then coach."

"I mean, if you couldn't play ball." Rabb stared harder at his thumbnails. Linda Rabb looked at the coffee table. Neither one spoke.

"Mrs. Rabb?"

She shook her head.

"How sure are you that if this all comes out you'll be suspended?" I said to Rabb.

"Sure," he said. "I threw some games. If the commissioner's office finds out, I'm finished for life."

"What if I confessed," Linda Rabb said. "If I told everyone about my past and no one said anything about the gambling part. I could say Marty didn't even know about me."

"They could still blackmail me with the fact I dumped the games," Rabb said.

"Not necessarily," I said. "If I could find a way to get Doerr out of it, we might be able to bargain with Maynard. If

Maynard told about you, he'd have to tell about himself. He'd be out of work too. With Maynard you'd have a standoff."

"Doesn't matter," Rabb said. He looked up from his thumbnails. "I won't let her." Linda Rabb was looking at me too.

"Could you get Doerr out of it, Spenser?"

"I don't know, Mrs. Rabb. If I can't, we're stuck. I guess I'll have to."

"She's not saying anything about it. What the hell kind of a man do you think I am?"

"How can you?" Linda Rabb said, and I realized we weren't paying attention to Marty.

"I don't know," I said.

"If you can, I'll do it," she said.

"No," Rabb said.

"Marty, if he can arrange it, I'll do it. It's for me too. I can't stand watching you pulled apart like this. You love two things, us and baseball, and you have to hurt one to help the other. I can't stand knowing that it's my fault, and I can't stand the tension and the fear and the uncertainty. If Spenser can do something about the other man, I will confess and we'll be free."

Rabb looked at me. "I'm warning you, Spenser."

"Grow up, Marty," I said. "The world's not all that clean. You do what you can, not what you oughta. You're involved in stuff that gets people dead. If you can get out of it with some snickers in the bullpen and some embarrassment for your wife, you call that good. You don't call it perfect. You call it better than it was."

Rabb was shaking his head. Linda Rabb was still looking at me. She nodded. I noticed that her body was still stiff and angular, but there was color in her face. Rabb said, "I . . ." and shook his head again.

I said, "We don't need to argue now. Let me see what I can do about Doerr. Maybe I can't do anything about him. Maybe he'll do something about me. But I'll take a look."

"Don't do anything without checking here," Rabb said.

I nodded. Linda Rabb got up and opened the door for

me. I got up and walked out. No one said be careful, or win this one for the Gipper, or it counts not if you win or lose but how you play the game. In fact, no one said anything, and all I heard as I left was the door closing behind me.

Outside on Mass Ave I looked at my watch: 1:30. I went home.

In my kitchen I opened a can of beer. I was having trouble getting Amstel these days and was drinking domestic stuff. Didn't make a hell of a lot of difference, though. The worst beer I ever had was wonderful. The apartment was very quiet. The hum of the air conditioner made it seem quieter. Doerr was the key. If I could take him out of this, I could reason with Maynard. All I had to do was figure out what to do about Doerr. I finished the beer. I didn't know what to do about Doerr. I applied one of Spenser's Rules: When in doubt, cook something and eat it. I took off my shirt, opened another can of beer, and studied the refrigerator.

Spareribs. Yeah. I doused them with Liquid Smoke and put them in the oven. Low. I had eaten once in a restaurant in Minneapolis, Charlie's something-or-other, and had barbecued spareribs with Charlie's own sauce. Since then I'd been trying to duplicate it. I didn't have it right yet, but I'd been getting close. This time I tried starting with chili sauce instead of ketchup. What did Doerr like? I'd been through that: money. What was he afraid of? Pain? Maybe. He hadn't liked me whacking his hand. I put a little less brown sugar in with the chili sauce this time. But maybe he hadn't liked me standing up to him. He was a weird guy and his reaction might be more complicated than just crying because his hand hurt. Two cloves of garlic this time. But first another beer, helps neutralize the garlic fumes. Either way I had got to him today. So what? I squeezed a couple of lemons and added the juice to my sauce. The smell of the spareribs was beginning to fill the kitchen. Even with the air conditioner on, the oven made the kitchen warm and sweat trickled down my bare chest.

Getting to Doerr and getting him to do what I wanted were different things. I had a feeling that right now if I saw him, I'd have to kill him. I never met a guy before who actually foamed at the mouth. If I killed him, I'd have to kill the Hog. Maybe a little red wine. I hadn't tried that before. I put in about half a cupful. Or would I? If Doerr were dead, the Hog might wither away like an uprooted weed. Best if I never found out. One dash of Tabasco? Why not? I opened another beer. If I were dead, I'd shrivel up like an uprooted weed. I put the sauce on to cook and began to consider what else to have. Maybe I could call Wally and Frank over and cook at them until they agreed to terms. Way to a man's heart and all that.

There was zucchini squash in the vegetable drawer, and I sliced it up and shook it in flour and set it aside while I made a beer batter. It always hurt me to pour beer into a bowl of flour, but the results were good. That's me. Mr. Results. Lemme see, what was I going to do about Frankie Doerr? The barbecue sauce began to bubble, and I turned the gas down to simmer. I put two dashes of Tabasco into the beer batter and stirred it and put it aside so the yeast in the beer would work on the flour.

I looked in the freezer. Last Sunday Susan Silverman and I had made bread all afternoon at her house while we watched the ball game and drank Rhine wine. She had mixed and I had kneaded and at the end of the day we had twelve loaves, baked and wrapped in foil. I'd brought home six that night and put them in the freezer. There were four left. I took one out and put it in the oven, still in the foil. Maybe old Suze would have an idea about what to do with Frankie Doerr, or how to get my barbecue sauce to taste like Charlie's or whether I was drinking too much lately. I looked at my watch: 3:30. She'd be home from school. I called her and let it ring ten times and she didn't answer, so I hung up. Brenda Loring? No. I wanted to talk about things I had trouble talking about. Brenda was for fun and wisecracks and she did a terrific picnic, but she wasn't much better than I was at talking about hard things.

The spareribs were done and the bread was hot. I

ROBERT B. PARKER

dipped my sliced zucchini in the beer batter and fried it in a little olive oil. I'd eaten alone before. Why didn't I like it better this time?

CHAPTER TWENTY-FOUR

I ATE AND DRANK and thought about my problem for the rest of the afternoon and went to bed early and woke up early. When I woke up, I knew what I was going to do. I didn't know how yet, but I knew what.

It was drizzly rainy along the Charles. I ran along the esplanade with my mind on other things, and it took a lot longer to do my three miles. It always does if you don't concentrate. I was on the curb by Arlington Street, looking to dash across Storrow Drive and head home, when a black Ford with a little antenna on the roof pulled alongside and Frank Belson stuck his head out the window on the passenger side and said, "Get in."

I got in the back seat and we pulled away. "Drive around for a while, Billy," Belson said to the other cop, and we headed west toward Allston.

Belson was leaning forward, trying to light a cigar butt with the lighter from the dashboard. When he got it going, he shifted around, put his left arm on the back of the front seat, and looked at me.

"I got a snitch tells me that Frank Doerr's going to blow you up."

"Frank personally?"

"That's what the snitch says. Says you roughed Frank up yesterday and he took it personally." Belson was thin,

308

with tight skin and a dark beard shaved close. "Marty thought you oughta know."

We stayed left where the river curved and drove out Soldiers Field Road, past the 'BZ radio tower.

"I thought Wally Hogg did that kind of work for Doerr."

"He does," Belson said. "But this one he's gonna do himself."

"If he can," I said.

"That ain't to say he might not have Wally around to hold you still," Belson said.

Billy U-turned over the safety island and headed back in toward town. He was young and stylish with a thick blond mustache and a haircut that hid his ears. Belson's sideburns were trimmed at the temple.

"Reliable snitch?"

Belson nodded. "Always solid in the past."

"How much you pay him for this stuff?"

"C-note," Belson said.

"I'm flattered," I said.

Belson shrugged. "Company money," he said.

We were passing Harvard Stadium. "You or Quirk got any thoughts about what I should do next?"

Belson shook his head.

"How about hiding?" Billy said. "Doerr will probably die in the next ten, twenty years."

"You think he's that tough?"

Billy shrugged. Belson said, "It's not tough so much. It's crazy. Doerr's crazy. Things don't work out, he wants to kill everybody. I hear he cut one guy up with a machete. I mean, cut him up. Dis-goddamn-membered him. Crazy."

"You don't think a dozen roses and a note of apology would do it, huh?"

Billy snorted. Belson didn't bother. We passed the Kenmore exit.

I said to Billy, "You know where I live?"

He nodded.

Belson said, "You got a piece on you?"

"Not when I'm running," I said.

"Then don't run," Belson said. "If I was Doerr, I coulda aced you right there at the curb when we picked you up."

I remembered my lecture to Lester about professionals. I had no comment. We swung off at Arlington and then right on Marlborough. Billy pulled up in front of my apartment.

"You're going up a one-way street," I said to Billy.

"Geez, I hope there's no cops around," Billy said.

I got out. "Thanks," I said to Belson.

He got out too. "I'll walk up to your place with you."

"With me? Frank, you old softy."

"Quirk told me to get you inside safe. After that you're on your own. We don't run a babysitting service. Not even for you, baby."

When I unlocked my apartment door, I noticed that Belson unbuttoned his coat. We went in. I looked around. The place was empty. Belson buttoned his coat.

"Watch your ass," he said and left.

From my front window I looked down while Belson got in the car and Billy U-turned and drove off. Now I knew what and was getting an idea of how. I took my gun from the bureau drawer and checked the load and brought it with me to the bathroom. I put it on the toilet seat while I took a shower and put it on the bed while I dressed. Then I stuck the holster in my hip pocket and clipped it to my belt. I was wearing broken-in jeans and white sneakers with a racing stripe and my black polo shirt with a beaver on the left breast. I wasn't up in the alligator bracket yet. I put on a seersucker jacket, my aviator sunglasses, and checked myself in the hall mirror. Battle dress.

I unlocked the front hall closet and got out a 12-gauge Iver Johnson pump gun and a box of double-aught shells. Then I went out. In the hall I put the shotgun down and closed a toothpick between the jamb and the hinge side of the door, a couple of inches up from the ground. I snapped it off so only the edge was visible at the crack of the door. It would be good to know if someone had gone in.

I picked up the shotgun and went out to my car. On the way down I passed another tenant. "Hunting season so early?" he said.

"Yeah."

Outside I locked the shotgun and the box of shells in the trunk of my car, got in, put the top down, and headed for the North Shore. I knew what and how, now I had to find where.

I drove Route 93 out of Boston through Somerville and Medford. Along the Mystic River across from Wellington Circle, reeds and head-high marsh grass still grew in an atmosphere made garish with neon and thick exhaust fumes. Past Medford Square, I turned off 93 and took the Lynn Fells Parkway east, looking at the woods and not seeing what I was looking for. Medford gave way to Melrose. I turned off the Fellsway and drove up around Spot Pond, past the MDC Zoo in Stoneham, and back into Melrose. Still nothing that looked right to me. I drove through Melrose, past red clay tennis courts by the lake, past the high school and the Christian Science Church. Just before I got to Route 1, I turned off into Breakhart Reservation. Past the MDC skating rink the road narrows to a single lane and becomes one way. I'd been there on a picnic once with Susan Silverman, and I knew that the road looped through the woods and returned here, one way all the way. There were saddle trails, and lakes, and picnic areas scattered through thick woods.

Thirty yards into the reservation I found the place. I pulled off the narrow hot top road, the bushes scraping my car fenders and crunching under the tires, and got out. A small hill sloped up from the road, and scooped out of the side of it was a hollow the size of a basketball court and the shape of a free-form pool. About in the middle was a flat-planed granite slab, higher than a man's head at one end that tapered into the ground in a shape vaguely like a shark fin.

The sides of the gully were yellow clay, streaked with erosion troughs, scattered with small white pines. The sides sloped steeply up to the somewhat gentler slope of the hill, which was thick with white pine and clustered birch saplings and bunches of sumac. I walked into the hollow and stood by the slab of granite. The high end was a foot above my head. There was a high hum of locust in the hot, still woods and the sound of birds. A squirrel shot down the trunk of a birch tree and up the trunk of a maple without pausing. I took my coat off and draped it over the rock. Then I scrambled up the slope of the gully and looked down. I walked around the rim of the hollow, looking at the woods and at the sun and down into the hollow. It would do. I looked at my watch: 2:00.

I went back down, put my coat on again, got in my car, and drove on around the loop and out of the reservation. There was a small shopping center next to the exit road and I parked my car in among a batch of others in front of a Purity Supreme Supermarket. There was a pay phone in the supermarket, and I used it to call Frank Doerr.

He wasn't in, but the solicitous soft-voiced guy that answered said he'd take a message.

"Okay," I said, "my name is Spenser. S-p-e-n-s-e-r, like the English poet. You know who I am?"

"Yeah, I know." No more solicitude.

"Tell Frank if he wants to talk to me, he should drive up to the Breakhart Reservation in Saugus. Come in by the skating rink entrance, drive thirty yards down the road. Park and walk into the little gully that's there. He'll know it. There's a big rock like a shark fin in the middle of the gully. You got that?"

"Yeah, but why should he want to see you? Frank wants to see someone he calls them into the office. He don't go riding around in the freaking woods."

"He'll ride around in them this time because if he doesn't, I am going to sing songs to the police that Frank will hate the sound of."

"If Frank does want to do this, and I ain't saying he will, when should he be there?"

"Six o'clock tonight."

"For crissake, what if he ain't around at that time?

Maybe he's busy. Who the Christ you think you're talking to?"

"Six o'clock tonight," I said, "or I'll be down on Berkeley Street crooning to the fuzz." I hung up.

CHAPTER TWENTY-FIVE

I BOUGHT A POUND of Hebrew National bologna, a loaf of pumpernickel, a jar of brown mustard, and a half gallon of milk and walked back to my car. I opened the trunk and got an old duffel bag from it. I put the shotgun, the shells, and my groceries in the duffel bag, closed the trunk, shouldered the duffel bag, and walked back toward Breakhart.

It took about fifteen minutes for me to walk back to my gully in the hillside. I climbed up the hill past it, halfway to the top of the hill, and found a thick stand of white pine screened by some dogberry bushes that let me look down into the hollow and the road below it. I took my groceries, my shotgun, and my ammunition out of the duffel bag, took off my coat, and put it in the duffel bag. I spread the bag on the ground, sat down on it, and loaded the shotgun. It took six shells. I put six extras in my hip pocket and cocked the shotgun and leaned it against the tree. Then I got out my groceries and made lunch. I spread the mustard on the bread with my pocketknife and used the folded paper bag as a plate. I drank the milk from the carton. Not bad. Nothing like dining al fresco. I looked at my watch: 2:45. I ate another sandwich. Three o'clock. The locusts keened at me. Some sparrows fluttered above me in the pines. On the road below cars with children and mothers and dogs and inflatable beach toys

drove slowly by every few minutes but less often as the afternoon wore on.

I finished the milk with my fourth sandwich and
wrapped the rest of the bread and bologna back up in the
paper sack and shoved it in the duffel bag. At four fifteen a
silver gray Lincoln Continental pulled off the road by the
gully and parked for a long time. Then the door opened and
Wally Hogg climbed out. He was alone. He stood and looked
carefully all over the hollow and up the hill at where I sat
behind my bushes and everywhere else. Finally he looked up
and down the road, reached back into the car, and came out
with a shoulder weapon. He held it inconspicuously down
along his leg and stepped away from the car and in behind
the trees along the road. The Lincoln started up and drove
away.

In the shelter of the trees Wally was less careful with
the weapon, and I got a good look at it. An M-16 rifle. Standard U.S. infantry weapon. 7.62 millimeter. Twenty rounds.
Fancy carry handle like the old BARs and a pistol grip back of
the trigger housing like the old Thompsons. M-16? Christ, I
was just getting used to the M-1.

Wally and his M-16 climbed the gully wall about opposite me. He was wearing stacked-heel shoes. He slipped once
on the steep sides and slid almost all the way back down.
Hah! I made it first try. When the Lincoln had arrived, I'd
picked up the shotgun and held it across my lap. I noticed
that my hands were a little sweaty as I held it. I looked at my
knuckles. They were white. Wally didn't climb as high as I
had. Too fat. Ought to jog mornings, Wally, get in shape. A
few yards above the gully edge he found some thick bushes
and settled in behind them. From the hollow he would be
invisible. Once he got settled, he didn't move and looked like
a big toad squatting in his ambush.

I looked at my watch again. Quarter of five. Some people went by on horseback, the shod hooves of the horses clat-
tering on the paved road. It was a sound you didn't hear
often, yet it brought back the times when I was small and the
milkman had a horse, and so did the trash people. And

manure in the street, and the sparrows. All three of the horses on the road below were a shiny, sweat-darkened chestnut color. The riders were kids. Two girls in white blouses and riding boots, a boy in jeans and no shirt.

The draft horses that used to pull the trash wagons were much different. Big splayed feet and massive, almost sumptuous haunches. Necks that curved in a stolid, muscular arch. When I was very small, I remembered, horses pulling a scoop were used to dig a cellar hole on the lot next to my house.

The riders disappeared and the clopping dwindled. Wally Hogg still sat there, silent and shapeless, watching the road. I heard a match scrape and smelled cigarette smoke. Careless Wally, what if I were just arriving and smelled the smoke? It carries out here in the woods. But Wally probably wasn't all that at home in the woods. Places Wally hung out you could probably smoke a length of garden hose and no one would smell it. The woods were dry, and I hoped he was careful with the cigarette. I didn't want this thing getting screwed up by a natural disaster.

I checked my watch again: 5:15. My chest felt tight, as if the diaphragm were rusty, and I had that old tingling toothache feeling in behind my navel. There was a lump in my throat. Above me the sky was still bright blue in the early summer evening, dappling through the green leaves. Five thirty, getting on toward supper. The road was empty now below me. The mommas and the kids and the dogs were going home to get supper going and eat with Daddy. Maybe a cookout. Too hot to eat in tonight. Maybe a couple of beers and some gin and tonic with a mint leaf in the glass. And after supper maybe the long quiet arc of the water from the hoses of men in shirt sleeves watering their lawns. My stomach rolled. Smooth. How come Gary Cooper's stomach never rolled? Oh, to be torn 'tween love and duty, what if I lose . . . Five forty. My fingertips tingled and the nerves along the insides of my arms tingled. The pectoral muscles, particularly near the outside of my chest, up by the shoulder, felt tight, and I flexed them, trying to loosen up. I took two pieces of gum out of my shirt pocket and peeled off the wrappers and folded the gum into my mouth. I rolled the wrappers up tight and put them in my shirt pocket and chewed on the gum. Quarter of six. I remembered in Korea, before we went in at Inchon, they'd fed us steak and eggs, not bologna and bread, but it hadn't mattered. My stomach rolled before Inchon too. And at Inchon I hadn't been alone. Ten of six.

I looked down at Wally Hogg. He hadn't moved. His throat wasn't almost closed, and he wasn't taking deep breaths and not getting enough oxygen. He thought he was going to sit up there and shoot me in the back when Frank Doerr gave the nod, which would be right after Frank Doerr found out exactly what I had on him and if I'd given anything to the cops. Or maybe Doerr wanted to fan me himself and Wally was just backup. Anyway, we'd find out pretty soon, wouldn't we? Seven of six. Christ, doesn't time flit by when you're having a big time and all?

I stood up. The shotgun was cocked and ready. I carried it muzzle down along my leg in my right hand and began to move down the hill in a half circle away from where Wally Hogg was. I was about 100 yards away. If I was careful, he wouldn't hear me. I was careful. It took me ten minutes to get down the slope to the road, maybe 50 yards down the road beyond the gully.

Still daylight and bright, but under the trees along the road a bit dimmer than midday. I stayed out of sight behind some trees just off the road and listened. At five past six I heard a car stop and a door open and close. With the shotgun still swinging along by my side, I walked up the road toward the dell. High-ho a dairy-o. The car was a maroon Coupe de Ville, pulled off on the shoulder of the road. No one was in it. I went past it and turned into the hollow. The sun was shining behind me and the hollow was bright and hot. Doerr was standing by the shark-fin rock. Maroon slacks, white shoes, white belt, black shirt, white tie, white safari jacket, black-rimmed sunglasses, white golf cap. A really neat dresser. Probably a real slick dancer too. His hands were empty as I walked in toward him. I didn't look up toward Wally. But I knew where he was, maybe thirty yards up and to my left. I kept the rock on his side of me as I walked into the gully. I kept the shotgun barrel toward the ground. Relaxed, casual. Just had it with me and thought I'd bring it along. Ten feet from Doerr, with the shark-fin rock not yet between me and Wally Hogg, I stopped. If I got behind the rock, Wally would move.

"What the hell is the shotgun for, Spenser?" Doerr said.

"Protection," I said. "You know how it is out in the woods. You might run into a rampaging squirrel or something."

I could feel Wally Hogg's presence up there to my left, thirty yards away. I could feel it along the rib cage and in my armpits and behind the knees. He wasn't moving around. I could hear him if he did; he wasn't that agile and he wasn't dressed for it. You can't sneak around in high-heeled shoes unless you take them off. I listened very hard and didn't hear him.

"I hear you have been bad-mouthing me, Frankie."

"What do you mean?"

"I mean you been saying you were going to blow me up."

Still no sound from Wally. I was about five feet from the shelter of the rock.

"Who told you that?"

I wished I hadn't thought about Wally taking his shoes off.

"Never mind who told me that. Say it ain't so, Frankie."

"Look, shit-for-brains. I didn't come out here into the freaking woods to talk shit with a shit-for-brains like you. You got something to say to me or not?"

"You haven't got the balls, Frankie."

Doerr's face was red. "To blow you up? A shit-for-brains pimple like you? I'll blow you up anytime I goddamned feel like it."

"You had the chance yesterday in your office, Frankie, and I took your piece away from you and made you cry."

Doerr's voice was getting hoarse. The level of it dropped. "You got me out here to talk shit at me or you got something to say?"

I was listening with all I had for Wally. So hard I could barely hear what Doerr was saying.

"I got you out here to tell you that you're a gutless, slobbering freak that couldn't handle an aggressive camp fire girl without hiring someone to help you." I was splitting my concentration, looking at Doerr as hard as I was listening for Wally, and the strain made the sweat run down my face. I almost grunted with the effort.

Doerr's voice was so hoarse and constricted he could barely talk. "Don't you dare talk to me that way," he said. And the oddly quaint phrase squeezed out like dust through a clogged filter.

"You gonna cry again, Frankie? What is it? Did your momma toilet-train you funny? Is that why you're such a god-damned freak-o?"

Doerr's face was scarlet and the carotid arteries stood out in his neck. His mouth moved, but nothing came out. Then he went for his gun. I knew he would sometime.

I brought the pump up level and shot him. The gun flew from his hand and clattered against the shark-fin rock and Doerr went over backwards. I didn't see him land; I dove for the rock and heard Wally's first burst of fire spatter the ground behind me. I landed on my right shoulder, rolled over and up on my feet. Wally's second burst hit the rock and sang off in several directions. I brought the shotgun down over the slope end of the rock where it was about shoulder-high and fanned five rounds into the woods in Wally Hogg's area as fast as I could pump.

I was back down behind the rock, feeding my extra rounds into the magazine, when I heard him fall. I looked and he came rolling through the brush down the side of the gully and came to a stop at the bottom, face up, the front of him already wet with blood. Leaves and twigs and dirt had stuck to the wetness as he rolled. I looked at Doerr. At ten feet the shotgun charge had taken most of his middle. I looked away. A thick and sour fluid rose in my throat and I choked it down. They were both dead. That's the thing about a shotgun. At close range you don't have to go around checking pulses after.

I sat down and leaned back against the rock. I hadn't planned to, and I didn't want someone to find me there. But I sat down anyway because I had to. My legs had gotten weak. I was taking deep breaths, yet I didn't seem to be getting enough oxygen. My body was soaking wet and in the early evening I was feeling cold. I shivered. The sour fluid came back and this time I couldn't keep it down. I threw up with my head between my knees and the two stiffs paying no attention.

Beautiful.

CHAPTER TWENTY-SIX

IT WAS QUARTER TO SEVEN. I had the shotgun back in the duffel bag and the duffel bag back in the trunk of my car and my car on the overpass where the Fellsway meets Route 1. I drove north on 1 toward Smithfield. On the way I stopped and bought a quart of Wild Turkey bourbon. Turning off Route 1 toward Smithfield Center, I twisted the top off, took a mouthful, rinsed my mouth, spit out the window, and drank about four ounces from the bottle. My stomach jumped when the booze hit it, but then it steadied and held. I was coming back. I drove past the old common, with its white church and meetinghouse, and turned left down Main Street. I'd been up here a year or so back on a case and since then had learned my way around the town pretty well. At least I knew the way

319

to Susan Silverman's house. She lived 100 yards up from the common in a small weathered shingle Cape with blue window boxes filled with red petunias. Her car was in the driveway. She was home. It hadn't occurred to me until now that she might not be.

I walked up the brick path to her front door. On either side of the path were strawberry plants, white blossoms, green fruit, and some occasional flashes of ripe red. A sprinkler arced slowly back and forth. The front door was open and I could hear music which sounded very much like Stan Kenton. "Artistry in Rhythm." Goddamn.

I rang her bell and leaned against the doorjamb, holding my bottle of Wild Turkey by the neck and letting it hang against my thigh. I was very tired. She came to the door. Every time I saw her I felt the same click in my solar plexus I'd felt the first time I saw her. This time was no different. She had on faded Levi cutoffs and a dark blue ribbed halter top. She was wearing octagonal horn-rimmed glasses and carried a book in her right hand, her forefinger keeping the place.

I said, "What are you reading?"

She said, "Erikson's biography of Gandhi."

I said, "I've always liked Leif's work."

She looked at the bourbon bottle, four ounces gone, and opened the door. I went in.

"You don't look good," she said.

"You guidance types don't miss a trick, do you?"

"Would it help if I kissed you?"

"Yeah, but not yet. I been throwing up. I need a shower. Then maybe we could sit down and talk and I'll drink the Wild Turkey."

"You know where," she said. I put the bourbon down on the coffee table in the living room and headed down the little hall to the bathroom. In the linen closet beside the bathroom was a shaving kit of mine with a toothbrush and other necessaries. I got it out and went into the bathroom. I brushed and showered and rinsed my mouth under the shower and soaped and scrubbed and shampooed and

320

lathered and rinsed and washed for about a half an hour. Out, out, damned spot.

When I got through, I toweled off and put on some tennis shorts I'd left there and went looking for Susan. The stereo was off, and she was on the back porch with my Wild Turkey, a bucket of ice, a glass, a sliced lemon, and a bottle of bitters.

I sat in a blue wicker armchair and took a long pull from the neck of the bottle.

"Were you bitten by a snake?" Susan said.

I shook my head. Beyond the screen porch the land sloped down in rough terraces to a stream. On the terraces were shade plants. Coleus, patient Lucy, ajuga, and a lot of vincas. Beyond the stream were trees that thickened into woods.

"Would you like something to eat?"

I shook my head again. "No," I said. "Thank you."

"Drinking bourbon instead of beer, and declining a snack. It's bad, isn't it?"

I nodded. "I think so," I said.

"Would you like to talk about it?"

"Yeah," I said, "but I don't quite know what to say."

I put some ice in the glass, added bitters and a squeeze of lemon, and filled the glass with bourbon. "You better drink a little," I said. "I'll be easier to take if you're a little drunk too."

She nodded her head. "Yes, I was thinking that," she said. "I'll get another glass." She did, and I made her a drink. In front of the house some kids were playing street hockey and their voices drifted back faintly. Birds still sang here and there in the woods, but it was beginning to get dark and the songs were fewer.

"How long ago did you get divorced?" I asked.

"Five years."

"Was it bad?"

"Yes."

"Is it bad now?"

"No. I don't think about it too much now. I don't feel

bad about myself anymore. And I don't miss him at all anymore. You have some part in all of that."

"Mr. Fixit," I said. My drink was gone and I made another.

"How does someone who ingests as much as you do get those muscle ridges in his stomach?" Susan said.

"God chose to make me beautiful instead of good," I said.

"How many sit-ups do you do a week?"

"Around a zillion," I said. I stretched my legs out in front of me and slid lower in the chair. It had gotten dark outside and some fireflies showed in the evening. The kids out front had gone in, and all I could hear was the sound of the stream and very faintly the sound of traffic on 128.

"There is a knife blade in the grass," I said. "And a tiger lies just outside the fire."

"My God, Spenser, that's bathetic. Either tell me about what hurts or don't. But for crissake, don't sit here and quote bad verse at me."

"Oh damn," I said. "I was just going to swing into *Hamlet*."

"You do and I'll call the cops."

"Okay," I said. "You're right. But bathetic? That's hard, Suze."

She made herself another drink. We drank. There was no light on the porch, just that which spilled out from the kitchen.

"I killed two guys earlier this evening," I said.

"Have you ever done that before?"

"Yeah," I said. "But I set these guys up."

"You mean you murdered them?"

"No, not exactly. Or . . . I don't know. Maybe."

She was quiet. Her face a pale blur in the semidarkness. She was sitting on the edge of a chaise opposite me. Her knees crossed, her chin on her fist, her elbow on her knee. I drank more bourbon.

"Spenser," she said, "I have known you for only a year or so. But I have known you very intensely. You are a good man. You are perhaps the best man I've ever known. If you killed two men, you did it because it had to be done. I know you. I believe that."

I put my drink on the floor and got up from the chair and stood over her. She raised her face toward me and I put one hand on each side of it and bent over and looked at her close. She had a very strong face, dark and intelligent, full of kinetic suggestion, with faint laugh lines at the corners of her mouth. She was still wearing her glasses, and her big dark eyes looked bigger through the lenses.

"Jesus Christ," I said.

She put her hands over mine and we stayed that way for a long time.

Finally she said, "Sit."

I sat and she leaned back on the chaise and pulled me down beside her and put my head against her breast. "Would you like to make love?" she said.

I was breathing in big low inhales. "No," I said. "Not now, let's just lie here and be still."

Her right arm was around me and she reached up and patted my cheek with her left hand. The stream murmured and after a while I fell asleep.

CHAPTER TWENTY-SEVEN

IT WAS A HOT, windy Tuesday when I finished breakfast with Susan and drove back into Boston. I stopped on the way to look at the papers. The *Herald American* had it, page one, below the fold: GANGLAND FIGURE GUNNED DOWN. Doerr and Wally Hogg had been found after midnight by two kids who'd slipped in there to neck. State and MDC police had no comment as yet.

Under the expressway, street grit was blowing about in the postcommuter lull as I pulled up and parked in front of Harbor Towers. I went through the routine with the houseman again and went up in the elevator. Bucky Maynard let me in. He was informal in a Boston Red Sox T-shirt stretched over his belly.

"What do you want, Spenser?" Informal didn't mean friendly. Lester leaned against the wall by the patio doors with his arms folded across his bare chest. He was wearing dark blue sweat pants and light blue track shoes with dark blue stripes. He blew a huge pink bubble and glared at me around it.

"It's hard to look tough blowing bubbles, Lester," I said. "You ever think about a pacifier?"

"Ah asked what you want, Spenser." Maynard still had his hand on the door.

I handed him the paper. "Below the fold," I said, "right side."

He looked at it, read the lead paragraph, and handed it to Lester.

"So?"

"So, maybe your troubles are over."

"Maybe they are," Maynard said.

"So are Marty Rabb's troubles over too?"

"Troubles?"

"Yeah, maybe you'll stop sucking on him now that Frank Doerr's not going to suck on you anymore."

"Spenser, y'all aren't making any sense. Ah'm not doing anything to Marty Rabb. Ah don't know, for a fact, what you are talking of."

"You're going to recoup your losses," I said. "You mean, stupid sonovabitch."

"No reason to stand there shaking your head, Spenser. Ah'm the one should be offended."

"Doerr bled Rabb through you, and you never got any blood. Now he's dead, you want yours."

"Ah think you ought to leave now, Spenser. You're becoming abusive."

Lester popped his bubble gum and tittered. There were newspapers on the coffee table, the *Globe* and the *Herald American*. They'd known before I got here, and Maynard had already figured out that he had the money machine now.

"Don't you want to know why I think you're stupid?" I said.

"No, ah don't."

"Because you were off the hook, clean. And you won't take the break."

"Move out," Lester said. "And just keep in mind, Spenser, if anybody was blackmailing Rabb, they could get him for throwing games just as much as for marrying a whore."

"Never mind, Lester," Maynard said sharply. "We don't know anything about it and Spenser is on his way out."

"I'd be glad to make him go faster, Buck."

"He's on his way, Lester. Aren't you, Spenser?"

"Yeah, I am, but as they say in all the movies, Bucky, I'll be back."

"Ah wouldn't if ah were you. Ah can't restrain Lester too much more."

"Well, do what you can," I said. "I don't want to kill him." Maynard opened the door. He'd never taken his hand off the knob.

"Hey, Spenser," Lester said, "I got something you haven't seen before." He put his hands behind his back and brought them back out front. In his right hand was a nickel-plated automatic pistol. It looked like a Beretta. "How's that look to you, Mr. Pro?"

I said, "Lester, if you point that thing at me again, I'll take it away from you and shoot you with it." Then I stomped out. The door closed behind me and I headed for the street.

Outside, the wind was hotter and stronger. I drove home in such a funk that I didn't even check the skirts on the girls, something I did normally as a matter of course, even on still days. Across the street from my apartment was a city car, and in it were Belson and the cop named Billy.

I walked over to the car. "You guys want something or are you hiding from the watch commander?"

"Lieutenant wants you," Billy said.

"Maybe I don't want him."

Belson was slumped down in the passenger seat with his hand over his eyes. He said, "Aw knock off the bullshit, Spenser. Get in the car. Quirk wants you and we both know you're going to come."

He was right, of course. The way I felt if someone said up I'd say down. I got in the back seat. In the two minutes it took us to drive to police headquarters no one said anything.

Quirk's office had moved since last time. He was third-floor front now, facing out onto Berkeley Street. With a view of the secretaries from the insurance companies when they broke for lunch. On his door it said COMMANDER, HOMICIDE.

Belson knocked and opened the door. "Here he is, Marty."

Quirk sat at a desk that had nothing on it but a phone and a clear plastic cube containing pictures of his family. He was immaculate and impervious, as he had been every other time I ever saw him. I wondered if his bedroom slippers had a spit shine. Probably didn't own bedroom slippers. Probably didn't sleep. He said, "Thanks, Frank. I'll see him alone."

Belson nodded and closed the door behind me. There was a straight chair in front of the desk. I sat in it. Quirk looked at me without saying anything. I looked back. There was a traffic cop outside at the Stuart Street intersection and I could hear his whistle as he moved cars around the construction.

Quirk said, "I think you burned those two studs up in Saugus."

I said, "Uh-huh."

"I think you set them up and burned them."

"Uh-huh."

"I went up and took a look early this morning. One of the MDC people asked me to. Informal. Doerr never fired his piece. Wally Hogg did, the magazine's nearly empty, there's a lot of brass up above the death scene in the woods, and there's ricochet marks on one side of the big rock. There's also six spent twelve-gauge shells on the ground on the other side of the rock. The shrubs are torn up around where the M-sixteen brass was. Like somebody fired off about five rounds of shotgun into the area."

"Uh-huh."

"You knew that Doerr was gunning for you. You let him know you'd be there and you figured they'd try to back-shoot you and you figured you could beat them. And you were right."

"That's really swell, Quirk, you got some swell imagination."

"It's more than imagination, Spenser. You're around buying me a drink, asking about Frank Doerr. Next day I get a tip that Doerr is going to blow you up, and this morning I was looking at Doerr and his gunsel dead up the woods. You got an alibi for yesterday afternoon and evening?"

"Do I need one?"

Quirk picked up the clear plastic cube on his desk and looked at the pictures of his family. In the outer office a phone rang. A typewriter clacked uncertainly. Quirk put the cube down again on the desk and looked at me.

"No," he said. "I don't think you do."

"You mean you didn't share your theories with the Saugus cops?"

"It's not my territory."

"Then why the hell am I sitting here nodding my head while you talk?"

"Because this is my territory." The hesitant typist in the outer office was still hunting and pecking. "Look, Spenser, I am not in sorrow's clutch because Frank Doerr and his animal went down. And I'm not even all that unhappy that you put them down. There's a lot of guys couldn't do it, and a lot of guys wouldn't try. I don't know why you did it, but I guess probably it wasn't for dough and maybe it wasn't even for protection. If I had to guess, I'd guess it might have been to take the squeeze off of someone else. The squeezee, you might say."

"You might," I said. "I wouldn't."

"Yeah. Anyway. I'm saying to you you didn't burn them in my city. And I'm kind of glad they're burnt. But . . ." Quirk paused and looked at me. His stare was as heavy and solid as his fist. "Don't do it ever in my city."

I said nothing.

"And," he said, "don't start thinking you're some kind of goddamned vigilante. If you get away with this, don't get tempted to do it again. Here or anywhere. You understand what I'm saying to you?"

"Yeah. I do."

"We've known each other awhile, Spenser, and maybe we got a certain amount of respect. But we're not friends. And I'm not a guy you know. I'm a cop."

"Nothing else?"

"Yeah," Quirk said, "something else. I'm a husband and a father and a cop. But the last one's the only thing that makes any difference to you."

"No, not quite. The husband and father makes a difference too. Nobody should be just a job."

"Okay, we agree. But believe what I tell you. I won't bite this bullet again."

"Got it," I said.

"Good."

I stood up, started for the door and stopped, and turned around and said, "Marty?"

"Yeah?"

"Shake," I said.

He put his hand out across his desk, and we did.

CHAPTER TWENTY-EIGHT

No ONE DROVE me home. It's a short walk from Berkeley Street to my place, and I liked the walk. It gave me time to think, and I needed time. A lot had happened in a short while, and not all of it was going my way. I hadn't thought it would, but there's always hope.

It was afternoon when I got home. I made two lettuce and tomato sandwiches on homemade wheat bread, poured a glass of milk, sat at the counter, and ate and drank the milk and thought about where I was at and where the Rabbs were at and where Bucky Marnard was at. I knew where Doerr and his gunner were at. I had a piece of rhubarb pie for dessert. Put the dishes in the dishwasher, wiped the counter off with a sponge, washed my hands and face, and headed for Church Park.

It was in walking distance and I walked. The wind was still strong, but there was less grit in the air along Marlborough Street, and what little there was rattled harmlessly on my sunglasses. Linda Rabb let me in.

"I heard on the radio that what's'isname Doerr and another man were killed," she said. She wore a loose sleeveless dress, striped black and white like mattress ticking, and white sandals. Her hair was in two braids, each tied with a small white ribbon, and her face was without makeup.

"Yeah, me too," I said. "Your husband home?"

"No, he's gone to the park."

"Your boy?"

"He's in nursery school."

"We need to talk," I said.

She nodded. "Would you like coffee or anything?"

"Yeah, coffee would be good."

"Instant okay?"

"Sure, black."

I sat in the living room while she made coffee. From the kitchen came the faintly hysterical sounds of daytime television. The set clicked off and Linda Rabb returned, carrying a round black tray with two cups of coffee on it. I took one.

"I've talked with Bucky Maynard," I said, and sipped the coffee. "He won't let go."

"Even though Doerr is dead?" Linda Rabb was sitting on an ottoman, her coffee on the floor beside her.

I nodded. "Now he wants his piece."

We were quiet. Linda Rabb sipped at her coffee, holding the cup in both hands, letting the steam warm her face. I drank some more of mine. It was too hot still, but I drank it anyway. The sound of my swallow seemed loud to me.

"We both know, don't we?" Linda Rabb said.

"I think so," I said.

"If I make a public statement about the way I used to be, we'll be free of Maynard, won't we?"

"I think so," I said. "He can still allege that Marty threw some games, but that implicates him too and he goes down the tube with you. I don't think he will. He gets nothing out of it. No money, nothing. And his career is shot as bad as Marty's."

She kept her face buried in the coffee cup.

"I can't think of another way," I said.

She lifted her face and looked at me and said, "Could you kill him?"

I said, "No."

She nodded, without expression. "What would be the best way to confess?"

"I will find you a reporter and you tell the story any way you wish, but leave out the blackmail. That way there's no press conferences, photographers, whatever. After he publishes the story, you refer all inquiry to me. You got any money in the house?"

"Of course."

"Okay, give me a dollar," I said.

She went to the kitchen and returned with a dollar bill. I took out one of my business cards and acknowledged receipt on the back of it and gave it to her.

"Now you are my client," I said. "I represent you."

She nodded again.

"How about Marty?" I said. "Don't you want to clear it with him or discuss it? Or something?"

"No," she said. "You get me the reporter. I'll give him my statement. Then I'll tell Marty. I never bother him before a game. It's one of our rules."

"Okay," I said. "Where's the phone?"

It was in the kitchen. A red wall phone with a long cord. I dialed a number at the *Globe* and talked to a police reporter named Jack Washington that I had gotten to know when I worked for the Suffolk County DA.

"You know the broad who writes that *Feminine Eye* column? The one that had the Nieman Fellowship to Harvard last year?"

"Yeah, she'd love to hear you call her a broad."

"She won't. Can you get her to come to an address I'll give you? If she'll come, she'll get a major news story exclusively. My word, but I can't tell you more than that."

"I can ask her," Washington said. There was silence and the distant sound of genderless voices. Then a woman's voice said, "Hello, this is Carol Curtis."

I repeated what I'd said to Washington.

"Why me, Mr. Spenser?"

"Because I read your column and you are a class person when you write. This is a story that needs more than who, what, when, and where. It involves a woman and a lot of pain, and more to come, and I don't want some heavy-handed slug with a press pass in his hatband screwing it up."

"I'll come. What's the address?"

I gave it to her and she hung up. So did I.

When I hung up, Linda Rabb asked, "Would you like more coffee? The water's hot."

"Yes, please."

She put a spoonful of instant coffee in my cup, added hot water, and stirred.

"Would you care for a piece of cake or some cookies or anything?"

I shook my head. "No, thanks," I said. "This is fine."

We went back to the living room and sat down as before. Me on the couch, Linda Rabb on the ottoman. We drank our coffee. It was quiet. There was nothing to say. At two fifteen the door buzzer buzzed. Linda Rabb got up and opened the door.

The woman at the door said, "Hello, I'm Carol Curtis."

"Come in, please. I'm Linda Rabb. Would you like coffee?"

"Yes, thank you."

Carol Curtis was small with brown hair cut short and a lively, innocent-looking face. There was a scatter of freckles across her nose and cheekbones, and her light blue eyes were shadowed with long thick lashes. She had on a pink dress with tan figures on it that looked expensive.

Linda Rabb said, "This is Mr. Spenser," and went to the kitchen. I shook hands with Carol Curtis. She had a gold wedding band on her left hand.

"You are the one who called," she said.

"Yeah."

"Jack told me a little about you. It sounded good." She sat on the couch beside me.

"He makes things up," I said.

Linda Rabb came back with coffee and a plate of cookies, which she placed on the coffee table in front of the couch. Then she sat back down on the ottoman and began to speak, looking directly at Carol Curtis as she did.

"My husband is Marty Rabb," she said. "The Red Sox pitcher. But my real name is not Linda, it's Donna, Donna Burlington. Before I married Marty, I was a prostitute in

332

New York and a performer in pornographic films when I met him."

Carol Curtis was saying, "Wait a minute, wait a minute," and rummaging in her purse for pad and pencil. Linda Rabb paused. Carol Curtis got the pad open and wrote rapidly in some kind of shorthand. "When did you meet your husband, Mrs. Rabb?"

"In New York, in what might be called the course of my profession," and off she went. She told it all, in a quiet, uninflected voice the way you might read a story to a child when you'd read it too often. Carol Curtis was a professional. She did not bat one of her thick-lashed eyes after the opening sentence. She asked very little. She understood her subject and she let Linda Rabb talk.

When it was over, she said, "And why are you telling me this?"

Linda Rabb said, "I've lived with it too long. I don't want a secret that will come along and haunt me, later, maybe when my son is older, maybe . . ." She let it hang. Listening, I had the feeling that she had given a real reason. Not the only reason, but a real one.

"Does your husband know?"

"He knows everything."

"Where is he now?"

"At the park."

"Does he know about this . . . ah . . . confession?"

"Yes, he does," Linda said without hesitation.

"And he approves?"

"Absolutely," Linda said.

"Mrs. Rabb," Carol Curtis said. And Linda Rabb shook her head.

"That's all," she said. "I'm sorry. Mr. Spenser represents me and anything else to be said about this he will say." Then she sat still with her hands folded in her lap and looked at me and Carol Curtis sitting on the couch.

I said, "No comment," and Carol Curtis smiled.

"I bet you'll say that often in the future when we talk, won't you?"

"No comment," I said.

"Why is a private detective representing Mrs. Rabb in this? Why not a lawyer or a PR man or perhaps a husband?"

"No comment," I said. And Carol Curtis said it silently along with me, nodding her head as she did so. She closed the notebook and stood up.

"Nice talking with you, Spenser," she said, and put out her hand. We shook. "Don't get up," she said. Then she turned to Linda Rabb.

"Mrs. Rabb," she said and put out her hand. Linda Rabb took it, and held it for a moment. "You are a saint, Mrs. Rabb. Not a sinner. That's the way I'll write this story."

Linda Rabb said, "Thank you."

"You are also," Carol Curtis said, "a hell of a woman."

CHAPTER TWENTY-NINE

WHEN CAROL CURTIS LEFT, I said to Linda Rabb, "Shall I stay with you?"

"I would rather be by myself," she said.

"Okay, but I want to call Harold Erskine and tell him what's coming. I took some of his money and I don't want him blindsided by this. I probably better resign his employ too."

She nodded.

"I'll call him from my office," I said. "Would you like me around when you tell Marty?"

"No," she said. "Thank you."

"I think this will work, kiddo," I said. "If you hear from Maynard, I want to know, right off. Okay?"

"Yes, certainly."

"You know what Carol Curtis said to you?"

She nodded.

"Me too," I said. "Me too."

She smiled at me slightly and didn't move. I let myself out of the apartment and left her sitting on her ottoman. Looking, as far as I could tell, at nothing at all.

I caught a cab to my office and called Harold Erskine. I told him what Linda Rabb had said in the papers and that it was likely to be on the street in the morning. I told him I'd found not a trace of evidence to suggest that Marty Rabb gambled or threw games or chewed snuff. He was not happy about Linda Rabb, and he was not happy that I didn't know more about it. Or wouldn't tell.

"Goddamnit, Spenser. You are not giving it to me straight. There's more there than you're saying. I hire a man I expect cooperation. You are holding out on me."

I told him I wasn't holding out, and if he thought so, he could refuse to pay my bill. He said he'd think about that too. And we hung up. On my desk were bills and some letters I should get to. I put them in the middle drawer of my desk and closed the drawer. I'd get to them later. Down the street a construction company was tearing down the buildings along the south side of Stuart Street to make room for a medical school. Since early spring they had been moving in on my building. I could hear the big iron wrecking ball thump into the old brick of the garment lofts and palm-reading parlors that used to be there. By next month I'd have to get a new office. What I should do right now is call a real estate broker and get humping on relocation. When you have to move in a hurry, you get screwed. That's just what I should do. Be smart, move before I had to. I looked at my watch: 4:45. I got up and went out of my office and headed for home. Once I got this cleared up with the Rabbs, I'd look into a new office.

As I walked across the Common, the Hare Krishnas were chanting and hopping around in their ankle-length saffron robes, Hush Puppies and sneakers with white sweat socks poking out beneath the hems. Did you have to look funny to be saved? If Christ were around today, He'd probably be wearing a chambray shirt and flared slacks. There were kids splashing in the wading pool and dogs on leashes and squirrels on the loose and pigeons. In the Public Garden the swan boats were still making their circuit of the duck pond under the little footbridge.

At home I got out a can of beer, read the morning *Globe,* warmed up some leftover beef stew for supper, ate it with Syrian bread while I watched the news, and settled down in my living room with my copy of Morison. I'd bought it in three-volume soft-cover and was halfway through the third volume. I stared at it for half an hour and made no progress at all. I looked at my watch: 7:20. Too early to go to bed. Brenda Loring? No. Susan Silverman? No. Over to the Harbor Health Club and lift a few and talk with Henry Cimoli? No. Nothing. I didn't want to talk with anyone. And I didn't want to read. I looked at the TV listings in the paper. There was nothing I could stand to look at. And I didn't feel like woodcarving and I didn't feel like sitting in my apartment. If I had a dog, I could take him for a walk. I could pretend.

I went out and strolled along Arlington to Commonwealth and up the mall on Commonwealth toward Kenmore Square. When I got there, I turned down Brookline Ave and went into a bar called Copperfield's and drank beer there till it closed. Then I walked back home and went to bed.

I didn't sleep much, but after a while it was morning and the *Globe* was delivered. There it was, page one, lower left, with a Carol Curtis by-line. SOX WIFE REVEALS OTHER LIFE. I read it, drinking coffee and eating corn bread with strawberry jam, and it was all it should have been. The facts were the way Linda Rabb had given them. The writing was sympathetic and intelligent. Inside on the sports page was a picture of Marty, and one of Linda, obviously taken in the stands on a happier occasion. Balls.

The phone rang. It was Marty Rabb.

"Spenser, the doorman says Maynard and another guy are here to see me. Linda said to call you."

"She there too?"

"Yes."

"I'll be over. Don't let them in until I come."

"Well, shit, I'm not scared . . ."

"Be scared. Lester's got a gun."

I hung up and ran for my car. In less than ten minutes I was in the lobby at Church Park and Bucky and Lester were glaring at me. The houseman called up and we three went together in the same elevator. No one said anything. But the silence in the elevator had the density of clay.

Marty Rabb opened the door and the three of us went in. Me first and Lester last. Linda Rabb came out of the bedroom with her little boy holding on to her hand. Rabb faced us in the middle of the living room. Legs slightly apart, hands on hips. He had on a short-sleeved white shirt, and his lean, wiry arms were tanned halfway up the forearms and pale thereafter. Must pitch with a sweat shirt on, I thought.

"Okay," he said. "Get it done, and then get the hell out of here. All three of you."

Bucky Maynard said, "Ah want to know just what in hell you think you gonna accomplish with that nonsense in the newspapers. You think that's gonna close the account between you and me? 'Cause if you think so, you better think on it some more, boy."

"I thought on it all I'm going to think on it, Maynard," Rabb said. "You and me got nothing else to say to each other."

"You think ah can't squeeze you some more, boy? Ah got records of every game you dumped, boy. Every inning you fudged a run for the office pools, and ah can talk just as good as your little girl to the newspapers, don't you think ah can't."

Lester was leaning bonelessly against the wall by the door with his arms across his chest and his jaws working. He was doing Che Guevara today, starched fatigue pants, engineer boots, a fatigue shirt with the sleeves cut off, and black beret. The shirt hung outside the pants. I wondered if he had the nickel-plated Beretta stuck in his belt.

"You can," I said. "But you won't."

Linda and the boy stood beside Marty, Linda's left hand touching his arm, her right holding the boy's.

"Ah won't?"

"Nope. Because you can't do it without sinking yourself too. You won't make any money by turning him in and you can't do it without getting caught yourself. Marty will be out of the league, okay. But so will you, fats."

Maynard's face got bright red. "You think so?" he said.

"Yeah. You say one word to anybody and you'll be calling drag races in Dalrymple, Georgia. And you know it."

Everybody looked at everybody. No one said anything. Lester cracked his gum. Then Rabb said, "So it looks like I got you and you got me. That's a tie, you fat bastard. And that's the way it'll end. But I tell you one time: I'll pitch and you broadcast, but you come near me or my wife or my kid and I will kill you."

Lester said, "You can't kill shit."

Rabb kept looking at Maynard. "And keep that goddamn freak away from me," he said, "or I'll kill him too."

Lester moved away from the wall, the slouch gone. He shrugged into his tae kwon do stance like a man putting on armor.

The little boy said, "Momma," not very loud, but with tears in it.

Marty said, "Get him out of here, Linda." And the woman and the boy backed away toward the bedroom. Maynard's face was red and sweaty.

"Hey, kid," Lester said, "your momma's a whore."

Rabb swung a looping left hand that Lester shucked off his forearm. He planted his left foot and swung his right around in a complete circle so that the back of his heel caught Rabb in the right side, at the kidneys. The kick had turned Lester all the way around. But he spun back forward like an unwinding spring. He was good. The kick staggered Rabb but didn't put him down. The next one would, and if it didn't, Lester would really hurt him. Maybe he already had. A kick like that will rupture a kidney.

Linda Rabb said, "Spenser." And grabbed hold of her husband, both arms around him. "Stop it, Marty," she said, "stop it." The boy pressed against her leg and his father's. Marty Rabb dragged his wife and son with him as he started back toward Lester. Lester was back in his stance, blowing a big bubble and chewing it back in again. He was about three feet to my left. I took one step and sucker-punched him in the neck, behind the ear. He fell down, his legs folding under him at the knees so that he sank to the floor like a penitent in prayer.

"Marty," I said, "get your wife and kid out of here. You don't want the kid seeing this. Look at him."

The kid was in a huddle of terror against his mother's leg. Marty reached down and picked him up, and with his other arm tight around Linda Rabb, he hustled them into the bedroom.

"I will say to you what Rabb did, you great sack of guts," I said. "You and your clotheshorse stay away from Rabb as long as you live or I will put you both in the hospital."

Lester came off the floor at me, but he was wobbly. He tried the kick again, but it was too slow. I leaned away from it. I moved in behind the kick and drove a left at his stomach. He blocked it and hit me in the solar plexus. I tensed for it, but it still made me numb. A good punch turning the fist over as it came, but there wasn't as much steam as there should have been behind it, and I was inside now, up against him. I had weight on him, maybe fifteen pounds, and I was stronger. As long as I stayed up against him, I could neutralize his quickness and I could outmuscle him. I rammed him against the wall. My chin was locked over his shoulder, and I hit him in the stomach with both fists. I hurt him. He grunted. He hammered on my back with both fists, but I had a lot of muscle layer to protect back there. Twenty years of working on the lats and the lateral obliques. I got hold of his shirtfront with both hands and pulled him away from the wall and slammed him back up against it. His hand whiplashed back and banged on the wall. It was plasterboard and it broke through. I slammed him again and he sagged. I brought my left fist up over his arms and hit him on the side of the face, at the temple, with the side of my clenched fist. Don't want to break the knuckles. A kind of pressure was building in me, and I saw everything indistinctly. I slammed him on the wall and then stepped back and hit him left, left, right, in the face. I could barely see his face now, white and disembodied in front of me. I hit it again. He started to sag, I got hold of his collar with my left hand and pulled him up and hit him with my right. He sagged heavier, and I jammed him against the wall with my left and hammered him with my right. His face was no longer white. It was bloody, and it bobbled limply when I hit him. I could feel my whole self surging up into my fist as I held him and hit him. The rhythm of the punches thundered in my head, and I couldn't hear anything else. I was vaguely aware of someone pulling at me and I brushed him away with my right hand. Then I could hear voices. I kept punching. Then I could hear Linda Rabb's voice. The pounding in my head modified a little.

"Stop it, Spenser. Stop it, Spenser. You're killing him. Stop it."

Someone had hold of my arm, and it was Marty Rabb, and Lester's face was a bloody mess, unconscious in front of me. Maynard was sitting openmouthed on the floor, blood trickling from his nose. It must have been him I brushed away.

"Stop it, stop it, stop it." Linda Rabb had hold of my left arm and was trying to pry my hand loose from Lester's shirtfront. I opened the fingers and stepped away, and Lester slid to the floor. Maynard slid over to him without getting up and with a handkerchief began to wipe the blood from Lester's face. I could see Lester's chest rising and falling as he breathed. I noticed I was breathing heavy too. Marty and Linda Rabb both stood in front of me, the kid holding Linda's hand. Tears were running down his cheeks and his eyes were wide with fright, but he was quiet.

"Jesus, Spenser," Rabb said. "What happened? You were crazy."

I was sweating now, as if a fever had broken. I shook my head. "A lot of strain," I said. "We've all had a lot of strain. I'm sorry the kid saw it."

Maynard had gone to the bathroom and come back with wet towels and was cleaning Lester up and putting a cold compress on his forehead. "Pay attention to what happened, Bucky boy," I said. "Don't irritate me."

Lester moved a little. His lips were swollen and one eye was closed. Maynard kept washing his face with the damp towel.

"It's okay, Lester," he said. "It's okay."

Lester sat up and pushed the towel away. "Help me up," he mumbled.

Maynard got up and got Lester on his feet.

"Let's get out of here," Lester said.

Maynard started to take him toward the door, his arm around Lester's back.

"Bucky," I said, "we agree about the tie? And how we got no further business?"

Maynard nodded. There was no color left in his face, just the slight smear of brown, drying blood on his lip.

"I want to go home, Bucky," Lester mumbled, and Bucky said, "Yeah, yeah, Lester, we'll go home." And out they went.

Linda Rabb sat on the floor with her son and held him against her and put her face in his hair. They rocked back and forth slightly on the floor, and Marty Rabb and I stood awkwardly above them and said nothing at all. Finally I said, "Okay, Marty. I think we've done all there is to do."

He put his hand out. "Thank you, Spenser, I guess. We were in a mess we couldn't have gotten out of without you. I can't say quite where we're at now, but thank you for what you did. Including Lester. I think probably he's too good at tae kwon dong or whatever it is for me."

"He might have been too good for me if I hadn't sucker-punched him first."

We shook hands. Linda Rabb didn't look up. I went out the front door. She didn't say goodbye.

I never saw her again.

CHAPTER THIRTY

"AND YOU KEPT HITTING him," Susan Silverman said.

We were sitting in a back booth in The Last Hurrah, looking at the menu and having the first drink of the evening. Mine was a stein of Harp; hers, a vodka gimlet.

"It all seemed to bubble up inside me and explode. It wasn't Lester; it was Doerr and Wally Hogg and me and the case and the way things worked out so everyone got hurt some. It all just exploded out of me, and I damn near killed the poor creep."

"From what you say he probably earned the beating."

"Yeah, he did. That's not what bothers me. I'm what bothers me. I'm not supposed to do that."

"I know, I've seen the big red S on your chest."

"That ain't all you seen, sweet patooti."

"I know, but it's all I remember."

"Oh," I said.

She smiled at me, that sunrise of a smile that colored her whole face and seemed to enliven her whole body. "Well, maybe I can remember something else if I think on it."

"Perhaps a refresher course later on tonight," I said.

"Perhaps."

The waiter came and took our order, went away, and returned shortly with another beer for me.

"The irony is," I said, "that Linda Rabb is married to one of the all-time greats of jockdom, and she's being helped by me, with the red S on my chest and the gun in my pocket, and she's the one that saves them. She's the one, while us two stud ducks are standing around flexing, that does what had

342

to be done. And it hurt and I couldn't save them and her husband couldn't save them. She saved herself and her husband."

"Maynard has stopped the blackmail?"

"Sure, he had to. He had nothing to gain and everything to lose." I drank some beer. The waiter brought us each a plate of oysters and a bottle of Chablis.

"The papers have been kind to Mrs. Rabb."

"Yeah, pretty good. There's been a lot of mail, some of it really ugly, but the club publicity people are handling it and she hasn't had to read much of it."

"How about Marty?"

"He went into the stands for some guy out in Minnesota and got a three-day suspension for it. Since then he's kept his mouth shut, but you can tell it hurts."

"And you?"

I shrugged. The waiter took away the empty oyster plates and put down two small crocks of crab and lobster stew.

"And you?" she said again.

"I killed two guys, and almost killed another one."

"Killing those two was what made it possible for Linda Rabb to do what she did."

"I know."

"You've killed people before."

"Yeah."

"They would have killed you."

"Yeah."

"Then it had to be, didn't it?"

"I set them up," I said. "I got them up there to kill them."

"Yes, and you walked in on them from the front, two of them to one of you, like a John Wayne movie. How many men do you think would have done that?"

I shook my head.

"Do you think they would have done it? They weren't doing it. They were trying to ambush you. And if they'd succeeded, would they be agonizing about it now?"

I shook my head again.

"You'd have had to kill them," Susan said. "Sometime. Now it's done. What does it matter how?"

"That's the part that does matter. How. It's the only part that matters."

"Honor?" Susan said.

"Yeah," I said. The waiter came and took the crocks and returned with scrod for Susan and steak for me. We ate a little.

"I am not making fun," Susan said, "but aren't you older and wiser than that?"

I shook my head. "Nope. Neither is Rabb. I know what's killing him. It's killing me too. The code didn't work."

"The code," Susan said.

"Yeah, jock ethic, honor, code, whatever. It didn't cover this situation."

"Can't it be adjusted?"

"Then it's not a code anymore. See, being a person is kind of random and arbitrary business. You may have noticed that. And you need to believe in something to keep it from being too random and arbitrary to handle. Some people take religion, or success, or patriotism, or family, but for a lot of guys those things don't work. A guy like me. I don't have religion or family, that sort of thing. So you accept some system of order, and you stick to it. For Rabb it's playing ball. You give it all you got and you play hurt and you don't complain and so on and if you're good you win and the better you are the more you win so the more you win the more you prove you're good. But for Rabb it's also taking care of the wife and kid, and the two systems came into conflict. He couldn't be true to both. And now he's compromised and he'll never have the same sense of self he had before."

"And you, Spenser?"

"Me too, I guess. I don't know if there is even a name for the system I've chosen, but it has to do with honor. And honor is behavior for its own reason. You know?"

"Who has it," Susan said, "he that died a Wednesday?"

"Yeah, sure, I know that too. But all I have is how I

act. It's the only system I fit into. Whatever the hell I am is based in part on not doing things I don't think I should do. Or don't want to do. That's why I couldn't last with the cops. That's the difference between me and Martin Quirk."

"Perhaps Quirk has simply chosen a different system," Susan said.

"Yeah. I think he has. You're catching on."

"And," Susan said, "two moral imperatives in your system are never to allow innocents to be victimized and never to kill people except involuntarily. Perhaps the words aren't quite the right ones, but that's the idea, isn't it?"

I nodded.

"And," she said, "this time you couldn't obey both those imperatives. You had to violate one."

I nodded again.

"I understand," she said.

We ate for a bit in silence.

"I can't make it better," she said.

"No," I said. "You can't."

We ate the rest of the entrée in silence.

The waiter brought coffee. "You will live a little diminished, won't you?" she said.

"Well, I got a small sniff of my own mortality. I guess everyone does once in a while. I don't know if that's diminishment or not. Maybe it's got to do with being human."

She looked at me over her coffee cup. "I think maybe it has to do with that," she said.

I didn't feel good, but I felt better. The waiter brought the check.

Outside on Tremont Street, Susan put her arm through mine. It was a warm night and there were stars out. We walked down toward the Common.

"Spenser," she said, "you are a classic case for the feminist movement. A captive of the male mystique, and all that. And I want to say, for God's sake, you fool, outgrow all that Hemingwayesque nonsense. And yet . . ." She leaned her head against my shoulder as she spoke. "And yet I'm not sure you're wrong. I'm not sure but what you are exactly what you

345

ought to be. What I am sure of is I'd care for you less if killing those people didn't bother you."

At Park Street we crossed to the Common and walked down the long walk toward the Public Garden. The swan boats were docked for the night. We crossed Arlington onto Marlborough Street and turned in at my apartment. We went up in silence. Her arm still through mine. I opened the door and she went in ahead of me. Inside the door, with the lights still out, I put my arms around her and said, "Suze, I think I can work you into my system."

"Enough with the love talk," she said. "Off with the clothes."

PROMISED LAND

For Joan, David and Daniel

CHAPTER ONE

I HAD BEEN urban-renewed right out of my office and had to
move uptown. My new place was on the second floor of a two-
story round turret that stuck out over the corner of Mass Ave
and Boylston Street above a cigar store. The previous tenant
had been a fortuneteller and I was standing in the window
scraping her patchy gilt lettering off the pane with a razor
blade when I saw him. He had on a pale green leisure suit
and a yellow shirt with long pointed collar, open at the neck
and spilling onto the lapels of the suit. He was checking the
address on a scrap of paper and looking unhappily at the
building.

"I've either got my first client in the new office," I said,
"or the last of Madam Sosostris'."

Behind me Susan Silverman, in cut-off jeans and a
blue-and-white-striped tank top, was working on the frosted
glass of the office door with Windex and a paper towel. She
stepped to the window and looked down.

"He doesn't look happy with the neighborhood," she
said.

"If I were in a neighborhood that would make him
happy, he couldn't afford me."

The man disappeared into the small door beside the

351

tobacco store and a minute later I heard his footsteps on the stairs. He paused, then a knock. Susan opened the door. He looked uncertainly in. There were files on the floor in cardboard boxes that said FALSTAFF on them, the walls still smelled of rubber-based paint and brushes and cans of paint clustered on newspaper to the left of the door. It was hot in the office and I was wearing only a pair of paint-stained jeans and worse sneakers.

"I'm looking for a man named Spenser," he said.

"Me," I said. "Come on in." I laid the razor blade on the windowsill and came around the desk to shake his hand. I needed a client. I bet Philo Vance never painted his own office.

"This is Mrs. Silverman," I said. "She's helping me to move in. The city knocked down my old office." I was conscious of the trickle of sweat that was running down my chest as I talked. Susan smiled and said hello.

"My name is Shepard," he said. "Harvey Shepard. I need to talk."

Susan said, "I'll go out and get a sandwich. It's close to lunchtime. Want me to bring you back something?"

I shook my head. "Just grab a Coke or something. When Mr. Shepard and I are finished I'll take you to lunch somwhere good."

"We'll see," she said. "Nice to have met you, Mr. Shepard."

When she was gone, Shepard said, "Your secretary?"

"No," I said. "Just a friend."

"Hey, I wish I had a friend like that."

"Guy with your kind of threads," I said, "shouldn't have any trouble."

"Yeah, well, I'm married. And I work all the time."

There was silence. He had a high-colored square face with crisp black hair. He was a little soft around the jowls and his features seemed a bit blurred, but he was a good-looking guy. Black Irish. He seemed like a guy who was used to talking and his failure to do so now was making him uncomfortable. I primed the pump.

352

"Who sent you to me, Mr. Shepard?"

"Harv," he said. "Call me Harv, everyone does."

I nodded.

"I know a reporter on the New Bedford *Standard Times.* He got your name for me."

"You from New Bedford, Harv?"

"No, Hyannis."

"You're gonna run for President and you want me for an advance man."

"No." He did a weak uncertain smile. "Oh, I get it, Hyannis, hah."

"Okay," I said, "you're not going to run for President. You don't want me as an advance man. What is your plan?"

"I want you to find my wife."

"Okay."

"She's run away, I think."

"They do that sometimes."

"I want her back."

"That I can't guarantee. I'll find her. But I don't do kidnaping. If she comes back is between you and her."

"She just left. Me and three kids. Just walked out on us."

"You been to the cops?"

He nodded.

"They don't suspect, if you'll pardon the expression, foul play?"

He shook his head. "No, she packed up her things in a suitcase and left. I know Deke Slade personally and he is convinced she's run off."

"Slade a cop?"

"Yes, Barnstable police."

"Okay. A hundred a day and expenses. The expenses are going to include a motel room and a lot of meals. I don't want to commute back and forth from Boston every day."

"Whatever it costs, I'll pay. You want something up front?"

"Harv, if you do run for President I will be your advance man."

He smiled his weak smile again. I wasn't taking his mind off his troubles.

"How much you want?"

"Five hundred."

He took a long wallet from his inside coat pocket and took five hundred-dollar bills out of it and gave them to me. I couldn't see how much was left in the wallet. I folded them up and stuck them in my pants pocket and tried to look like they were joining others.

"I'll come down in the morning. You be home?"

"Yeah. I'm on Ocean Street, eighteen Ocean Street. When do you think you'll get there? I got just a ton of work to do. Jesus, what a time for her to walk out on us."

"I'll be there at nine o'clock. If you got pictures of her, get them ready, I'll have copies made. If you have any letters, phone bills, charge-card receipts, that sort of thing, dig them out, I'll want to see them. Check stubs? List of friends or family she might go to? How about another man?"

"Pam? Naw. She's not interested much in sex."

"She might be interested in love."

"I give her that, Spenser. All she could ever use."

"Well, whatever. How about the kids? Can I talk in front of them?"

"Yeah, we don't hide things. They know she took off. They're old enough anyway, the youngest is twelve."

"They have any thoughts on their mother's whereabouts?"

"I don't think so. They say they don't."

"But you're not certain?"

"It's just, I'm not sure they'd tell me. I mean I haven't talked with them much lately as much as I should. I don't know for sure that they're leveling with me. Especially the girls."

"I have that feeling all the time about everybody. Don't feel bad."

"Easy for you."

"Yeah, you're right. You have anything else to tell me?"

He shook his head.

"Okay, I'll see you tomorrow at nine."

We shook hands.

"You know how to get there?"

"Yes," I said. "I know Hyannis pretty well. I'll find you."

"Will you find her, Spenser?"

"Yep."

CHAPTER TWO

WHEN SUSAN SILVERMAN CAME back from her Coke I was sitting at the desk with the five one-hundred-dollar bills spread out in front of me.

"Whose picture is on a one-hundred-dollar bill?" I said.

"Nelson Rockefeller."

"Wrong."

"David Rockefeller?"

"Never mind."

"Laurance Rockefeller?"

"Where would you like to go to lunch?"

"You shouldn't have shown me the money. I was ready to settle for Ugi's steak and onion subs. Now I'm thinking about Pier 4."

"Pier 4 it is. Think I'll have to change?"

"At least wipe the sweat off your chest."

"Come on, we'll go back to my place and suit up."

"When you get a client," Susan said, "you really galvanize into action, don't you?"

"Yes, ma'am. I move immediately for the nearest restaurant."

I clipped my gun on my right hip, put on my shirt and

left the shirttail out to hide the gun and we left. It was a ten-minute walk to my apartment, most of it down the mall on Commonwealth Ave. When we got there, Susan took the first shower and I had a bottle of Amstel while I called for reservations. In fact I had three.

Pier 4 looms up on the waterfront like a kind of Colonial Stonehenge. Used brick, old beams and a Hudson River excursion boat docked alongside for cocktails. A monument to the expense account, a temple of business lunches. One of the costumed kids at the door parked my convertible with an embarrassed look. Most of the cars in the lot were newer and almost none that I could see had as much gray tape patching the upholstery.

"That young man seemed disdainful of your car," Susan said.

"One of the troubles with the culture," I said. "No respect for age."

There'd be a wait for our table. Would we care for a cocktail in the lounge? We would. We walked across the enclosed gangplank to the excursion boat and sat and looked at Boston Harbor. Susan had a Margarita, I had some Heinekens. Nobody has Amstel. Not even Pier 4.

"What does your client want you to do?"

"Find his wife."

"Does it sound difficult?"

"No. Sounds like she's simply run off. If she has she'll be easy to find. Most wives who run off don't run very far. The majority of them, in fact, want to be found and want to come home."

"That doesn't sound particularly liberated."

"It isn't particularly liberated but it's the way it is. For the first time the number of runaway wives exceeds the number of runaway husbands. They read two issues of *Ms.* Magazine, see Marlo Thomas on a talk show and decide they can't go on. So they take off. Then they find out that they have no marketable skills. That ten or fifteen years of housewifing has prepared them for nothing else and they end up washing dishes or waiting tables or pushing a mop and they want out. Also lots of them get lonesome."

"And they can't just go home," Susan said, "because they are embarrassed and they can't just go crawling back."

"Right. So they hang around and hope someone looks for them."

"And if someone does look for them it's a kind of communicative act. That is, the husband cared enough about them to try to find them. It's a gesture, in its odd way, of affection."

"Right again. But the guilt, particularly if they have kids, the guilt is killing them. And when they get home things are usually worse than they were when they left."

Susan sipped at her Margarita. "The husband has a new club to beat her with."

I nodded. "Yep. And partly he's right. Partly he's saying, hey, you son of a bitch. You ducked out on us. You left me and the kids in the goddamned lurch and you ran. That's no reason for pride, sweetheart. You owe us."

"But," Susan said.

"Of course, but. Always but. But she's lived her life in terms of them and she needs a chance to live it in terms of her. Natch." I shrugged and drank the rest of my beer.

"You make it sound so routine."

"It is routine in a way," I said. "I've seen it enough. In the sixties I spent most of my time looking for runaway kids. Now I spend it looking for runaway mommas. The mommas don't vary the story too much."

"You also make it sound, oh I don't know, trivial. Or, commonplace. As if you didn't care. As if they were only items in your work. Things to look for."

"I don't see much point to talking with a tremor in my voice. I care enough about them to look for them. I do it for the money too, but money's not hard to make. The thing, in my line of work at least, is not to get too wrapped up in caring. It tends to be bad for you." I gestured to the waitress for another beer. I looked at Susan's drink. She shook her head.

Across the harbor a 747 lifted improbably off the runway at Logan and swung slowly upward in a lumbering circle before heading west. L.A.? San Francisco?

"Suze," I said. "You and I ought to be on that."

"On what?"

"The plane, heading west. Loosing the surly bonds of earth."

"I don't like flying."

"Whoops," I said, "I have trod on a toe."

"Why do you think so?"

"Tone, babe, tone of voice. Length of sentence, attitude of head. I am, remember, a trained investigator. Clues are my game. What are you mad at?"

"I don't know."

"That's a start."

"Don't make fun of me, Spenser. I don't exactly know. I'm mad at you, or at least in that area. Maybe I've read *Ms.* Magazine, maybe I spend too much time seeing Marlo Thomas on talk shows. I was married and divorced and maybe I know better than you do what this man's wife might be going through."

"Maybe you do," I said. The maître d' had our table and we were silent as we followed him to it. The menus were large and done in a stylish typeface. The price of lobster was discreetly omitted.

"But say you do," I picked up. "Say you understand her problem better than I do. What's making you mad?"

She looked at her menu. "Smug," she said. "That's the word I was looking for, a kind of smugness about that woman's silly little fling."

The waitress appeared. I looked at Susan. "Escargots," she said to the waitress. "And the cold crab." I ordered assorted hot hors d'oeuvres and a steak. The waitress went away.

"I don't buy smug," I said. "Flip, maybe, but not smug."

"Condescending," Susan said.

"No," I said. "Annoyed, maybe, if you push me. But not

at her, at all the silliness in the world. I'm sick of movements. I'm sick of people who think that a new system will take care of everything. I'm sick of people who put the cause ahead of the person. And I am sick of people, whatever sex, who dump the kids and run off: to work, to booze, to sex, to success. It's irresponsible."

The waitress reappeared with our first course. My platter of hot hors d'oeuvres included a clam casino, an oyster Rockefeller, a fried shrimp, a soused shrimp and a stuffed mushroom cap.

"I'll trade you a mushroom cap for a snail," I said to Susan.

She picked a snail up in the tongs and put it on my plate. "I don't want the mushroom," she said.

"No need for a hunger strike, Suze, just because you're mad." I poked the snail out of its shell and ate it. "Last chance for the mushroom."

She shook her head. I ate the mushroom.

Susan said, "You don't know why she ran off."

"Neither of us does."

"But you assumed a feminist reason."

"I should not have. You are right."

"I'll take that soused shrimp," Susan said. I put it on her plate with my fork.

I said, "You know they're my favorite."

She said, "And I know you don't care that much for the mushroom caps."

"Bitch."

Susan smiled. "The way to a man's remorse," she said, "is through his stomach."

The smile did it, it always did it. Susan's smile was Technicolor, Cinemascope and stereophonic sound. I felt my stomach muscles tighten, like they always did when she smiled, like they always did when I really looked at her.

"Where in hell were you," I said, "twenty years ago?"

"Marrying the wrong guy," she said. She put her right hand out and ran her forefinger over the knuckles on my left hand as it lay on the tabletop. The smile stayed but it was a serious smile now. "Better late than never," she said.

The waitress came with the salad.

CHAPTER THREE

I WAS UP EARLY and on my way to Hyannis before the heavy rush hour traffic started in Boston. Route 3 to the Cape is superhighway to the Sagamore Bridge. Twenty years ago there was no superhighway and you went to the Cape along Route 28 through the small southern Mass towns like Randolph. It was slow but it was interesting and you could look at people and front yards and brown mongrel dogs, and stop at diners and eat hamburgers that were cooked before your very eyes. Driving down Route 3 that morning the only person I saw outside a car was a guy changing a tire near a sign that said PLYMOUTH.

As I arched up over the Cape Cod Canal at the Sagamore Bridge, Route 3 became Route 6, the Mid-Cape Highway. In the center strip and along each roadside was scrub white pine, and some taller, an occasional maple tree and some small oak trees. At high points on the road you could see ocean on both sides, Buzzards Bay to the south, Cape Cod Bay to the north. In fact the whole Cape echoed with a sense of the ocean, not necessarily its sight and not always its scent or sound. Sometimes just the sense of vast space on each side of you. Of open brightness stretching a long way under the sun.

Route 132 took me into Hyannis center. The soothing excitements of scrub pine and wide sea gave way to McDonald's and Holiday Inn and prefab fence companies, shopping malls and Sheraton Motor Inns, and a host of less likely places where you could sleep and eat and drink in surroundings indistinguishable from the ones you'd left at home. Except there'd be a fishnet on the wall. If Bartholomew Gosnold had approached the Cape from this direction he'd have kept on going.

At the airport circle, I headed east on Main Street. Hyannis is surprisingly congested and citylike as you drive into it. Main Street is lined with stores, many of them branches of Boston and New York stores. The motel I wanted was at the east end of town, a big handsome resort motel with a health club and a good restaurant of Victorian décor. A big green sign out front said DUNFEY'S. I had stayed there two months ago with Brenda Loring and had a nice time.

I was in my room and unpacked by nine-thirty. I called Shepard. He was home and waiting for me. Ocean Street is five minutes from the motel, an extension of Sea Street, profuse with weathered shingles and blue shutters. Shepard's house was no exception. A big Colonial with white cedar shingles weathered silver, and blue shutters at all the windows. It was on a slight rise of ground on the ocean side of Ocean Street. A white Caddie convertible with the top down was parked in front. A curving brick path ran up to the front door and small evergreens clustered along the foundation. The front door was blue. I rang the bell and heard it go bing-bong inside. To the left of the house was a beach, where the street curved. To the right was a high hedge concealing the neighbors' house next door. A blond teenage girl in a very small lime green bikini answered the door. She looked maybe seventeen. I carefully did not leer at her when I said, "My name's Spenser to see Mr. Shepard."

The girl said, "Come in."

I stepped into the front hallway and she left me standing while she went to get her father. I closed the door behind me. The front hall was floored in flagstone and the walls appeared to be cedar paneling. There were doors on both sides and in the rear, and a stairway leading up. The ceilings were white and evenly rough, the kind of plaster ceiling that is sprayed on and shows no mark of human hand.

Shepard's daughter came back. I eyed her surreptitiously behind my sunglasses. Surreptitious is not leering. She might be too young, but it was hard to tell.

"My dad's got company right now, he says can you wait a minute?"

"Sure."

She walked off and left me standing in the hall. I didn't insist on port in the drawing room, but standing in the hall seemed a bit cool. Maybe she was distraught by her mother's disappearance. She didn't look distraught. She looked sullen. Probably mad at having to answer the door. Probably going to paint her toenails when I'd interrupted. Terrific-looking thighs though. For a little kid.

Shepard appeared from the door past the stairs. With him was a tall black man with a bald head and high cheekbones. He had on a powder blue leisure suit and a pink silk shirt with a big collar. The shirt was unbuttoned to the waist and the chest and stomach that showed were as hard and unadorned as ebony. He took a pair of wraparound sunglasses from the breast pocket of the jacket and as he put them on, he stared at me over their rims until very slowly the lenses covered his eyes and he stared at me through them.

I looked back. "Hawk," I said.

"Spenser."

Shepard said, "You know each other?"

Hawk nodded.

I said, "Yeah."

Shepard said to Hawk, "I've asked Spenser here to see if he can find my wife, Pam."

Hawk said, "I'll bet he can. He's a real firecracker for finding things. He'll find the ass off of a thing. Ain't that right, Spenser?"

"You always been one of my heroes too, Hawk. Where you staying?"

"Ah'm over amongst de ofays at de Holiday Inn, Marse Spensah."

"We don't say ofays anymore, Hawk. We say honkies. And you don't do that Kingfish dialect any better than you used to."

"Maybe not, but you should hear me sing 'Shortnin' Bread,' babe."

"Yeah, I'll bet," I said.

Hawk turned toward Shepard. "I'll be in touch, Mr. Shepard," he said. They shook hands and Hawk left. Shepard and I watched him from the front door as he walked down toward the Caddie. His walk was graceful and easy yet there was about him an aura of taut muscle, of tight coiled potential, that made it seem as if he were about to leap.

He looked at my '68 Chevy, and looked back at me with a big grin. "Still first cabin all the way, huh, baby?"

I let that pass and Hawk slid into his Cadillac and drove away. Ostentatious.

Shepard said, "How do you know him?"

"We used to fight on the same card twenty years ago. Worked out in some of the same gyms."

"Isn't that amazing, and twenty years later you run into him here."

"Oh, I've seen him since then. Our work brings us into occasional contact."

"Really?"

"Yeah."

"You know, I could sense that you knew each other pretty well. Salesman's instinct at sizing people up, I guess. Come on in. Have a cup of coffee or something? It's pretty early for a drink, I guess."

We went into the kitchen. Shepard said, "Instant okay?"

I said, "Sure," and Shepard set water to boiling in a red porcelain teakettle.

The kitchen was long with a divider separating the cooking area from the dining area. In the dining area was a big rough hewn picnic table with benches on all four sides. The table was stained a driftwood color and contrasted very nicely with the blue floor and counter tops.

"So you used to be a fighter, huh?"

I nodded.

"That how your nose got broken?"

"Yep."

"And the scar under your eye, too, I'll bet."

"Yep."

"Geez, you look in good shape, bet you could still go a few rounds today, right?"

"Depends on who I went them with."

"You fight heavyweight?"

I nodded again. The coffee water boiled. Shepard spooned some Taster's Choice from a big jar into each cup. "Cream and sugar?"

"No thank you," I said.

He brought the coffee to the table and sat down across from me. I'd been hoping, maybe for a doughnut, or a muffin. I wondered if Hawk had gotten one.

"Cheers," Shepard said, and raised his cup at me.

"Harv," I said, "you got more troubles than a missing wife."

"What do you mean by that?"

"I mean I know Hawk, I know what he does. He's an enforcer, what the kids on my corner used to call a leg-breaker. He freelances and these days he freelances most often for King Powers."

"Now wait a minute. I hired you to find my wife. Whatever business I'm in with Hawk is my business. Not yours. I'm not paying you to nose around in my business."

"That's true," I said. "But if you are dealing with Hawk, you are dealing with pain. Hawk's a hurter. You owe Powers money?"

"I don't know a goddamned thing about Powers. Don't worry about Powers or Hawk or anybody else. I want you looking for my wife, not peeking into my books, you know?"

"Yeah, I know. But I've spent a lot of years doing my business with people like Hawk. I know how it goes. This time Hawk came and talked to you, pleasantly enough,

364

spelled out how much you owed and how far behind you were on the vig and when you had to pay it by."

"How the hell do you know what we were talking about."

"And at the end he told you, with a friendly enough smile, what would happen if you didn't pay. And then I came and he said goodby politely and he left."

"Spenser, are you going to talk about this anymore or are you going to get to work on what I hired you for."

"Harv. Hawk means it. Hawk is a bad man. But he keeps his word. If you owe money, pay it. If you haven't the money, tell me now, and we can work on the problem. But don't bullshit me, and don't bullshit yourself. If you're dealing with Hawk you are in way, way, far way, over your head."

"There's nothing to talk about. Now that's it. There's no more to say about it."

"You may even be in over mine," I said.

CHAPTER FOUR

I HAD A SENSE, call it a hunch, that Shepard didn't want to talk about his dealings with Hawk, or King Powers or anybody else. He wanted to talk about his wife.

"Your wife's name is Pam, right?"

"Right."

"Maiden name?"

"What difference does that make?"

"She might start using it when she took off."

"Pam Neal." He spelled it.

"Folks living?"

"No."

"Siblings?"

He looked blank.

"Brothers or sisters," I said.

"No. She's an only child."

"Where'd she grow up?"

"Belfast, Maine. On the coast, near Searsport."

"I know where it is. She have friends up there she might visit?"

"No. She left there after college. Then her folks died. She hasn't been back in fifteen years, I'd bet."

"Where'd she go to college?"

"Colby."

"In Waterville?"

"Yeah."

"What year she graduate?"

"Nineteen fifty-four, both of us. College sweethearts."

"How about college friends?"

"Oh, hell, I don't know. I mean we still see a lot of people we went to school with. You think she might be visiting someone?"

"Well, if she ran off, she had to run somewhere. She ever work?"

He shook his head strongly. "No way. We got married right after graduation. I've supported her since her father stopped."

"She ever travel without you, separate vacations, that sort of thing?"

"No, Christ, she gets lost in a phone booth. I mean she's scared to travel. Anywhere we've ever gone, I've taken her."

"So if you were her, no work experience, no travel skills, no family other than this one, and you ran off, where would you go?"

He shrugged.

"She take money," I said.

"Not much. I gave her the food money and her house money on Monday and she took off Thursday, and she'd already done the food shopping. She couldn't a had more than twenty bucks."

"Okay, so we're back to where could she go. She needed help. There's not a lot you can do on twenty bucks. What friends could she have gone to?"

"Well, I mean most of her friends were my friends too, you know. I mean I know the husband and she knows the wife. I don't think she could be hiding out anywhere like that. One of the guys would tell me."

"Unmarried friend?"

"Hey, that's a problem, I don't think I know anybody who isn't married."

"Does your wife?"

"Not that I know. But, hell, I don't keep track of her every move. I mean she had some friends from college, I don't think ever married. Some of them weren't bad either."

"Could you give me their names, last known address, that sort of thing?"

"Jesus, I don't know. I'll try, but you gotta give me a little time. I don't really know too much about what she did during the day. I mean maybe she wrote to some of them, I don't know."

"Any who live around here?"

"I just don't know, Spenser. Maybe Millie might know."

"Your daughter?"

"Yeah, she's sixteen. That's old enough for them to have girl talk and stuff, I imagine. Maybe she's got something you could use. Want me to get her?"

"Yeah, and old phone bills, letters, that kind of thing, might be able to give us a clue as to where she'd go. And I'll need a picture."

"Yeah, okay. I'll get Millie first, and I'll look for that stuff while you're talking with her." He hadn't come right home and done it like I told him. Maybe I lacked leadership qualities.

Millie didn't look happy to talk with me. She sat at the table and turned her father's empty coffee cup in a continuous circle in front of her. Shepard went off to collect the phone bills and letters. Millie didn't speak.

"Any thoughts on where your mother might be, Millie?"

She shook her head.

"Does that mean you don't know or you won't say."

She shrugged and continued to turn the coffee cup carefully.

"You want her back?"

She shrugged again. When I turn on the charm they melt like butter.

"Why do you think she ran off?"

"I don't know," she said, staring at the cup. Already she was starting to pour out her heart to me.

"If you were she," I said, "would you run off?"

"I wouldn't leave my children," she said and there was some emphasis on the *my*.

"Would you leave your husband?"

"I'd leave him," she said and jerked her head toward the door her father had gone through.

"Why?"

"He's a jerk."

"What's jerky about him?"

She shrugged.

"Work too hard? Spend too much time away from the family?"

She shrugged again.

"Honey," I said. "On the corner I hang out, when you call someone a jerk you're supposed to say why, especially if it's family."

"Big deal," she said.

"It's one of the things that separate adults from children," I said.

"Who wants to be an adult?"

"I been both and adult is better than kid."

"Sure," she said.

"Who's your mother's best friend?" I said.

She shrugged again. I thought about getting up and

368

throwing her through the window. It made me feel good for a minute, but people would probably call me a bully.

"You love your mother?"

She rolled her eyes at the ceiling and gave a sigh. "Course," she said and looked back at the circles she was making with the coffee cup. Perhaps I could throw it through the window instead.

"How do you know she's not in trouble?"

"I don't know."

"How do you know she's not kidnaped?"

"I don't know."

"Or sick someplace with no one to help her." Ah, the fertility of my imagination. Maybe she was the captive of a dark mysterious count in a castle on the English moors. Should I mention to the kid a fate worse than death?

"I don't know. I mean my father just said she ran away. Isn't he supposed to know?"

"He doesn't know. He's guessing. And he's trying to spare you in his jerky way from worse worry."

"Well, why doesn't he find out?"

"Ahhh, oh giant of brain, come the light. What the hell do you think he's hired me for?"

"Well, why don't you find out." She had stopped turning the coffee cup.

"That's what I'm trying to do. Why don't you help? So far your contribution to her rescue is four I-don't-knows and six shrugs. Plus telling me your old man's a jerk but you don't know why."

"What if she really did run away and doesn't want to come back?"

"Then she doesn't come back. I almost never use my leg irons on women anymore."

"I don't know where she is."

"Why do you suppose she left?"

"You already asked me that."

"You didn't answer."

"My father got on her nerves."

"Like how?"

369

"Like, I don't know. He was always grabbing at her, you know. Patting her ass, or saying gimme a kiss when she was trying to vacuum. That kind of stuff. She didn't like it."

"They ever talk about it?"

"Not in front of me."

"What did they talk about in front of you?"

"Money. That is, my old man did. My old lady just kind of listened. My old man talks about money and business all the time. Keeps talking about making it big. Jerk."

"Your father ever mistreat your mother?"

"You mean hit her or something?"

"Whatever."

"No. He treated her like a goddamned queen, actually. That's what was driving her crazy. I mean he was all over her. It was gross. He was sucking after her all the time. You know?"

"Did she have any friends that weren't friends of your father's?"

She frowned a little bit, and shook her head. "I don't think so. I don't know any."

"She ever go out with other men?"

"My mother?"

"It happens."

"Not my mother. No way."

"Is there anything you can think of, Millie, that would help me find your mother?"

"No, nothing. Don't you think I'd like her back. I have to do all the cooking and look out for my brother and sister and make sure the cleaning lady comes and a lot of other stuff."

"Where's your brother and sister?"

"At the beach club, the lucky stiffs. I have to stay home for you."

"For me?"

"Yeah, my father says I have to be the hostess and stuff till my mother comes home. I'm missing the races and everything."

"Life's hard sometimes," I said. She made a sulky gesture with her mouth. We were silent for a minute.

"The races go on all week," she said. "Everybody's there. All the summer kids and everybody."

"And you're missing them," I said. "That's a bitch."

"Well, it is. All my friends are there. It's the biggest time of the summer."

So young to have developed her tragic sense so highly.

Shepard came back in the room with a cardboard carton filled with letters and bills. On top was an 8½ × 11 studio photo in a gold filigree frame. "Here you go, Spenser. This is everything I could find."

"You sort through any of it?" I asked.

"Nope. That's what I hired you for. I'm a salesman, not a detective. I believe in a man doing what he does best. Right, Mill?"

Millie didn't answer. She was probably thinking about the races.

"A man's gotta believe in something," I said. "You know where I'm staying if anything comes up."

"Dunfey's, right? Hey, mention my name to the maître d' in The Last Hurrah, get you a nice table."

I said I would. Shepard walked me to the door. Millie didn't. "You remember that. You mention my name to Paul over there. He'll really treat you good."

As I drove away I wondered what races they were running down at the beach club.

CHAPTER FIVE

I ASKED AT THE TOWN hall for directions to the police station. The lady at the counter in the clerk's office told me in an English accent that it was on Elm Street off Barnstable Road. She also gave me the wrong directions to Barnstable Road, but what can you expect from a foreigner. A guy in a Sunoco station straightened me out on the directions and I pulled into the parking lot across the street from the station a little before noon.

It was a square brick building with a hip roof and two small A dormers in front. There were four or five police cruisers in the lot beside the station: dark blue with white tops and white front fenders. On the side was printed BARNSTABLE PO-LICE. Hyannis is part of Barnstable Township. I know that but I never did know what a township was and I never found anyone else who knew.

I entered a small front room. To the left behind a low rail sat the duty officer with switchboard and radio equipment. To the right a long bench where the plaintiffs and felons and penitents could sit in discomfort while waiting for the captain. All police stations had a captain you waited for when you came in. Didn't matter what it was.

"Deke Slade in?" I asked the cop behind the rail.

"Captain's busy right now. Can I help you?"

"Nope, I'd like to see him." I gave the cop my business card. He looked at it with no visible excitement.

"Have a seat," he said, nodding at the bench. "Captain'll be with you when he's free." It's a phrase they learn in the police academy. I sat and looked at the color prints of game birds on the walls on my side of the office.

I was very sick of looking at them when, about one-ten, a gray-haired man stuck his head through the door on my side of the railing and said, "Spenser?"

I said, "Yeah."

He jerked his head and said, "In here." The head jerk is another one they learn in the police academy. I followed the head jerk into a square shabby office. One window looked out onto the lot where the cruisers parked. And beyond that a ragged growth of lilacs. There was a green metal filing cabinet and a gray metal desk with matching swivel chair. The desk was littered with requisitions and flyers and such. A sign on one corner said CAPTAIN SLADE.

Slade nodded at the gray metal straight chair on my side of the desk. "Sit," he said. Slade matched his office. Square, uncluttered and gray. His hair was short and curly, the face square as a child's block, outdoors tan, with a gray blue sheen of heavy beard kept close shave. He was short, maybe five-eight, and blocky, like an offensive guard from a small college. The kind of guy that should be running to fat when he got forty, but wasn't. "What'll you have," he said.

"Harv Shepard hired me to look for his wife. I figured you might be able to point me in the right direction."

"License?"

I took out my wallet, slipped out the plasticized photostat of my license and put it in front of him on the desk. His uniform blouse had short sleeves and his bare arms were folded across his chest. He looked at the license without unfolding his arms, then at me and back at the license again.

"Okay," he said.

I picked up the license, slipped it back in my wallet.

"Got a gun permit?"

I nodded, slipped that out of the wallet and laid it in front of him. He gave it the same treatment and said, "Okay."

I put that away, put the wallet away and settled back in the chair.

Slade said, "Far as I can tell she ran off. Voluntary. No

foul play. Can't find any evidence that she went with someone. Took an Almeida bus to New Bedford and that's as far as
we've gone. New Bedford cops got her description and all, but
they got things more pressing. My guess is she'll be back in a
week or so dragging her ass."

"How about another man?"

"She probably spent the night prior to her disappearance with a guy down the Silver Seas Motel. But when she got
on the bus she appeared to be alone."

"What's the guy's name she was with?"

"We don't know." Slade rocked back in his chair.

"And you haven't been busting your tail looking to find
out either."

"Nope. No need to. There's no crime here. If I looked
into every episode of extramarital fornication around here I'd
have the whole force out on condom patrol. Some babe gets
sick of her husband, starts screwing around a little, then
takes off. You know how often that happens?" Slade's arms
were still folded.

"Yeah."

"Guy's got money, he hires somebody like you to look.
The guy he hires fusses around for a week or so, runs up a big
bill at the motel and the wife comes back on her own because
she doesn't know what else to do. You get a week on the Cape
and a nice tan, the husband gets a tax deduction, the broad
starts sleeping around locally again."

"You do much marriage counseling?"

He shook his head. "Nope, I try to catch people that
did crimes and put them in jail. You ever been a cop? I mean a
real one, not a private license?"

"I used to be on the States," I said. "Worked out of the
Suffolk County D.A.'s office."

"Why'd you quit?"

"I wanted to do more than you do."

"Social work," he said. He was disgusted.

"Any regular boyfriends you know of?"

He shrugged. "I know she slept around a little, but I
don't think anybody steady."

"She been sleeping around long or has this developed lately?"

"Don't know."

I shook my head.

Slade said, "Spenser, you want to see my duty roster? You know how many bodies I got to work with here. You know what a summer weekend is like when the weather's good and the Kennedys are all out going to Mass on Sunday."

"You got any suggestions who I might talk to in town that could get my wheels turning?" I said.

"Go down the Silver Seas, talk with the bartender, Rudy. Tell him I sent you. He pays a lot of attention and the Silver Seas is where a lot of spit gets swapped. Pam Shepard hung out down there."

I got up. "Thank you, captain."

"You got questions I can answer, lemme know."

"I don't want to take up too much of your time."

"Don't be a smart-ass, Spenser, I'll do what I can. But I got a lot of things to look at and Pam Shepard's just one of them. You need help, gimme a call. If I can, I'll give you some."

"Yeah," I said. "Okay." We shook hands and I left.

It was two-fifteen when I pulled into the lot in front of the Silver Seas Motel. I was hungry and thirsty. While I took care of that I could talk to Rudy, start running up that big bar bill. Slade was probably right, but I'd give Shepard his money's worth before she showed up. If she was going to.

There's something about a bar on the Cape in the daytime. The brightness of lowland surrounded by ocean maybe makes the air-conditioned dimness of the bar more striking. Maybe there's more people there and they are vacationers rather than the unemployed. Whatever it is, the bar at the Silver Seas Motel had it. And I liked it.

On the outside, the Silver Seas Motel was two-storied, weathered shingles, with a verandah across both stories in front. It was tucked into the seaward side of Main Street in the middle of town between a hardware store and a store that sold scallop shell ashtrays and blue pennants that said CAPE

COD on them. The bar was on the right, off the lobby, at one end of the dining room. A lot of people were eating lunch and several were just drinking. Most of the people looked like college kids, cut-offs and T-shirts, sandals and halter tops. The décor in the place was surfwood and fishnet. Two oars crossed on one wall, a harpoon that was probably made in Hong Kong hung above the mirror behind the bar. The bartender was middle-aged and big-bellied. His straight black hair was streaked here and there with gray and hung shoulder length. He wore a white shirt with a black string bow tie like a riverboat gambler. The cuffs were turned neatly back in two careful folds. His hands were thick with long tapering fingers that looked manicured.

"Draft beer?" I asked.

"Schlitz," he said. He had a flat nose and dark coppery skin. American Indian? Maybe.

"I'll have one." He drew it in a tall straight glass. Very good. No steins, or schooners or tulip shapes. Just a tall glass the way the hops god had intended. He put down a paper coaster and put the beer on it, fed the check into the register, rang up the sale and put the check on the bar near me.

"What have you got for lunch," I said.

He took a menu out from under the bar and put it in front of me. I sipped the beer and read the menu. I was working on sipping. Susan Silverman had lately taken to reprimanding me for my tendency to empty the glass in two swallows and order another. The menu said linguica on a crusty roll. My heart beat faster. I'd forgotten about linguica since I'd been down here last. I ordered two. And another beer. Sip. Sip.

The juke box was playing something by Elton John. At least the box wasn't loud. They'd probably never heard of Johnny Hartman here. Rudy brought the sandwiches and looked at my half-sipped glass. I finished it—simple politeness, otherwise he'd have had to wait while I sipped—and he refilled the glass.

"You ever hear of Johnny Hartman," I said.

376

"Yeah. Great singer. Never copped out and started singing this shit." He nodded at the juke box.

"You Rudy," I said.

"Yeah."

"Deke Slade told me to come talk with you." I gave him a card. "I'm looking for a woman named Pam Shepard."

"I heard she was gone."

"Any idea where?" I took a large bite of the linguica sandwich. Excellent. The linguica had been split and fried and in each sandwich someone had put a fresh green pepper ring.

"How should I know?"

"You knew Johnny Hartman, and you add green peppers to your linguica sandwich."

"Yeah, well, I don't know where she went. And the cook does the sandwiches. I don't like green pepper in mine."

"Okay, so you got good taste in music and bad taste in food. Mrs. Shepard come in here much?"

"Lately, yeah. She's been in regular."

"With anyone?"

"With everyone."

"Anyone special?"

"Mostly young guys. In a dim light you might have a shot."

"Why?"

"You're too old, but you got the build. She went for the jocks and the muscle men."

"Was she in here with someone before she took off? That would have been a week ago Monday." I started on my second linguica sandwich.

"I don't keep that close a count. But it was about then. She was in here with a guy named Eddie Taylor. Shovel operator."

"They spend the night upstairs?"

"Don't know. I don't handle the desk. Just tend bar. I'd guess they did, the way she was climbing on him." A customer signaled Rudy for another stinger on the rocks. Rudy stepped down the bar, mixed the drink, poured it, rang up the price and came back to me. I finished my second sandwich while he did that. When he came back my beer glass was empty and he filled that without being asked. Well, I couldn't very well refuse, could I. Three with lunch was about right anyway.

"Where can I find Eddie Taylor?" I said.

"He's working on a job in Cotuit these days. But he normally gets off work at four and is in here by four-thirty to rinse out his mouth."

I looked at the clock behind the bar: 3:35. I could wait and sip my beer slowly. I had nothing better to do anyway. "I'll wait," I said.

"Fine with me," Rudy said. "One thing though, Eddie's sorta hard to handle. He's big and strong and thinks he's tough. And he's too young to know better yet."

"I'm big-city fuzz, Rudy. I'll dazzle him with wit and sophistication."

"Yeah, you probably will. But don't mention it was me that sicked you on to him. I don't want to have to dazzle him too."

CHAPTER SIX

IT WAS FOUR-TWENTY when Rudy said, "Hi, Eddie" to a big blond kid who came in. He was wearing work shoes and cut-off jeans and a blue tank top with red trim. He was a weight-lifter: lots of tricep definition and overdeveloped pectoral muscles. And he carried himself as if he were wearing a medal. I'd have been more impressed with him if he weren't carrying a twenty-pound roll around his middle. He said to Rudy, "Hey, Kemo Sabe, howsa kid?"

Rudy nodded and without being asked put a shot of

rye and a glass of draft beer on the bar in front of Eddie. Eddie popped down the shot and sipped at the beer.

"Heap good, red man," he said. "Paleface workem ass off today." He talked loudly, aware of an audience, assuming his Lone Ranger Indian dialect was funny. He turned around on the barstool, hooked his elbows over the bar and surveyed the room. "How's the quiff situation, Rudy?" he said.

"Same as always, Eddie. You don't usually seem to have any trouble." Eddie was staring across the room at two college-age girls drinking Tom Collinses. I got up and walked down the bar and slipped onto the stool beside him. I said, "You Eddie Taylor?"

"Who wants to know?" he said, still staring at the girls.

"There's a fresh line," I said.

He turned to look at me now. "Who the hell are you?"

I took a card out of my jacket pocket, handed it to him. "I'm looking for Pam Shepard," I said.

"Where'd she go?" he said.

"If I knew I'd go there and look for her. I was wondering if you could help me."

"Buzz off," he said and turned his stare back at the girls.

"I understand you spent the night with her just before she disappeared."

"Who says?"

"Me, I just said it."

"What if I did? I wouldn't be the first guy. What's it to you?"

"Poetry," I said. "Pure poetry when you talk."

"I told you once, buzz off. You hear me. You don't want to get hurt, you buzz off."

"She good in bed?"

"Yeah, she was all right. What's it to you?"

"I figure you had a lot of experience down here, and I'm new on the scene, you know? Just asking."

"Yeah, I've tagged a few around the Cape. She was all right. I mean for an old broad she had a nice tight body, you know. And, man, she was eager. I thought I was gonna have to nail her right here in the bar. Ask Rudy. Huh, Rudy? Wasn't that Shepard broad all over me the other night?"

"You say so, Eddie." Rudy was cleaning his thumbnail with a matchbook cover. "I never notice what the customers do."

"So you did spend the night with her?" I said.

"Yeah. Christ, if I hadn't she'd have dropped her pants right here in the bar."

"You already said that."

"Well, it's goddamned so, Jack, you better believe it."

Eddie dropped another shot of bar whiskey and sipped at a second beer chaser that Rudy had brought without being asked.

"Did you know her before you picked her up?"

"Hell, I didn't pick her up, she picked me up. I was just sitting here looking over the field and she came right over and sat down and started talking to me."

"Well, then, did you know her before she picked you up?"

Eddie shrugged, and gestured his shot glass at Rudy. "I'd seen her around. I didn't really know her, but I knew she was around, you know, that she was easy tail if you were looking." Eddie drank his shot as soon as Rudy poured it, and when he put the glass back on the bar Rudy filled it again.

"She been on the market long," I said. Me and Eddie were really rapping now, just a couple of good old boys, talking shop. Eddie drained his beer chaser, burped loudly, laughed at his burp. Maybe I wouldn't be able to dazzle him with my sophistication.

"On the market? Oh, you mean, yeah, I get you. No, not so long. I don't think I noticed her or heard much about her before this year. Maybe after Christmas, guy I know banged her. That's about the first I heard." His tongue was getting a little thick and his S's were getting slushy.

"Was your parting friendly?" I said.

"Huh?"

"What was it like in the morning when you woke up and said goodby to each other?"

"You're a nosy bastard," he said and looked away, staring at the two college girls across the room.

"People have said that."

"Well, I'm saying it."

"Yes, you are. And beautifully."

Eddie turned his stare at me. "What are you, a wise guy?"

"People have said that too."

"Well, I don't like wise guys."

"I sort of figured you wouldn't."

"So get lost or I'll knock you on your ass."

"And I sort of figured you'd put it just that way."

"You looking for trouble, Jack. I'm just the man to give it to you."

"I got all the trouble I need," I said. "What I'm looking for is information. What kind of mood was Pam Shepard in the morning after she'd been all over you?"

Eddie got off the barstool and stood in front of me. "I'm telling you for the last time. Get lost or get hurt." Rudy started drifting toward the phone. I checked the amount of room in front of the bar. Maybe ten feet. Enough. I said to Rudy, "It's okay. No one will get hurt. I'm just going to show him something."

I stood up. "Tubbo," I said to Eddie, "if you make me, I can put you in the hospital, and I will. But you probably don't believe me, so I'll have to prove it. Go ahead. Take your shot."

He took it, a right-hand punch that missed my head when I moved. He followed up with a left that missed by about the same margin when I moved the other way.

"You'll last about two minutes doing that," I said. He rushed at me and I rolled around him. "Meanwhile," I said, "if I wanted to I could be hitting you here." I tapped him open-handed on the right cheek very fast three times. He swung again and I stepped a little inside the punch and caught it on my left forearm. I caught the second one on my right. "Or here," I said and patted him rat-a-tat with both hands on

381

each cheek. The way a grandma pats a child. I stepped back away from him. He was already starting to breathe hard. "Some shape you're in, kid. In another minute you won't be able to get your arms up."

"Back off, Eddie," Rudy said from behind the bar. "He's a pro, for crissake, he'll kill you if you keep shoving him."

"I'll shove the son of a bitch," Eddie said and made a grab at me. I moved a step to my right and put a left hook into his stomach. Hard. His breath came out in a hoarse grunt and he sat down suddenly. His face blank, the wind knocked out of him, fighting to get his breath. "Or there," I said.

Eddie got his breath partially back and climbed to his feet. Without looking at anyone he headed, wobbly legged, for the men's room. Rudy said to me, "You got some good punch there."

"It's because my heart is pure," I said.

"I hope he don't puke all over the floor in there," Rudy said.

The other people in the room, quiet while the trouble had flared, began to talk again. The two college girls got up and left, their drinks unfinished, their mothers' parting fears confirmed. Eddie came back from the men's room, his face pale and wet where he'd probably splashed it with water.

"The boilermakers will do it to you," I said. "Slow you down and tear up your stomach."

"I know guys could take you," Eddie said. There was no starch in his voice when he said it and he didn't look at me.

"I do too," I said. "And I know guys who can take them. After a while counting doesn't make much sense. You just got into something I know more about than you do."

Eddie hiccupped.

"Tell me about how you left each other in the morning," I said. We were sitting at the bar again.

"What if I don't?" Eddie was looking at the small area of bar top encircled by his forearms.

"Then you don't. I don't plan to keep punching you in the stomach."

"We woke up in the morning and I wanted to go one more time, you know, sort of a farewell pop, and she wouldn't let me touch her. Called me a pig. Said if I touched her she'd kill me. Said I made her sick. That wasn't what she said before. We were screwing our brains out half the night and next morning she calls me a pig. Well, I don't need that shit, you know? So I belted her and walked out. Last I seen her she was lying on her back on the bed crying loud as a bastard. Just staring up at the ceiling and screaming crying." He shook his head. "What a weird bitch," he said. "I mean five hours before she was screwing her brains out for me."

I said, "Thanks, Eddie." I took a twenty-dollar bill out of my wallet and put it on the bar. "Take his out too, Rudy, and keep what's left."

When I left, Eddie was still looking at the bar top inside his forearms.

CHAPTER SEVEN

I HAD LAMB STEW and a bottle of Burgundy for supper and then headed into my room to start on the box of bills and letters Shepard had given me. I went through the personal mail first and found it sparse and unenlightening. Most people throw away personal mail that would be enlightening, I'd found. I got all the phone bills together and made a list of the phone numbers and charted them for frequency. Then I cross-charted them for locations. A real sleuth, sitting on the motel bed in my shorts shuffling names and numbers. There were three calls in the past month to a number in New Bedford, the rest were local. I assembled all the gasoline credit-card receipts. She had bought gasoline twice that month in New

Bedford. The rest were around home. I catalogued the other credit-card receipts. There were three charges from a New Bedford restaurant. All for more than thirty dollars. The other charges were local. It was almost midnight when I got through all of the papers. I made a note of the phone number called in New Bedford, of the New Bedford restaurant and the name of the gas station in New Bedford, then I stuffed all the paper back in the carton, put the carton in the closet and went to bed. I spent most of the night dreaming about phone bills and charge receipts and woke up in the morning feeling like Bartleby the Scrivener.

I had room service bring me coffee and corn muffins and at 9:05 put in a call to the telephone business office in New Bedford. A service rep answered.

"Hi," I said. "Ed MacIntyre at the Back Bay business office in Boston. I need a listing for telephone number 555-3688, please."

"Yes, Mr. MacIntyre, one moment please . . . that listing is Alexander, Rose. Three Centre Street, in New Bedford."

I complimented her on the speed with which she found the listing, implied perhaps a word dropped to the district manager down there, said goodby with smily pleasant overtones in my voice and hung up. Flawless.

I showered and shaved and got dressed. Six hours of paper shuffling had led me to a surmise that the Hyannis cops had begun by checking the bus terminal. She was in New Bedford. But I had an address, maybe not for her, but for someone. It pays to do business with your local gumshoe. Personalized service.

The drive to New Bedford up Route 6 was forty-five miles and took about an hour through small towns like Wareham and Onset, Marion and Mattapoisett. Over the bridge from Fairhaven across the interflow of the harbor and the Acushnet River, New Bedford rose steeply from the docks. Or what was left of it. The hillside from the bridge to the crest looked like newsreel footage of the Warsaw ghetto. Much of the center of the city had been demolished and urban renewal was in full cry. Purchase Street, one of the main streets the last time I'd been in New Bedford, was now a pedestrian mall. I drove around aimlessly in the bulldozed wasteland for perhaps ten minutes before I pulled off into a rutted parking area and stopped. I got out, opened the trunk of my car and got out a street directory for Massachusetts.

Centre Street was down back of the Whaling Museum. I knew the hill and turned left past the public library. Out front they still had the heroic statue of the harpooner in the whaleboat. A dead whale or a stove boat. The choices then were simple, if drastic. I turned left down the hill toward the water, then onto Johnny Cake Hill and parked near the Whaling Museum, in front of the Seaman's Bethel.

I checked my street map again and walked around the Whaling Museum to the street behind it and looked and there was Centre Street. It was a short street, no more than four or five buildings long, and it ran from North Water Street, behind the museum, to Front Street, which paralleled the water. It was an old street, weedy and dank. Number three was a narrow two story building with siding of gray asbestos shingles and a crumbly looking red brick chimney in the center of the roof. The roof shingles were old and dappled in various shades as though someone had patched it periodically with what he had at hand. It needed more patching. There was worn green paint on the trim here and there and the front door on the right side of the building face was painted red. It had the quality of an old whore wearing lipstick.

I hoped she wasn't in there. I wanted to find her but I hated to think of her coming from the big sunny house in Hyannis to burrow in rat's alley. What to do now? No one knew me, neither Rose Alexander or Pam Shepard, nor, as far as I knew, anyone in New Bedford. In fact the number of places where I could go and remain anonymous continuously amazed me. I could enter on any pretext and look around. Or I could knock on the door and ask for Pam Shepard. The safest thing was to stand around and watch. I liked to know as much as I could before I went in where I hadn't been before. That would take time, but I wouldn't run the risk of scaring anyone off. I looked at my watch: 12:15. I went back up toward what was left of the business district and found a restaurant. I had fried clams and cole slaw and two bottles of beer. Then I strolled back down to Centre Street and took up station about five past one. On North Water Street a municipal crew was at work with a backhoe and some jackhammers, while several guys with shirts and ties and yellow hard hats walked around with clipboards and conferred. Nobody came down Centre Street, or up it. Nobody had anything to do with Centre Street. No evidence of life appeared at number three. I had picked up a copy of the New Bedford *Standard Times* on my way back from lunch and I read it while I leaned on a telephone pole on the corner of North Water and Centre. I read everything, glancing regularly over the rim of the paper to check the house. I read about a bean supper at the Congregational church in Mattapoisett, about a father-son baseball game at the junior high school field in Rochester, about a local debutante's ball at the Wamsutta Club. I read the horoscope, the obituaries, the editorial, which took a strong stand against the incursion of Russian trawlers into local waters. I read "Dondi" and hated it. When I finished the paper, I folded it up, walked the short length of Centre Street and leaned against the doorway of an apparently empty warehouse on the corner of Centre and Front streets.

At three o'clock a wino in a gray suit, a khaki shirt and an orange flowered tie stumbled into my doorway and urinated in the other corner. When he got through I offered to brush him off and hand him a towel but he paid me no attention and stumbled off. What is your occupation, sir? I'm an outdoor men's room attendant. I wondered if anyone had ever whizzed on Allan Pinkerton's shoe.

At four-fifteen Pam Shepard came out of the shabby house with another woman. Pam was slim and Radcliffy looking with a good tan and her brown hair back in a tight French twist. She was wearing a chino pantsuit that displayed a fine-looking backside. I'd have to get closer but she looked worth finding. The woman she was with was smaller and sturdier looking. Short black hair, tan corduroy jeans and a pink muslin shirt like Indira Gandhi. They headed up the street toward the museum and turned left on the Purchase Street pedestrian mall. The mall had been created by curbing across the intersection streets and had a homemade look to it. Pam Shepard and her friend went into a supermarket and I stood under the awning of a pawnshop across the street and watched them through the plate-glass window. They bought some groceries, consulting a shopping list as they went, and in about a half-hour they were back out on the street, each with a large brown paper sack in her arms. I followed them back to the house on Centre Street and watched them disappear inside. Well, at least I knew where she was. I resumed my telephone pole. The warehouse door had lost some of its appeal.

It got dark and nothing else happened. I was beginning to hope for the wino again. I was also hungry enough to eat at a Hot Shoppe. I had some thinking it over to do and while I always did that better eating, the fried clams had not sold me on New Bedford cuisine and I would probably have to sleep sometime later on anyway. So I went back and got my car and headed back for Hyannis. There was a parking ticket under the wiper but it blew off somewhere near a bowling alley in Mattapoisett.

During the ride back to Hyannis I decided that the best move would be to go back to New Bedford in the morning and talk with Pam Shepard. In a sense I'd done what I hired on for. That is, I had her located and could report that she was alive and under no duress. It should be up to Shepard to go and get her. But it didn't go down right, giving him the address and going back to Boston. I kept thinking of Eddie Taylor's final look at her, lying on the bed on her back screaming at the ceiling. There had been a pathetic overdressed quality to her as she came out of the shabby two-story on Centre Street. She'd had on pendant earrings.

It was nine-thirty when I got back to the motel. The dining room was still open so I went in and had six oysters and a half bottle of Chablis and a one-pound steak with Béarnaise sauce and a liter of beer. The salad had an excellent house dressing and the whole procedure was a great deal more pleasant than hanging around in a doorway with an incontinent wino. After dinner I went back to my room and caught the last three innings of the Sox game on channel six.

CHAPTER EIGHT

IN THE MORNING I was up and away to New Bedford before eight. I stopped at a Dunkin' Donuts shop for a training-table breakfast to go, and ate my doughnuts and drank my coffee as I headed up the Cape with the sun at my back. I hit New Bedford at commuter time and while it wasn't that big a city its street system was so confused that the traffic jam backed up across the bridge into Fairhaven. It was nine-forty when I got out of the car and headed for the incongruous front door at 3 Centre Street. There was no doorbell and no knocker so I rapped on the red panels with my knuckles. Not too hard, the door might fold.

A big, strong-looking young woman with light brown hair in a long single braid opened the door. She had on jeans and what looked like a black leotard top. She was obviously braless, and, less noticeably, shoeless.

"Good morning," I said, "I'd like to speak with Pam Shepard, please."

"I'm sorry, there's no Pam Shepard here."

"Will she be back soon?" I was giving her my most engaging smile. Boyish. Open. Mr. Warm.

"I don't know any such person," she said.

"Do you live here?" I said.

"Yes."

"Are you Rose Alexander?"

"No." Once I give them the engaging smile they just slobber all over me.

"Is she in?"

"Who are you?"

"I asked you first," I said.

Her face closed down and she started to shut the door. I put my hand flat against it and held it open. She shoved harder and I held it open harder. She seemed determined.

"Madam," I said, "if you will stop shoving that door at me, I will speak the truth to you. Even though, I do not believe you have spoken the truth to me."

She paid no attention. She was a big woman and it was getting hard to hold the door open effortlessly.

"I stood outside this house most of yesterday and saw Pam Shepard and another woman come out, go shopping and return with groceries. The phone here is listed to Rose Alexander." My shoulder was beginning to ache. "I will talk civilly with Pam Shepard and I won't drag her back to her husband."

Behind the young woman a voice said, "What the hell is going on here, Jane?"

Jane made no reply. She kept shoving at the door. The smaller, black-haired woman I'd seen with Pam Shepard yesterday appeared. I said, "Rose Alexander?" She nodded. "I need to talk with Pam Shepard," I said.

"I don't . . ." Rose Alexander started.

"You do too," I said. "I'm a detective and I know such things: If you'll get your Amazon to unhand the door we can talk this all out very pleasantly."

Rose Alexander put her hand on Jane's arm. "You'd better let him in, Jane," she said gently. Jane stepped away from the door and glared at me. There were two bright smudges of color on her cheekbones, but no other sign of exertion. I stepped into the hall. My shoulder felt quite numb as I took my hand off the door. I wanted to rub it but was too proud. What price machismo?

"May I see some identification?" Rose Alexander said.

"Certainly." I took the plastic-coated photostat of my license out of my wallet and showed it to her.

"You're not with the police then," she said.

"No, I am self-employed," I said.

"Why do you wish to talk with me?"

"I don't," I said. "I wish to talk with Pam Shepard."

"Why do you wish to talk with her?"

"Her husband hired me to find her."

"And what were you to do when you did?"

"He didn't say. But he wants her back."

"And you intend to take her?"

"No, I intend to talk with her. Establish that she's well and under no duress, explain to her how her husband feels and see if she'd like to return."

"And if she would not like to return?"

"I won't force her."

Jane said, "That's for sure," and glared at me.

"Does her husband know she's here?" Rose Alexander asked.

"No."

"Because you've not told him?"

"That's right."

"Why?"

"I don't know. I guess I just wanted to see what was happening in the china shop before I brought in the bull."

"I don't trust you," Rose Alexander said. "What do you think, Jane?"

Jane shook her head.

"I'm not here with her husband, am I?"

"But we don't know how close he is," Rose Alexander said.

"Or who's with him," Jane said.

"Who's with him?" I was getting confused.

Rose said, "You wouldn't be the first man to take a woman by force and never doubt your right."

"Oh," I said.

"We back down from you now," Jane said, "and it will be easier next time. So we'll draw the line here, up front, first time."

"But if you do," I said, "you'll make me use force. Not to take anyone, but to see that she's in fact okay."

"You saw that yesterday," Jane said. The color was higher on her cheekbones now, and more intense. "You told me you saw Pam and Rose go shopping together."

"I don't think you've got her chained in the attic," I said. "But duress includes managing the truth. If she has no chance to hear me and reject me for herself she's not free, she's under a kind of duress."

"Don't you try to force your way in," Jane said. "You'll regret it, I promise you." She had stepped back away from me and shifted into a martial arts stance, her feet balanced at right angles to each other in a kind of T stance, her open hands held in front of her in another kind of T, the left hand vertical, the right horizontal above it. She looked like she was calling for time out. Her lips were pulled back and her breath made a hissing sound as it squeezed out between her teeth.

"You had lessons?" I asked.

Rose Alexander said, "Jane is very advanced in karate. Do not treat her lightly. I don't wish to hurt you, but you must leave." Her black eyes were quite wide and bright as she spoke. Her round pleasant face was flushed. I didn't believe the part about not wishing to hurt me.

"Well, I'm between a rock and a hard place right now. I don't want you to hurt me either, and I don't take Jane lightly. On the other hand the more you don't want me to see Pam Shepard, the more I think I ought to. I could probably go for the cops, but by the time we got back, Pam Shepard would be gone. I guess I'm going to have to insist."

Jane kicked me in the balls. Groin just doesn't say it. I'd never fought with a woman before and I wasn't ready. It felt like it always does: nausea, weakness, pain and an irresistible compulsion to double over. I did double over. Jane chopped down on the back of my neck. I twisted away and the blow landed on the big trapezious muscles without doing any serious damage. I straightened up. It hurt but not as much as it was going to if I didn't make a comeback. Jane aimed the heel of her hand at the tip of my nose. I banged her hand aside with my right forearm and hit her as hard a left hook as I've used lately, on the side of her face, near the hinge of her jaw. She went over backward and lay on the floor without motion. I'd never hit a woman before and it scared me a little. Had I hit her too hard? She was a big woman but I must have outweighed her by forty pounds. Rose Alexander dropped to her knees beside Jane, and having got there didn't know what to do. I got down too, painfully, and felt her pulse. It was nice and strong and her chest heaved and fell steadily. "She's okay," I said. "Probably better than I am."

At the far end of the hall was a raised panel door that had been painted black. It opened and Pam Shepard came through it. There were tears running down her face. "It's me," she said. "It's my fault, they were just trying to protect me. If you've hurt her it's my fault."

Jane opened her eyes and stared up blankly at us. She moved her head. Rose Alexander said, "Jane?"

I said, "She's going to be all right, Mrs. Shepard. You didn't make her kick me in the groin."

She too got down on the floor beside Jane. I got out of the way and leaned on the door jamb with my arms folded, trying to get the sick feeling to go away, and trying not to show it. People did not seem to be warming to me down here. I hoped Jane and Eddie never got together.

Jane was on her feet, Pam Shepard holding one arm and Rose Alexander the other. They went down the hall toward the black door. I followed along. Through the door was a big kitchen. A big old curvy-legged gas stove on one wall, a big oilcloth-covered table in the middle of the room, a couch with a brown corduroy spread along another wall. There was a pantry at the right rear and the walls were wainscoted narrow deal boards that reminded me of my grandmother's house. They sat Jane down in a black leather upholstered rocker. Rose went to the pantry and returned with a wet cloth. She washed Jane's face while Pam Shepard squeezed Jane's hand. "I'm all right," Jane said and pushed the wet cloth away. "How the hell did you do that," she said to me. "That kick was supposed to finish you right there."

"I am a professional thug," I said.

"It shouldn't matter," she said, frowning in puzzlement. "A kick in the groin is a kick in the groin."

"Ever do it for real before?"

"I've put in hours on the mat."

"No, not instruction. Fighting. For real."

"No," she said. "But I wasn't scared. I did it right."

"Yeah, you did, but you got the wrong guy. One of the things that a kick in the groin will do is scare the kickee. Aside from the pain and all, it's not something he's used to and he cares about the area and he tends to double over and freeze. But I've been kicked before and I know that it hurts, but it's not fatal. Not even to my sex life. And so I can force myself through the pain."

"But . . ." She shook her head.

"I know," I said. "You thought you had a weapon that made you impregnable. That would keep people from shoving you around and the first time you use it you get cold-cocked. I can bench-press three hundred pounds. I used to be a fighter. And I scuffle for a living. The karate will still work for you. But you gotta remember it's not a sport in the street."

"You think, goddamn you, you think it's because you're a man . . ."

"Nope. It's because a good big person will beat a good small person every time. Most men aren't as good as I am. A lot of them aren't as good as you are."

They were all looking at me and I felt isolated, unwelcome and uneasy. I wished there were another guy there. I said to Pam Shepard, "Can we talk?"

Rose Alexander said, "You don't have to say a word to him, Pam."

Jane said, "There's no point in it, Pam. You know how you feel."

I looked at Pam Shepard. She had sucked in both lips so they were not visible, and her mouth was a thin line. She looked back at me and we held the pose for about thirty seconds.

"Twenty-two years," I said. "And you knew him before

you got married. More than twenty-two years you've known Harvey Shepard. Doesn't that earn him five minutes of talk. Even if you don't like him? Even simple duration eventually obliges you."

She nodded her head, to herself, I think, more than to me.

"Tell him about obligation, I've known him since nineteen fifty," she said.

I shrugged. "He's forking out a hundred dollars a day and expenses to find you."

"That's his style, the big gesture. 'See how much I love you,' but is he looking? No, you're looking."

"Better than no one looking."

"Is it?" There was color on her cheekbones now. "Is it really? Why isn't it worse? Why isn't it intrusive? Why isn't it a big pain in the ass? Why don't you all just leave me the goddamned hell alone?"

"I'm guessing," I said, "but I think it's because he loves you."

"Loves me, what the hell has that got to do with anything. He probably does love me. I never doubted that he did. So what. Does that mean I have to love him? His way? By his definition?"

Rose Alexander said, "It's an argument men have used since the Middle Ages to keep women in subjugation."

"Was that a master-slave relationship Jane was trying to establish with me?" I said.

"You may joke all you wish," Rose said, "but it is perfectly clear that men have used love as a way of obligating women. You even used the term yourself." Rose was apparently the theoretician of the group.

"Rosie," I said. "I am not here to argue sexism with you. It exists and I'm against it. But what we've got here is not a theory, it's a man and a woman who've known each other a long time and conspired to produce children. I want to talk with her about that."

"You cannot," Rose said, "separate the theory from its application. And"—her look was very forceful—"you cannot get the advantage of me by using the diminutive of my name. I'm quite aware of your tricks."

"Take a walk with me," I said to Pam Shepard.

"Don't do it, Pam," Jane said.

"You'll not take her from this house," Rose said.

I ignored them and looked at Pam Shepard. "A walk," I said, "down toward the bridge. We can stand and look at the water and talk and then we'll walk back."

She nodded. "Yes," she said, "I'll walk with you. Maybe you can make him understand."

Chapter nine

PROTESTS, EXCURSION and alarums followed Pam Shepard's decision but in the end it was agreed that we would, in fact, stroll down toward the harbor and that Jane and Rose would follow along, at a discreet distance in case I tried to chloroform her and stuff her in a sack.

As we walked along Front Street the light was strong on her face and I realized she was probably around my age. There were faint lines of adulthood at her eyes and the corners of her mouth. They didn't detract, in fact they added a little, I thought, to her appeal. She didn't look like someone who'd need to pick up overweight shovel operators in bars. Hell, she could have her choice of sophisticated private eyes. I wondered if she'd object to the urine stain on my shoe.

We turned onto the bridge and walked far enough out on it to look at the water. The water made the city look good. Oil slick, cigarette wrappers, dead fish, gelatinous-looking pieces of water-soaked driftwood, an unraveled condom looking like an eel skin against the coffee-colored water. Had it looked like this when Melville shipped out on a whaler 130 years ago? Christ, I hope not.

"What did you say your name was?" Pam Shepard asked.

"Spenser," I said. We leaned our forearms on the railing and stared out toward the transmitter tower on one of the harbor islands. The wind off the ocean was very pleasant despite the condition of the water.

"What do you want to talk about?" Today she had on a dark blue polo shirt, white shorts and white Tretorn tennis shoes. Her legs were tan and smooth.

"Mrs. Shepard, I've found you and I don't know what to do about it. You are clearly here by choice, and you don't seem to want to go home. I hired on to find you, and if I call your husband and tell him where you are I'll have earned my pay. But then he'll come up here and ask you to come home, and you'll say no, and he'll make a fuss, and Jane will kick him in the vas deferens, and unless that permanently discourages him, and it is discouraging, you'll have to move."

"So don't tell him."

"But he's hired me. I owe him something."

"I can't hire you," she said. "I have no money."

Jane and Rose stood alertly across the roadway on the other side of the bridge and watched my every move. *Semper paratus*.

"I don't want you to hire me. I'm not trying to hold you up. I'm trying to get a sense of what I should do."

"Isn't that your problem?" Her elbows were resting on the railing and her hands were clasped. The diamond-wedding ring combination on her left hand caught the sun and glinted.

"Yes it is," I said, "but I can't solve it until I know who and what I'm dealing with. I have a sense of your husband. I need to get a sense of you."

"For someone like you, I'd think the *sanctity of marriage* would be all you'd need. A woman who runs out on her family deserves no sympathy. She's lucky her husband will

396

take her back." I noticed the knuckles of her clasped hands were whitening a little.

"Sanctity of marriage is an abstraction, Mrs. Shepard. I don't deal in those. I deal in what it is fashionable to call people. Bodies. Your basic human being. I don't give a goddamn about the sanctity of marriage. But I occasionally worry about whether people are happy."

"Isn't happiness itself an abstraction?"

"Nope. It's a feeling. Feelings are real. They are hard to talk about so people sometimes pretend they're abstractions, or they pretend that ideas, which are easy to talk about, are more important."

"Is the equality of men and women an abstraction?"

"I think so."

She looked at me a little scornfully. "Yet the failure of that equality makes a great many people unhappy."

"Yeah. So let's work on the unhappiness. I don't know what in hell equality means. I don't know what it means in the Declaration of Independence. What's making you unhappy with your husband?"

She sighed in a deep breath and heaved it out quickly. "Oh, God," she said. "Where to begin." She stared at the transmitter tower. I waited. Cars went by behind us.

"He love you?"

She looked at me with more than scorn. I thought for a minute she was going to spit. "Yes," she said. "He loves me. It's as if that were the only basis for a relationship. 'I love you. I love you. Do you love me? Love. Love.' Shit!"

"It's better than I hate you. Do you hate me?" I said.

"Oh, don't be so goddamned superficial," she said. "A relationship can't function on one emotion. Love or hate. He's like a . . ." She fumbled for an appropriate comparison. "He's like when one of the kids eats cotton candy at a carnival on a hot day and it gets all over her and then all over you and you're sticky and sweaty and the day's been a long one, and horrible, and the kids are whiny. If you don't get away by yourself and take a shower you'll just start screaming. You have any children, Mr. Spenser?"

"No."

"Then maybe you don't know. Are you married?"

"No."

"Then certainly you don't know."

I was silent.

"Every time I walk by him he wants to hug me. Or he gives me a pat on the ass. Every minute of every day that I am with him I feel the pressure of his love and him wanting a response until I want to kick him."

"Old Jane would probably help you," I said.

"She was protecting me," Pam Shepard said.

"I know," I said. "Do you love him?"

"Harvey? Not, probably, by his terms. But in mine. Or at least I did. Until he wore me down. At first it was one of his appeals that he loved me so totally. I liked that. I liked the certainty. But the pressure of that . . ." She shook her head.

I nodded at her encouragingly. Me and Carl Rogers.

"In bed," she said. "If I didn't have multiple orgasms I felt I was letting him down."

"Have many," I said.

"No."

"And you're worried about being frigid."

She nodded.

"I don't know what that means either," I said.

"It's a term men invented," she said. "The sexual model, like everything else, has always been male."

"Don't start quoting Rose at me," I said. "That may or may not be true, but it doesn't do a hell of a lot for our problem at the moment."

"You have a problem," Pam Shepard said. "I do not."

"Yes you do," I said. "I've been talking with Eddie Taylor."

She looked blank.

"Eddie Taylor," I said, "big blond kid, runs a power shovel. Fat around the middle, and a loud mouth."

She nodded and continued to as I described him, the lines at the corners of her mouth deepening. "And why is he a problem?"

"He isn't. But unless he made it all up, and he's not bright enough to make it up, you're not as comfortably in charge of your own destiny as you seem to be."

"I'll bet he couldn't wait to tell you every detail. Probably embellished a great deal."

"No. As a matter of fact he was quite reluctant. I had to strike him in the solar plexus."

She made a slight smiling motion with her mouth for a moment. "I must say you don't talk the way I'd have expected."

"I read a lot," I said.

"So what is my problem?"

"I don't read that much," I said. "I assume you are insecure about your sexuality and ambivalent about it. But that doesn't mean anything that either one of us can bite into."

"Well, don't we have all the psychological jargon down pat. If my husband slept around would you assume he was insecure and ambivalent?"

"I might," I said. "Especially if he had a paroxysm the morning after and was last seen crying on the bed."

Her face got a little pink for a moment. "He was revolting. You've seen him. How I could have, with a pig like that. A drunken, foul, sweaty animal. To let him use me like that." She shivered. Across the street Jane and Rose stood poised, eyes fixed upon us, ready to spring. I felt like a cobra at a mongoose festival. "He didn't give a damn about me. Didn't care about how I felt. About what I wanted. About sharing pleasure. He just wanted to rut like a hog and when it was over roll off and go to sleep."

"He didn't strike me too much as the Continental type," I said.

"It's not funny."

"No, it isn't no more than everything else. Laughing is better than crying though. When you can."

"Well, isn't that just so folksy and down home," she said. "What the hell do you know about laughing and crying?"

"I observe it a lot," I said. "But what I know isn't an

399

issue. If Eddie Taylor was so revolting, why did you pick him up?"

"Because I goddamned well felt like it. Because I felt like going out and getting laid without complications. Just a simple straightforward screw without a lot of lovey-dovey—did-you-like-that-do-you-love-me crap."

"You do that much?"

"Yes. When I felt like it, and I've been feeling like it a lot these last few years."

"You usually enjoy it more than you did with old Eddie?"

"Of course, I—oh hell, I don't know. It's very nice sometimes when it happens, but afterwards I'm still hung up on guilt. I can't get over all those years of nice-girls-don't-do-it, I guess."

"A guy told me you always went for the big young jocko types. Muscle and youth."

"You have yourself in mind? You're not all that young."

"I would love to go to bed with you. You are an excellent-looking person. But I'm still trying to talk about you."

"I'm sorry," she said. "That was flirtatious, and I'm trying to change. Sometimes it's hard after a long time of being something else. Flirtatious was practically the only basis for male-female relationship through much of my life."

"I know," I said. "But what about the guy who says you go for jockos. He right?"

She was silent awhile. An old Plymouth convertible went by with the top down and radio up loud. I heard a fragment of Roberta Flack as the sound dopplered past.

"I guess I do. I never really gave it much thought but I guess the kind of guy I seek out is big and young and strong looking. Maybe I'm hoping for some kind of rejuvenation."

"And a nice uncomplicated screw."

"That too."

"But not with someone who just wants to rut and roll off."

She frowned. "Oh, don't split hairs with me. You know what I mean."

"No," I said. "I don't know what you mean. And I don't think you know what you mean. I'm not trying to chop logic with you. I'm trying to find out how your head is. And I think it's a mare's nest."

"What's a mare's nest?"

"Something confused."

"Well, I'm not a mare's nest. I know what I want and what I don't want."

"Yeah? What?"

"What do you mean what?"

"I mean what do you want and what do you not want."

"I don't want to live the way I have been for twenty years."

"And what do you want?"

"Something different."

"Such as?"

"Oh"—tears showed in her eyes—"I don't know. God-damn it, leave me alone. How the hell do I know what I want. I want you to leave me the goddamned hell alone." The tears were on her cheeks now, and her voice had thickened. Across the bridge Rose and Jane were in animated conference. I had the feeling Jane was to be unleashed in a moment. I took out one of my cards and gave it to her.

"Here," I said. "If you need me, call me. You got any money?"

She shook her head. I took ten of her husband's ten-dollar bills out of my wallet and gave them to her. The wallet was quite thin without them.

"I won't tell him where you are," I said, and walked off the bridge and back up the hill toward my car back of the museum.

CHAPTER TEN

HARVEY SHEPARD HAD a large purple bruise under his right eye and it seemed to hurt him when he frowned. But he frowned anyway. "Goddamnit," he said. "I laid out five hundred bucks for that information and you sit there and tell me I can't have it. What kind of a goddamned business is that?"

"I'll refund your advance if you want, but I won't tell you where she is. She's well, and voluntarily absent. I think she's confused and unhappy but she's safe enough."

"How do I know you've even seen her. How do I know you're not trying to rip me off for five bills and expenses without even looking for her?"

"Because I offered to give it back," I said.

"Yeah, lots of people offer but try to get the money."

"She was wearing a blue polo shirt, white shorts, white Tretorn tennis shoes. Recognize the clothes?"

He shrugged.

"How'd you get the mouse?" I said.

"The what?"

"The bruise on your face. How'd you get it?"

"For crissake, don't change the subject. You owe me information and I want it. I'll take you right the hell into court if I have to."

"Hawk lay that on you?"

"Lay what?"

"The mouse. Hawk give it to you?"

"You keep your nose out of my business, Spenser. I hired you to find my wife, and you won't even do that. Never mind about Hawk."

We were in his office on the second floor overlooking Main Street. He was behind his big Danish modern desk. I was in the white leather director's chair. I got up and walked to the door.

"Come here," I said. "I want you to see something in the outer office."

"What the hell is out there?"

"Just get up and come here, and you'll see."

He made a snort and got up, slowly and stiffly, and walked like an old man, holding himself very carefully. Keeping his upper body still. When he got to the door, I said, "Never mind."

He started to frown, but his eye hurt, so he stopped and swore at me. "Jesus Christ! What are you trying to do?"

"You been beat up," I said. He forgot himself for a moment, turned sharply toward me, grunted with pain and put his hand against the wall to keep steady.

"Get out of here," he said as hard as he could without raising his voice.

"Somebody worked you over. I thought so when I saw the mouse, and I knew so when you tried to walk. You are in money trouble with someone Hawk works for and this is your second notice."

"You don't know what you're talking about."

"Yeah, I do. Hawk works that way. Lots of pressure on the body, where it doesn't show. Actually I'm surprised that there's any mark on your face."

"You're crazy," Shepard said. "I fell downstairs yesterday. Tripped on a rug. I don't owe anybody anything. I'm just doing business with Hawk."

I shook my head. "Hawk doesn't do business. It bores him. Hawk collects money, and guards bodies, that sort of thing. You're with him one day and the next you can hardly walk. Too big a coincidence. You better tell me."

Shepard had edged his way back to the desk and gotten seated. His hands shook a little as he folded them in front of him on the desk.

"You're fired," he said. "Get out of here. I'm going to

403

sue you for every cent I gave you. You'll be hearing from my lawyer."

"Don't be a goddamned fool, Shepard. If you don't get out of what you're in, I'll be hearing from your embalmer. You got three kids and no wife. What happens to the kids if you get planted?"

Shepard made a weak attempt at a confident smile. "Listen, Spenser, I appreciate your concern, but this is a private matter, and it's nothing I can't handle. I'm a businessman, I know how to handle a business deal." His hands, clasped on the desk in front of him, were rigid, white-knuckled like his wife's had been on the New Bedford-Fairhaven bridge. Probably for the same reason. He was scared to death.

"One last try, Shepard. Are you doing business with King Powers?"

"I told you, Spenser, it is not your business." His voice did a chord change. "Stop trying to hustle yourself up some business. You and I are through. I want a check for five hundred dollars in the mail to me tomorrow or you'll find yourself in court." His voice was hitting the upper registers now. The tin clatter of hysteria.

"You know where to reach me," I said and walked out.

Living around Boston for a long time you tend to think of Cape Cod as the promised land. Sea, sun, sky, health, ease, boisterous camaraderie, a kind of real-life beer commercial. Since I'd arrived no one had liked me, and several people had told me to go away. Two had assaulted me. You're sure to fall in love with old Cape Cod.

I drove to the end of Sea Street and parked illegally and walked on the beach. I seemed to be unemployed. There was no reason I could not pack up and go home. I looked at my watch. I could call Susan Silverman from the motel and in two hours we could be having a late lunch and going to the Museum of Fine Arts to look at the Vermeer exhibit that had just arrived. Giving Shepard back his retainer didn't thrill me, maybe Suze would pick up the lunch tab, but telling Shepard where his wife was didn't thrill me either.

I liked the idea of seeing Susan. I hadn't seen her in

four days. Lately I had found myself missing her when I didn't see her. It made me nervous.

The beach was crowded and a lot of kids were swimming off a float anchored fifty yards from shore. Down the curve of the beach there was a point and beyond I could see part of the Kennedy compound. I found some open beach and sat down and took off my shirt. A fat woman in a flowered bathing suit eyed the gun clipped to my belt. I took it off and wrapped it in the shirt and used the package for a pillow. The woman got up and folded her beach chair and moved to a different spot. At least people were consistent in their response. I closed my eyes and listened to the sound of the water and the children and occasionally a dog. Down the beach someone's portable radio was playing something about a man who'd been crying for a million years, so many tears. Where have you gone, Cole Porter?

It was a mess, too big a mess. I couldn't walk away from it. How big a mess, I didn't know, but a mess. More mess than even Shepard could handle, I thought.

I got up, clipped the gun back on my hip, stuck the holster in my hip pocket, put on my pale blue madras shirt with the epaulets and let it hang out to cover up the gun. I walked back to my car, got in and drove to my motel. It was nearly noontime.

From my room I called Susan Silverman at home. No answer. I went to the restaurant and had oyster stew and two draft beers and came back and called again. No answer. I called Deke Slade. He was in.

"Spenser," I said, "known in crime-detection circles as Mr. Sleuth."

"Yeah?"

"I have a couple of theories I'd like to share with you on some possible criminal activity in your jurisdiction. Want me to come in?"

"Criminal activity in my jurisdiction? You gotta stop watching those TV crime shows. You sound like Perry Mason."

"Just because you don't know how to talk right, Slade,

405

is no reason to put me down. You want to hear my theories or not."

"Come on in," he said and hung up. He didn't sound excited.

CHAPTER ELEVEN

"What's Hawk's full name?" Slade said.

"I don't know," I said. "Just Hawk."

"He's gotta have a full name."

"Yeah, I know, but I don't know what it is. I've known him about twenty years and I've never heard him called anything but Hawk."

Slade shrugged and wrote Hawk on his pad of yellow, legal sized lined paper. "Okay," he said. "So you figure that Shepard owes money and isn't paying and the guy he owes it to has sent a bone-breaker down. What's Shepard's story?"

"He has none," I said. "He says he's in business with Hawk and it's got nothing to do with me."

"And you don't believe him."

"Nope. First place Hawk doesn't do business, with a big B like Shepard means. Hawk's a free spirit."

"Like you," Slade said.

I shook my head. "Nope, not like me. I don't hire out for the things Hawk does."

"I heard you might," Slade said.

"From who?"

"Oh, guys I know up in Boston. I made a couple of calls about you."

"I thought you were too busy keeping a close tail on the litterbugs," I said.

"I did it on my lunch hour," Slade said.

"Well, don't believe all you hear," I said.

Slade almost smiled. "Not likely," he said. "How sure are you he was beat up?"

"Shepard? Certain. I've seen it done before, fact I've had it done before. I know the look and feel of it."

"Yeah, it does stiffen you up some," Slade said. "What's Shepard's story?"

"Says he fell downstairs."

Slade wrote on his yellow pad again. "You got thoughts on who hired Hawk?"

"I'm guessing King Powers. Hawk normally gives first refusal to Powers." Slade wrote some more on his pad. "Powers is a shylock," I said. "Used to . . ."

"I know Powers," Slade said.

"Anyway, he's in trouble. Bad, I would guess, and he's too scared to yell for help."

"Or maybe too crooked."

I raised both eyebrows at Slade. "You know something I don't," I said.

Slade shook his head. "No, just wondering. Harv has always been very eager to get ahead. Not crooked really, just very ambitious. This leisure community he's building is causing a lot of hassle and it doesn't seem to be going up very fast, and people are beginning to wonder if something's wrong."

"Is there?"

"Hell," Slade said, "I don't know. You ever looked into a land swindle? It takes a hundred C.P.A.s and a hundred lawyers a hundred years just to find out if there's anything to look into." Slade made a disgusted motion with his mouth. "You usually can't find out who owns the goddamned property."

"Shepard doesn't strike me as crooked," I said.

"Adolf Hitler was fond of dogs," Slade said. "Say he's not crooked, say he's just overextended. Could be."

"Yeah," I said, "could be. But what are we going to do about it?"

"How the hell do I know. Am I the whiz-bang from the

city? You tell me. We got, to my knowledge, no crime, no victim, no violation of what you big-city types would call the criminal statutes. I'll have the patrol cars swing by his place more often and have everyone keep an eye out for him. I'll see if the A.G.'s office has anything on Shepard's land operation. You got any other thoughts?"

I shook my head.

"You find his wife?" Slade asked.

"Yeah."

"She coming home?"

"I don't think so."

"What's he going to do about that?"

"Nothing he can do."

"He can go get her and drag her ass home."

"He doesn't know where she is. I wouldn't tell him."

Slade frowned at me for about thirty seconds. "You are a pisser," Slade said. "I'll give you that."

"Yeah."

"Shepard take that okay?"

"No, he fired me. Told me that he was going to sue me."

"So you're unemployed."

"I guess so."

"Just another tourist."

"Yep."

Slade did smile this time. A big smile that spread slowly across his face making deep furrows, one on each cheek. "Goddamn," he said and shook his head. "Goddamn."

I smiled back at him, warmly, got up and left. Back in my car, on the hot seats, with the top down, I thought something I've thought before. I don't know what to do, I thought. I started the car, turned on the radio and sat with the motor idling. I didn't even know where to go. Mrs. Shepard sure wasn't happy, and Mr. Shepard sure wasn't happy. That didn't make them unusual of course. I wasn't right at the moment all that goddamned happy myself. I supposed I ought to go home. Home's where you can go and they have to take you in. Who said that? I couldn't remember. Cynical bastard though. I put the car in gear and drove slowly down Main

Street toward the motel. Course at my home there wasn't any they. There was just me. I'd take me in any time. I stopped for a light. A red-haired girl wearing powder blue flared denim slacks and a lime-colored halter top strolled by. The slacks were so tight I could see the brief line of her underpants slanting across her buttocks. She looked at the car in a friendly fashion. I could offer her a drink and a swim and dazzle her with my Australian crawl. But she looked like a college kid and she'd probably want me to do some dope and rap about the need for love and a new consciousness. The light turned green and I moved on. A middle-aged grump with nowhere to go. It was a little after one when I pulled into the parking lot at my motel. Time for lunch. With renewed vigor I strode into the lobby, turned left past the desk and headed down the corridor toward my room. A fast wash, and then on to lunch. Who'd have thought but moments ago that I was without purpose. When I opened the door to my room Susan Silverman was lying on the bed reading a book by Erik Erikson and looking like she should.

I said, "Jesus Christ, I'm glad to see you."

With her finger in the book to keep her place she turned her head toward me and said, "Likewise, I'm sure" and grinned. Often she smiled, but sometimes she didn't smile, she grinned. This was a grin. I never knew for sure what the difference was but it had something to do with gleeful wickedness. Her smile was beautiful and good, but in her grin there was just a hint of evil. I dove on top of her on the bed, breaking the impact of my weight with my arms, and grabbed her and hugged her.

"Ow," she said. I eased up a little on the hug, and we kissed each other. When we stopped I said, "I am not going to ask how you got in here because I know that you can do anything you want to, and getting the management to aid and abet you in a B and E would be child's play for you."

"Child's play," she said. "How has it been with you, blue eyes?"

We lay on our backs on the bed beside each other while I told her. When I finished telling her I suggested an afternoon of sensual delight, starting now. But she suggested that it start after lunch and after a brief scuffle I agreed.

"Suze," I said in the dining room starting my first stein of Harp while she sipped a Margarita, "you seemed uncommonly amused by the part where Jane tried to caponize me."

She laughed. "I think your hips are beginning to widen out," she said. "Are you still shaving?"

"Naw," I said, "it did no damage. If it had, all the waitresses here would be wearing black armbands and the flag would fly half-mast at Radcliffe."

"Well, we'll see, later, when there's nothing better to do."

"There's never anything better to do," I said. She yawned elaborately.

The waitress came and took our order. When she'd departed Susan said, "What are you going to do?"

"Jesus, I don't know."

"Want me to hang around with you while you do it?"

"Very much," I said. "I think I'm in over my head with Pam, Rose and Jane."

"Good, I brought my suitcase on the chance you might want me to stay."

"Yeah, and I noted you unpacked it and hung up your clothes. Confidence."

"Oh, you noticed. I keep forgetting you are a detective."

"Spenser's the name, clues are my game," I said. The waitress brought me a half-dozen oysters and Susan six soused shrimp. Susan looked at the oysters.

"Trying to make a comeback?"

"No," I said, "planning ahead."

We ate our seafood.

"What makes you say you're in over your head?" Susan asked.

"I don't feel easy. It's an element I'm not comfortable in. I'm good with my hands, and I'm persevering, but . . . Pam Shepard asked me if I had children and I said no. And she said I probably couldn't understand, and she asked if I

410

were married and I said no and she said then for sure I couldn't understand." I shrugged.

"I've never had children either," Susan said. "And marriage wasn't the best thing that ever happened to me. Nor the most permanent. I don't know. There's all the clichés about you don't have to be able to cook a soufflé to know when one's bad. But . . . at school, I know, parents come in sometimes for counseling with the kids and they say, but you don't know. You don't have children . . . there's probably something to it. Say there is. So what? You've been involved in a lot of things that you haven't experienced firsthand, as I recall. Why is this one different?"

"I don't know that it is," I said.

"I think it is. I've never heard you talk about things like this before. On a scale of ten you normally test out about fifteen in confidence."

"Yeah, I think it is too."

"Of course, as you explain it, the case is no longer your business because the case no longer exists."

"There's that," I said.

"Then why worry about it. If it's not your element, anyway, why not settle for that. We'll eat and swim and walk on the beach for a few days and go home."

The waitress came with steak for each of us, and salad, and rolls and another beer for me. We ate in silence for maybe two minutes.

"I can't think of anything else to do," I said.

"Try to control your enthusiasm," Susan said.

"I'm sorry," I said. "I didn't mean it that way. It's just bothering me. I've been with two people whose lives are screwed up to hell and I can't seem to get them out of it at all."

"Of course you can't," she said. "You also can't do a great deal about famine, war, pestilence and death."

"A great backfield," I said.

"You also can't be everyone's father. It is paternalistic of you to assume that Pam Shepard with the support of several other women cannot work out her own future without you. She may in fact do very well. I have."

"Me paternalistic? Don't be absurd. Eat your steak and shut up or I'll spank you."

CHAPTER TWELVE

AFTER LUNCH we took coffee on the terrace by the pool, sitting at a little white table made of curlicued iron shaded by a blue and white umbrella. It was mostly kids in the pool, splashing and yelling while their mothers rubbed oil on their legs. Susan Silverman was sipping coffee from a cup she held with both hands and looking past me. I saw her eyes widen behind her lavender sunglasses and I turned and there was Hawk.

He said, "Spenser."

I said, "Hawk."

He said, "Mind if I join you?"

I said, "Have a seat. Susan, this is Hawk. Hawk, this is Susan Silverman."

Hawk smiled at her and she said, "Hello, Hawk."

Hawk pulled a chair around from the next table, and sat with us. Behind him was a big guy with a sunburned face and an Oriental dragon tattooed on the inside of his left forearm. As Hawk pulled his chair over he nodded at the next table and the tattooed man sat down at it. "That's Powell," Hawk said. Powell didn't say anything. He just sat with his arms folded and stared at us.

"Coffee?" I said to Hawk.

He nodded. "Make it iced coffee though." I gestured to the waitress, ordered Hawk his iced coffee.

"Hawk," I said, "you gotta overcome this impulse

toward anonymity you've got. I mean why not start to dress so people will notice you instead of always fading into the background like you do."

"I'm just a retiring guy, Spenser, just my nature." He stressed the first syllable in retiring. "Don't see no reason to be a clotheshorse." Hawk was wearing white Puma track shoes with a black slash on them. White linen slacks, and a matching white linen vest with no shirt. Powell was more conservatively dressed in a maroon-and-yellow-striped tank top and maroon slacks.

The waitress brought Hawk his iced coffee. "You and Susan having a vacation down here?"

"Yep."

"Sure is nice, isn't it? Always like the Cape. Got atmosphere you don't usually find. You know? Hard to define it, but it's kind of leisure spirit. Don't you think, Spenser?"

"I'll tell you if you'll tell me."

"Susan," Hawk said, "this man is a straight-ahead man, you know? Just puts it right out front, hell of a quality, I'd say."

Susan smiled at him and nodded. He smiled back.

"Come on, Hawk, knock off the Goody Two-shoes shtick. You want to know what I'm doing with Shepard and I want to know what you're doing with Shepard."

"Actually, it's a little more than that, babe, or a little less, whichever way you look at it. It ain't that I so much care what you're doing with Shepard as it is I want you to stop doing it."

"Ah-ha," I said. "A threat. That explains why you brought Eric the Red along. You knew Susan was with me and you didn't want to be outnumbered."

Powell said from his table, "What did you call me?"

Hawk smiled. "Still got that agile mind, Spenser."

Powell said again, "What did you call me?"

"It is hard, Powell," I said to him, "to look tough when your nose is peeling. Why not try some Sun Ban, excellent, greaseless, filters out the harmful ultraviolet rays."

413

Powell stood up. "Don't smart-mouth me, man. You wising off at me?"

"That a picture of your mom you got tattooed on your left arm?" I said.

He looked down at the dragon tattoo on his forearm for a minute and then back at me. His face got redder and he said, "You wise bastard. I'm going to straighten you out right now."

Hawk said, "Powell, I wouldn't if I was you."

"I don't have to take a lot of shit from a guy like this," Powell said.

"Don't swear in front of the lady," Hawk said. "You gotta take about whatever he gives you 'cause you can't handle him."

"He don't look so tough to me," Powell said. He was standing and people around the pool were beginning to look.

"That's cause you are stupid, Powell," Hawk said. "He is tough, he may be damn near as tough as me. But you want to try him, go ahead."

Powell reached down and grabbed me by the shirt front. Susan Silverman inhaled sharply.

Hawk said, "Don't kill him, Spenser, he runs errands for me."

Powell yanked me out of the chair. I went with the yank and hit him in the Adam's apple with my forearm. He said something like "ark" and let go of my shirt front and stepped back. I hit him with two left hooks, the second one with a lot of shoulder turned into it, and Powell fell over backward into the pool. Hawk was grinning as I turned toward him.

"The hayshakers are all the same, aren't they," he said. "Just don't seem to know the difference between amateurs and professionals." He shook his head. "That's a good lady you got there though." He nodded at Susan, who was on her feet holding a beer bottle she'd apparently picked up off another table.

Hawk got up and walked to the pool and dragged

414

Powell out of it negligently, with one hand, as if the dead weight of a 200-pound man were no more than a flounder.

The silence around the pool was heavy. The kids were still hanging on to the edge of the pool, staring at us. Hawk said, "Come on, let's walk out to my car and talk." He let Powell slump to the ground by the table and strolled back in through the lobby. Susan and I went with him. As we passed the desk we saw the manager come out of his office and hurry toward the terrace.

I said, "Why don't you go down to the room, Suze. I'll be along in a minute. Hawk just wants me to give him some pointers on poolside fighting." The tip of her tongue was stuck out through her closed mouth and she was obviously biting on it. "Don't bite your tongue," I said. "Save some for me." She shook her head.

"I'll stay with you," she said.

Hawk opened the door on the passenger's side of the Cadillac. "My pleasure," he said to Susan. If Hawk and I were going to fight he wouldn't pick a convertible for the place. I got in after Susan. Hawk went around and got in the driver's side. He pushed a button and the roof went up smoothly. He started the engine and turned on the air conditioning. A blue and white Barnstable Township police car pulled into the parking lot and two cops got out and walked into the motel.

Hawk said, "Let's ride around." I nodded and he put us in gear and slipped out of the parking lot.

"Where the hell did you get him?" I said to Hawk as we drove.

"Powell? Oh, man, I don't know. He's a local dude. People that hired me told me to work with him."

"They trying to set up an apprentice program?"

Hawk shrugged. "Beats me, baby, he got a long way to go though, don't he?"

"It bother you that the cops are going to ask him what he was doing fighting with a tourist, and who the tourist was and who was the black stud in the funny outfit?"

Hawk shook his head. "He won't say nothing. He dumb, but he ain't that dumb."

Between us on the front seat Susan Silverman said, "What are we doing?"

Hawk laughed. "A fair question, Susan. What in hell are we doing?"

"Let me see if I can guess," I said. "I guess that Harv Shepard owes money to a man, probably King Powers, and Hawk has been asked to collect it. Or maybe just oversee the disbursement of funds, whatever, and that things are going the way they should." I said to Susan, "Hawk does this stuff, quite well. And then surprise, I appear, and I'm working for Shepard. And Hawk and his employer, probably King Powers, wonder if Harv hired me to counteract Hawk. So Hawk has dropped by to inquire about my relationship with Harv Shepard, and to urge me to sever that relationship."

The Caddie went almost soundless along the Mid-Cape Highway, down Cape, toward Provincetown. I said, "How close, Hawk?"

He shrugged. "I have explained to the people that employ me about how you are. I don't expect to frighten you away, and I don't expect to bribe you, but my employer would like to compensate you for any loss if you were to withdraw from the case."

"Hawk," I said. "All this time I've known you I never could figure out why sometimes you talk like an account exec from Merrill Lynch and sometimes you talk like Br'er Bear."

"Ah is the product of a ghetto education." He pronounced both t's in ghetto. "Sometimes my heritage keep popping up."

"Lawdy me, yes," I said. "What part of the ghetto you living in now?"

Hawk grinned at Susan. "Beacon Hill," he said. He U-turned the Caddie over the center strip and headed back up Cape toward Hyannis. "Anyway, I told the people you weren't gonna do what they wanted, whatever I said, but they give me money to talk to you, so I'm talking. What your interest in Shepard?"

"He hired me to look for his wife."

"That all?"

"Yes."

"You find her?"

"Yes."

"Where?"

"I won't say."

"Don't matter, Shepard'll tell me. If I need to know."

"No." I shook my head. "He doesn't know either."

"You won't tell him?"

"Nope."

"Why not, man? That's what you hired on for."

"She doesn't want to be found."

Hawk shook his head again. "You complicate your life, Spenser. You think about things too much."

"That's one of the things that makes me not you, Hawk."

"Maybe," Hawk said, "and maybe you a lot more like me than you want to say. 'Cept you ain't as good looking."

"Yeah, but I dress better."

Hawk snorted, "Shit. Excuse me, Susan. Anyway, my problem now is whether I believe you. It sounds right. Sounds just about your speed, Spenser. Course you ain't just fell off the sugar-beet truck going through town, and if you was lying it would sound good. You still work for Shepard?"

"No, he canned me. He says he's going to sue me."

"Ah wouldn't worry all that much about the suing," Hawk said. "Harv's kinda busy."

"Is it Powers?" I said.

"Maybe it is, maybe it ain't. You gonna stay out of this, Spenser?"

"Maybe I will, maybe I won't."

Hawk nodded. We drove a way in silence.

"Who's King Powers?" Susan said.

"A thief," I said. "Loan sharking, numbers, prostitution, laundromats, motels, trucking, produce, Boston, Brockton, Fall River, New Bedford."

Hawk said, "Not Brockton anymore. Angie Degamo has got Brockton now."

"Angie chase Powers out?"

"Naw, some kind of business deal. I wasn't in it."

"Anyway," I said to Susan, "Powers is like that."

"And you work for him," she said to Hawk.

"Some."

"Hawk's a free-lance," I said. "But Powers asks him early when he's got Hawk's kind of work."

"And what is Hawk's kind of work?" Susan said, still to Hawk.

"He does muscle and gun work."

"Ah prefer the term soldier of fortune, honey," Hawk said to me.

"Doesn't it bother you," Susan said, "to hurt people for money?"

"No more than it does him." Hawk nodded to me.

"I don't think he does it for money," she said.

"That's why ah'm bopping down the Cape in a new Eldorado and he's driving that eight-year-old hog with the gray tape on the upholstery."

"But . . ." Susan looked for the right words. "But he does what he must, his aim is to help. Yours is to hurt."

"Not right," Hawk said. "Maybe he aiming to help. But he also like the work. You know? I mean he could be a social worker if he just want to help. I get nothing out of hurting people. Sometimes just happens that way. Just don't be so sure me and old Spenser are so damn different, Susan."

We pulled back into the parking lot at the motel. The blue and white was gone. I said, "You people through discussing me yet, I got a couple things to say, but I don't want to interrupt. The subject is so goddamned fascinating."

Susan just shook her head.

"Okay," I said. "This is straight, Hawk. I'm not working for Shepard, or anybody, at the moment. But I can't go home and let you and Powers do what you want. I'm gonna hang around, I think, and see if I can get you off Shepard's back."

Hawk looked at me without expression. "That's what I told them," he said. "I told them that's what you'd say if I came around and talked. But they paying the money. I'll tell them I was right. I don't think it gonna scare them."

"I don't suppose it would," I said.

I opened the door and got out and held it open for Susan. She slid out, and then leaned back in and spoke to Hawk. "Goodby," she said. "I'm not sure what to say. Glad to have met you wouldn't do, exactly. But"—she shrugged—"thanks for the ride."

Hawk smiled at her. "My pleasure, Susan. Maybe I'll see you again."

I closed the door and Hawk slid the car out of the parking lot, soundless and smooth, like a shark cruising in still water.

CHAPTER THIRTEEN

SUSAN SAID, "I want a drink."

We went in and sat on two barstools, at the corner, where the bar turns. Susan ordered a martini and I had a beer. "Martini?" I said.

She nodded. "I said I wanted a drink. I meant it." She drank half the martini in a single pull and put the glass back on the bar.

"How different?" she said, and looked at me.

"You mean me and Hawk?"

"Uh huh."

"I don't know. I don't beat people up for money. I don't kill people for money. He does."

"But sometimes you'll do it for nothing. Like this afternoon."

"Powell?"

"Powell. You didn't have to fight him. You needled him into it."

I shrugged.

"Didn't you?" Susan said.

I shrugged again. She belted back the rest of the martini.

"Why?"

I gestured the bartender down. "Another round," I said.

We were silent while he put the martini together and drew the beer and placed them before us.

"Got any peanuts," I said.

He nodded and brought a bowl up from under the bar. The place was almost deserted, a couple having a late lunch across the room, and four guys, who looked like they'd been golfing, drinking mixed drinks at a table behind us. Susan sipped at her second martini.

"How can you drink those things?" I said. "They taste like a toothache cure."

"It's how I prove I'm tough," she said.

"Oh," I said. I ate some of the peanuts. The voices of the golf foursome were loud. Full of jovial good fellowship like the voice of a game-show host. A little desperate.

"Millions of guys spend their lives that way," I said. "Sitting around pretending to be a good fellow with guys they have nothing to say to."

Susan nodded. "Not just guys," she said.

"I always thought women did that better though," I said.

"Early training," Susan said, "at being a phony, so men would like you. You going to answer my question?"

"About why I badgered Powell?"

"Uh huh."

"You don't give up easy, do you?"

"Un unh."

"I don't know exactly why I pushed him. He annoyed me sitting there, but it also seemed about the right move to make at the time."

420

"To show Hawk you weren't afraid?"

"No, I don't think it impressed Hawk one way or the other. It was a gut reaction. A lot of what I do is a gut reaction. You're a linear thinker, you want to know why and how come and what the source of the problem is and how to work out a solution to it. I assume it comes, in part, with being a guidance type."

"You're reversing the stereotype, you know," Susan said.

"What? Women emotional, men rational? Yeah. But that was always horseshit anyway. Mostly, I think it's just the opposite. In my case anyway. I don't think in ABC order. I've gotten to be over forty and done a lot of things, and I've learned to trust my impulses usually. I tend to perceive in images and patterns and—what to call it—whole situations."

"Gestalt," Susan said.

"Whatever, so when you say why I feel like the best I can do is describe the situation. If I had a video tape of the situation I would point at it and say, "See, that's why.""

"Would you have done the same thing if I weren't there?"

"You mean was I showing off?" The bartender came down and looked at our glasses. I nodded and he took them away for refill. "Maybe." The bartender brought the drinks back. "Would you have hit someone with that beer bottle if I needed it?"

"You insufferable egotist," Susan said. "Why don't you think I picked the bottle up to defend myself?"

"You got me," I said. "I never thought of that. Is that why you picked it up?"

"No," she said. "And stop grinning like a goddamned idiot." She drank some of her third martini. "Smug bastard," she said.

"You did it because I'm such terrific tail, didn't you."

"No," she said. The force of her face and eyes were on me. "I did it because I love you."

The couple across the room got up from the table and headed out. She was Clairol blond, her hair stiff and brittle, he was wearing white loafers and a matching belt. As they left the dining room their hands brushed and he took hers and held it. I drank the rest of my beer. Susan sipped at her martini. "Traditionally," she said, "the gentleman's response to that remark is, 'I love you too.'" She wasn't looking at me now. She was studying the olive in the bottom of her martini.

"Suze," I said. "Do we have to complicate it?"

"You can't say the traditional thing?"

"It's not saying 'I love you,' it's what comes after."

"You mean love and marriage, they go together like a horse and carriage?"

I shrugged. "I don't suppose they have to, I've seen a lot of marriages without love. I guess it could work the other way."

Susan said, "Um hum" and looked at me steadily again.

"The way we're going now seems nice," I said.

"No," she said. "It is momentary and therefore finally pointless. It has no larger commitment, it involves no risk, and therefore no real relationship."

"To have a real relationship you gotta suffer?"

"You have to risk it," she said. "You have to know that if it gets homely and unpleasant you can't just walk away."

"And that means marriage? Lots of people walk away from marriage. For crissake, I got a lady client at this moment who has done just that."

"After what, twenty-two years?" Susan said.

"One point for your side," I said. "She didn't run off at the first sprinkle of rain, did she. But does that make the difference? Some J.P. reading from the Bible?"

"No," Susan said. "But the ceremony is the visible symbol of the commitment. We ritualize our deepest meanings usually, and marriage is the way we've ritualized love. Or one of the ways."

"Are you saying we should get married?"

"At the moment I'm saying I love you and I'm waiting for a response."

"It's not that simple, Suze."

"And I believe I've gotten the response." She got up from the bar and walked out. I finished my beer, left a ten on the bar and walked back to my room. She wasn't there. She also was not on the terrace or in the lobby or in the parking lot. I looked for her small blue Chevy Nova and didn't see it. I went back to the room. Her suitcase was still on the rack, her clothes hanging in the closet. She wouldn't go home without her clothes. Without me maybe, but not without her clothes. I sat down on the bed and looked at the red chair in the corner. The seat was one form of molded plastic, the legs four thin rounds of dark wood with little brass booties on the bottom. Elegant. I was much too damn big and tough to cry. Too old also. It wasn't that goddamned simple.

On the top of the bureau was a card that said, "Enjoy our health club and sauna." I got undressed, dug a pair of white shorts and a gray T-shirt out of the bureau, put them on and laced up my white Adidas track shoes with the three black stripes, no socks. Susan always bitched at me about no socks when we played tennis, but I liked the look. Besides, it was a bother putting socks on.

The health club was one level down, plaid-carpeted, several rooms, facilities for steam, sauna, rubdowns, and an exercise room with a Universal Trainer. A wiry middle-aged man in white slacks and a white T-shirt gave me a big smile when I came in.

"Looking for a nice workout, sir?"

"Yeah."

"Well, we've got the equipment. You familiar with a Universal, sir?"

"Yeah."

"It is, as you can see, a weightlifting machine that operates on pulleys and runs, thus allowing a full workout without the time-consumning inconvenience of changing plates on a barbell."

"I know," I said.

"Let me give you an idea of how ours works. There are eight positions on the central unit here, the bench press, curls, over-the head press . . ."

"I know," I said.

"The weight numbering on the left is beginning weight, the markings on the right are overload weights resulting from the diminishment of fulcrum . . ."

I got on the bench, shoved the pin into the slot marked 300, took a big breath and blew the weight up to arm's length and let it back. I did it two more times. The trainer said, "I guess you've done this before."

"Yeah," I said.

He went back toward the trainer's room. "You want anything, you let me know," he said.

I moved to the lat machine, did 15 pull downs with 150, did 15 tricep presses with 90, moved to the curl bar, then to the bench again. I didn't normally lift that heavy on the bench but I needed to bust a gut or something and 300-pound bench presses were just right for that. I did four sets of everything and the sweat was soaking through my shirt and running down the insides of my arms, so I had to keep wiping my hands to keep a grip on the weight bars. I finished up doing twenty-five dips, and when I stepped away my arms were trembling and my breath was coming in gasps. It was a slow day for the health club. I was the only one in there, and the trainer had come out after a while and watched.

"Hey," he said, "you really work out, don't you?"

"Yeah," I said. There was a heavy bag in one corner of the training room. "You got gloves for that thing?" I said.

"Got some speed gloves," the trainer said.

"Gimme," I said.

He brought them out and I put them on and leaned against the wall, getting my breath under control and waiting for my arms to stop feeling rubbery. It didn't used to take as long. In about five minutes, I was ready for the bag. I stood close to it, maybe six inches away, and punched it in combinations as hard as I could. Two lefts, a right. Left jab, left hook, right cross, left jab, left jab, step-back right uppercut. It's hard to hit a heavy bag with an uppercut. It has no chin. I hit the bag for as long as I could, as hard as I could. Grunting with the effort. Staying up against it and trying to get all the power I could into the six-inch punches. If you've never done it you have no idea how tiring it is to punch something. Every couple of minutes I had to back away and lean on the wall and recover.

The trainer said to me, "You used to fight?"

"Yeah," I said.

"You can always tell," he said. "Everybody comes in here slaps at the bag, or gives it a punch. They can't resist it. But one guy in a hundred actually hits it and knows what he's doing."

"Yeah." I went back to the bag, driving my left fist into it, alternating jabs and hooks, trying to punch through it. The sweat rolled down my face and dripped from my arms and legs. My shirt was soaking and I was beginning to see black spots dancing like visions of sugar plums before my eyes.

"You want some salt," the trainer said. I shook my head. My gray T-shirt was soaked black with sweat. Sweat ran down my arms and legs. My hair was dripping wet. I stepped back from the bag and leaned on the wall. My breath was heaving in and out and my arms were numb and rubbery. I slid my back down the wall and sat on the floor, knees up, back against the wall, my forearms resting on my knees, my head hanging, and waited while the breath got under control and the spots went away. The speed gloves were slippery with sweat as I peeled them off. I got up and handed them to the trainer.

"Thanks," I said.

"Sure," he said. "When you work out, man, you work out, don't you?"

"Yeah," I said.

I walked slowly out of the training room and up the stairs. Several people looked at me as I crossed the lobby toward my room. The floor of the lobby was done in rust-colored quarry tile, about 8″ × 8″. In my room I turned up the air conditioner and took a shower, standing a long time under the hard needle spray. Susan's make-up kit was still on the vanity. I toweled dry, put on a blue and white tank top, white slacks and black loafers. I looked at my gun lying on the bureau. "Screw it." I headed clean and tired and unarmed down the corridor, back to the bar, and began to drink bourbon.

CHAPTER FOURTEEN

I WOKE UP at eight-fifteen the next morning feeling like a failed suicide. The other bed had not been slept in. At twenty to nine I got out of bed and shuffled to the bathroom, took two aspirin and another shower. At nine-fifteen I walked stiffly and slow down to the coffee shop and drank two large orange juices and three cups of black coffee. At ten of ten I walked less stiffly, but still slow, back to my room and called my answering service. In desperate times, habit helps give form to our lives.

Pam Shepard had called and would call again. "She said it was urgent, Spenser."

"Thank you, Lillian. When she calls again give her this number." I hung up and waited. Ten minutes later the phone rang.

"Spenser," I said.

"I need help," she said. "I've got to talk with you."

"Talk," I said.

"I don't want to talk on the phone, I need to see you, and be with you when I talk. I'm scared. I don't know who else to call."

"Okay, I'll come up to your place."

"No, we're not there anymore. Do you know where Plimoth Plantation is?"

"Yes."

"I'll meet you there. Walk down the main street of the village. I'll see you."

426

"Okay, I'll leave now. See you there about noon?"

"Yes. I mustn't be found. Don't let anyone know you're going to see me. Don't let anyone follow you."

"You want to give me a hint of what your problem is?"

"No," she said. "Just meet me where we said."

"I'll be there."

We hung up. It was ten-thirty. Shouldn't take more than half an hour to drive to Plymouth. Susan's clothes were still in the closet. She'd come back for them, and the make-up kit. She must have been incensed beyond reason to have left that. She'd probably checked into another motel. Maybe even another room in this one. I could wait an hour. Maybe she'd come back for her clothes. I got a piece of stationery and an envelope from the drawer of the desk, wrote a note, sealed it in the envelope and wrote Susan's name on the outside. I got Susan's cosmetic case from the bathroom and put it on the desk. I propped the note against it, and sat down in a chair near the bathroom door.

At eleven-thirteen someone knocked softly on my door. I got up and stepped into the bathroom, out of sight, behind the open bathroom door. Another knock. A wait. And then a key in the lock. Through the crack of the hinge end of the bathroom door I could see the motel room door open. Susan came in. Must have gotten the key at the desk. Probably said she'd lost hers. She walked out of sight toward the desk top where the note was. I heard her tear open the envelope. The note said, "Lurking in the bathroom is a horse's ass. It requires the kiss of a beautiful woman to turn him into a handsome prince again." I stepped out from behind the door, into the room. Susan put the note down, turned and saw me. With no change of expression she walked over and gave me a small kiss on the mouth. Then she stepped back and studied me closely. She shook her head. "Didn't work," she said. "You're still a horse's ass."

"It was the low-voltage kiss," I said. "Transforming a horse's ass into a handsome prince is a high-intensity task."

"I'll try once more," she said. And put both arms around me and kissed me hard on the mouth. The kiss held, and developed into much more and relaxed in post-climactic languor without a sound. Without even breaking the kiss. At close range I could see Susan's eyes still closed.

I took my mouth from hers and said, "You wanta go to Plimoth Plantation?"

Susan opened her eyes and looked at me. "Anywhere at all," she said. "You are still a horse's ass, but you are my horse's ass."

I said, "I love you."

She closed her eyes again and pushed her face against the hollow of my neck and shoulder for a moment. Then she pulled her head back and opened her eyes and nodded her head. "Okay, prince," she said. "Let's get to Plimoth."

Our clothes were in a scattered tangle on the floor and by the time we sorted them out and got them back on it was noon. "We are late," I said.

"I hurried as fast as I could," Susan said. She was putting on her lipstick in the mirror, bending way over the dresser to do it.

"We were fast," I said. "A half-hour from horse's ass to handsome prince. I think that fulfills the legal definition of a quickie."

"You're the one in a hurry to go see Plimoth Plantation. Given the choice between sensual delight and historical restoration, I'd have predicted a different decision on your part."

"I've got to see someone there, and it may help if you're with me. Perhaps later we can reconsider the choice."

"I'm ready," she said. And we went out of the room to my car. On the drive up Route 3 to Plymouth I told Susan what little I knew about why we were going.

Susan said, "Won't she panic or something if I show up with you? She did say something about alone."

"We won't go in together," I said. "When I find her, I'll explain who you are and introduce you. You been to the Plantation before?"

She nodded. "Well, then, you can just walk down the central street a bit ahead of me and hang around till I holler."

"Always the woman's lot," she said.

I grunted. A sign on my left said Plimoth Plantation Road and I turned in. The road wound up through a meadow toward a stand of pines. Behind the pines was a parking lot and at one edge of the parking lot was a ticket booth. I parked and Susan got out and walked ahead, bought a ticket and went through the entrance. When she was out of sight I got out and did the same thing. Beyond the ticket booth was a rustic building containing a gift shop, lunch room and information service. I went on past it and headed down the soft path between the high pines toward the Plantation itself. A few years back I had been reading Samuel Eliot Morison's big book of American history, and got hooked and drove around the East going to Colonial restorations. Williamsburg is the most dazzling, and Sturbridge is grand, but Plimoth Plantation is always a small pleasure.

I rounded the curve by the administration building and saw the blockhouse of dark wood and the stockade around the little town and beyond it the sea. The area was entirely surrounded by woods and if you were careful you could see no sign of the twentieth century. If you weren't careful and looked too closely you could see Bert's Restaurant and somebody else's motel down along the shore. But for a moment I could go back, as I could every time I came, to the small cluster of zealous Christians in the wilderness of seventeenth-century America, and experience a sense of the desolation they must have felt, minute and remote and resolute in the vast woods.

I saw Susan on top of the blockhouse, looking out at the village, her arms folded on the parapet, and I came back to business and walked up the hill, past the blockhouse and into the Plantation. There was one street, narrow and rutted, leading downhill toward the ocean. Thatched houses along each side, behind the herb gardens, some livestock and a number of people dressed in Colonial costume. Lots of children, lots of Kodak Instamatics. I walked down the hill, slowly, letting Pam Shepard have ample time to spot me and see that I wasn't followed. I went the whole length of the street and started back up. As I passed Myles Standish's house, Pam came out of the door wearing huge sunglasses and fell into step beside me.

"You're alone."

"No, I have a friend with me. A woman." It seemed important to say it was a woman.

"Why," she said. Her eyes were wide and dark.

"You are in trouble, and maybe she could help. She's an A-1 woman. And I had the impression you weren't into men much lately."

"Can I trust her?"

"Yes."

"Can I trust you?"

"Yes."

"I suppose you wouldn't say so if I couldn't anyway, would you?" She was wearing a faded denim pants and jacket combo over a funky-looking multicolored T-shirt. She was exactly as immaculate and neat and fresh-from-the-shower-and-make-up-table as she had been the last time I saw her.

"No, I wouldn't. Come on, I'll introduce you to my friend, then we can go someplace and sit down and maybe have a drink or a snack or both and talk about whatever you'd like to talk about."

She looked all around her as if she might dart back into one of the thatched houses and hide in the loft. Then she took a deep breath and said, "Okay, but I mustn't be seen."

"Seen by who?"

"By anyone, by anyone who would recognize me."

"Okay, we'll get Susan and we'll go someplace obscure." I walked back up the street toward the gate to the blockhouse, Pam Shepard close by me as if trying to stay in my shadow. Near the top of the hill Susan Silverman met us. I nodded at her and she smiled.

"Pam Shepard," I said. "Susan Silverman." Susan put out her hand and smiled.

Pam Shepard said, "Hello."

I said, "Come on, we'll head back to the car."

In the car Pam Shepard talked with Susan. "Are you a detective too, Susan?"

"No, I'm a guidance counselor at Smithfield High School," Susan said.

"Oh, really? That must be very interesting."

"Yes," Susan said, "it is. It's tiresome, sometimes, like most things, but I love it."

"I never worked," Pam said. "I always just stayed home with the kids."

"But that must be interesting too," Susan said. "And tiresome. I never had much chance to do that."

"You're not married?"

"Not now, I was divorced quite some time ago."

"Children?"

Susan shook her head, I pulled into the parking lot at Bert's. "You know anybody in this town," I said to Pam.

"No."

"Okay, then this place ought to be fairly safe. It doesn't look like a spot people would drive up from the Cape to go to."

Bert's was a two-story building done in weathered shingles fronting on the ocean. Inside, the dining room was bright, pleasant, informal and not very full. We sat by the window and looked at the waves come in and go out. The waitress came. Susan didn't want a drink. Pam Shepard had a stinger on the rocks. I ordered a draft beer. The waitress said they had none. "I've learned," I said, "to live with disappointment." The waitress said she could bring me a bottle of Heineken. I said it would do. The menu leaned heavily toward fried seafood. Not my favorite, but the worst meal I ever had was wonderful. At least they didn't feature things like the John Alden Burger or Pilgrim Soup.

The waitress brought the drinks and took our food order. I drank some of my Heineken. "Okay, Mrs. Shepard," I said. "What's up?"

She looked around. There was no one near us. She drank some of her stinger. "I . . . I'm involved in a murder."

I nodded. Susan sat quietly with her hands folded in front of her on the table.

"We . . . there was . . ." She took another gulp of the stinger. "We robbed a bank in New Bedford, and the bank guard, an old man with a red face, he . . . Jane shot him and he's dead."

The tide was apparently ebbing. The mark was traced close to the restaurant by an uneven line of seaweed and driftwood and occasional scraps of rubbish. Much cleaner than New Bedford harbor. I wondered what flotsam was. I'd have to look that up sometime when I got home. And jetsam.

"What bank?" I said.

"Bristol Security," she said. "On Kempton Street."

"Were you identified?"

"I don't know. I was wearing these sunglasses."

"Okay, that's a start. Take them off."

"But . . ."

"Take them off, they're no longer a disguise, they are an identification." She reached up quickly and took them off and put them in her purse.

"Not in your purse, give them to me." She did, and I slipped them in Susan Silverman's purse. "We'll ditch them on the way out," I said.

"I never thought," she said.

"No, probably you don't have all that much experience at robbery and murder. You'll get better as you go along."

Susan said, "Spenser."

I said, "Yeah, I know. I'm sorry."

"I didn't know," Pam Shepard said. "I didn't know Jane would really shoot. I just went along. It seemed . . . it seemed I ought to—they'd stood by me and all."

Susan was nodding. "And you felt you had to stand by them. Anyone would."

The waitress brought the food, crab salad for Susan, lobster stew for Pam, fisherman's plate for me. I ordered another beer.

"What was the purpose of the robbery?" Susan said.

"We needed money for guns."

"Jesus Christ," I said.

"Rose and Jane are organizing . . . I shouldn't tell you this . . ."

"Babe," I said, "you better goddamned well tell me everything you can think of. If you want me to get your ass out of this."

Susan frowned at me.

"Don't be mad at me," Pam Shepard said.

"Bullshit," I said. "You want me to bring you flowers for being a goddamn thief and a murderer? Sweets for the sweet, my love. Hope the old guy didn't have an old wife who can't get along without him. Once you all get guns you can liberate her too."

Susan said, "Spenser," quite sharply. "She feels bad enough."

"No she doesn't," I said. "She doesn't feel anywhere near bad enough. Neither do you. You're so goddamned empathetic you've jumped into her frame. 'And you felt you had to stand by them. Anyone would.' Balls. Anyone wouldn't. You wouldn't."

I snarled at Pam Shepard. "How about it. You thought you were going to a dance recital when you went into that bank with guns to steal the money? You thought you were Faye Dunaway, la de da, we'll take the money and run and the theme music will come up and the banjos will play and all the shots will miss?" I bit a fried shrimp in half. Not bad. Tears were rolling down Pam Shepard's face. Susan looked very grim. But she was silent.

"All right? Okay. We start there. You committed a vicious and mindless goddamned crime and I'm going to try and get you out of the consequences. But let's not clutter up the surface with a lot of horseshit about who stood by who and how you shouldn't tell secrets, and oh-of-course-anyone-would-have."

Susan said, between her teeth, "Spenser."

I drank some beer and ate a scallop. "Now start at the beginning and tell me everything that happened."

Pam Shepard said, "You will help me?"

"Yes."

She dried her eyes with her napkin. Snuffled a little. Susan gave her a Kleenex and she blew her nose. Delicately. My fisherman's platter had fried haddock in it. I pushed it aside, over behind the French fries, and ate a fried clam.

"Rose and Jane are organizing a women's movement. They feel we must overcome our own passivity and arouse our sisters to do the same. I think they want to model it on the Black Panthers, and to do that we need guns. Rose says we won't have to use them. But to have them will make a great psychological difference. It will increase the level of militancy and it will represent power, even, Jane says, a threat to phallic power."

"Phallic power?"

She nodded.

I said, "Go ahead."

"So they talked about it, and some other women came over and we had a meeting, and decided that we either had to steal the guns or the money to buy them. Jane had a gun, but that was all. Rose said it was easier to steal money than guns, and Jane said that it would be easy as pie to steal from a bank because banks always instruct their employees to cooperate with robbers anyway. What do they care, they are insured. And banks are where the money is. So that's where we should go."

I didn't say anything. Susan ate some crab salad. Pam Shepard seemed to have no interest in her lobster stew. Looked good too.

"So Rose and Jane said they would do the actual work," she said. "And I—I don't know exactly why—I said I'd go with them. And Jane said that was terrific of me and proved that I was really into the women's movement. And Rose said a bank was the ideal symbol of masculine-capitalist oppression. And one of the other women, I don't know her name, she was a black woman, Cape Verdean I think, said that capitalism was itself masculine, and racist as well, so that the bank was a really perfect place to strike. And I said I wanted to go."

434

"Like an initiation," I said.

Susan nodded. Pam Shepard looked puzzled and shrugged. "Maybe, I don't know. Anyway we went and Jane and Rose and I all wore sunglasses and big hats. And Jane had the gun."

"Jane has all the fun," I said. Susan glared at me. Pam Shepard didn't seem to notice.

"Anyway, we went in and Rose and Jane went to the counter and I stayed by the door as a . . . a lookout . . . and Rose gave the girl, woman, behind the counter a note and Jane showed her the gun. And the woman did what it said. She took all her money from the cash drawer and put it in a bag that Rose gave her and we started to leave when that foolish old man tried to stop us. Why did he do that? What possessed him to take that chance?"

"Maybe he thought that was his job."

She shook her head. "Foolish old man. What is an old man like that working as a bank guard for anyway?"

"Probably a retired cop. Stood at an intersection for forty years and directed traffic and then retired and couldn't live on the pension. So he's got a gun and he hires out at the bank."

"But why try to stop us, an old man like that. I mean he saw Jane had a gun. It wasn't his money."

"Maybe he thought he ought to. Maybe he figured that if he were taking the money to guard the bank when the robbers didn't come, he ought to guard it when they did. Sort of a question of honor, maybe."

She shook her head. "Nonsense, that's the machismo convention. It gets people killed and for what. Life isn't a John Wayne movie."

"Yeah, maybe. But machismo didn't kill that old guy. Jane killed him."

"But she had to. She's fighting for a cause. For freedom. Not only for women but for men as well, freedom from all the old imperatives, freedom from the burden of machismo for you as well as for us."

"Right on," I said. "Off the bank guard."

Susan said, "What happened after Jane shot the guard?"

"We ran," Pam said. "Another woman, Grace something, I never knew her last name, was waiting for us in her Volkswagen station wagon, and we got in and drove back to the house."

"The one on Centre Street?" I asked.

She nodded. "And we decided there that we better split up. That we couldn't stay there because maybe they could identify us from the cameras. There were two in the bank that Rose spotted. I didn't know where to go so I went to the bus station in New Bedford and took the first bus going out, which was coming to Plymouth. The only time I'd ever been to Plymouth was when we took the kids to Plimoth Plantation when they were smaller. So I got off the bus and walked here. And then I didn't know what to do, so I sat in the snack bar at the reception center for a while and I counted what money I had, most of the hundred dollars you gave me, and I saw your card in my wallet and called you." She paused and stared out the window. "I almost called my husband. But that would have just been running home with my tail between my legs. And I started to call you and hung up a couple of times. I . . . Did I have to have a man to get me out of trouble? But then I had nowhere else to go and nothing else to try so I called." She kept looking out the window. The butter in her lobster stew was starting to form a skin as the stew cooled. "And after I called you I walked up and down the main street of the village and in and out of the houses and thought, here I am, forty-three years old and in the worst trouble of my life and I've got no one to call but a guy I've met once in my life, that I don't even know, no one else at all." She was crying now and her voice shook as she talked. She turned her head away farther toward the window to hide it. The tide had gone out some more since I'd last looked and the dark water rounded rocks beyond the beach and made a kind of cobbled pattern with the sea breaking and foaming over them. It had gotten quite dark now, though it was early afternoon, and spits of rain splattered on the window. "And you think I'm a goddamned fool,"

436

she said. She had her hand on her mouth and it muffled her speech. "And I am."

Susan put her hand on Pam Shepard's shoulder. "I think I know how you feel," Susan said. "But it's the kind of thing he can do and others can't. You did what you felt you had to do, and you need help now, and you have the right person to help you. You did the right thing to call him. He can fix this. He doesn't think you are a fool. He's grouchy about other things, about me, and about himself, a lot of things and he leaned on you too hard. But he can help you with this. He can fix it."

"Can he make that old man alive again?"

"We don't work that way," I said. "We don't look around and see where we were. And we don't look down the road and see what's coming. We don't have anything to do but deal with what we know. We look at the facts and we don't speculate. We just keep looking right at this and we don't say what if, or I wish or if only. We just take it as it comes. First you need someplace to stay besides Plimoth Plantation. I'm not using my apartment because I'm down here working on things. So you can stay there. Come on, we'll go there now." I gestured for the check. "Suze," I said, "you and Pam go get in my car, I'll pay up here."

Pam Shepard said, "I have money."

I shook my head as the waitress came. Susan and Pam got up and went out. I paid the check, left a tip neither too big nor too small—I didn't want her to remember us—and went to the car after them.

CHAPTER FIFTEEN

IT'S FORTY-FIVE MINUTES from Plymouth to Boston and the traffic was light in midafternoon. We were on Marlborough Street in front of my apartment at three-fifteen. On the ride up Pam Shepard had given me nothing else I could use. She didn't know where Rose and Jane were. She didn't know how to find them. She didn't know who had the money, she assumed Rose. They had agreed, if they got separated, to put an ad in the New Bedford *Standard Times* personals column. She didn't know where Rose and Jane had expected to get the guns. She didn't know if they had any gun permit or FID card.

"Can't you just go someplace and buy them?" she said.

"Not in this state," I said.

She didn't know what kind of guns they had planned to buy. She didn't really know that guns came in various kinds. She didn't know anyone's name in the group except Rose and Jane and Grace and the only last name she knew was Alexander.

"It's a case I can really sink my teeth into," I said. "Lot of hard facts, lot of data. You're sure I've got your name right?"

She nodded.

"What's the wording for your ad," I said.

"If we get separated? We just say, 'Sisters, call me at' —then we give a phone number and sign our first name."

"And you run it in the *Standard Times*?"

"Yes, in the personal column."

438

We got out of the car and Pam said, "Oh, what a pretty location. There's the Common right down there."

"Actually the Public Garden. The Common's on the other side of Charles Street," I said. We went up to my apartment, second floor front. I opened the door.

Pam Shepard said, "Oh, very nice. Why it's as neat as a pin. I always pictured bachelor apartments with socks thrown around and whiskey bottles on the floor and wastebaskets spilling onto the floor."

"I have a cleaning person, comes in once a week."

"Very nice. Who did the woodcarvings?"

"I have a woodcarver come in once a week."

Susan said, "Don't listen to him. He does them."

"Isn't that interesting, and look at all the books. Have you read all these books?"

"Most of them, my lips get awful tired though. The kitchen is in here. There should be a fair supply of food laid in."

"And booze," Susan said.

"That too," I said. "In case the food runs out you can starve to death happy."

I opened the refrigerator and took out a bottle of Amstel. "Want a drink?" Both Susan and Pam said no. I opened the beer and drank some from the bottle.

"There's some bread and cheese and eggs in the refrigerator. There's quite a bit of meat in the freezer. It's labeled. And Syrian bread. There's coffee in the cupboard here." I opened the cupboard door. "Peanut butter, rice, canned tomatoes, flour, so forth. We can get you some vegetables and stuff later. You can make a list of what else you need."

I showed her the bathroom and the bedroom. "The sheets are clean." I said. "The person changes them each week, and she was here yesterday. You will need clothes and things." She nodded. "Why don't you make a list of food and clothes and toiletries and whatever that you need and Suze and I will go out and get them for you." I gave her a pad and pencil. She sat at the kitchen counter to write. While she did I talked at her. "When we leave," I said, "stay in here. Don't answer the door. I've got a key and Suze has a key and no one else has. So you won't have to open the door for us and no one else has reason to come here. Don't go out."

"What are you going to do?" she asked.

"I don't know," I said. "I'll have to think about it."

"I think maybe I'll have that drink you offered," she said.

"Okay, what would you like?"

"Scotch and water?"

"Sure."

I made her the drink, lots of ice, lots of Scotch, a dash of water. She sipped it while she finished her list.

When she gave it to me she also offered me her money.

"No," I said. "You may need it. I'll keep track of all this and when it's over I'll give you a bill."

She nodded. "If you want more Scotch," I said, "you know where it is."

Susan and I went out to shop. At the Prudential Center on Boylston Street we split up. I went into the Star Market for food and she went up to the shopping mall for clothes and toiletries. I was quicker with the food than she was with her part and I had to hang around for a while on the plaza by the funny statue of Atlas or Prometheus or whoever he was supposed to be. Across the way a movie house was running an action-packed double feature: *The Devil in Miss Jones* and *Deep Throat*. They don't make them like they used to. Whatever happened to Ken Maynard and his great horse, Tarzan? I looked some more at the statue. It looked like someone had done a takeoff on Michelangelo, and been taken seriously. Did Ken Maynard really have a great horse named Tarzan? If Ken were still working, his great horse would probably be named Bruce and be a leather freak. A young woman went by wearing a white T-shirt and no bra. On the T-shirt was stenciled TONY'S PX, GREAT FALLS, MONTANA. I was watching her walk away when Susan arrived with several ornate shopping bags.

"That a suspect?" Susan said.

"Remember I'm a licensed law officer. I was checking whether those cut-off jeans were of legal length."

440

"Were they?"

"I don't think so." I picked up the groceries and one of Susan's shopping bags and we headed for the car. When we got home Pam Shepard was sitting by the front window looking out at Marlborough Street. She hadn't so far as I could see done anything else except perhaps freshen her drink. It was five o'clock and Susan agreed to join Pam for a drink while I made supper. I pounded some lamb steaks I'd bought for lamb cutlets. Dipped them in flour, then egg, then bread crumbs. When they were what Julia Child calls nicely coated I put them aside and peeled four potatoes. I cut them into little egg-shaped oblongs, which took a while, and started them cooking in a little oil, rolling them around to get them brown all over. I also started the cutlets in another pan. When the potatoes were evenly browned I covered them, turned down the heat and left them to cook through. When the cutlets had browned, I poured off the fat, added some Chablis and some fresh mint, covered them and let them cook. Susan came out into the kitchen once to make two new drinks. I made a Greek salad with feta cheese and ripe olives and Susan set the table while I took the lamb cutlets out of the pan and cooked down the wine. I shut off the heat, put in a lump of unsalted butter, swirled it through the wine essence and poured it over the cutlets. With the meal we had warm Syrian bread and most of a half gallon of California Burgundy. Pam Shepard told me it was excellent and what a good cook I was.

"I never liked it all that much," Pam said. 'When I was a kid my mother never wanted me in the kitchen. She said I'd be messy. So when I got married I couldn't cook anything."

Susan said, "I couldn't cook, really, when I got married either."

"Harv taught me," Pam said. "I think he kind of liked to cook, but . . ." She shrugged. "That was the wife's job. So I did it. Funny how you cut yourself off from things you like because of . . . of nothing. Just convention, other people's assumptions about what you ought to be and do."

"Yet often they are our own assumptions, aren't they," Susan said. "I mean where do we get our assumptions about how things are or ought to be? How much is there really a discrete identifiable self trying to get out?" I drank some Burgundy.

"I'm not sure I follow," Pam said.

"It's the old controversy," Susan said. "Nature-nurture. Are you what you are because of genetics or because of environment? Do men make history or does history make men?"

Pam Shepard smiled briefly. "Oh yes, nature-nurture, Child Growth and Development, Ed. 103. I don't know, but I know I got shoved into a corner I didn't want to be in." She drank some of her wine, and held her glass toward the bottle. Not fully liberated. Fully liberated you pour the wine yourself. Or maybe the half-gallon bottle was too heavy. I filled her glass. She looked at the wine a minute. "So did Harvey," she said.

"Get shoved in a corner?" Susan said.

"Money?" Susan asked.

"No, not really. Not money exactly. It was more being important, being a man that mattered, being a man that knew the score, knew what was happening. A mover and shaker. I don't think he cared all that much about the money, except it proved that he was on top. Does that make sense?" She looked at me.

"Yeah, like making the football team," I said. "I understand that."

"You ought to," Susan said.

Pam Shepard said, "Are you like that?"

I shrugged. Susan said, "Yes, he's like that. In a specialized way."

Pam Shepard said, "I would have thought he wasn't but I don't know him very well."

Susan smiled. "Well, he isn't exactly, but he is if that makes any sense."

I said, "What the hell am I, a pot roast, I sit here and you discuss me?"

Susan said, "I think you described yourself quite well this morning."

442

"Before or after you smothered me with passionate kisses?"

"Long before," she said.

"Oh," I said.

Pam Shepard said, "Well, why aren't you in the race? Why aren't you grunting and sweating to make the team, be a star, whatever the hell it is that Harvey and his friends are trying to do?"

"It's not easy to say. It's an embarrassing question because it requires me to start talking about integrity and self-respect and stuff you recently lumped under John Wayne movies. Like honor. I try to be honorable. I know that's embarrassing to hear. It's embarrassing to say. But I believe most of the nonsense that Thoreau was preaching. And I have spent a long time working on getting myself to where I could do it. Where I could live life largely on my own terms."

"Thoreau?" Pam Shepard said. "You really did read all those books, didn't you."

"And yet," Susan said, "you constantly get yourself involved in other lives and in other people's troubles. This is not Walden Pond you've withdrawn to."

I shrugged again. It was hard to say it all. "Everybody's got to do something," I said.

"But isn't what you do dangerous?" Pam Shepard said.

"Yeah, sometimes."

"He likes that part," Susan said. "He's very into tough. He won't admit it, maybe not even to himself, but half of what he's doing all the time is testing himself against other men. Proving how good he is. It's competition, like football."

"Is that so?" Pam Shepard said to me.

"Maybe. It goes with the job."

"And yet it cuts you off from a lot of things," Susan said. "You've cut yourself off from family, from home, from marriage."

"I don't know," I said. "Maybe."

"More than maybe," Susan said. "It's autonomy. You are the most autonomous person I've ever seen and you don't let anything into that. Sometimes I think the muscle you've built is like a shield, like armor, and you keep yourself private and alone inside there. The integrity complete, unviolated, impervious, safe even from love."

"We've gone some distance away from Harv Shepard, Suze," I said. I felt as if I'd been breathing shallow for a long time and needed a deep inhale.

"Not as far as it looks," Susan said. "One reason you're not into the corner that Pam's husband is in is because he took the chance. He married. He had kids. He took the risk of love and relationship and the risk of compromise that goes with it."

"But I don't think Harvey was working for us, Susan," Pam Shepard said.

"It's probably not that easy," I said. "It's probably not something you can cut up like that. Working for us, working for him."

"Well," Pam Shepard said. "There's certainly a difference."

"Sometimes I think there's never a difference and things never divide into column A and column B," I said. "Perhaps he had to be a certain kind of man for you, because he felt that was what you deserved. Perhaps to him it meant manhood, and perhaps he wanted to be a man for you."

Pam said, "Machismo again."

"Yeah, but machismo isn't another word for rape and murder. Machismo is really about honorable behavior."

"Then why does it lead so often to violence?"

"I don't know that it does, but if it does it might be because that's one of the places that you can be honorable."

"That's nonsense," Pam Shepard said.

"You can't be honorable when it's easy," I said. "Only when it's hard."

"When the going gets tough, the tough get going?" The scorn in Pam Shepard's voice had more body than the wine. "You sound like Nixon."

I did my David Frye impression. "I am not a crook," I said and looked shifty.

"Oh, hell, I don't know," she said. "I don't even know

444

what we're talking about anymore. I just know it hasn't worked. None of it, not Harv, not the kids, not me, not the house and the business and the club and growing older, nothing."

"Yeah," I said, "but we're working on it, my love."

She nodded her head and began to cry.

CHAPTER SIXTEEN

I COULDN'T THINK of much to do about Pam Shepard crying so I cleared the table and hoped that Susan would come up with something. She didn't. And when we left, Pam Shepard was still snuffling and teary. It was nearly eleven and we were overfed and sleepy. Susan invited me up to Smithfield to spend the night and I accepted, quite graciously, I thought, considering the aggravation she'd been giving me.

"You haven't been slipping off to encounter groups under an assumed name, have you?" I said.

She shook her head. "I don't quite know why I'm so bitchy lately," she said.

"It's not bitchy, exactly. It's pushy. I feel from you a kind of steady pressure. An obligation to explain myself."

"And you don't like a pushy broad, right?"

"Don't start up again, and don't be so goddamned sensitive. You know I don't mean the cliché. If you think I worry about role reversal and who keeps in whose place, you've spent a lot of time paying no attention to me."

"True," she said. "I'm getting a little hyped about the whole subject."

"What whole subject? That's one of my problems. I

445

think I know the rules of the game all right, but I don't know what the game is."

"Man–woman relationships, I guess."

"All of them or me and you."

"Both."

"Terrific, Suze, now we've got it narrowed down."

"Don't make fun. I think being middle-aged and female and single one must think about feminism, if you wish, women's rights and women vis-à-vis men. And of course that includes you and me. We care about each other, we see each other, we go on, but it doesn't develop. It seems directionless."

"You mean marriage?"

"I don't know. I don't think I mean just that. My God, am I still that conventional? I just know there's a feeling of incompleteness in us. Or, I suppose I can only speak for me, in me, and in the way I perceive our relationship."

"It ain't just wham-bam-thank-you-ma'am."

"No, I know that. That's not a relationship. I know I'm more than good tail. I know I matter to you. But . . ."

I paid my fifteen cents on the Mystic River Bridge and headed down its north slope, past the construction barricades that I think were installed when the bridge was built.

"I don't know what's wrong with me," she said.

"Maybe it's wrong with me," I said.

There weren't many cars on the Northeast Expressway at this time of night. There was a light fog and the headlights made a scalloped apron of light in front of us as we drove.

"Maybe," she said. Far right across the salt marshes the lights of the G.E. River Works gleamed. Commerce never rests.

"Explaining myself is not one of the things I do really well, like drinking beer, or taking a nap. Explaining myself is clumsy stuff. You really ought to watch what I do, and, pretty much, I think, you'll know what I am. Actually I always thought you knew what I am."

Promised Land

"I think I do. Much of it is very good, a lot of it is the best I've ever seen."

"Ah-ha," I said.

"I don't mean that," Susan said. The mercury arc lights at the newly renovated Saugus Circle made the wispy fog bluish and the Blue Star Bar look stark and unreal across Route 1.

"I know pretty well what you are," she said. "It's what we are that is bothersome. What the hell are we, Spenser?"

I swung off Route 1 at the Walnut Street exit and headed in toward Smithfield. "We're together," I said. "Why have we got to catalogue. Are we a couple? A pair? I don't know. You pick one."

"Are we lovers?"

On the right Hawkes Pond gleamed through a very thin fringe of trees. It was a long narrow pond and across it the land rose up in a wooded hill crowned with power lines. In the moonlight, with a wispy fog, it looked pretty good.

"Yeah," I said. "Yeah. We're lovers."

"For how long?" Susan said.

"For as long as we live," I said. "Or until you can't bear me anymore. Whichever comes first."

We were in Smithfield now, past the country club on the left, past the low reedy meadow that was a bird sanctuary, and the place where they used to have a cider mill, to Summer Street, almost to Smithfield Center. Almost to Susan's house.

"For as long as we live will come first," Susan said.

I drove past Smithfield Center with its old meeting house on the triangular common. A banner stretched across the street announced some kind of barbecue, I couldn't catch what in the dark. I put my hand out and Susan took it and we held hands to her house.

Everything was wet and glistening in the dark, picking up glints from the streetlights. It wasn't quite raining, but the fog was very damp and the dew was falling. Susan's house was a small cape, weathered shingles, flagstone walk, lots of shrubs. The front door was a Colonial red with small bull's-

447

eye glass windows in the top. Susan unlocked it and went in. I followed her and shut the door. In the dark silent living room, I put my hands on Susan's shoulders and turned her slowly toward me, and put my arms around her. She put her face against my chest and we stood that way, wordless and still for a long time.

"For as long as we live," I said.

"Maybe longer," Susan said. There was an old steeple clock with brass works on the mantel in the living room and while I couldn't see in the dark, I could hear it ticking loudly as we stood there pressed against each other. I thought about how nice Susan smelled, and about how strong her body felt, and about how difficult it is to say what you feel. And I said, "Come on, honey, let's go to bed." She didn't move, just pressed harder against me and I reached down with my left hand and scooped up her legs and carried her to the bedroom. I'd been there before and had no trouble in the dark.

CHAPTER SEVENTEEN

IN THE MORNING, still damp from the shower, we headed back for the Cape, stopped on the way for steak and eggs in a diner and got to the hotel room I still owned about noon. The fog had lifted and the sun was as clean and bright as we were, though less splendidly dressed. In my mailbox was a note to call Harv Shepard.

I called him from my room while Susan changed into her bathing suit.

"Spenser," I said, "what do you want?"

"You gotta help me."

"That's what I was telling you just a little while back," I said.

"I gotta see you, it's, it's outta control. I can't handle it. I need help. That, that goddamned nigger shoved one of my kids. I need help."

"Okay," I said. "I'll come over."

"No," he said. "I don't want you here. I'll come there. You in the hotel?"

"Yep." I gave him my room number. "I'll wait for you."

Susan was wiggling her way into a one-piece bathing suit.

"Anything?" she said.

"Yeah, Shepard's coming apart. I guess Hawk made a move at one of the kids and Shepard's in a panic. He's coming over."

"Hawk scares me," Susan said. She slipped her arms through the shoulder straps.

"He scares me too, my love."

"He's . . ." She shrugged. "Don't go against him."

"Better me than Shepard," I said.

"Why better you than Shepard?"

"Because I got a chance and Shepard has none."

"Why not the police?"

"We'll have to ask Shepard that. Police are okay by me. I got no special interest in playing Russian roulette with Hawk. Shepard called him a nigger."

Susan shrugged. "What's that got to do?"

"I don't know," I said. "But I wish he hadn't done that. It's insulting."

"My God, Spenser, Hawk has threatened this man's life, beaten him up, abused his children, and you're worried about a racial slur?"

"Hawk's kind of different," I said.

She shook her head. "So the hell are you," she said. "I'm off to the pool to work on my tan. When you get through you can join me there. Unless you decide to elope with Hawk."

"Miscegenation," I said. "Frightful."

She left. About two minutes later Shepard arrived. He

449

was moving better now. Some of the stiffness had gone from his walk, but confidence had not replaced it. He had on a western-cut, black-checked leisure suit and a white shirt with black stitching, the collar out over the lapels of the suit. There was a high shine on his black-tassled loafers and his face was gray with fear.

"You got a drink here," he said.

"No, but I'll get one. What do you like?"

"Bourbon."

I called room service and ordered bourbon and ice. Shepard walked across the room and stared out the window at the golf course. He sat down in the armchair by the window and got right up again. "Spenser," he said. "I'm scared shit."

"I don't blame you," I said.

"I never thought . . . I always thought I could handle business, you know? I mean I'm a businessman and a businessman is supposed to be able to handle business. I'm supposed to know how to put a deal together and how to make it work. I'm supposed to be able to manage people. But this. I'm no goddamned candy-ass. I been around and all, but these people . . ."

"I know about these people."

"I mean that goddamned nigger . . ."

"His name's Hawk," I said. "Call him Hawk."

"What are you, the NAACP?"

"Call him Hawk."

"Yeah, okay, Hawk. My youngest came in the room while they were talking to me and Hawk grabbed him by the shirt and put him out the door. Right in front of me. The black bastard."

"Who are they?"

"They?"

"You said your kid came in while they were talking to you."

"Oh, yeah," Shepard walked back to the window and looked out again. "Hawk and a guy named Powers. White guy. I guess Hawk works for him."

"Yeah, I know Powers."

The room service waiter came with the booze on a tray. I signed the check and tipped him a buck. Shepard rummaged in his pocket. "Hey, let me get that," he said.

"I'll put it on your bill," I said. "What did Powers want? No, better, I'll tell you what he wanted. You owe him money and you can't pay him and he's going to let you off the hook a little if you let him into your business a lot."

"Yeah." Shepard poured a big shot over ice from the bottle of bourbon and slurped at it. "How the hell did you know?"

"Like I said, I know Powers. It's also not a very new idea. Powers and a lot of guys like him have done it before. A guy like you mismanages the money, or sees a chance for a big break or overextends himself at the wrong time and can't get financing. Powers comes along, gives you the break, charges an exorbitant weekly interest. You can't pay, he sends Hawk around to convince you it's serious. You still can't pay so Powers comes around and says you can give me part of the business or you can cha-cha once more with Hawk. You're lucky, you got me to run to. Most guys got no one but the cops."

"I didn't mismanage the money."

"Yeah, course not. Why not go to the cops?"

"No cops," Shepard said. He drank some more bourbon.

"Why not?"

"They'll start wanting to know why I needed money from Powers."

"And you were cutting a few corners?"

"Goddamnit, I had to. Everybody cuts a few corners."

"Tell me about the ones you cut."

"Why? What do you need to know that for?"

"I won't know till you tell me."

Shepard drank some more bourbon. "I was in a box. I had to do something." The drape on the right side of the window hung crookedly. Shepard straightened it. I waited. "I was in business with an outfit called Estate Management Corporation. They go around to different vacation-type areas and

451

develop leisure homes in conjunction with a local guy. Around here I was the local guy. What we did was set up a separate company with me as president. I did the developing, dealt with the town planning board, building inspector, that stuff, and supervised the actual construction. They provided architects, planners and financing and the sales force. It's a little more complicated than that, but you get the idea. My company was a wholly owned subsidiary of Estate Management. You follow that okay?"

"Yeah. I got that. I'm not a shrewd-o-business tycoon like you, but if you talk slowly and I can watch your lips move, I can keep up, I think. What was the name of your company?"

"We called the development Promised Land. And the company was Promised Land, Inc."

"Promised Land." I whistled. "Cu-ute," I said. "Were you aiming at an exclusive Jewish clientele?"

"Huh? Jewish? Why Jewish? Anybody was welcome. I mean we wouldn't be thrilled if the Shvartzes moved in maybe, but we didn't care about religion."

I wished I hadn't said it. "Okay," I said. "So you're president of Promised Land, Inc., a wholly owned subsidiary of Estate Management, Inc. Then what?"

"Estate Management went under."

"Bankrupt?"

"Yeah." Shepard emptied his bourbon and I poured some more in the glass. I offered ice and he shook his head. "The way it worked was the Estate Management people would see the land, really high-powered stuff, contact people, closers, free trips to Florida, the whole bag. The buyer would put a deposit on the land and would also sign a contract for the kind of house he wanted. We had about six models to choose from. He'd put a deposit on the house as well, and that deposit would go into an escrow account."

"What happened to the land deposit?"

"Went to Estate Management."

"Okay, and who controlled the house escrow?"

Shepard said, "Me."

"And when Estate Management pulled out, and you were stuck with a lot of money invested and no backing, you dipped into the escrow."

"Yeah, I used it all. I had to. When Estate Management folded, the town held up on the building permits. All there was was the building sites staked off. We hadn't brought the utilities in yet. You know, water, sewage, that kind of thing."

I nodded.

"Well, the town said, nobody gets a permit to build anything until the utilities are in. They really screwed me. I mean, I guess they had to. Things smelled awful funny when Estate went bankrupt. A lot of money disappeared, all those land deposits, and a lot of people started wondering about what happened. It smelled awful bad. But I was humped. I had all my capital tied up in the goddamned land and the only way I was going to get it back was to build the houses and sell them. But I couldn't do that because I couldn't get a permit until I put in the utilities. And I couldn't put in the utilities because I didn't have any money. And nobody wanted to finance the thing. Banks only want to give you money when you can prove you don't need it, you know that. And they really didn't want to have anything to do with Promised Land, because by now the story was all around financial circles and the IRS and the SEC and the Mass attorney general's office and the FCC and a bunch of other people were starting to investigate Estate Management, and a group of people who'd bought land were suing Estate Management. So I scooped the escrow money. I was stuck. It was that or close up shop and start looking for work without enough money to have my résumé typed. I'm forty-five years old."

"Yeah, I know. Let me guess the next thing that happened. The group that was suing Estate Management also decided to get its house deposit back."

Shepard nodded.

"And of course, since you'd used it to start bringing in utilities, you couldn't give it back."

He kept nodding as I talked.

"So you found Powers someplace and he lent you the dough. What was the interest rate? Three percent a week?"

"Three and a half."

"And, of course, payment on the principal."

Shepard nodded some more.

"And you couldn't make it."

Nod.

"And Hawk beat you up."

"Yeah. Actually he didn't do it himself. He had two guys do it, and he, like, supervised."

"Hawk's moving up. Executive level. He was always a comer."

"He said he just does the killing now, the sweaty work he delegates."

"And so here we are."

"Yeah," Shepard said. He leaned his head against the window. "The thing is, Powers' money bailed me out. I was coming back. The only money I owe is Powers and I can't pay. It's like—I'm so close and the only way to win is to lose."

CHAPTER EIGHTEEN

SHEPARD LOOKED AT ME expectantly when he was through telling me his sins.

"What do you want," I said, "absolution? Say two Our Fathers and three Hail Marys and make a good act of contrition? Confession may be good for the soul but it's not going to help your body any if we can't figure a way out."

"What could I do," he said. "I was in a corner, I had to crib on the escrow money. Estate Management got off with four or five million bucks. Was I supposed to watch it all go down the pipe? Everything I've been working for? Everything I am?"

"Someday we can talk about just what the hell you were working for, and maybe even what you are. Not now. How hot is Powers breathing on your neck?"

"We've got a meeting set up for tomorrow."

"Where?"

"At Hawk's room in the Holiday Inn."

"Okay, I'll go with you."

"What are you going to do?"

"I don't know. I've got to think. But it's better than going alone, isn't it."

Shepard's breath came out in a rush. "Oh, hell, yes," he said, and finished the bourbon.

"Maybe we can talk them into an extension," I said. "The more time I got, the more chance to work out something."

"But what can we do?"

"I don't know. What Powers is doing, remember, is illegal. If we get really stuck we can blow the whistle and you can be state's evidence against Powers and get out of it with a tongue-lashing."

"But I'm ruined."

"Depends how you define ruined," I said. "Being King Powers' partner, rich or poor, would be awful close to ruination. Being dead also."

"No," he said. "I can't go to the cops."

"Not yet you can't. Maybe later you'll have to."

"How would I get Pam back? Broke, no business, my name in the papers for being a goddamned crook? You think she'd come back and live with me in a four-room cottage while I collected welfare?"

"I don't know. She doesn't seem to be coming back to you while, as far as she knows, you're up on top."

"You don't know her. She's always watching. Who's got how much, whose house is better or worse than ours, whose lawn is greener or browner. You don't know her."

"She's another problem," I said. "We'll work on her too,

but we can't get into marriage encounter until this problem is solved."

"Yeah, but just remember, what I told you is absolutely confidential. I can't risk everything. There's got to be another way."

"Harv," I said. "You're acting like you got lots of options. You don't. You reduced your options when you dipped into the escrow, and you goddamned near eliminated them when you took some of Powers' money. We're talking about people who might shoot you. Remember that."

Shepard nodded. "There's got to be a way."

"Yeah, there probably is. Let me think about it. What time's the meeting tomorrow?"

"One o'clock."

"I'll pick you up at your house about twelve forty-five. Go home, stay there. If I need you I want to be able to reach you."

"What are you going to do?"

"I'm going to think."

Shepard left. Half sloshed and a little relieved. Talking about a problem sometimes gives you the illusion you've done something about it. At least he wasn't trying to handle it alone. Nice clientele I had. The cops wanted Pam and the crooks wanted Harv.

I went out to the pool. Susan was sitting in a chaise in her red-flowered one-piece suit reading *The Children of the Dream,* by Bruno Bettelheim. She had on big, gold-rimmed sunglasses and a large white straw hat with a red band that matched the bathing suit. I stopped before she saw me and looked at her. Jesus Christ, I thought. How could anyone have ever divorced her? Maybe she'd divorced him. We'd never really talked much about it. But even so, where was he? If she'd divorced me, I'd have followed her around for the rest of our lives. I walked over, put my arms on either side of her and did a push-up on the chaise. Lowering myself until our noses touched.

"If you and I were married, and you divorced me, I would follow you around the rest of my life," I said.

"No you wouldn't," she said. "You'd be too proud."

"I would assault anyone you dated."

"That I believe. But you're not married to me and get off of me, you goof. You're just showing off."

I did five or six push-ups over her on the chaise.

"Why do you say that?" I said.

She poked me with her index finger in the solar plexus. "Off," she said.

I did one more push-up. "You know what this makes me think of?"

"Of course I know what it makes you think of. Now get the hell off me, you're bending my book."

I snapped off one more push-up and bounced off the chaise the way a gymnast dismounts the parallel bars. Straightening to attention as my feet hit.

"Once you put adolescence behind you," Susan said, "you'll be quite an attractive guy, a bit physical but . . . attractive. What did Shepard want?"

"Help," I said. "He's into a loan shark as we assumed, and the loan shark wants his business." I got a folding chair from across the pool and brought it back and sat beside Susan and told her about Shepard and his problem.

"That means you are going to have to deal with Hawk," Susan said.

"Maybe," I said.

She clamped her mouth in a thin line and took a deep breath through her nose. "What are you going to do?"

"I don't know. I thought I'd go down and sit in the bar and think. Want to come?"

She shook her head. "No, I'll stay here and read and maybe swim in a while. When you think of something, let me know. We can have lunch or something to celebrate."

I leaned over and kissed her on the shoulder, and went to the bar. There were people having lunch, but not many drinking. I sat at the far end of the bar, ordered a Harp on draft and started in on the peanuts in the dark wooden bowl in front of me.

I had two problems. I had to take King Powers off of

Shepard's back and I had to get Pam Shepard off the hook for armed robbery and murder. Saps. I was disgusted with both of them. It's an occupational hazard, I thought. Everyone gets contemptuous after a while of his clients. Teachers get scornful of students, doctors of patients, bartenders of drinkers, salesmen of buyers, clerks of customers. But, Jesus, they were saps. The Promised Land. Holy Christ. I had another beer. The peanut bowl was empty. I rattled it on the bar until the bartender came down and refilled it. Scornfully, I thought. Guns, I thought. Get guns and disarm phallic power. Where the hell were they going to get guns? They could look in the Yellow Pages under gunrunner. I could put them in touch with somebody like King Powers. Then when he sold them the guns they could shoot him and that would solve Shepard's problem . . . or I could frame Powers. No, frame wasn't right. Entrapment. That's the word. I could entrap Powers. Not for sharking: That would get Shepard in the soup too. But for illegal gun sales. Done right it would get him off Shepard's back for quite a long time. It would also get Rose and Jane out of Pam Shepard's life. But why wouldn't they take Pam with them? Because I could deal with the local D.A.: Powers and two radical feminists on a fresh roll, if he kept the Shepards out of it. I liked it. It needed a little more shape and substance. But I liked it. It could work. My only other idea was appealing to Powers' better instincts. That didn't hold much promise. Entrapment was better. I was going to flimflam the old King. A little Scott Joplin music in the background, maybe. I had another beer and ate more peanuts and thought some more.

Susan came in from the pool with a thigh-length white lace thing over her bathing suit, and slid onto the barstool next to me.

"Cogito ergo sum," I said.

"Oh absolutely," she said. "You've always been sicklied over with the pale cast of thought."

"Wait'll you hear," I said.

CHAPTER NINETEEN

AFTER LUNCH I called the New Bedford *Standard Times* and inserted an ad in the personals column of the classified section: "Sisters, call me at 555-1434. Pam."

Then I called 555-1434. Pam Shepard answered the first ring.

"Listen," I said. And read her the ad. "I just put that in the New Bedford *Standard Times*. When the sisters call you arrange for us to meet. You, me, them."

"Oh, they won't like that. They won't trust you."

"You'll have to get them to do it anyway. Talk to them of obligation and sororal affiliation. Tell them I've got a gun dealer who wants to talk. How you get us together is up to you, but do it."

"Why is it so important?"

"To save your hide and Harv's and make the world safe for democracy. Just do it. It's too complicated to explain. You getting stir-crazy there?"

"No, it's not too bad. I've seen a lot of daytime television."

"Don't watch too much, it'll rot your teeth."

"Spenser?"

"Yeah."

"What's wrong with Harvey? What did you mean about saving Harvey's hide?"

"Nothing you need worry about now. I'm just concerned with his value system."

"He's all right?"

"Sure."

"And the kids?"

"Of course. They miss you, Harv, too, but they're fine otherwise." Ah, Spenser, you glib devil you. How the hell did I know how they were? I'd seen one of them my first day on the case.

"Funny," she said. "I don't know if I miss them or not, sometimes I think I do, but sometimes I just think I ought to and am feeling guilty because I don't. It's hard to get in touch with your feelings sometimes."

"Yeah, it is. Anything you need right now before I hang up?"

"No, no thanks, I'm okay."

"Good. Suze or I will be in touch."

I hung up.

Susan in faded jeans and a dark blue blouse was heading down Cape to look at antiques. "And I may pick up some young stud still in college and fulfill my wildest fantasies," she said.

I said, "Grrrrrr."

"Women my age are at the peak of their erotic power," she said. "Men your age are in steep decline."

"I'm young at heart," I said. Susan was out the door. She stuck her head back in. "I wasn't talking about heart," she said. And went. I looked at my watch. It was one-fifteen. I went in the bathroom, splashed some water on my face, toweled dry and headed for New Bedford.

At five after two I was illegally parked outside the New Bedford police station on Spring Street. It was three stories, brick, with A dormers on the roof and a kind of cream yellow trim. Flanking the entrance, just like in the Bowery Boys movies, were white globes on black iron columns. On the globes it said NEW BEDFORD POLICE in black letters. A couple of tan police cruisers with blue shields on the door were parked out front. One of them was occupied, and I noticed that the New Bedford cops wore white hats. I wondered if the crooks wore black ones.

At the desk I asked a woman cop who was handling the Bristol Security robbery. She had light hair and blue eyeshadow and shiny lipstick and she looked at me hard for about ten seconds.

"Who wants to know?" she said.

Not sex nor age nor national origin makes any difference. Cops are cops.

"My name's Spenser," I said. "I'm a private license from Boston and I have some information that's going to get someone promoted to sergeant."

"I'll bet you do," she said. "Why don't you lay a little on me and see if I'm impressed."

"You on the case?"

"I'm on the desk, but impress me anyway."

I shook my head. "Detectives," I said. "I only deal with detectives."

"Everybody only deals with detectives. Every day I sit here with my butt getting wider, and every day guys like you come in and want to talk with a detective." She picked up the phone on the desk, dialed a four-digit number and said into the mouthpiece, "Sylvia there? Margaret on the desk. Yeah. Well, tell him there's a guy down here says he's got information on Bristol Security. Okay." She hung up. "Guy in charge is a detective named Jackie Sylvia. Sit over there, he'll be down in a minute."

It was more like five before he showed up. A squat bald man with dark skin. He was as dapper as a guy can be who stands five six and weighs two hundred. Pink-flowered shirt, a beige leisure suit, coppery brown patent leather loafers with a couple of bright gold links on the tops. It was hard to tell how old he was. His round face was without lines, but the close-cropped hair that remained below his glistening bald spot was mostly gray. He walked over to me with a light step and I suspected he might not be as fat as he looked.

"My name's Sylvia," he said. "You looking for me?"

"I am if you're running the Bristol Security investigation."

"Yeah."

"Can we go someplace and talk?"

Sylvia nodded toward the stairs past the desk and I

followed him to the second floor. We went through a door marked ROBBERY and into a room that overlooked Second Street. There were six desks butted together in groups of two, each with a push-button phone and a light maple swivel chair. In the far corner an office had been partitioned off. On the door was a sign that read SGT. CRUZ. At one of the desks a skinny cop with scraggly blond hair sat with his feet up talking on the phone. He was wearing a black T-shirt, and on his right forearm he had a tattoo of a thunderbird and the words FIGHTING 45TH. A cigarette burned on the edge of the desk, a long ash forming. Sylvia grabbed a straight chair from beside one of the other desks and dragged it over beside his. "Sit," he said. I sat and he slid into his swivel chair and tilted it back, his small feet resting on the base of the chair. He wasn't wearing socks. A big floor fan in the far corner moved hot air back and forth across the desk tops as it scanned the room.

On Sylvia's desk was a paper coffee cup, empty, and part of a peanut butter sandwich on white bread. "Okay," Sylvia said. "Shoot."

"You know who King Powers is?" I said.

"Yeah."

"I can give you the people who did the Bristol Security and I can give you Powers, but there's got to be a trade."

"Powers don't do banks."

"I know. I can give him to you for something else, and I can give you the bank people and I can tie them together, but I gotta have something back from you."

"What do you want?"

"I want two people who are in this, left out of this."

"One of them you?"

"No, I don't do banks either."

"Let me see something that tells me what you do do."

I showed him my license. He looked at it, handed it back. "Boston, huh. You know a guy named Abel Markum up there, works out of Robbery?"

"Nope."

"Who do you know?"

"I know a homicide lieutenant named Quirk. A dick

462

named Frank Belson. Guy in Robbery named Herschel Patton. And I have a friend that's a school-crossing guard in Billerica named . . ."

Sylvia cut me off. "Okay, okay, I done business with Patton." He took some grape-flavored sugarless bubble gum from his shirt pocket and put two pieces in his mouth. He didn't offer any to me. "You know, if you're in possession of evidence of the commission of a felony that you have no legal right to withhold that evidence."

"Can I have a piece of bubble gum?"

Sylvia reached into his pocket, took out the pack and tossed it on the desk in front of me. There were three pieces left. I took one.

"Take at least two," Sylvia said. "You can't work up a bubble with one. Stuff's lousy."

I took another piece, peeled off the paper and chewed it. Sylvia was right. It was lousy.

"Remember when Double Bubble used to put out the nice lump of pink bubble gum and it was all you needed to get a good bubble?"

"Times change," Sylvia said. "Withholding information of a felony is illegal."

I blew a small purple bubble. "Yeah, I know. You want to talk about trade?"

"How about we slap you in a cell for a while as an accessory to a felony?"

I worked on the bubble gum. It wasn't elastic enough. I could only produce a small bubble, maybe as big as a Ping-Pong ball, before it broke with a sharp little snap.

"How about while you're in the cell we interrogate you a while. We got some guys down here can interrogate the shit out of a person. You know?"

"This stuff sticks to your teeth," I said.

"Not if you don't have any," Sylvia said.

"Why the hell would someone make gum that sticks to your teeth," I said. "Christ, you can't trust anyone."

"You don't like it, spit it out. I don't make you chew it."

"It's better than nothing," I said.

"You gonna talk to me about the Bristol Security job?"

"I'm gonna talk to you about a trade."

"Goddamnit, Spenser, you can't come waltzing in here and tell me what kind of deal you'll make with me. I don't know what kind of crap you get away with up in Boston, but down here I tell you what kind of deal there is."

"Very good," I said. "One look at my license and you remembered my name. I didn't even see your lips move when you looked at it either."

"Don't smart-ass with me, Johnny, or you'll be looking very close at the floor. Understand what I'm saying to you?"

"Aw come on, Sylvia, stop terrifying me. When I get panicky I tend to violence and there's only two of you in the room." The scraggly haired cop with the tattoo had hung up the phone and drifted over to listen.

"Want me to open the window, Jackie," he said. "Then if he gets mean we can scream for help?"

"Or jump," Sylvia said. "It's two floors but it would be better than trying to deal with an animal like this."

I said, "You guys want to talk trade yet, or are you working up a nightclub act?"

"How do I know you can deliver," Sylvia said.

"If I don't what have you lost. You're no worse off than you are now."

"No entrapment," scraggly hair said. "At least nothing that looks like entrapment in court. We been burned on that a couple of times."

"No sweat," I said.

"How bad are the people you want left out?"

"They are no harm to anybody but themselves," I said. "They ran after the wrong promise and got into things they couldn't control."

"The bank guard that got killed," Sylvia said, "I knew him. Used to be in the department here, you know."

"I know," I said. "My people didn't want it to happen."

"Homicide during the commission of a felony is murder one."

"I know that too," I said. "And I know that these peo-

ple are a good swap for what I can give you. Somebody's got to
go down for the bank guard."

Sylvia interrupted. "Fitzgerald, his name was. Everybody called him Fitzy."

"Like I say, somebody has to go down for that. And
somebody will. I just want to save a couple of goddamned
fools."

Scraggly hair looked at Sylvia. "So far we got zip on
the thing, Jackie. Air."

"You got a plan," Sylvia said.

I nodded.

"There's no guarantee. Whatever you got, I'm going to
have to check you out first."

"I know that."

"Okay, tell me."

"I thought you'd never ask," I said.

CHAPTER TWENTY

SCRAGGLY HAIR'S NAME turned out to be McDermott. He and
Jackie Sylvia listened without comment while I laid it out
and when I was through Sylvia said, "Okay, we'll think about
it. Where can I reach you?"

"Dunfey's in Hyannis. Or my service if I'm not there. I
check with the service every day." I gave him the number.

"We'll get back to you."

On the drive back to Hyannis the grape bubble gum
got harder and harder to chew. I gave up in Wareham and
spit it out the window in front of the hospital. The muscles at
my jaw hinges were sore, and I felt slightly nauseous. When I

pulled into the parking lot at Dunfey's it was suppertime and the nausea had given way to hunger.

Susan was back from her antiquing foray and had a Tiffany style glass lampshade for which she'd paid $125. We went down to the dining room, had two vodka gimlets each, parslied rack of lamb and blackberry cheesecake. After dinner we had some cassis and then went down to the ballroom and danced all the slow numbers until midnight. We brought a bottle of champagne back to the room and drank it and went to bed and didn't sleep until nearly three.

It was ten-forty when I woke up. Susan was still asleep, her back to me, the covers up tight around her neck. I picked up the phone and ordered breakfast, softly. "Don't knock," I said. "Just leave it outside the door. My friend is still asleep."

I showered and shaved and with a towel around my waist opened the door and brought in the cart. I drank coffee and ate from a basket of assorted muffins while I dressed. Susan woke up as I was slipping my gun into the hip holster. I clipped the holster on to my belt. She lay on her back with her hands behind her head and watched me. I slipped on my summer blazer with the brass buttons and adjusted my shirt collar so it rolled out nicely over the lapels. Seductive.

"You going to see Hawk and what's'isname?" Susan said.

"Powers," I said. "Yeah. Me and Harv Shepard."

She continued to look at me.

"Want some coffee?" I said.

She shook her head. "Not yet."

I ate a corn muffin.

"Are you scared? Susan asked.

"I don't know. I don't think much about it. I don't see anything very scary happening today."

"Do you like it?"

"Yeah. I wouldn't do it if I didn't like it."

"I mean this particularly. I know you like the work. But do you like this? You are going to frame a very dangerous man. That should scare you, or excite you or something."

"I'm not going to frame him. I'm going to entrap him, in fact."

"You know what I mean. If it doesn't work right he'll kill you."

"No, he'll have it done."

"Don't do that. Don't pick up the less important part of what I'm saying. You know what I'm after. What kind of man does the kinds of things you do? What kind of man gets up in the morning and showers and shaves and checks the cartridges in his gun?"

"Couldn't we talk over the transports of delight in which we soared last evening?"

"Do you laugh at everything?"

"No, but we're spending too much time on this kind of talk. The kind of man I am is not a suitable topic, you know. It's not what one talks about."

"Why?"

"Because it's not."

"The code? A man doesn't succumb to self-analysis? It's weak? It's womanish?"

"It's pointless. What I am is what I do. Finding the right words for it is no improvement. It isn't important whether I'm scared or excited. It's important whether or not I do it. It doesn't matter to Shepard why. It matters to Shepard if."

"You're wrong. It matters more than that. It matters why."

"Maybe it matters mostly how."

"My, aren't we epigrammatic. Spencer Tracy and Katharine Hepburn. Repartee."

"He spells his name differently," I said.

Susan turned over on her side, her back to me, and was quiet. I had some more coffee. The murmurous rush of the air conditioner seemed quite loud. I'd asked for the New Bedford *Standard Times* with breakfast, and in the quiet, I picked it up and turned to the classified section. My ad was there under personals. "Sisters, call me at 555-1434, Pam." I looked at the sports page and finished my coffee. It was ten after twelve. I folded the paper and put it on the room service cart.

"Gotta go, Suze," I said.

She nodded without turning over.

I got up, put on my sunglasses and opened the door. "Spenser," she said, "I don't want us to be mad at each other."

"Me either," I said. I still had hold of the doorknob.

"Come back when you can," she said. "I miss you when you're gone."

"Me too," I said. I left the door open and went back and kissed her on the cheekbone, up near the temple. She rolled over on her back and looked up at me. Her eyes were wet. "Bye-bye," I said.

"Bye-bye."

I went out and closed the door and headed for Harv Shepard's place with my stomach feeling odd.

I don't know if I was scared or not, but Shepard was so scared his face didn't fit. The skin was stretched much too tight over the bones and he swallowed a lot, and loudly, as we drove out Main Street to the Holiday Inn.

"You don't need to know what I'm up to," I said. "I think you'll do better if you don't. Just take it that I've got something working that might get you out of this."

"Why can't you tell me?"

"Because it requires some deception and I don't think you're up to it."

"You're probably right," he said.

Hawk had a room on the second floor, overlooking the pool. He answered the door when we knocked, and Shepard and I went in. There was assorted booze on the bureau to the right, and a thin guy with horn-rimmed glasses reading the *Wall Street Journal* on one of the beds. King Powers was sitting at a round table with an open ledger in front of him, his hands folded on the edge of the table. Stagey bastard.

"What is that you have with you," Powers said in a flat Rudy Vallee voice.

"We're friends," I said. "We go everywhere together."

Powers was a tall, soft-looking man with pale skin and

reddish hair trimmed long like a Dutch boy, and augmented with fuzzy mutton-chop sideburns. His wardrobe looked like Robert Hall Mod. Maroon-checked doubleknit leisure suit, white belt, white shoes, white silk shirt with the collar out over the lapels. A turquoise arrowhead was fastened around his neck on a leather thong and stuck straight out, like a gesture of derision.

"I didn't tell you to bring no friends," Powers said to Shepard.

"You'll be glad he did," I said. "I got a package for you that will put a lot of change in your purse."

"I don't use no goddamned purse," Powers said.

"Oh," I said. "I'm sorry. I thought that was your mistress on the bed."

Behind me Hawk murmured. "Hot damn" to himself. The guy on the bed looked up from his *Wall Street Journal* and frowned.

Powers said, "Hawk, get him the fuck out of here."

Hawk said. "This is Spenser. I told you about him. He likes to kid around but he don't mean harm. Leastwise he don't always mean harm."

"Hawk, you hear me. I told you move him out."

"He talking money, King. Maybe you should listen."

"You working for me, Hawk? You do what you're told."

"Naw, I only do what I want. I never do what I'm told. Same with old Spenser here. You yell your ass off at him, if you want, but he ain't going to do a goddamned thing he don't want to do. You and Macey listen to him. He talking about money, he probably ain't bullshitting. You don't like what you hear. Then I'll move him out."

"Aw right, aw right. Let's hear it, for crissake. Spit it out." Powers' pale face was a little red and he was looking at me hard. Macey, on the bed, had sat up, and put his feet on the floor. He still held the *Journal* in his left hand, his forefinger keeping the place.

"Okay, King. First. Harv can't pay up, at this time."

"Then his ass is grass and I'm a fucking lawnmower," Powers said.

"Trendy," I said.

"Huh?"

"Trendy as a bastard, that slick maroon and white combo. And to top it off you talk so good. You're just an altogether with-it guy."

"You keep fucking around with me, Spenser, and you're going to wish you never did."

"Whyn't you get to the part about the bread, Spenser," Hawk said. "In the purse. Whyn't you talk on that."

"I got a buyer with about a hundred thousand dollars who is looking for some guns. I will trade you the buyer for Shepard."

"What makes you think I can get guns?"

"King, for a hundred thousand skins you could get a dancing aardvark." He smiled. His lips were puffy and when he smiled the inside of his upper lip turned out. And his gums showed above his top teeth.

"Yeah, maybe I could," he said. "But Shepard's into me for a lot of fucking dough." He ran his eyes down the ledger page in front of him. "Thirty big ones. I took a lot of risk with that dough, just on a handshake, you know? It ain't easy to trade that off."

"Okay," I said. "See you, we'll take it elsewhere," I said. "Come on, Harv."

Powers said, "You're choice, but your pal better have the payment on him now, or we're going to be awful mad."

"The payment's in the offer. You turned it down, you got no bitch." I turned to go. Hawk was between us and the door. His hands resting delicately on his hips.

"Hawk," Powers said. "Shepard don't leave."

"Hundred thousand's a lotta vegetable matter, King," Hawk said.

"Hawk's right, Mr. Powers." Macey on the bed had dropped his *Journal* and brought out a neat-looking little .25 automatic with a pearl handle and nickel plating. Probably matched his cuff links.

"What's in it for you, Spencer?" Powers said.

"Thirty percent," I said. "You can use it to pay off Shepard's loan."

Powers was quiet. We all were. It was like a stop frame in instant replay.

Hawk at ease in front of the door. Shepard with his skin squeezing tight on his body, Macey with his cute gun. Powers sitting at the table, thinking.

The window was behind him and the light coming in framed him like a back-lit photograph. The little tendrils of fuzz in the double-knit were silhouetted and clear along his coat sleeves and the tops of the shoulders. The muttonchop sideburns where the whiskers individuated at the outer edge were more gold than copper against the light.

"Who's your customer?" King said. Hawk whistled shave-and-a-haircut-two-bits between his teeth. Softly.

"If I told you that I probably wouldn't be needed as go-between, would I?"

Powers turned his lip up again and giggled. Then he turned to the thin guy. "Macey," he said, "I got some golf to play. Set this thing up." He looked at me. "This better be straight," he said. "If it ain't you are going to be pushing up your fucking daisies. You unnerstand? Fucking daisies you'll be pushing up." He got up and walked past me toward the door.

"Daisies," I said.

He went out. Macey put the .25 away and said, "Okay, let's get to work."

I said, "Is he going to play golf in his Anderson-Little cutaway?"

"He's going to change in the clubhouse," Macey said. "Haven't you ever played golf?"

"Naw, we were into aggravated assault when I was a kid."

Macey smiled once, on and off like a blinking light. Hawk went and lay down on the bed and closed his eyes. Shepard went stiffly to the bureau where the booze was and made a big drink. Macey sat down at the round table and I joined him. "Okay," he said, "give me the deal."

CHAPTER TWENTY-ONE

THERE WASN'T ALL THAT MUCH to set up with Macey yet. I told him I'd have to get in touch with the other principals first and get back to him, but that the 100 grand was firm and he should start getting in touch with his sources.

"The guns would be top dollar," Macey said. "There's the risk factor, and the added problem of market impact. Large quantity like this causes ripples, as you must know."

"I know. And I know you can manage it. That's why I came to you."

Macey said, "Um-hum" and took a business card from the breast pocket of his seersucker suit. "Call me," he said, "when you've talked to the other party."

I took the card and put it in my wallet. "We're in business then," I said.

"Certainly," Macey said. "Assuming the deal is as you represent it."

"Yeah, that too," I said. "That means if we're in business that you folks will lay off old Harv here. Right?"

"Of course," Macey said. "You heard Mr. Powers. We borrow and lend, we're not animals. There's no problem there."

"Maybe not," I said. "But I want a little more reassurance. Hawk?"

Hawk was motionless on the bed, his hands folded over his solar plexus, his eyes closed. Without opening his eyes he said, "Shepard'll be okay."

I nodded. "Okay," I said. "Let's go, Harv."

Shepard put down what was left of his drink, and went

out of the room without even looking around. I followed him. Nobody said goodby.

When we got in my car and started out of the parking lot, Shepard said, "How do we know they'll keep their word?"

"About staying off your back?" I said.

Shepard nodded.

"Hawk said so," I said.

"Hawk? The nigger? He's the one beat me up last time."

"He keeps his word," I said. "And I told you before, call him Hawk. I'm not going to tell you again."

"Yeah, sure, sorry, I forgot. But, Jesus, trusting him. I mean the guy Macey seems reasonable, like a guy you can do business with . . . But Hawk."

"You don't know anything," I said. "Macey would take out your eyeballs for a dollar. You think he's a guy you can deal with 'cause he talks like he went to the Wharton School. Maybe he did, but he's got no more honor than a toad. He'll do anything. Hawk won't. There's things Hawk won't do."

"Like what?"

"He won't say *yes* and do *no*."

"Well, I guess you know your business. Where the hell are you getting the money?"

"That's not your problem," I said. We pulled up in front of Shepard's house. He'd banged back two big drinks while I was talking with Macey and his mouth was a little slow.

"Thanks, Spenser," he said. "Just for going, let alone for making that gun deal. I was scared shit."

"You should have been," I said. We shook hands, Shepard got out and went in the house. I cruised back to the motel. Susan wasn't around and her car wasn't in the lot. I called Pam Shepard from my hotel room.

"You hear from the girls?" I said.

"From Rose, yes. They'll meet us. I know you're being funny, but please don't call them girls."

"Where?"

"Where will they meet us?"

"Yeah."

"In Milton. There's an observatory on top of the Great Blue Hill. Do you know where that is?"

"Yeah."

"They'll meet us in the observatory. This afternoon at five."

I looked at my watch: 1:25. There was time. "Okay," I said. "I'll come pick you up and we'll go. I'll leave now, should be there around three. Start looking out the window then. I'll park on the street and when you see me, come on down."

"What are we going to do?"

"I'll talk with you about it while we drive to Milton."

"All right."

"You bored?"

"Oh God, I'm going crazy."

"Not too much longer," I said.

"I hope not."

We hung up, I went back to my car and set out for Boston again. If I made the trip many more times I'd be able to sleep on the way. I pulled up in front of my apartment at ten after three. In about forty seconds Pam Shepard came out the front door and got in the car. And we were off again for the Blue Hills.

The top was down and Pam Shepard leaned her head back against the seat and took a big inhale. "Good God, it's good to get out of there," she said.

"That's my home you're speaking of," I said. "I was kind of wishing I could get in there."

"I didn't mean it's not nice, and it's not even so much that it's been that long, it's just that, when you know you can't go out, it's almost like claustrophobia."

Her clean brown hair was pulled back, still in the French twist she'd worn since I met her, and the wind didn't bother it much. I went out along Park Drive and the Jamaicaway and the Arborway south on Route 28. Just across the Neponset River, Route 138 branched off from Route 28 and we went with it, taking our time. We pulled into the Blue Hills Reservation and parked near the Trailside Museum at four o'clock.

"We're awfully early," Pam Shepard said.

"Plan ahead," I said. "I want to be here waiting. I don't want them to get nervous waiting for us and leave."

"I don't mind," she said. "What are we going to do?"

"We'll walk up to the observatory on the top. And when they come, I'll tell them I have a seller for them."

"A seller?"

"A gun broker. I've got a guy who'll sell them all the guns they can afford."

"But why? Why would you do that?"

"Isn't that why you stole the money?"

"Yes, but you don't approve of us, do you? You don't want to arm us certainly."

"That doesn't matter. I'm working on a very fancy move, and I don't want you trying to pretend you don't know. So I won't tell you. Then you won't have to pretend. You just assume I'm in your corner, and you vouch for me every time the question comes up."

"I've done that already. On the phone when they called. They don't trust you and they don't like you."

"Hard to imagine, isn't it," I said.

She smiled, and closed her eyes and shook her head slightly.

"Come on," I said, "let's get out and walk."

The blue hills are actually spruce green and they form the center of a large reservation of woods and ponds in an upper-middle-class suburb that abuts Boston. The biggest of the blue hills supports on its flank a nature museum, and on its crest a fieldstone observatory from which one gets a fine view of Boston's skyline, and an excellent wind for kite flying on the downside pitch of the hill below the building. It's a hike of maybe fifteen minutes to the top, through woods and over small gullies, and there are usually Cub Scout packs and Audubon members clambering among the slate-colored outcroppings. I offered Pam Shepard a hand over one of the gullies and she declined. I didn't offer on the next one. I'm a quick study.

The observatory at the top had two sets of stairs and

two balconies and kids were running up and down the stairs and shouting at each other from the balconies. Several kites danced above us, one of them shaped like a large bat. "That's auspicious," I said to Pam, and nodded at the bat.

She smiled. "They have all sorts of fancy ones like that now," she said. "The kids went through the kite stage. Harvey and I could never get them to fly. . . . Or us either, now that I think of it."

"It can be done," I said. "I've seen it done."

She shrugged and smiled again and shook her head. We stood on the upper balcony of the observatory and looked at the Boston skyline to the north. "What is it," Pam Shepard said, "about a cluster of skyscrapers in the distance that makes you feel . . . What? . . . Romantic? Melancholy? Excited? Excited probably."

"Promise," I said.

"Of what?"

"Of everything," I said. "From a distance they promise everything, whatever you're after. They look clean and permanent against the sky like that. Up close you notice dog litter around the foundations."

"Are you saying it's not real? The look of the skyscrapers from a distance."

"No. It's real enough, I think. But so is the dog litter and if you spend all your time looking at the spires you're going to step in it."

"Into each life some shit must fall?"

"Ah," I said, "you put it so much more gracefully than I."

She laughed.

Below us to the left Jane emerged from behind some trees where the trail opened out into a small meadow below the observatory. She looked around carefully and then looked up at us on the balcony. Pam Shepard waved. I smiled inoffensively. Jane turned her head and said something and Rose emerged from the trees and stood beside her. Pam waved again and Rose waved back. My smile became even more inoffensive. And earnest. I fairly vibrated with earnestness. This was going to be the tough part. Guys like Powers you can get with money, or the hope of it. Or fear, if you're in a position to scare them. But people like Rose, they were hard. Zealots were always hard. Zeal distorts them. Makes the normal impulses convolute. Makes people fearless and greedless and loveless and finally monstrous. I was against zeal. But being against it didn't make it go away. I had to persuade these two zealots to go along with the plan or the plan washed away and maybe so did the Shepards.

They trudged up the hill to the observatory warily, alert for an ambush among the kite-flying kids and the Cub Scouts looking at lichen growth on the north side of rocks. They disappeared below us as they went into the stairwell and then appeared coming up the stairs behind us. As Rose reached the top of the stairs Pam Shepard went to her and embraced her. Rose patted her back as they hugged. With one arm still around Rose, Pam took Jane's hand and squeezed it.

"It's good to see you both," she said.

Rose said, "Are you all right?"

Jane said, "Have you got a place to stay?"

"Yes, yes, I'm all right, I'm fine, I've been using his apartment."

"With him?" Rose looked suddenly menopausal.

"No," I said. The way I used to say it to my mother. "No, I've been down the Cape, working on a case. Besides I have a girlfriend, ah woman, ah, I have a person, I . . . I'm with Susan Silverman."

Rose said to Pam Shepard, "That's good of him."

Jane said to Rose and Pam Shepard, "I still don't trust him."

"You can," Pam said. "You really can. I trust him. He's a good man."

I smiled harder. Ingratiation. Jane eyes me for vulnerable points.

Rose said, "Well, whether or not we can trust him, we can talk some business with him at least. I'll reserve my opinion of his trustworthiness. What is his offer exactly?" And, while she hadn't yet addressed me directly, she looked at me.

Once they did that I always had them. I think it was the puckish charm. "Well?" she said. Yeah, it was the puckish charm.

"I can get you all the guns you need, one hundred thousand dollars' worth. And bullets. No questions asked."

"Why?"

"I get a broker's fee."

Rose nodded. Jane said, "Perhaps that's why we can trust him."

Rose said, "I suppose we give you the money and then you have the guns delivered? Something like that perhaps? And when we get tired of waiting for delivery and call you up you seem to have moved?"

Pam Shepard said, "No. Rose, believe me, you can trust him. He's not dishonest."

"Pam, almost everyone is dishonest. He's as dishonest as anyone else. I don't want to do business with him."

"That's dumb," I said. "It's the kind of dumb that smart people get because they think they're smart."

"What the hell does that mean?" Jane said.

"It means that if everyone's dishonest you aren't going to do better elsewhere. And the devil you know is better than the devil you don't know. I got one character witness. Where you going to find a gun dealer that has that many?"

Rose said, "We are not fools. You assume women can't manage this sort of thing? That gunrunning is a masculine profession?"

"I don't assume anything. What I know is that amateurs can't handle this sort of thing. You will get ripped off if you're lucky and ripped off and busted if you're not." Ah, Spenser, master of the revolutionary argot. Word maven of the counterculture.

"And why should we believe you won't rip us off?" Jane said.

"You got my word, and the assurance of one of your own people. Have I lied to you yet? Have I turned Pam in to her husband, or the fuzz? You held up a bank and killed an old man. He used to be a cop and the New Bedford cops are not going to forget that. They are going to be looking for you until Harvard wins the Rose Bowl. You are fugitives from justice as the saying goes. And you are in no position to be advertising for a gun dealer. If the word gets out that a group of women are looking to make a gun buy, who do you think the first dealer will be? The easy one, the one that shows up one day and says he's got what you want?"

"So far," Rose said, "it seems to be you."

"Yeah, and you know who I am. The next one will be somebody undercover. An FBI informant, a special services cop, an agent from the Treasury Department, maybe a woman, a nice black woman with all the proper hatreds who wants to help a sister. And you show up with the cash and she shows up with thirteen cops and the paddy wagon."

"He's right, you know," Pam Shepard said. "He knows about this kind of thing, and we don't. Who would get us guns that we could trust better?"

"Perhaps," Rose said, "we can merely sit on the money for a while."

I shook my head. "No, you can't. Then you're just a felon, a robber and murderer. Now you're a revolutionary who killed because she had to. If you don't do what you set out to do then you have no justification for murdering that old man and the guilt will get you."

"I killed the guard," Jane said. "Rose didn't. He tried to stop us and I shot him." She seemed proud.

"Same, same," I said. "She's an accessory and as responsible as you are. Doesn't matter who squeezed off the round."

"We can do without the amateur psychoanalyzing, Spenser," Rose said. "How do we prevent you from taking our money and running?"

"I'll just be the broker. You and the gun dealer meet face to face. You see the guns, he sees the money."

"And if they're defective?"

"Examine them before you buy."

They were silent.

"If you're not familiar with the particular type of

weapon, I'll examine it too. Have you thought of what kinds of guns you want?"

"Any kind," Jane said. "Just so they fire."

"No, Jane. Let's be honest. We don't know much about guns. You know that anyway. We want guns appropriate for guerrilla fighting. Including handguns that we can conceal easily, and, I should think, some kind of machine guns."

"You mean hand-held automatic weapons, you don't mean something you'd mount on a tripod."

"That's right. Whatever the proper terminology. Does that seem sensible to you?"

"Yeah. Let me check with my dealer. Any other preferences?"

"Just so they shoot," Jane said.

"Are we in business?" I said.

"Let us talk a bit, Mr. Spenser," Rose said. And the three women walked to the other end of the balcony and huddled.

On the walls of the observatory, mostly in spray paint, were graffiti. Mostly names, but also a pitch for gay liberation, a suggestion that blacks be bused to Africa and some remarks about the sister of somebody named Mangan. The conference broke up and Rose came back and said, "All right, we're agreed. When can you get the guns?"

"I'll have to be in touch with you," I said. "Couple days, probably."

"We're not giving you an address or phone number."

"No need to." I gave her my card. "You have my number. I'll leave a message with my answering service. Call every day at noon and check in. Collect is okay."

"We'll pay our way, Mr. Spenser."

"Of course you will, I was just being pleasant."

"Perhaps you shouldn't bother, Mr. Spenser. It seems very hard for you."

CHAPTER TWENTY-TWO

ROSE AND JANE LEFT as furtively as they'd come. They were hooked. I might pull it off. Jane hadn't even kicked me.

"It's going to work," I said to Pam Shepard.

"Are they going to get hurt?"

"That's my worry, not yours."

"But I'm like the Judas goat if they are. They are trusting you because of me."

We were driving back into Boston passing the outbound commuting traffic. "Somebody has to go down," I said, "for the bank guard. It isn't going to be you and that's all you have to concentrate on."

"Damnit, Spenser, am I selling them out?"

"Yes," I said.

"You son of a bitch."

"If you kick me in the groin while I'm driving a traffic accident might ensue."

"I won't do it. I'll warn them now. As soon as I get home."

"First, you don't know how to reach them except through an ad in the paper, which you can't do right now. Second, if you warn them you will screw yourself and your husband, whose troubles are as serious as yours and whose salvation is tied to selling out Rose and Jane."

"What's wrong? What's the matter with Harvey? Are the kids okay?"

"Everyone's okay at the moment. But Harv's in hock to a loan shark. I didn't want to tell you all this but you can't trust me if I lie to you. You kept asking."

"You have no right to manipulate me. Not even for my own good. You have not got that right maybe especially for my own good."

"I know. That's why I'm telling you. You're better off not knowing, but you have the right to know and I don't have the right to decide for you."

"So what in hell is going on?"

I told her. By the time I got through we were heading down Boylston Street through Copley Square with the sun reflecting off the empty John Hancock Building and the fountain sparkling in the plaza. I left out only the part about Hawk shoving one of the kids. Paternalism is hard to shake.

"Good Jesus," she said. "What the hell have we become."

"You've become endangered species among other things. The only way out for you is to do what I say. That includes throwing Rose and Jane off the back of the sleigh."

"I can't . . . double-cross them. I know that sounds melodramatic but I don't know how else to put it."

"It's better than saying you can't betray them. But however you put it, you're wrong. You've gotten yourself into a place where all the choices are lousy. But they seem clear. You've got kids that need a mother, you've got a husband that needs a wife. You've got a life and it needs you to live it. You're a handsome intelligent broad in the middle of something that could still be a good life." I turned left at Bonwit's onto Berkeley Street. "Somebody has got to go inside for that old cop. And I won't be crying if it's Rose and Jane. They snuffed him like a candle when he got in their way. And if we can hook King Powers on the same line, I say we've done good."

I turned right onto Marlborough Street and pulled into the curb by the hydrant in front of my apartment. We went up in silence. And we were silent when we got inside. The silence got awkward inside because it was pregnant with self-awareness. We were awkwardly aware that we were alone together in my apartment and that awareness hung between us as if Kate Millett had never been born. "I'll make us some supper," I said. "Want a drink first?" My voice was a little husky but I didn't want to clear my throat. That would have been embarrassing, like an old Leon Errol movie.

"Are you having one?" she said.

"I'm having a beer." My voice had gone from husky to hoarse. I coughed to conceal the fact that I was clearing it.

"I'll have one too," she said.

I got two cans of Utica Club cream ale out of the refrigerator.

"Glass?" I said.

"No, can's fine," she said.

"Ever try this," I said. "Really very good. Since they stopped importing Amstel, I've been experimenting around."

"It's very nice," she said.

"Want spaghetti?"

"Sure, that would be fine."

I took a container of sauce from the freezer and ran it under hot water and popped the crimson block of frozen sauce out into a saucepan. I put the gas on very low under the pan, covered it and drank some Utica Club cream ale.

"When I was a kid, I remember being out in western Mass somewhere and they used to advertise Utica Club with a little character made out of the U and the C. I think he was called Ukie." I coughed again, and finished the beer. Pam Shepard was leaning her backside on one of the two counter stools in my kitchen, her legs straight out in front of her and slightly apart so that the light summer print dress she wore pulled tight over the tops of her thighs. I wondered if tumescent could be a noun. I am a tumescent? Sounded good. She sipped a little of the beer from the can.

"Like it?" I said.

She nodded.

"And the plan? How about that."

She shook her head.

"All right, you don't like it. But will you go along? Don't waste yourself. Go along. I can get you out of this mess. Let me."

"Yes," she said. "I'm not pleased with myself, but I'll go

483

along. For Harvey and for the children and for myself. Probably mostly for myself . . ."

Ah-ha, the old puckish charm. I must use this power only for good.

I said, "Whew" and popped the top off another can of Utica Club. I put the water on for the spaghetti and started to tear lettuce for the salad.

"Want another beer?" I said. I put the lettuce in some ice water to crisp.

"Not yet," she said. She sat still and sipped on the beer and watched me. I glanced at her occasionally and smiled and tried not to look too long at her thighs.

"I can't figure you out," she said. I sliced a red onion paper thin with a wide-bladed butcher knife.

"You mean how someone with my looks and talent ended up in this kind of business?"

"I was thinking more about all the conflicts in your character. You reek of machismo, and yet you are a very caring person. You have all these muscles and yet you read all those books. You're sarcastic and a wise guy and you make fun of everything; and yet you were really afraid I'd say no a little while ago and two people you don't even like all that well would get into trouble. And now here you are cooking me my supper and you're obviously nervous at being alone with me in your apartment."

"Obviously?"

"Obviously."

"And you?"

"I too. But I'm just somebody's middle-class housewife. I would have assumed that you were used to such things. Surely I can't be the first woman you've made supper for?"

"I cook for Suze a lot," I said. I cut some native tomatoes into wedges. And started on a green pepper.

"And for no one else?"

"Lately, just for Suze."

"So what's different about me? Why is there this sense of strain?"

"I'm not sure. It has to do with you being desirable and

484

me being randy. I know that much. But it also has to do with a sense that we should leave it at that."

"Why?" She had put the beer can down and her arms were folded under her breasts.

"I'm trying to get you and Harv back together and making a move at you doesn't seem the best way to get that done. And, I don't think Suze would like it all that much either."

"Why would she have to know?"

"Because if I didn't tell her then there would be things I kept from her. She couldn't trust me."

"But she wouldn't know she couldn't trust you."

"Yeah, but she couldn't."

"That's crazy."

"No. See the fact would be that she couldn't trust me. That I am not trustworthy. The fact that she didn't know it would be simply another deception."

"So you confess every indiscretion?"

"Every one she has a right to know about."

"Have there been many?"

"Some."

"And Susan objects?"

"No. Not generally. But she doesn't know them. And she knows you. I think this would hurt her. Especially now. We're at some kind of juncture. I'm not quite sure what, but I think this would be wrong. Damnit."

"She is, I think, a very lucky woman."

"Would you be willing to swear to that. Just recently she called me a horse's ass."

"That's possible," Pam Shepard said.

I sliced up three small pickling cucumbers, skin and all, and added them to my salad. I took the lettuce out of the water and patted it with a towel and then wrapped it and put it in the refrigerator. I checked my sauce, it was nearly melted. I added some seedless green grapes to the salad bowl. "The thing is, all that explanation didn't do much for the randiness. I don't think it's fatal, but you can't say I'm resting comfortably."

Pam Shepard laughed. "That's good to know. In fact, I thought about us going to bed together and the thought was pleasant. You look like you'd hurt and somehow I know you wouldn't."

"Tough but oh so gentle," I said.

"But it isn't going to happen, and it's probably just as well. I don't usually feel so good about myself after I've made it with someone but Harvey." She laughed again, but this time harshly. "Come to think about it, I didn't feel all that good the last few times I made it with Harvey."

"Was that recently?"

She looked away from me. "Two years ago."

"That embarrass you?"

She looked back. "Yes," she said. "Very much. Don't you think it should?"

"Yeah, maybe. On the other hand you're not a sex vendomatic. He drops in two quarters and you come across. I guess you didn't want to sleep with him."

"I couldn't stand it."

"And you both figured you were frigid. So you hustled out evenings to prove you weren't."

"I guess so. Not very pretty, is it?"

"Nope. Unhappiness never is. How about Harv, what was he doing to dissipate tension?"

"Dissipate tension. My God, I don't think I've ever heard anyone talk the way you do. I don't know what he was doing. Masturbation perhaps. I don't think he was with other women."

"Why not?"

"Loyalty, masochism, maybe love, who knows."

"Maybe a way to grind the guilt in deeper too."

"Maybe, maybe all that."

"It's almost always all that. It seems the longer I'm in business, the more it's always everything working at the same time." I took two cans of Utica Club from the refrigerator and popped the tops and handed one to her.

"The thing is," she said, "I never found out."

"If you were frigid?"

486

"Yes. I'd get drunk and I'd thrash around and bite and moan and do anything anyone wanted done, but part of it all was faking and the next day I was always disgusted. I think one reason I wanted to ball you was so I could ask you afterwards if you thought I was frigid." Her voice had a harsh sound to it, and when she said "ball you" it sounded wrong in her mouth. I knew the harsh sound. Disgust, I'd heard it before.

"For one thing, you're asking the wrong question. Frigid isn't a very useful word. You pointed that out to me a while ago. It doesn't have a meaning. It simply means you don't want to do something that someone else wants you to do. If you don't enjoy screwing old Harv then why not say that. Why generalize. Say I don't enjoy screwing Harvey, or, even better, I didn't enjoy it last evening. Why turn it into an immutable law."

"It's not that simple."

"Sometimes I wonder. Sometimes I think everything is that simple. But you're probably right. Sex is as natural as breathing except it takes a partner and what one can do with ease, two mangle."

"Does Susan . . . I'm sorry, I have no right to ask that."

"Does Susan like to have sexual intercourse? Sometimes she does and sometimes she doesn't. Occasionally, just occasionally now, that's true of me. The occasions are more frequent than they were when I was nineteen."

She smiled.

I took the lettuce out of the refrigerator, unwrapped it and tossed it in the bowl with the rest of the vegetables. My sauce was starting to bubble gently and I took enough spaghetti for two and tossed it into my boiling pot. "Plenty of water," I said, "makes it less sticky, and it comes right back to a boil so it starts cooking right away. See that. I am a spaghetti superstar."

"Why do you want Harvey and me back together? I'm not sure that's your business. Or is it just American and apple pie. Marriages are made in heaven, they should never break up?"

"I just don't think you've given it a real shot."

"A real shot. Twenty-two years? That's not a real shot?"

"That's a long shot, but not a real one. You've been trying to be what you aren't until you can't swallow it anymore and now you think you're frigid. He's been panting after greatness all his life and he can't catch it because he thinks it's success."

"If I'm not what I've been trying to be, what am I?"

"I don't know. Maybe you could find out if you no longer decided that what you ought to be was what your husband expected you to be."

"I'm not sure I know what you're talking about."

"You too, huh? Well, look, if he's disappointed in you it doesn't mean you're wrong. It could mean he's wrong."

She shook her head. "Of course, I mean that's no news flash. That's every woman's problem. I know that."

"Don't generalize on me. I don't know if it's every woman's problem, or if it's only a woman's problem. What I do know is that it might be one of your problems. If so, it can be solved. It's one thing to know something. It's another to feel it, to act as if it were so, in short, to believe it."

"And how does one learn to believe something?"

"One talks for a while with a good psychotherapist."

"Oh God, a shrink?"

"There's good ones and bad ones. Like private eyes. I can put you in touch with some good ones."

"Former clients?"

"No, Suze knows a lot about that stuff. She's a guidance person and takes it seriously."

"Is that the answer, a damned shrink? Everything that happens some psychiatrist is in on it. Every time some kid gets an F the shrink's got to have his two cents' worth."

"You ever try it?"

"No."

"Harv?"

"No. He wanted me to, see if they could find out why I was frigid. But he didn't want to go too. Said there was nothing wrong with him. Didn't want some goddamned headshrinker prying around in his business trying to convince him he was sick."

"Doesn't have to be a psychiatrist, you know. Could be a good social worker. You ought to talk with Suze about it. But Harv's got the wrong language again, just like frigid. Doesn't help to talk about 'wrong' with a big W. You got a problem. They can help. Sometimes."

"What about all these people they commit to asylums for no reason and how in murder cases they can't agree on anything. One side gets a shrink to say he's crazy and the other side gets one to say he's sane."

"Okay, psychiatry boasts as many turkeys as any other business, maybe more. But the kinds of things you're talking about aren't relevant. Those things come from asking psychiatrists to do what they aren't equipped to do. Good ones know that, I think. Good ones know that what they can do is help people work out problems. I don't think they are very good at curing schizophrenia or deciding whether someone is legally sane. That's bullshit. But they might be quite useful in helping you get over defining yourself in your husband's terms, or helping your husband get over defining himself in Cotton Mather's terms."

"Cotton Mather?"

"Yeah, you know, the old Puritan ethic."

"Oh, that Cotton Mather. You do read the books, don't you?"

"I got a lotta time," I said. The timer buzzed and I twirled out a strand of spaghetti and tried it. "Al dente," I said. "His brother Sam used to play for the Red Sox." The spaghetti was done, I turned it into a colander, emptied the pan, shook the colander to drain the spaghetti, turned it back into the pan, added a little butter and some Parmesean cheese and tossed it.

"You made that up."

"What?"

"About Al Dente's brother."

"Nope, truth. Sam Dente used to play with the Sox about thirty years ago. Infielder. Left-handed batter." The spaghetti sauce was bubbling. I poured it into a big gravy boat and put two big heaps of spaghetti on two plates. I poured the salad dressing over the salad, tossed it and set everything on the kitchen counter. "Silverware in the drawer there," I said. I got some Gallo Burgundy in a half-gallon bottle and two wine glasses out of the cupboard.

We sat at the counter and ate and drank. "Did you make the spaghetti sauce?" she said.

"Yeah. A secret recipe I got off the back of the tomato paste can."

"And the salad dressing? Is there honey in it?"

"Yep. Got that from my mother."

She shook her head. "Fighter, lover, gourmet cook? Amazing."

"Nope. I'll take the fighter, lover, but the gourmet cook is a sexist remark."

"Why?"

"If you'd cooked this no one would say you were a gourmet cook. It's because I'm a man. A man who cooks and is interested in it is called a gourmet. A woman is called a housewife. Now eat the goddamned spaghetti," I said. She did. Me too.

CHAPTER TWENTY-THREE

I SLEPT ON THE COUCH. A triumph once more of virtue over tumescence. I was up and showered and away before Pam Shepard woke up. At 10:00 A.M. I was having coffee with King Powers' man Macey in the Holiday Inn in Hyannis.

"Care for some fruit?" Macey said.

"No thanks. The coffee will do. When can you deliver the guns?"

"Tomorrow maybe, day after for sure."

"What you got?"

"M2 carbines, in perfect condition, one hundred rounds apiece."

"How many?"

"Four hundred and fifty."

"Jesus Christ, that's more than two bills apiece."

Macey shrugged. "Ammo's included, don't forget."

"Christ, you can pick 'em up in the gun shop for less than half that."

"Four hundred and fifty of them? M2s?"

"There's that," I said. "But a hundred grand for four hundred and fifty pieces. I don't think my people will like that."

"You came to us, Spence. You asked us. Remember."

I loved being called Spence. "And remember there's thirty thousand out for your share."

"Which you're keeping."

"Hey, Spence, it's owed us. We wouldn't be long in business if we didn't demand financial responsibility from our clients. We didn't go to Harvey either. He came to us. Just like you. You don't like the deal, you're free to make another one someplace else. Just see to it that Harvey comes up with the thirty thousand dollars he owes us. Which, incidentally, will increase as of Monday."

"Oh yeah, you private-service firms seem to work on an escalated interest scale, don't you."

Macey smiled and shrugged and spread his hands. "What can I tell you, Spence? We have our methods and we attract clients. We must be doing something right." He folded his arms. "You want the guns or don't you?"

"Yes."

"Good, then we have a deal. When do you wish to take delivery? I can guarantee day after tomorrow." He checked his calendar watch. "The twenty-seventh. Sooner is iffy."

491

"The twenty-seventh is fine."

"And where do you wish to take delivery?"

"Doesn't matter. You got a spot?"

"Yes. Do you know the market terminal in Chelsea?"

"Yeah."

"There, day after tomorrow at six A.M. There are a lot of trucks loading and unloading at that time. No one will pay us any mind. Your principals have a truck?"

"Yeah."

"Okay. We've got a deal. You going to be there with your people?"

"Yeah."

"I won't be. But you should have ready for the man in charge one hundred thousand dollars in cash. Go to the restaurant there in the market center. You know where it is." I nodded. "Have a cup of coffee or whatever. You'll be contacted."

"No good," I said.

"Why not?"

"King's got to deliver them himself."

"Why?"

"My people want to do business with the principals. They don't like working through me. They might want to do more business and they want to deal direct."

"Perhaps I can go."

"No. It's gotta be King. They want to be sure they don't get burned. They figure doing business with the boss is like earnest money. If he does it himself they figure it'll go right, there won't be anything sour, like selling us ten crates of lead pipe. Or shooting us and taking the money and going away. They figure King wouldn't want to be involved in that kind of goings-on himself. Too much risk. So, King delivers personally or it's no deal."

"Mr. Powers doesn't like being told what to do," Macey said.

"Me either, but we been reasonable, and you're getting your price. He can bend on this one."

"I can assure you there will be no contrivances or

double dealing on this. This is an on-the-table, straight-ahead business deal."

"That's good to know, Macey. And I believe you 'cause I'm here looking into your sincere brown eyes but my clients, they're not here. They don't know how sincere you are and they don't trust you. Even after I mentioned how you been to college and everything."

"How about we just cancel the whole thing and fore-close on Harvey."

"We go to the cops."

"And Harvey explains why he needed all that money we advanced him?"

"Better than explaining to you people why he can't pay."

"That would be a bad mistake."

"Yeah, maybe, but it would be a bad one for you too. Even if you wasted Harvey you'd have the fuzzy-wuzzies fol-lowing you around and you'd have me mad at you and trying to get you busted and for what? All because King was too lazy to get up one morning for a six o'clock appointment?"

Macey looked at me for maybe thirty seconds.

"You don't want to maneuver me and Harv into a place where we got no options. You don't want to make the law look more attractive than you guys. You don't want to arrange something where Harv's got nothing to lose by talkin to the D.A. My people are adamant on this. They are interested in doing business with the man. And you ain't him. King is the man."

Macey said, "I'll check with him. I'm not authorized to commit him to something like this."

"You're not authorized to zip your fly without asking King. We both know that, preppy. Call him." Macey looked at me another thirty seconds. Then he got up and went into the next room.

He was gone maybe fifteen minutes. I drank my coffee and admired my Adidas Varsities, in rust-colored suede. Ex-cellent for tennis, jogging and avoiding injury through flight. I poured another cup of coffee from the room service thermos

493

pitcher. It was not hot. I left the cup on the table and went to the window and looked down at the pool. It was as blue as heaven and full of people, largely young ones, splashing and swimming and diving. A lot of flesh was darkening on beach chairs around the pool and some of it was pleasant to see. I should probably call Susan. I hadn't been back last night. Maybe she'd be worried. I should have called her last night. Hard to keep everything in my head sometimes. Pam Shepard and Harvey and Rose and Jane and King Powers and Hawk, and the New Bedford cops and getting it to work. And the tumescence. There was that to deal with too. A girl with long straight blond hair appeared from under one of the sun umbrellas wearing a bikini so brief as to seem pointless. I was looking at her closely when Macey came back into the room.

"King okayed it."

"Say, isn't that good," I said. "Not only is he a King but he's a Prince. Right, Macey?"

"He wasn't easy to persuade, Spence. You've got me to thank for this deal. He was going to have you blown away when I first told him what you wanted."

"And you saved me. Macey, you've put it all together today, kid."

"You laugh, but I'm telling you it was a near thing. This better go smooth or King'll do it. Take my word. He'll do it, Spence."

"Macey," I said. "If you call me Spence again I'll break your glasses."

CHAPTER TWENTY-FOUR

IT WAS ELEVEN-TWENTY when I got back to my motel. There was a note on the bureau. "I'm walking on the beach," it said. "Be back around lunchtime. Maybe I didn't come home all night either." I looked at my watch: 11:22. I called my service and left word for Rose to call me at the motel. At five past twelve she did.

"You know where the New England Produce Center is in Chelsea?" I said.

"No."

"I'm going to tell you, so get a pencil and write it down."

"I have one."

I told her. "When you get there," I said, "go to the restaurant and sit at the counter and have a cup of coffee. I'll be there by quarter of six."

"I want Pamela to be there as well."

"Why?"

"I'll trust you more if she's there."

"That's sort of like using a sister," I said.

"We use what we must. The cause requires it."

"Always does," I said.

"She'll be there?"

"I'll bring her with me."

"We will be there, with our part of the bargain."

"You'll need a truck."

"How large?"

"Not large, an Econoline van, something like that."

"We'll rent one. Will you help us load?"

"Yes."

"Very well. See you there." She hung up.

I wrote a note to Susan, told her I'd be back to take her to dinner, put twenty-seven X's at the bottom and replaced the one she'd written me. Then I called New Bedford. Jackie Sylvia said he and McDermott would meet me at the Bristol County Court House on County Street. They were there when I arrived, leaning on each side of a white pillar out front.

"Come on," Sylvia said when I got out of the car. "We got to talk with Linhares."

We went into the red brick courthouse, past the clerk's office, up some stairs and into an office that said ANTON LINHARES, ASST. DIST. ATT., on the door. Linhares stood, came around the desk and shook hands with me when we went in. He was medium-size and trim with a neat Afro haircut, a dark three-piece suit and a white shirt with a black and red regimental stripe tie. His shoes looked like Gucci and his suit looked like Pierre Cardin and he looked like a future D.A. His handshake was firm and he smelled of after shave lotion. Canoe I bet.

"Sit down, Spenser, good to see you. Jackie and Rich have me wired in on the case. I don't see any problem. When's it going down?"

"Day after tomorrow," I said, "at six in the morning, at the market terminal in Chelsea."

"That Suffolk or Middlesex County?"

"Suffolk," I said.

"You sure?"

"I used to work for the Suffolk County D.A. Everett's Middlesex, Chelsea's Suffolk."

"Okay, I'm going to need some cooperation from Suffolk." He looked at his wristwatch. It was big and had a luminous green face and you pressed a button to get the time displayed in digits. "That's no sweat," he said. "I'll get Jim Clancy on the horn up there. He'll go along."

He leaned back in his swivel chair, cocked one foot up on a slightly open drawer and looked at me. "What's the setup?" he said. I told him.

496

"So we set up around there ahead of time," Sylvia said, "and when they are in the middle of the transaction . . ." He raised an open hand and clamped it shut.

Linhares nodded. "Right. We've got them no matter what part of the swap they're in. One of them will have stolen money and the others will have stolen guns. I want to be there. I want part of this one."

McDermott said. "We thought you might, Anton."

Linhares smiled without irritation. "I didn't take this job to stay in it all my life."

Sylvia said, "Yeah, but let's make sure this doesn't get leaked to the press before it happens."

Linhares grinned again. "Gentlemen," he said. He shook his head in friendly despair. "Gentlemen. How unkind."

"Sylvia's right," I said. "These are very careful people. King Powers by habit. Rose and Jane by temperament. They'll be very skittish."

"Fair enough," Linhares said. "Now what about your people. How you want to handle that?"

"I want them not to exist," I said. "They can be referred to as two anonymous undercover operatives whose identity must be protected. Me too. If my name gets into this it may drag theirs in with it. They're both clients."

Linhares said, "I'll need the names. Not to prosecute but to bury. If they get scooped up in the net I've got to know who to let go."

I told him. "They're related?" he said.

"Yeah, husband and wife."

"And you put this thing together for them?"

"Yeah."

"How'd Suffolk ever let you get away?"

"Hard to figure," I said.

"Okay." Linhares looked at his watch again. He liked pushing the button. "Jackie, you and Rich get up there tomorrow with Spenser here and set this thing up. I'll call Jimmy Clancy and have him waiting for you."

"We gotta check with the squad," McDermott said.

"I'll take care of that," Linhares said. "I'll call Sergeant Cruz and have you assigned to me for a couple of days. Manny and I are buddies. He'll go along. You get hold of Bobby Santos, he'll go up with you tomorrow so he can brief me for the bust." He reached over and punched an intercom on his phone and said into it, "Peggy, get me Jimmy Clancy up in the Suffolk D.A.'s office." With one hand over the mouthpiece he said to me, "Good seeing you, Spenser. Nice job on this one." And to Sylvia and McDermott, "You, too, guys, nice job all around."

He took his hand away and said into the phone, "Jimmy, Anton Linhares. I got a live one for you, kid." We got up and went out.

"Who's this Santos?" I said to Jackie Sylvia.

"State dick, works out of this office. He's okay. Wants to be public safety commissioner, but what the hell, nothing wrong with ambition. Right Rich?"

"I don't know," McDermott said. "I never had any. You want to ride up with us tomorrow, Spenser, or you want to meet us there?"

"I'll meet you there," I said. "In Clancy's office. About ten."

"Catch you then," Sylvia said. We reached my car. There was a parking ticket under the windshield wiper. I took it out and slipped it into the breast pocket of Sylvia's maroon blazer. "Show me the kind of clout you got around here," I said. "Fix that." I got in the car. As I pulled away Sylvia took the ticket out of his pocket and tore it in two. As I pulled around the corner on County Street he was giving half to McDermott.

I was into the maze again and on my first pass at the Fairhaven Bridge I ended up going out Acushnet Street parallel to the river. There was a parking lot by the unemployment office and I pulled in to turn around. There was a long line at the unemployment office and a man with a pushcart and a striped umbrella was selling hot dogs, soft drinks, popcorn and peanuts. Festive.

I made the bridge on my second try, and headed back

down the Cape. The sun was at my back now and ahead was maybe a swim, some tennis and supper. I hoped Susan hadn't eaten. It was five-twenty when I got back to the motel. I spotted Susan's Nova in the lot. When I unlocked the door to the room she was there. Sitting in front of the mirror with a piece of Kleenex in her hand, her hair up in big rollers, a lot of cream on her face, wearing a flowered robe and unlaced sneakers.

"Arrrgh," I said.

"You weren't supposed to be back yet," she said, wiping at some of the cream with her Kleenex.

"Never mind that shit, lady," I said, "what have you done with Susan Silverman?"

"It's time you knew, sweetie, this is the real me."

"Heavens," I said.

"Does this mean it's over?"

"No, but tell me the fake you will reappear in a while."

"Twenty minutes," she said, "I've made us reservations at the Coonamessett Inn for seven."

"How about a swim first and then some tennis, or vice versa."

"No. I just washed my hair. I don't want to get it wet and sweaty. Or vice versa. Why don't you swim while I conceal the real me. Then we can have a drink and a leisurely drive to the inn and you can explain yourself and where the hell you've been and what you've been doing and with or to whom, and that sort of thing."

I swam for a half-hour. The pool was only about fifty feet long so I did a lot of turns, but it was a nice little workout and I went back to the room with the blood moving in my veins. Susan didn't do anything to slow it down. The hair was unrolled and the robe and cream had disappeared. And she was wearing a pale sleeveless dress the color of an eggshell, and jade earrings. She was putting her lipstick on when I came in, leaning close to the mirror to make sure it was right.

I took a shower and shaved and brushed my teeth with a fluoride toothpaste that tasted like Christmas candy. I put on my dark blue summer suit with brass buttons on the coat and vest, a pale blue oxford button-down shirt and a white tie with blue and gold stripes. Dark socks, black tassel loafers. I checked myself in the mirror. Clear-eyed, and splendid. I clipped my gun on under my coat. I really ought to get a dress gun sometime. A pearl handle perhaps, in a patent leather holster.

"Stay close to me," I said to Susan on the way out to the car. "The Hyannis Women's Club may try to kidnap me and treat me as a sex object."

Susan put her arm through mine. "Death before dishonor," she said.

In the car Susan put a kerchief over her hair and I drove slowly with the top down to the inn. We had a Margarita in the bar and got a table by the window where you could look out on the lake.

We had a second Margarita while we looked at the menu. "No beer?" Susan asked.

"Didn't seem to go with the mood or the occasion," I said. "I'll have some with dinner."

I ordered raw oysters and lobster thermidor. Susan chose oysters and baked stuffed lobster.

"It's all falling into place, Suze," I said. "I think I can do it."

"I hope so," she said. "Have you seen Pam Shepard?"

"Last night."

"Oh?"

"Yeah, I slept in my apartment last night."

"Oh? How is she?"

"Oh, nowhere near as good as you," I said.

"I don't mean that. I mean how is her state of mind."

"Okay, I think you should talk with her. She's screwed up pretty good, and I think she needs some kind of therapy."

"Why? You made a pass at her and she turned you down?"

"Just talk with her. I figure you can direct her someplace good. She and her husband can't agree on what she ought to be and she feels a lot of guilt about that."

Susan nodded. "Of course I'll talk with her. When?"

"After this is over, day after tomorrow it should be."

"I'll be glad to."

"I didn't make a pass at her."

"I didn't ask," Susan said.

"It was a funny scene though. I mean we talked about it a lot. She's not a fool, but she's misled, maybe unadult, it's hard to put my finger on it. She believes some very destructive things. What's that Frost line, 'He will not go behind his father's saying'?"

" 'Mending Wall,' " Susan said.

"Yeah, she's like that, like she never went beyond her mother's sayings, or her father's and when they didn't work she still didn't go beyond them. She just found someone with a new set of sayings, and never went beyond them."

"Rose and Jane?" Susan said.

"You have a fine memory," I said. "It helps make up for your real appearance."

"There's a lot of women like that. I see a lot of them at school, and a lot of them at school parties. Wives of teachers and principals. I see a lot of them coming in with their daughters and I see a lot of daughters that will grow into that kind of woman."

"Frost was writing about a guy," I said.

"Yes, I know. I see." The waitress brought our oysters. "It's not just women, is it."

"No, ma'am. Old Harv is just as bad, just as far into the sayings of his father and just as blind to what's beyond them as Pam is."

"Doesn't he need therapy too?"

The oysters were outstanding. Very fresh, very young. "Yeah, I imagine. But I think she might be brighter, and have more guts. I don't think he's got the guts for therapy. Maybe not the brains either. But I've only seen him under stress. Maybe he's better than he looks," I said. "He loves her. Loves the crap out of her."

"Maybe that's just another saying of his father's that he can't go behind."

"Maybe everything's a saying. Maybe there isn't anything but saying. You have to believe in something. Loving the crap out of someone isn't the worst one."

"Ah, you sweet talker you," Susan said. "How elegantly you put it. Do you love the crap out of anyone?"

"You got it, sweetheart," I said.

"Is that your Bogart impression again?"

"Yeah, I work on it in the car mirror driving back and forth between here and Boston and New Bedford."

The oysters departed and the lobster came. While we worked on it I told Susan everything we had set up for next day. Few people can match Susan Silverman for lobster eating. She leaves no claw uncracked, no crevice unpried. And all the while she doesn't get any on her and she doesn't look savage.

I tend to hurt myself when I attack a baked stuffed lobster. So I normally get thermidor, or salad, or stew or whatever they offered that had been shelled for me.

When I got through talking Susan said, "It's hard to keep it all in your head, isn't it. So many things depend on so many other things. So much is unresolved and will remain so unless everything goes in sequence."

"Yeah, it's nervous-making."

"You don't seem nervous."

"It's what I do," I said. "I'm good at it. It'll probably work."

"And if it doesn't."

"Then it's a mess and I'll have to think of something else. But I've done what I can. I try not to worry about things I can't control."

"And you assume if it breaks you can fix it, don't you?"

"I guess so. Something like that. I've always been able to do most of what I needed to do."

We each had a very good wild blueberry tart for dessert and retired to the bar for Irish coffee. On the ride back to the motel, Susan put her head back against the seat without the kerchief and let her hair blow about.

"Want to go look at the ocean," I said. "Yes," she said.

I drove down Sea Street to the beach and parked in

the lot. It was late and there was no one there. Susan left her shoes in the car and we walked along the sand in the bright darkness with the ocean rolling in gently to our left. I took her hand and we walked in silence. Off somewhere to the right, inland, someone was playing an old Tommy Dorsey album and a vocal group was singing "Once in a while." The sound in the late stillness drifted out across the water. Quaint and sort of old-fashioned now, and familiar.

"Want to swim," I said.

We dropped our clothes in a heap on the beach and went into the ebony water and swam beside each other parallel to the shore perhaps a quarter of a mile. Susan was a strong swimmer and I didn't have to slow down for her. I dropped back slightly so I could watch the white movement of her arms and shoulders as they sliced almost soundlessly through the water. We could still hear the stereo. A boy singer was doing "East of the Sun and West of the Moon" with a male vocal group for backing. Ahead of me Susan stopped and stood breast deep in the water. I stopped beside her and put my arms around her slick body. She was breathing deeply, though not badly out of breath, and I could feel her heart beating strongly against my chest. She kissed me and the salt taste of ocean mixed with the sweet taste of her lipstick. She pulled her head back and looked up at me with her hair plastered tight against her scalp. And the beads of sea water glistening on her face. Her teeth seemed very shiny to me, up close like that when she smiled.

"In the water?" she said.

"Never tried it in the water," I said. My voice was hoarse again.

"I'll drown," she said and turned and dove toward the shore. I plunged after her and caught her at the tidal margin and we lay in the wet sand and made love while Frank Sinatra and the Pied Pipers sang "There Are Such Things" and the waves washed about our legs. By the time we had finished the late-night listener had put on an Artie Shaw album and we were listening to "Dancing in the Dark." We were motionless for a bit, letting the waves flow over us. The tide seemed to be coming in. A wave larger than the ones before it broke over us, and for a moment we were underwater. We came up, both of us blowing water from our mouths, and looked at each other and began to laugh. "Deborah Kerr," I said.

"Burt Lancaster," she said.

"From here to eternity," I said.

"That far, at least," she said. And we snuggled in the wet sand with the sea breaking over us until our teeth began to chatter.

CHAPTER TWENTY-FIVE

WE GOT DRESSED and went back to the motel and took a long hot shower together and ordered a bottle of Burgundy from room service and got into bed and sipped the wine and watched the late movie, *Fort Apache,* one of my favorites, and fell asleep.

In the morning we had breakfast in the room and when I left for Boston about eight-thirty, Susan was still in bed, drinking a cup of coffee and watching the *Today* program.

The Suffolk County Court House in Pemberton Square is a very large gray building that's hard to see because it's halfway up the east flank of Beacon Hill and the new Government Center buildings shield it from what I still call Bowdoin Square and Scollay Square. I parked down in Bowdoin Square in front of the Saltonstall State Office Building and walked up the hill to the courthouse.

Jim Clancy had an Errol Flynn mustache, and it looked funny because his face was round and shiny and his light hair had receded hastily from his forehead. Sylvia and McDermott were there already, along with a guy who looked like Ricardo Montalban and one who looked like a Fed. McDermott introduced me. Ricardo turned out in fact to be Bobby Santos who might someday be public safety commissioner. The Fed turned out to be a man named Klaus from Treasury.

"We'll meet some people from Chelsea over there," McDermott said. "We've already filled Bobby in, and we're about to brief these gentlemen."

McDermott was wearing a green T-shirt today, with a pocket over the left breast, and gray corduroy pants, and sandals. His gun was stuck in his belt under the T-shirt, just above his belt buckle, and bulged like a prosthetic device. Klaus, in a Palm Beach suit, white broadcloth shirt and polka dot bow tie, looked at him like a virus. He spoke to Sylvia.

"What's Spenser's role in this?"

Sylvia said, "Why not ask him?"

"I'm asking you," Klaus said.

Sylvia looked at McDermott and raised his eyebrows. McDermott said, "Good heavens."

"Did I ever explain to you," Sylvia said to McDermott, "why faggots wear bow ties?"

I said to Klaus, "I'm the guy set it up. I'm the one knows the people and I'm the one that supervises the swap. I'm what you might call your key man."

Clancy said, "Go ahead, McDermott. Lay it out for us, we want to get the arrangements set."

McDermott lit a miserable-looking cigarette from the pack he kept in the pocket of his T-shirt.

"Well," he said, "me and Jackie was sitting around the squad room one day, thinking about crime and stuff, it was kind of a slow day, and here comes this key man here."

Klaus said, "For crissake, get on with it."

Santos said, "Rich."

McDermott said, "Yeah, yeah, okay, Bobby. I just don't want to go too fast for the G-man."

"Say it all, Rich," Santos said.

He did. The plan called for two vans, produce trucks, with Sylvia, McDermott, Santos, Linhares, Klaus and several Chelsea cops and two Staties from Clancy's staff to arrive in the area about five-thirty, park at a couple of unloading docks, one on one side and one on the other side of the restaurant, and await developments. When the time was right I'd signal by putting both hands in my hip pockets, and "Like locusts," McDermott said, "me and Jackie and J. Edgar over here will be on 'em."

Clancy opened a manila folder on his desk and handed around 8 × 10 glossy mug shots of King Powers. "That's Powers," Clancy said. "We have him on file."

"The two women," I said, "I'll have to describe." And I did. Klaus took notes, Sylvia cleaned his fingers with the small blade of a pocketknife. The others just sat and looked at me. When I got through, Klaus said, "Good descriptions, Spenser."

McDermott and Sylvia looked at each other. Tomorrow it would be good if they were in one truck and Klaus was in another.

Clancy said, "Okay, any questions."

Santos said, "Warrants?"

Clancy said, "That's in the works, we'll have them ready for tomorrow."

Santos said, "How about entrapment."

"What entrapment," Sylvia said. "We got a tip from an informant that an illegal gun sale was going down, we staked it out and we were lucky."

Clancy nodded. "It should be clean, all we're arranging is the stakeout. We had nothing to do with Spenser double-crossing them."

"One of my people's going to be there, Pam Shepard. You'll probably have to pick her up. If you do, keep her separate from the others and give her to me as soon as the others are taken away."

"Who in hell are you talking to, Spenser," Klaus said. "You sound like you're in charge of the operation."

506

McDermott said, "Operation, Jackie. That's what we're in, an operation."

Clancy said, "We agreed, Clyde. We trade the broad and her husband for Powers and the libbers."

"Clyde?" Sylvia said to McDermott.

"Clyde Klaus?" McDermott's face was beautiful with pleasure.

Klaus's face flushed slightly.

"Clyde Klaus." McDermott and Sylvia spoke in unison, their voices breaking on the very edge of a giggle.

Santos said, "You two clowns wanna knock off the horseshit. We got serious work to do here. Cruz got you detached to me on this thing, you know. You listen to what I tell you."

Sylvia and McDermott forced their faces into solemnity behind which the giggles still smirked.

"Anything else?" Clancy said. He turned his head in a half circle, covering all of us, one at a time. "Okay, let's go look at the site."

"I'll skip that one," I said. "I'll take a look at it later. But if any of the bad persons got it under what Klaus would call surveillance I don't want to be spotted with a group of strange, fuzzy-looking men."

"And if they see you looking it over on your own," Santos said, "they'll assume you're just careful. Like they are. Yeah. Good idea."

"You know the place?" Clancy said.

"Yeah."

"Okay, the Chelsea people are going to be under command of a lieutenant named Kaplan if you want to check on something over there."

I nodded. "Thanks, Clancy, nice to have met you gentlemen. See you tomorrow." I went out of Clancy's office. With the door ajar I reached back in with my right hand, gave it the thumbs-up gesture and said, "Good hunting, Clyde," and left. Behind me I could hear Sylvia and McDermott giggling again, now openly. Klaus said, "Listen," as I closed the door.

Outside I bought two hot dogs and a bottle of cream

soda from a street vendor and ate sitting by the fountain in City Hall Plaza. A lot of women employed in the Government Center buildings were lunching also on the plaza and I ranked them in the order of general desirability. I was down to sixteenth when my lunch was finished and I had to go to work. I'd have ranked the top twenty-five in that time normally, but there was a three-way tie for seventh and I lost a great deal of time trying to resolve it.

Chelsea is a shabby town, beloved by its residents, across the Mystic River from Boston. There was a scatter of junk dealers, rag merchants and wholesale tire outlets, a large weedy open area where a huge fire had swallowed half the city, leaving what must be the world's largest vacant lot. On the northwest edge of the city where it abuts Everett is the New England Produce Center, one of two big market terminals on the fringes of Boston that funnel most of the food into the city. It was an ungainly place, next door to the Everett oil farm, but it sports a restaurant housed in an old railroad car. I pulled my car in by the restaurant and went in. It bothered me a little, as I sat at the counter and looked out at it, that my car seemed to integrate so aptly with the surroundings.

I had a piece of custard pie and a cup of black coffee and looked things over. It was a largely idle gesture. There was no way I could know where the swap would take place. There wasn't a hell of a lot for me to gain by surveying the scene. I had to depend on the buttons to show up, like they would when I put my hands in my hip pockets.

The restaurant wasn't very busy, more empty than full, and I glanced around to see if anyone was casing me. Or looked suspicious. No one was polishing a machine gun, no one was picking his teeth with a switchblade, no one was paying me any attention at all. I was used to it. I sometimes went days when people paid no attention to me at all. The bottom crust on my custard pie was soggy. I paid the bill and left.

I drove back into Boston through Everett and Charlestown. The elevated had been dismantled in Charlestown and

City Square looked strangely naked and vulnerable without it. Like someone without his accustomed eyeglasses. They could have left it up and hung plants from it.

For reasons that have never been clear to me the midday traffic in Boston is as bad as the commuter traffic and it took me nearly thirty-five minutes to get to my apartment. Pam Shepard let me in looking neat but stir-crazy.

"I was just having a cup of soup," she said. "Want some?"

"I ate lunch," I said, "but I'll sit with you and have a cup of coffee while you eat. We're going to have to spend another night together."

"And?"

"And then I think we'll have it whipped. Then I think you can go home."

We sat at my counter and she had her tomato soup and I had a cup of instant coffee.

"Home," she said. "My God, that seems so far away."

"Homesick?"

"Oh, yes, very much. But . . . I don't know. I don't know about going home. I mean, what has changed since I left."

"I don't know. I guess you'll have to go home and find out. Maybe nothing has changed. But tomorrow Rose and Jane are going to be in the jug and you can't sleep here forever. My restraint is not limitless."

She smiled. "It's kind of you to say so."

"After tomorrow we can talk about it. I won't kick you out."

"What happens tomorrow?"

"We do it," I said. "We go over to the Chelsea Market about six in the morning and we set up the gun sale and when it is what you might call consummated, the cops come with the net and you and Harv get another crack at it."

"Why do I have to go? I don't mean I won't, or shouldn't, but what good will I do?"

"You're kind of a hostage . . . Rose figures if you're

implicated too, I won't double-cross them. She doesn't trust me, but she knows I'm looking out for you."

"You mean if she gets arrested, I'll get arrested too?"

"That seems her theory. I told her that didn't seem sisterly. She said something about the cause."

"Jesus Christ, maybe you are the only person I can depend on."

I shrugged.

CHAPTER TWENTY-SIX

IT WAS RAINING like hell and still dark when I woke up with a crick in my neck on the sofa in my living room. I shut off the alarm and dragged myself out of bed. It was quarter of five. I took a shower, and got dressed before I banged on my bedroom door, at five o'clock.

Pam Shepard said, "I'm awake."

She came out of the bedroom wearing my bathrobe and looking her age and went into the bathroom. I checked my gun. I stood in my front window and looked down at Marlborough Street and at the rain circles forming in the wet street. I thought about making coffee and decided we wouldn't have time and we could get some in the railroad car. I got out my red warm-up jacket that said LOWELL CHIEFS on it and put it on. I tried getting the gun off my hip while wearing it, and I left it unbuttoned. It wasn't bad. At five-twenty Pam Shepard came out of the bathroom with her hair combed and her make-up on and my robe still folded around her, and went back into my bedroom and shut the door. I took my car keys out of my hip pocket and put them in my coat pocket. I went to the window and looked at the rain some more. It always excited me when it rained. The wet streets seemed more promising than the dry ones, and the city was quieter. At five-thirty Pam Shepard came out of my bedroom wearing yellow slacks and a chocolate-colored blouse with long lapels. She put on a powder blue slicker and a wide-brimmed rain hat that matched and said, "I'm ready."

"The wardrobe for every occasion," I said. "I have the feeling you had Susan buy you a safari hat just in case you had to shoot tiger while you stayed here."

She smiled but there wasn't much oomph in it. She was scared.

"This is going to be a milk run," I said. "There will be more cops than fruit flies there. And me, I will be right with you."

We went down the front stairs and got in my car and it started and we were off.

"I know," she said. "I know it'll be all right. There's just been so much, and now this. Police and gangsters and it's early in the morning and raining and so much depends on this."

"You and me babe," I said, "we'll be fine." I patted her leg. It was a gesture my father used to make. It combined, when he did it, affection and reassurance. It didn't seem to do a hell of a lot for Pam Shepard. At twelve minutes of six in the morning we pulled into the restaurant parking lot. It was daylight now, but a gray and dismal daylight, cold as hell, for summer, and the warm yellow of the lighted windows in the railroad car looked good. There were a lot of trucks and cars parked. The terminal does its work very early. I assumed that two of the trucks contained our side but there was no telling which ones.

Inside we sat in a booth and ordered two coffees and two English muffins. Pam didn't eat hers. At about two minutes past six King Powers came in wearing a trench coat and a plaid golf cap. Macey was with him in a London Fog, and outside in the entryway I could see Hawk in what looked like a white leather cape with a hood.

"Good morning, Kingo-babe," I said. "Care for a cup of java? English muffin? I think my date's not going to eat hers."

Powers sat down and looked at Pam Shepard. "This the buyer," he said.

"One of them. The ones with the bread haven't shown up yet."

"They fucking better show up," King said. Macey sat in the booth beside Powers.

"That's a most fetching hat, King," I said. "I remember my Aunt Bertha used to wear one very much like it on rainy days. Said you get your head wet you got the miseries."

Powers paid no attention to me. "I say fucking six o'clock I mean fucking six o'clock. I don't mean five after. You know what I'm saying."

Rose and Jane came into the restaurant.

"Speak of coincidence, King," I said. "There they are."

I gestured toward Rose and Jane and pointed outside. They turned and left. "Let us join them," I said, "outside where fewer people will stand around and listen to us."

Powers got up, Macey went right after him and Pam and I followed along. As we went out the door I looked closely at Hawk. It was a white leather cape. With a hood. Hawk said, "Pow'ful nice mawning, ain't it, boss."

I said, "Mind if I rub your head for luck?"

I could see Hawk's shoulders moving with silent laughter. He drifted along behind me. In the parking lot I said, "King, Macey, Hawk, Rose, Jane, Pam. There now, we're all introduced, let us get it done."

Powers said, "You got the money?"

Jane showed him a shopping bag she was carrying under her black rubber raincoat.

"Macey, take it to the truck and count it."

Rose said, "How do we know he won't run off with it?"

Powers said, "Jesus Christ, sister, what's wrong with you?"

Rose said, "We want to see the guns."

"They're in the back of the truck," Macey said. "We'll

get in and you can look at the guns while I count the money. That way we don't waste time and we both are assured."

Powers said, "Good. You do that. I'm getting out of the fucking rain. Hawk, you and Macey help them load the pieces when Macey's satisfied."

Powers got up in the cab of a yellow Ryder Rental Truck and closed the door. Rose and Jane and Macey went to the back of the truck. Macey opened the door and the three of them climbed in. Hawk and I and Pam Shepard stood in the rain. In about one minute Rose leaned out of the back of the truck.

"Spenser," she said, "would you check this equipment for us?"

I said to Pam, "You stand right there. I'll be right back." Hawk was motionless beside her, leaning against the front fender of the truck. I went around back and climbed in. The guns were there. Still in the original cases. M2 carbines. I checked two or three. "Yeah," I said, "they're good. You can waste platoons of old men now."

Rose ignored me. "All right, Jane bring the truck over here. Spenser, you said you'd help us load the truck."

"Yes, ma'am," I said. "Me and Hawk."

Macey took the shopping bag that said FILENE'S on it, jumped down and went around to where Powers sat in the cab. He handed the money in to Powers and came back to the tailgate. "What do you think, Spenser. This okay to make the swap."

We were to the side of and nearly behind the restaurant. "Sure," I said. "This looks fine. Nobody around. Nobody pays any attention anyway. They load and unload all day around here."

Macey nodded. Jane backed in a blue Ford Econoline van, parked it tail to tail with Powers' truck, got out and opened the back doors. I went back to the front of the truck where Pam and Hawk were standing. "Hawk," I said softly, "the cops are coming. This is a setup." Macey and Rose and Jane were conspiring to move one case of guns from the truck to the van. "Hawk," Macey yelled, "you and Spenser want to give us a hand." Hawk walked silently around the front of the truck behind the restaurant and disappeared. I put my hands in my hip pockets. "Stay right beside me," I said to Pam Shepard.

From a truck that said ROLLIE'S PRODUCE Sylvia and McDermott and two state cops emerged with shotguns.

Jane screamed, "Rose," and dropped her end of the crate. She fumbled in the pocket of her raincoat and came out with a gun. Sylvia chopped it out of her hand with the barrel of the shotgun and she doubled over, clutching her arm against her. Rose said, "Jane," and put her arms around her. Macey dodged around the end of the van and ran into the muzzle of Bobby Santos' service revolver, which Santos pressed firmly into Macey's neck. King Powers never moved. Klaus and three Chelsea cops came around the other side of the truck and opened the door. One of the Chelsea cops, a fat guy with a boozer's nose, reached in and yanked him out by the coat front. Powers said nothing and did nothing except look at me.

I said to King, "Peekaboo, I see you," nodded at Jackie Sylvia, took Pam Shepard's hand and walked away. At seven we were in a deli on Tremont Street eating hash and eggs and toasted bagels and cream cheese and looking at the rain on the Common across the street.

"Why did you warn that black man?" Pam Shepard said, putting cream cheese on her bagel. She had skipped the hash and eggs, which showed you what she knew about breakfasts. The waitress came and poured more coffee in both our cups.

"I don't know. I've known him a long time. He was a fighter when I was. We used to train together sometimes."

"But isn't he one of them? I mean isn't he the, what, the muscle man, the enforcer, for those people?"

"Yeah."

"Doesn't that make a difference? I mean you just let him go."

"I've known him a long time," I said.

CHAPTER TWENTY-SEVEN

IT WAS STILL RAINING when we drove back to my apartment to get Pam's things, and it was still raining when we set out at about eight-thirty for Hyannis. There's an FM station in Boston that plays jazz from six in the morning until eleven. I turned it on. Carmen McRae was singing "Skyliner." The rain had settled in and came steadily against the windshield as if it planned to stay awhile. My roof leaked in one corner and dripped on the back seat.

Pam Shepard sat quietly and looked out the side window of the car. The Carmen McRae record was replaced by an album of Lee Wiley singing with Bobby Hackett's cornet and Joe Bushkin's piano. Sweet Bird of Youth. There wasn't much traffic on Route 3. Nobody much went to the Cape on a rainy midweek morning.

"When I was a little kid," I said, "I used to love to ride in the rain, in a car. It always seemed so self-contained, so private." There we were in the warm car with the music playing, and the rest of the world was out in the rain getting wet and shivering. "Still like it, in fact."

Pam Shepard kept looking out the side window. "Is it over, do you think?" she said.

"What?"

"Everything. The bank robbery, the trouble Harvey is in, the hiding out and being scared? The feeling so awful?"

"I think so," I said.

"What is going to happen to Harvey and me?"

"Depends, I guess. I think you and he can make it work better than it has worked."

"Why?"

"Love. There's love in the relationship."

"Shit," she said.

"Not shit," I said. "Love doesn't solve everything and it isn't the only thing that's important, but it has a big head start on everything else. If there's love, then there's a place to begin."

"That's romantic goo," Pam Shepard said. "Believe me. Harvey's preached the gospel of love at me for nearly twenty years. It's crap. Believe me, I know."

"No, you don't know. You've had a bad experience, so you think it's the only experience. You're just as wrong as Harvey. It didn't work, doesn't mean it won't work. You're intelligent, and you've got guts. You can do therapy. Maybe you can get Harv to do it. Maybe when you've gotten through talking about yourself with someone intelligent you'll decide to roll Harv anyway. But it'll be for the right reasons, not because you think you're frigid, or he thinks you're frigid. And if you decide to roll Harv you'll have some alternatives beside screwing sweaty drunks in one night cheap hotels, or living in a feminist commune with two cuckoos."

"Is it that ugly," she said.

"Of course it's that ugly. You don't screw people to prove things. You screw people because you like the screwing or the people or both. Preferably the last. Some people even refer to it as making love."

"I know," she said, "I know."

"And the two dimwits you took up with. They're theoreticians. They have nothing much to do with life. They have little connection with phallic power and patterns of dominance and blowing away old men in the service of things like that."

She stopped looking out the window and looked at me. "Why so angry," she said.

"I don't know exactly. Thoreau said something once about judging the cost of things in terms of how much life he had to expend to get it. You and Harv aren't getting your money's worth. Thrift, I guess. It violates my sense of thrift."

516

She laughed a little bit and shook her head. "My God, I like you," she said. "I like you very much."

"It was only a matter of time," I said.

She looked back out the window and we were quiet most of the rest of the drive down. I hadn't said it right. Maybe Suze could. Maybe nobody could. Maybe saying didn't have much effect anyway.

We got to the motel a little after ten and found Susan in the coffee shop drinking coffee and reading the *New York Times.*

"Was it okay," Susan said.

"Yeah, just the way it should have been."

"He warned one of them," Pam Shepard said. "And he got away."

Susan raised her eyebrows at me.

"Hawk," I said.

"Do you understand that," Pam Shepard said.

"Maybe," Susan said.

"I don't."

"And I'll bet he didn't give you a suitable explanation, did he?" Susan said.

"Hardly," Pam said.

"Everything else was good though?" Susan said.

I nodded.

"Are you going home, Pam?"

"I guess I am. I haven't really faced that, even driving down. But here I am, half a mile from my house. I guess I am going home."

"Good."

"I'm going to call Harv," I said. "How about I ask him to join us and we can talk about everything and maybe Suze can talk a little."

"Yes," she said. "I'm scared to see him again. I'd like to see him with you here and without the children."

I went back to the room and called Shepard and told him what had happened. It took him ten minutes to arrive. I met him in the lobby.

"Is Powers in jail?" he said.

517

I looked at my watch. "No, probably not. They've booked him by now, and his lawyer is there arranging bail and King's sitting around in the anteroom waiting to go home."

"Jesus Christ," Shepard said. "You mean he's going to be out loose knowing we set him up?"

"Life's hard sometimes," I said.

"But, for crissake, won't he come looking for us? You didn't tell me they'd let him out on bail. He'll be after us. He'll know we double-crossed him. He'll be coming."

"If I'd told you, you wouldn't have done it. He won't come after you."

"What the hell is wrong with them, letting him out on bail. You got no right to screw around with my life like that."

"He won't come after you, Shepard. Your wife's waiting for you in the coffee shop."

"Jesus, how is she?"

"She's fine."

"No, I mean, like what's her frame of mind? I mean, what's she been saying about me? Did she say she's going to come back?"

"She's in the coffee shop with my friend Susan Silverman. She wants to see you and she wants us to be there and what she's going to do is something you and she will decide. She's planning, right now, I think, to stay. Don't screw it up."

Shepard took a big inhale and let it out through his nose. We went into the coffee shop. Susan and Pam Shepard were sitting opposite each other in a booth. I slid in beside Susan. Shepard stood and looked down at Pam Shepard. She looked up at him and said, "Hello, Harv."

"Hello, Pam."

"Sit down, Harv," she said. He sat, beside her. "How have you been?" she said.

He nodded his head. He was looking at his hands, close together on the table before him.

"Kids okay?"

He nodded again. He put his right hand out and rested it on her back between the shoulder blades, the fingers spread. His eyes were watery and when he spoke his voice was very thick. "You coming back?"

She nodded. "For now," she said and there was strain now in her voice too.

"Forever," he said.

"For now, anyway," she said.

His hand was moving in a slow circle between her shoulder blades. His face was wet now. "Whatever you want," he said in his squeezed voice. "Whatever you want. I'll get you anything you want, we can start over and I'll be back up on top for you in a year. Anything. Anything you want."

"It's not up on top I want, Harvey." I felt like a voyeur. "It's, it's different. They think we need psychiatric help." She nodded toward me and Suze.

"What do they know about it or us, or anything?"

"I won't stay if we don't get help, Harvey. We're not just unhappy. We're sick. We need to be cured."

"Who do we go to? I don't even know any shrinks."

"Susan will tell us," Pam said. "She knows about these things."

"If that's what will bring you back, that's what I'll do." His voice was easing a little, but the tears were still running down his face. He kept rubbing her back in the little circles. "Whatever you want."

I stood up. "You folks are going to make it. And while you are, I'm going to make a call."

They paid me very little heed and I left feeling about as useful as a faucet on a clock. Back in the room I called Clancy in the Suffolk County D.A.'s office.

"Spenser," I said when he came on. "Powers out of the calaboose yet?"

"Lemme check."

I listened to the vague sounds that a telephone makes on hold for maybe three minutes. Then Clancy came back on. "Yep."

"Dandy," I said.

"You knew he would be," Clancy said. "You know the score."

"Yeah, thanks." I hung up.

Back in the coffee shop Pam was saying, "It's too heavy. It's too heavy to carry the weight of being the center of everybody's life."

The waitress brought me another cup of coffee.

"Well, what are we supposed to do," Harv said. "Not love you. I tell the kids, knock it off on the love. It's too much for your mother? Is that what we do?"

Pam Shepard shook her head. "It's just . . . no of course, I want to be loved, but it's being the *only* thing you love, and the kids, being so central, feeling all that . . . I don't know . . . responsibility, maybe, I want to scream and run."

"Boy"—Harv shook his head—"I wish I had that problem, having somebody love me too much. I'd trade you in a goddamned second."

"No you wouldn't."

"Yeah, well, I wouldn't be taking off on you either. I don't even know where you been. You know where I been."

"And what you've been doing," she said. "You goddamned fool."

Harv looked at me. "You bastard, Spenser, you told her."

"I had to," I said.

"Well, I was doing it for you and the kids. I mean, what kind of man would I be if I let it all go down the freaking tube and you and the kids had shit? What kind of a man is that?"

"See," Pam said. "See, it's always me, always my responsibility. Everything you do is for me."

"Bullshit. I do what a man's supposed to do. There's nothing peculiar about a man looking out for the family. Dedicating his life to his family. That's not peculiar. That's right."

"Submerging your own ego to that extent is unusual," Susan said.

"Meaning what?"

Shepard's voice had lost its strangled quality and had gotten tinny. He spoke too loudly for the room.

"Don't yell at Suze, Harv," I said.

"I'm not yelling, but I mean, Christ, Spenser, she's telling me that dedication and self-sacrifice is a sign of being sick."

"No she's not, Harv. She's asking you to think why you can't do anything in your own interest. Why you have to perceive it in terms of self-sacrifice."

"I, I don't perceive . . . I mean I can do things I want to . . . for myself."

"Like what?" I said.

"Well, shit, I . . . Well, I want money too, and good things for the family . . . and . . . aw, bullshit. Whose side are you on in this?"

Pam Shepard put her face in her hands. "Oh God," she said. "Oh God, Jesus goddamned Christ," she said.

CHAPTER TWENTY-EIGHT

THE SHEPARDS WENT HOME after a while, uneasy, uncertain, but in the same car with the promise that Susan and I would join them for dinner that night. The rain stopped and the sun came out. Susan and I went down to Sea Street beach and swam and lay on the beach. I listened to the Sox play the Indians on a little red Panasonic portable that Susan had given me for my birthday. Susan read Erikson and the wind blew very gently off Nantucket Sound. I wondered when Powers would show up. Nothing much to do about that. When he showed he'd show. There was no way to prepare for it.

The Sox lost to Cleveland and a disc jockey came on and started to play "Fly Robin Fly."

I shut off the radio.

"You think they'll make it?" I said.

Susan shrugged. "He's not encouraging, is he?"

"No, but he loves her."

"I know." She paused. "Think we'll make it?"

"Yeah. We already have."

"Have we?"

"Yeah."

"That means that the status remains quo?"

"Nope."

"What does it mean?"

"Means I'm going to propose marriage."

Susan closed her book. She looked at me without saying anything. And she smiled. "Are you really?" she said.

"Yeah."

"Was that it?"

"I guess it was, would you care to marry me?"

She was quiet. The water on the sound was quiet. Easy swells looking green and deep rolled in quietly toward us and broke gently onto the beach.

Susan said, "I don't know."

"I was under a different impression," I said.

"So was I."

"I was under the impression that you wanted to marry me and were angry that I had not yet asked."

"That was the impression I was under too," Susan said. "Songs unheard are sweeter far," I said.

"No, it's not that, availability makes you no less lovable. It's . . . I don't know. Isn't that amazing. I think I wanted the assurance of your asking more than I wanted the consummated fact."

"Consummation would hardly be a new treat for us," I said.

"You know what I mean," she said.

"Yeah, I do. How are you going to go about deciding whether you want to marry me or not?"

"I don't know. One way would be to have you threaten to leave. I wouldn't want to lose you."

"You won't lose me," I said.

"No, I don't think I will. That's one of the lovely qualities about you. I have the freedom, in a way, to vacillate. It's safe to be hesitant, if you understand that."

I nodded. "You also won't shake me," I said.

"I don't want to."

"And this isn't free-to-be-you-and-me-stuff. This is free to be us, no sharesies. No dibs, like we used to say in the schoolyard."

"How dreadfully conventional of you." Susan smiled at me. "But I don't want to shake you and take up with another man. And I'm not hesitating because I want to experiment around. I've done that. I know what I need to know about that. Both of us do. I'm aware you might be difficult about sharing me with guys at the singles bar."

"I'll say."

"There are things we have to think about though."

"Like what?"

"Where would we live?"

I was still lying flat and she was half sitting, propped up on her left elbow, her dark hair falling a little forward. Her interior energy almost tangible. "Ah-ha," I said.

She leaned over and kissed me on the mouth. "That's one of your great charms, you understand so quickly."

"You don't want to leave your house, your work."

"Or a town I've lived in nearly twenty years where I have friends, and patterns of life I care about."

"I don't belong out there, Suze," I said.

"Of course you don't. Look at you. You are the ultimate man, the ultimate adult in some ways, the great powerful protecting father. And yet you are the biggest goddamned kid I ever saw. You would have no business in the suburbs, in a Cape Cod house, cutting the lawn, having a swim at the club. I mean you once strangled a man to death, did not you?"

"Yeah, name was Phil. Never knew his other name, just Phil. I didn't like it."

"No, but you like the kind of work where that kind of thing comes up."

"I'm not sure that's childish."

"In the best sense it is. There's an element of play in it for you, a concern for means more than ends. It comes very close to worrying about honor."

"It often has to do with life and death, sweetie."

"Of course it does, but that only makes it a more significant game. My neighbors in Smithfield are more serious. They are dealing with success or failure. For most of them it's no fun."

"You've thought about me some," I said.

"You bet your ass I have. You're not going to give up your work, I'm not going to stop mine. I'm not going to move to Boston. You're not going to live in Smithfield."

"I might," I said. "We could work something out there, I think. No one's asking you to give up your work, or me to give up mine."

"No, I guess not. But it's the kind of thing we need to think on."

"So a firm I-don't-know is your final position on this?"

"I think so."

I put my hands up and pulled her down on top of me. "You impetuous bitch," I said. Her face pressed against my chest. It made her speech muffled.

"On the other hand," she mumbled, "I ain't never going to leave you."

"That's for sure," I said. "Let's go have dinner and consummate our friendship."

"Maybe," Susan said as we drove back to the motel, "we should consummate it before dinner."

"Better still," I said, "how about before and after dinner?"

"You're as young as you feel, lovey," Susan said.

CHAPTER TWENTY-NINE

WE RANG THE BELL at the Shepards' house at seven-thirty, me with a bottle of Hungarian red wine in a brown paper bag, and Hawk opened the door and pointed a Colt .357 Magnum at me.

"Do come in," he said.

We did. In the living room were King Powers and Powell, the stiff I had knocked in the pool, and Macey and the Shepards. The Shepards were sitting on the couch together with Powell standing by with his gun out, looking at them, hard as nails. Macey stood by the mantel with his slim-line briefcase and Powers was in a wing chair by the fireplace. Shepard's face was damp and he looked sick. Getting beaten up tends to take a lot of starch out of a person and Shepard looked like he was having trouble holding it together. His wife had no expression at all. It was as if she'd gone inside somewhere and was holding there, waiting.

"Where's the kids?" I said.

Hawk smiled. "They not here. Harv and the Mrs., I guess, thought they'd have a quiet time together, 'fore you come, so they shipped 'em off to neighbors for the night. That do make it cozier, I say."

Powers said, "Shut up, Hawk. You'd fuck around at your own funeral."

Hawk winked at me. "Mr. Powers a very grumpy man and I do believe I know who he grumpy at, babe."

"I figured I'd be seeing you, King," I said.

"You figured fucking right, too, smart guy. I got something for you, you son of a bitch. You think you can drop me into the bag like that and walk away, you don't know nothing about King Powers."

Macey said, "King, this is just more trouble. We don't need this. Why don't we just get going."

"Nope, first I burn this son of a bitch." Powers stood up. He was a paunchy man who looked like he'd once been thin, and his feet pointed out to the side like a duck's. "Hawk, take his gun away."

"On the wall, kid, you know the scene."

I turned and leaned against the wall and let him take the gun off my hip. He didn't have to search around. He knew right where it was. Probably smelled it. I stepped away from the wall. "How come you walk like a duck, King?" I said. Powers' red face deepened a bit. He stepped close to me and hit me in the face with his closed fist. I rocked back from the waist and didn't fall.

"Quack," I said. Powers hit me again, and cut my lip. It would be very fat in an hour. If I was around in an hour.

Susan said, "Hawk."

He shook his head at her. "Sit on the couch," he said.

Shepard said, "You gonna shoot us?" There wasn't much vitality in his voice.

"I'm fucking-A-well going to shoot this smart scumbag," Powers said. "Then maybe I'll like it so much I'll shoot the whole fucking bag of you. How's that sound to you, you fucking welcher."

"She's not in it," Shepard said, moving his head toward his wife. "Let her go. We got four kids. They never done anything to you."

Powers laughed with the inside of his upper lip showing. "But you did. You screwed me out of a lot of money, you gonna have to make that good to me."

"I'll make it good, with interest. Let her go."

"We'll talk about it, welcher. But I want to finish with this smart bastard first." He turned back to me and started to hit me again. I stepped inside and hit him hard in the side over the kidneys. His body was soft. He grunted with pain and buckled to his knees.

526

Macey brought out his little automatic and Powell turned his gun from the Shepards toward me.

Hawk said, "Hold it." There was no Amos and Andy mockery in it now.

Powers sat on the floor, his body twisted sideways, trying to ease the pain. His face red and the freckles looking pale against it.

"Kill him," he said. "Kill the fucker. Kill him, Hawk."

Susan said, "Hawk."

I kept my eyes on Hawk. Macey wouldn't have the stomach for it. He'd do it to save his ass, if he couldn't run. But not just standing there; that took something Macey didn't get in business school. Powell would do what he was told, but so far no one had told him. Hawk was the one. He stood as motionless as a tree. From the corner of my eye, I could see Shepard's hand go out and rest in the middle of his wife's back, between the shoulder blades.

Susan said again, "Hawk."

Powers, still sitting on the floor with his knees up and his white socks showing above his brown loafers, said, "Hawk, you bastard, do what you're told. Burn him. Blow him away. Right now. Kill him."

Hawk shook his head. "Naw."

Powers was on his knees now, struggling to his feet. He was so out of shape that just getting off the floor was hard for him. "No? Who the fuck you saying no to, nigger. Who pays your fucking ass? You do what you're told . . ."

Hawk's face widened into a bright smile. "Naw, I don't guess I am going to do what I'm told. I think I'm going to leave that up to you, boss."

Powell said, "I'll do it, Mr. Powers."

Hawk shook his head. "No, not you, Powell. You put the piece down and take a walk. You too, Macey. This gonna be King and Spenser here, one on one."

"Hawk, you gotta be out of your mind," Macey said.

"Hawk, what the fuck are you doing?" Powers said.

"Move it out, Macey," Hawk said. "You and Powell lay the pieces down on the coffee table and walk on away."

527

Powell said, "Hawk, for crissake . . ."

Hawk said. "Do it. Or you know I'll kill you."

Macey and Powell put the guns on the coffee table and walked toward the front door.

"What the fuck is happening here," Powers said. The color was down in his face now, and his voice was up an octave. "You don't take orders from this fucking coon, you take them from me."

"Racial invective," Hawk said to me.

"It's ugly," I said. "Ugly talk."

Powers said, "Macey. Call the cops when you get out, Macey. You hear me, you call the cops. They're going to kill me. This crazy nigger is trying to kill me."

Macey and Powell went out and closed the door. Powers' voice was high now. "Macey, goddamnit. Macey."

Hawk said, "They gone, King. Time for you to finish Spenser off, like you started to."

"I don't have a gun. You know that, Hawk. I never carry a piece. Lemme have Macey's."

"No guns, King. Just slap him around like you was doing before." Hawk put his .357 under his coat and leaned against the door with his arms folded and his glistening ebony face without expression. Powers, on his feet now, backed away two steps.

"Hey, wait up, now, hey, Hawk, you know I can't go on Spenser just me and him. I don't even know if you could. I mean that ain't fair, you know. I mean that ain't the way I work."

Hawk's face was blank. Harvey Shepard got off the couch and took a looping amateurish roundhouse righthand haymaker at Powers. It connected up high on the side of Powers' head near his right ear and staggered him. It also probably broke a knuckle in Shepard's hand. It's a dumb way to hit someone but Harv didn't seem to mind. He plowed on toward Powers, catching him with a left hand on the face and knocking him down. Powers scrambled for the two guns on the coffee table as Shepard tried to kick him. I stepped between him and the guns and he lunged at my leg and bit me in the right calf.

I said, "Jesus Christ," and reached down and jerked him to his feet. He clawed at my face with both hands and I twisted him away from me and slammed him hard against the wall. He stayed that way for a moment, face against the wall, then turned slowly away from the wall, rolling on his left shoulder so that when he got through turning, his back was against the wall. Shepard started toward him again and I put my hand out. "Enough," I said. Shepard kept coming and I had to take his shoulder and push him back. He strained against me.

From the couch Pam Shepard said, "Don't, Harvey." Shepard stopped straining and turned toward her. "Jesus," he said and went and sat on the couch beside her and put his arms awkwardly around her and she leaned against him, a little stiffly, but without resistance.

Susan got up and walked over and put her hands on Hawk's shoulders and, standing on her toes to reach, kissed him on the mouth.

"Why not, Hawk? I knew you wouldn't, but I don't know why."

Hawk shrugged. "Me and your old man there are a lot alike. I told you that already. There ain't all that many of us left, guys like old Spenser and me. He was gone there'd be one less. I'd have missed him. And I owed him one from this morning."

"You wouldn't have done it anyway," Susan said. "Even if he hadn't warned you about the police."

"Don't be too sure, honey. I done it lots of times before."

"Anyway, babe," Hawk said to me, "we even. Besides" —Hawk looked back at Susan and grinned—"Powers a foul-mouthed bastard, never did like a guy swore in front of ladies that way." He stepped across, dropped my gun on the table, picked up those belonging to Macey and Powell and walked out. "See y'all again," he said. And then he was gone.

I looked at Powers. "I think we got you on assault with

intent to murder, King. It ain't gonna help iron out the trouble you're already in in Boston, is it."

"Fuck you," Powers said and let his legs go limp and slid onto the floor and sat still.

"Hawk was right, King," I said. "Nobody likes a garbage mouth."

About the Author

ROBERT B. PARKER is the author of twenty-three books. Since his first Spenser novel, *The Godwulf Manuscript,* he has had numerous bestsellers, including *Pale Kings and Princes, Crimson Joy, Valediction, A Catskill Eagle* and *Taming a Sea-Horse; Poodle Springs,* his best-selling collaboration with Raymond Chandler; and the more recent *Stardust* and *Playmates.* Mr. Parker currently lives in Boston with his wife, Joan.